GW01319827

# A Loafer's Guide To Living

# A Loafer's Guide To Living

The Goldman Trilogy Book 2

***W.L. Liberman***

Published 2019 by Magnum Opus – A Next Chapter Imprint
Cover art by Cover Mint
Edited by Marilyn Wagner

*This book is dedicated to Finn Michael Liberman, born June 30, 2019. May you walk among giants and one day become a giant yourself.*

# 1

Toronto, 2002

It was the perfect moment. A loafable moment. And these were exceedingly rare. My wife had sashayed off to the gym. The twins played basketball outside. I wore my grey fleece cardigan with the overly large wingtip collar. I'd zipped it up to my chin with the collar covering my ears like the flaps of a leather helmet that had been up-ended. I lay prone with three large pillows supporting my head and my mother's old seersucker bathrobe covering my feet. I can remember the day perfectly. It was late April and the winter had been long, frigid and forbidding, enough to make a person feel like a northerner when there was everything about that idea that I loathed. No, give me sun and sand and light winds on the beach. But on this day, milder weather had flounced in and although it brought an underlying chill, the heat of the sun overlaid the cold air like an insulating blanket. I opened the windows to the bedroom for circulation. I don't think they'd been open since the previous September and it felt stuffy. And stale. That's why I wore the fleece cardigan, to keep me warm and cozy as I melted into the comforter on our bed. It was bliss, sheer bliss. The closest to nothingness a human being, specifically, a male, could achieve. With the exception, perhaps, of the swaying hammock beneath the leafy maple tree on a hot day. That wasn't bad, either. Pretty damned close I'd say.

Tragically, the moment remained short-lived. No sooner had I drifted off into unconscious tranquillity, than I heard a fiddling with the lock and the front door swung open with a bang. Basketballs bounced in cacophonic rhythm on the ceramic tile floor in the hall. Their voices had deepened with the onset of puberty and they didn't so much as talk as growl or croak in a verbal assault one might have mistaken for dialogue, interspersed as their conversation was, with lyrics from the latest rap ditty that repeated the phrase, "On your feet, muthafucka".

"Shit."

I kicked the robe away and rolled off the bed, unzipped the fleece cardigan and shrugged it off, leaving it in a heap on the floor. I shoved my feet into some slippers and pounded into the kitchen where the teenage mongrels devoured cookies between gulps of orange juice straight from the jug, passing it between them as if it were a coveted prize.

"What happened to basketball?"

They shrugged. "It was boring," Nathan said, then crammed a cookie into his mouth. "Nobody was there," he continued spitting crumbs and bits of chocolate chip on to his T-shirt. His brother, Sean, pointed and laughed at him. We don't get along, he and I. I'd describe our relationship as pointedly tense.

My name is Bernard Goldman and I used to be a writer. Several years ago, I published a book, *Spinning Through Time*, a semi-autobiographical examination of my family and my father, in particular. My father, Eph Goldman, is now a retired history professor who wrote a seminal work, *The Global View*. This book has proved extraordinarily popular for decades and it built and sustained my father's reputation. He is now living in Tuscany with his second wife, Catherine, a woman barely older than I am. Of me, my father would remark sardonically, "At least in this case, history is not repeating itself." That says a lot about our relationship. Not warm. Hardly fuzzy.

I'm working two manuscripts at the moment bouncing from one to the other. The first is called, *Memories* and is about a man who has amnesia but I keep forgetting where I am in the story. The second is called *Das Vidaniya* and details the life of a Jewish warrior who finds himself thrust into tough situations during The Second World War. Basically, the main character, cuts a swath of violence from Stalingrad to Berlin. But at least, I tell myself, he isn't a victim. I have grown exceedingly tired of books about Jews during the War portrayed as victims.

I met Hugo at the local community centre. Now 87, he had been a tank commander in the Soviet Army. Still vigorous, each day I see the ruthless side of him. We play basketball and I have not beaten him once in the previous seven years. Over 568 consecutive games of "21", my highest score has been an "8". Hugo put up an arcing shot and the ball swished through the basket.

"That's 569, I think."

"Bastard," I muttered, bent over, panting like a winded turtle.

Hugo broke out into a broad grin. "Want to go again?" he rasped.

I shook my head. "I am going for a swim."

Hugo ran a gnarled hand through his stiff, iron-grey hair. "Good. So am I."

I groaned. It was always the same but he had good stories to tell.

After the swim, I went into the office. I had rather foolishly ploughed some of the fees I collected from the first book into a magazine about Writers and Writing. Titled *Bookology*, it has just lurched into its fifth year of near-death survival. We subsist on the meagre advertising I can dredge up and those who take pity on us and actually buy a subscription. The pitiers number some 1200 now and I am proud to say, the subscribership has leapt some three or four percent since we began. In total, we print 15,000 copies of Bookology and circulate them across the country through retail outlets, newsstands, college and university writing programs and those who seem to be interested in getting published.

I spend my days fending off would-be writers, fawning on real writers, putting off creditors and badgering advertisers, many of whom are book publishers and moments away from declaring bankruptcy themselves. Yet it is my task to squeeze some advertising out of them to keep us afloat. This includes my own publisher, Julian de Groot of the House of Erasmus. Julian is a very successful publisher and my book made him a lot of money. While he waits for me to turn out my next masterpiece, he throws some mad money my way as an incentive.

"How are the manuscripts coming?" Julian de Groot drawled during his weekly call. "How many are there now? I've lost count, is it three or four?"

"Just two," I replied. "Incidentally, you haven't paid our last invoice. I sent it out two months ago."

"Oh dear, I must have Clarisse look into that right away." Clarisse was the bookkeeper.

"Do that."

"You haven't answered my question, dear boy."

"No, I haven't." I imagined de Groot, all six foot six of him, dressed in a white suit, long silvery hair hanging about his pristine collar, his yellowed fingers dangling a cigarette in a silver holder. "As well as can be expected actually."

"When will you have something to show me?"

"I don't know."

"Ollie North is looking for a good biographer, you know."

"So you said."

"So is Alan Greenspan."

"Julian, I don't want to do biographies. I only did the last one to get me started. It's time to move on, to expand, to grow."

I could hear him draw on the cigarette through the phone, then exhale languidly. "Well then, you need some Miracle Grow on the plants, old boy because things have been a little stunted lately, hmm?"

"Don't forget the invoice."

I hung up the phone and cursed. He always got my goat but then he was a publisher waiting for something he could publish. I held up the gravy boat. Didn't qualify as a train.

Despite all the moaning and fumbling, Bookology, almost in spite of itself and despite my heroic leadership, gained a reputation in the industry that meant I was invited to all of the main line parties and publishing events. As both an author and a magazine publisher, I had sat on panels in conferences that examined the business of book publishing and the nuts and bolts of getting published. I had been asked to speak about the writer's life and offer advice on getting published in what is a brutal, cut-throat sort of business. My talks tended to be short and to the point. "Have a famous father," I'd say. I wasn't often asked back but it was the best I could do and it had worked for me. Speak and write from personal experience was a common axiom exhorted to young up and comers, the sort I loathe really. The sort that actually get somewhere because they are talented. How irritating in the extreme when the opportunities dwindled down.

So in my natural discombobulated state, I stood in the loo taking a whizz. I came to my senses upon feeling a warm, wet sensation on my right leg. I looked down.

"Oh shit."

At that moment, my nemesis of sorts, one Eric Schwilden, found me standing, sans pants, in front of the hand dryer desperately rubbing the legs together and cursing under my breath.

"Goldman," he smirked. "Wet yourself, have you?"

"No, of course not," I retorted.

"And that's why you're standing there half-naked drying your pants with the hand warmer?"

"It was coffee actually. My hand slipped and the cup spilled. Pretty clumsy, I'll admit."

Schwilden gave me a knowing grin. "Sure. If that's the way you want to play it."

"It's the truth."

Schwilden smiled and shook his head of perfectly groomed hair that rounded the backs of his ears and just covered the nape of his long neck. He stood tall and slim, about 30 and wore clothes well. They just hung on him properly like you see on runway models, no silly bags or bulges. His teeth were even and white and he seemed to have a perpetual tan. Schwilden was a partner in a successful software company and drove a Porsche Targa. I knew this because his parking spot sat next to mine. His car made my 12-year old Saab, held together by rust and diminishing paint, look like a found object in the forest. He dated only beautiful, intelligent women. I hated him ever since he tried hitting on my wife, a tall, well-proportioned redhead who, at age 37, could still make them whistle. Sharon and I married at 22, just after she finished her accountancy exams. I stood five-eleven and weighed in at 155 pounds and when I examined myself in the mirror, I looked gawky and uncoordinated. I went to the community centre and put up with the indignities foisted on me by Hugo so I wouldn't turn into one of those paunchy dads who wore a baseball cap, Bermuda shorts, knee-high, white socks and open-toed sandals.

Schwilden dried his hands on some paper and grinned at me sardonically while I continued to air out my trousers. Then, he cocked a finger at me, dropped the paper in the bin and took his leave. I could hear him laughing all the way down the corridor. I looked in the mirror. What a yutz, the image said back to me.

Back in the office with my trousers nicely heated, I contemplated the "loafable" moment and decided that today I wouldn't find one. It was difficult. There was no office in fact, but a large open space shared by myself, my editorial assistant Jessica, my partner Roberto, his graphic assistant, the lissome Angela and our crusty, wheezy receptionist, Ruth. Ruth was a dumpy little woman who travelled on a cloud of nicotine trailing wisps of cat hair in her wake. She lived for her two cats. Otherwise, she took surly and mean-spiritedness to new levels but unfortunately remained the only living entity that understood our convoluted invoicing system. Without her, we'd be bankrupt in short order and she knew it. My partner, Roberto, spent more time worrying about what he was going to have for lunch than working. He didn't put any money into the business but brought a lot of computer equipment and in exchange I gave him a minority interest. If he wasn't talking about food, on the phone with his mother, his wife, any of his several sisters or his children, he kibitzed with the lovely Angela, who, at six feet and gorgeous, intimidated us all. No, we stood together as a community and, as such, lived in close quarters. No chance for obvious loafing, I'm afraid. Without walls, it seemed virtually impossible, except for Angela, who, having a date the evening before or attended the latest rave, would simply put her head down and fall asleep. We never said a word. I didn't dare tell Sharon, or she'd scream bloody murder that we hadn't fired the girl for this sort of behaviour. But you see, we liked Angela and I didn't want to fire her. She was good company and a crack graphic artist when she was awake. Needless to say, Schwilden hit on her constantly. So far, to my delight, she had turned him down flat, thinking him a stuck-up poser. I couldn't be more pleased.

I suspected my assistant, Jessica, harboured deep thoughts and conflicted emotions yet barely a word came out of her mouth. She was tall and slender with remarkably long, brown hair. Although she would reply when spoken to or asked a question. Thankfully, she was dedicated and extremely diligent, picking up where I slacked off. If I was having a bad day, which truthfully, could be any day, she'd pick up after me. I wouldn't feel like writing the intros or the blurbs or transcribing the interviews or taking calls from press agents and publicists. Some days, I wanted to shut it all down. Jessica would smoothly take over with a shy smile and a quiet demeanour. I think she was very intuitive. Perhaps those that don't speak much are that way.

While I'm confessing, I might as well get it all out. I was conducting a cyber affair with a young woman in my wife's office. A graphic designer named Charlotte. We met at the Cablestar Christmas party, the media conglomerate that Sharon manages as the CFO, the previous year and have been carrying on a lively correspondence ever since. I should say that's all it has been and likely ever will be. Charlotte is married as I am but I've suspected it is a marriage of convenience, more like a friendship, really. Her husband, Michael, is Australian and needed to stay in the country. Charlotte hasn't admitted as much but she travels a good deal, usually on her own. No children, obviously. We talk art and books and movies and architecture, the sorts of things that bore Sharon to tears and for which, she really has no time, focused as she is on the pragmatic things in life. Finance, for instance, which is her field, after all.

As I returned to my desk and punched up my email, a message pinged from Charlotte. My heart always quickened a bit. I couldn't shake the feeling this was something very elicit yet I couldn't say we were doing anything wrong. After all, I corresponded with a lot of people. Sharon did the same and probably more. Her inbox regularly had a couple hundred messages every morning. I was lucky if I had ten or twenty but that was more than enough. Corresponding with writers was never brief. Some of the emails I received ran five pages and more. So why did I feel a pang of pleasurable guilt when Charlotte's name and address came up?

Charlotte wrote: Hey you. Went to the Bergman festival last night. Simply fab. I'd forgotten how eerie and dark Seventh Seal was. Creepy really but creepy in a good kind of way. Afterward we retired to the Irish pub and got a bit smashed but it was good fun. I was drinking Guinness, which I never do, so that tells you I was in a strange mood after the film. You know, dark, brooding story, dark ale. There's a psychic connection, don't you think? Umm, I know we've never done this before but I'm going to the new China exhibit opening at the museum Friday evening. Care to join me? C.

My mouth went very dry as I read that last bit. This was a turn of events and I began to panic. As I got up from my desk to go to the water cooler for a drink, I tripped over the lamp cord and it came crashing down bringing a load of files with it. Jessica jumped up.

"No need to panic. I'll get it," I said as Roberto and Angela looked up from where they were huddling. Ruth twisted her fuzzy lips in what I interpreted as a smirk.

"Just an accident."

And bent down to pick up the papers and file folders that lay spread out on the pitted hardwood floor. Before I could protest, Jessica swept things up while I fumbled and cursed under my breath.

"Really, there's no need."

She moved quickly for a wraith revealing a coiled strength in her sinewy arms as she stacked everything back in proper order on the surface of my old, glass-topped desk.

"Thank you."

Her smile appeared; a grim crease that quickly sent crackling lines running up her face. Perhaps that's why she smiled so seldom, preferring a composed complexion that suited her better, I'll admit. At certain angles, she was a lovely looking girl, pert nose, a bit pointy and a pale complexion, too pale, almost ghostly.

"Sure," she said and bustled back to her computer and immediately began pounding the keys as if she'd never left or merely paused in mid-strike. The others turned away, back to their scheming or worse, loafing.

Charlotte had thrown me and I was stymied with indecision, a natural state of being for a loafer. It was easier and less stressful not to do anything, or put things off while tucking them away from active thought. Don't do anything, I told myself, there is danger in every direction. I liked Charlotte, I really did and I was attracted to her, no question. But I also loved and was attracted to Sharon and had been faithful these past 16 years, not a slip or a hint of a slip in all that time. No desire, in fact.

Lately, our sex life had been wanting. One night she was tired and the next I felt like going right to sleep. I put in long days rising at five in the morning to get to the community centre so I could be outclassed by bloody Hugo and then home by seven-thirty, just in time to nag Sean and Nathan to get ready for school while Sharon headed out the door for work. Beside my soiled Saab, her massive, four-wheel drive, Lincoln Navigator, a shrunken motor home in leather, made me feel like I belonged in a trailer park. And so, I was legitimately tired, coming home at five-thirty, making dinner, helping the kids with their homework, tidying up, settling down to the inevitable reading I'd bring home, then a little television, around ten-thirty came the tedious ritual of badgering Sean and Nathan into bed, a half-hour ordeal at the very least.

Finally, around eleven, we could tuck in. When home, Sharon would get herself ready, flossing and brushing and washing while I chased the twins up and down the stairs, in and out of rooms while they conspired to elude me and by the time they'd settled in, Sharon would have the light out and was gently snoring. This insidious habit of hers infuriated me further having been aggravated enough frolicking with two idiots who happened to be our children. That is, when Sharon wasn't working late or on the road travelling or spending time with her personal trainer, Sven, at her exclusive club near her office.

Truthfully, it could be months or more. I reacted in one of two ways. The first meant moving through the day in a boil, a perpetual state of lust. Then

I felt sort of dead as I experienced life being sucked out of the marrow of my bones. *Bookology* dragged me down into the mire and along with the lack of co-operation from my confreres, the plotting, the wheedling that went with being a 'businessman', something I was supremely ill-prepared to be. The inertia in my own work that plodded from sentence to sentence, paragraph to paragraph. Was there no bright light? Apparently not. When I was in that frame of being, a porno queen couldn't rouse me if she sat in my lap naked and gyrated to a boogie beat. So, maybe I was ripe for Charlotte. Perhaps it was time?

What stopped me? Was it guilt, the Jewish mother's invention? Nope. In pondering this, I think it was the magnetism of inertia. Running around with Charlotte meant activity, expending energy, plotting, planning and God knows what else. Secretive dinners. Finding a time and place to be alone. I didn't want to be disappointed in her and I didn't want her to be disappointed in me. It was inevitable, I reasoned after the first guilty rush of emotion engorged us. And then? Back to the mundane things. The things that taught us to be disdainful and over time, show contempt. The familiarity thing. I didn't want that for either of us. So I made a decision. I returned Charlotte's email.

I wrote: Hi C. Friday isn't going to work for me. Let me get back to you. B.

How was that for inaction?

Loafing through life was a grand thing but it took so much work to organize. The arrangements required to ensure that everyone in your life was running in the right direction, away in this case, to give you, the loafee, some leisure time. This required a great deal of coordination, planning and strategic thinking.

# 2

Every Saturday morning around ten, I met some of my cohorts at the local coffee bistro, BoBo's where we would commiserate over the dilemma each of us faced. Nook, a Burmese national, married with a child and toiled as a software engineer. His daughter just turned seven. His wife was a lawyer and had a steel trap mind to go with it. Ramon hailed from Peru and spent his days in social work. He had no children but his wife, Luisa, was a nurse who worked shifts. She wanted to have children but Ramon kept hedging, knowing he'd have to give in eventually. I liked BoBo's and loved to inhale the smell of the different blends of coffee. It's just too bad that I gave up drinking coffee. I sacrificed myself because coffee gave me heart palpitations. We all managed to sneak out on the pretext of picking up the paper and bagels and cream cheese, in my case, at least. When I left the house, everyone remained fast asleep. By the time I got back, the boys would likely still be asleep and Sharon would have gone to the gym. I saved myself that humiliation on the weekends knowing I could barely take the psychological beating during the week. It just went with everything else. Hugo wanted to show me how to use the various weight machines. It seemed like there were hundreds of them, all very complicated looking. More ineptitude awaited me.

"What's your excuse?" asked Nook, sipping a mochaccino.

I dropped the paper and bagels onto the empty seat beside him. "Same as always. You?"

Nook lifted his paper and a sack of milk, smiling ruefully. Ramon looked up from his extra large, black Colombian. Misery itself would have looked more pleased.

"Luisa's pregnant." There reverberated a stunned silence. Neither Nook or I knew what to say. We avoided each other's eyes until finally, I couldn't stand it.

"Think of it this way," I said. "There's always things to be running out for. Diapers. Formula. Wipes. Not to mention the cravings. When Sharon was pregnant, I had to buy her double double chocolate fudge or a Fatso's superburger with the works. Mind you, that was almost always after midnight."

"Thanks," Ramon replied, glumly dropping his wide chin to his narrow chest.

Nook polished his glasses on a paper napkin. "How far along is she?"

"Eight weeks."

"You never know, things can happen in the first trimester. It's a delicate time. The data is pretty clear, according to a bunch of research studies."

Ramon's face clouded. "I don't want her to lose the baby."

"No, of course not," I interjected and shot Nook an angry look. He shrugged in that Buddha-like way. He should never have shaved his head. He looked like the Dalai Lama... or his younger brother.

"It's just that I know it's going to be a lot of work. Babies are a lot of work, right?"

Nook and I exchanged glances, we knew how much work it was.

"Right," I said. Nook didn't answer, just took another sip from the mochaccino that left a white moustache on his upper lip. Nook drove a new Saab and was considering switching to a Volvo, more space he thought and better for travelling with the family when they visited his mother-in-law who lived out of town. He glanced down at the paper and took in the headlines.

"We'll help you," I said.

"That's right," Nook chimed in.

"We'll call you up and ask you out, make up things."

"It's her shifts that worry me the most," Ramon said. "If she's working nights or weekends, then I'm stuck."

"Bring the baby with you," said Nook. "We've all done it. I used to strap Liliana to my chest. When she started to cry, I gave her a bottle or walked around a little bit to quiet her down. It wasn't a problem."

"I used to bring the kids in the stroller. Same thing," I said.

Ramon looked at us skeptically. One thing about loafers, much went on below the surface. We had an intuitive understanding of each other. There wasn't a great deal of overt conversation or anything mildly active. We'd sip whatever we ordered, chat about whatever, glance at the newspaper and be on our way.

Simple, easy and no stress. That's what we wanted. Ramon's interjection had been the most meaningful thing we'd heard in months. It put us right on the edge, actually. That was another implied rule. Stick to the trivial and even, the inane when possible. But it was all right to muse on things as long as the others weren't required to respond in any meaningful way.

For instance, whenever I wrote the Editor's Notes for *Bookology* or even conducted an interview, I often fell asleep. Nodded off right at the computer. Something about expending mental energy that drained me like a leaky battery. I could barely keep my eyes open and it was a bit embarrassing when it happened in front of the staff, even if it only lasted a few seconds. Jessica would politely tap me on the shoulder and quietly smile. I didn't fall asleep during phone conversations but if it were a particularly long or tedious call, then no guarantees. Phone interviews were the worst of the lot as writers tended to drone on and on about their work and really, if the truth be known, who cared what they thought? Certainly, I didn't but it was all a sort of continuum, you see. I had to keep the writers happy to keep the book publishers happy so they would continue to advertise with us so I could continue to pay my bills and even that was dicey at best. I had to admit that some of my suppliers were very good about it.

"If you don't cut me a cheque and send it by courier today, I won't print your magazine, Mr. Goldman," shouted John Hawthorne, owner of Vantone Press, our printer of the moment.

"But I've got a lot of money tied up in that issue," I protested.

"I know. That's why you'll need to get it printed, won't you?" Hawthorne growled.

"But I can't pay you until I send out all the invoices and I can't do that until the damn thing is printed."

"So you're asking me to add to your bill by printing the magazine so you can do your billing?"

"That's right."

"I'm not a bloody banker, Goldman. If you want to see the magazine in print, then you'd better send a cheque." He hung up. And what happened? I was stuck, of course. I just didn't have $12,000 sitting around in the corporate bank account. It was more like $250. So, the contingency was, I dug into my personal line of credit and coughed it up. I had to be very quiet about this when it happened. If she found out, Sharon would rupture a few ovaries. She was very,

very responsible, fiscally. But then she could afford to be, earning a significant six-figure salary as the Chief Financial Officer at Cablestar.

These were the sorts of things I lapsed into when I was ensconced at BoBo's, cradling my bagels and cream cheese. I couldn't blame Hawthorne but he was a bastard all the same.

"He's gone again," Nook remarked.

"I swear, Bernie, your mind is drifting like a paralyzed tuna," Ramon said mysteriously.

"I didn't know a tuna could be paralyzed," I replied.

Ramon pointed a finger at me. "You don't know everything." And he drained his large, black Colombian and signalled for another.

I picked up my bagels and cream cheese. "Later boys." Nook nodded, Ramon shrugged, the quintessential loafer's response. Spare the energy.

When I got home, I found Nathan at the computer playing some sort of strategy game that involved a lot of shooting and simulated blood. I made him put the headphones on. The last thing I wanted to hear on a Saturday morning were the agonized cries of the dead and dying, simulated or not.

"Bagels and cream cheese," I said.

There was no response. Louder. "Bagels and cream cheese."

"What?"

I held up the bag. "Bernie, you always get bagels and cream cheese. I know that's what you've got. You do that every Saturday after you hang out with your geeky friends." Nathan paused the game to tell me this.

"My friends are geeky?" I put the bag down on the counter. "You have the nerve tell me my friends are geeky. At least we don't have our faces pressed into a computer screen all day long playing Cosmic Cowboy Blast-Off or something else equally inane."

Nathan looked at me woefully. "First of all, Bernie, this is a very cool game that demands a higher order of thinking, strategy and hand-eye coordination, the sort of strategy game employed in the top gun fighter ace schools in the United States Air Force, so don't presume to tell me what is inane or not." With a contemptuous gesture, he returned the headphones to his ears and unpaused the game. I wish I had a comeback to that or simply grounded the little bugger for the rest of his life. Instead, I picked up the newspaper and went into the living room to read.

Just as I was about to nod off, Sharon came bursting in, flushed from her workout, and dropped her gear by the couch with a thump. My heart still fluttered when I saw her and to my familiar eye, she looked and appeared eminently desirable. Wearing form-fitting stretch pants and a tight T-shirt sprayed on her elegant but fulsome figure stirred something in me. It usually did. Her auburn hair had been cut recently and it looked good on her, gave her an air of youth and vitality even though we were the same age. I, on the other hand, felt mummified by comparison.

"Hallo lazy bones," she called. "Where are the boys, then?" Her Irishness came out subtlely in her speech when she was in a good mood, not so subtlely when she wasn't.

"Nathan's on the computer, destroying western civilization as we know it and Sean is sleeping through it all."

Sharon glanced at her watch. "He is, is he? Jesus, it's almost eleven-thirty and thirteen hours of sleep is enough, even for a teenager." She stomped off to wake him. I followed her undulating buttocks as she climbed the stairs. As if picking up my thoughts on radar, she stopped midway.

"What is it?" I shrugged, then grinned sheepishly.

"You dirty-minded bastard. Well perhaps, if you're a good boy." And she continued on her way.

Somehow, she took the wind out of me. I mean, when put that way. I felt as if I had been scolded by my mother, hardly a lustful thought. I felt myself wilt a little bit and a piece of my soul shrank too. I know it's no good to dwell on the past but it wasn't like it had been before. Even when the kids were small, we'd just enjoy each other for the sake of it. There were no conditions or strings that tagged along. Is this what getting older is all about and naturally, my thoughts went to Charlotte and her invitation for next Friday. I had written my reply but in true layabout form, I hadn't sent it yet, relegating the message to my outbox so I might have the time to ruminate a bit further. I returned to the paper that I read quickly and cursorily as my main objective was to get to the crossword and finish it just after lunch. Then I would scout out any pending leisure moments.

"Dad?" Nathan appeared in front of me, sticking his dark face over the newspaper.

"What?" I was annoyed. He could be a very annoying child.

"I need a lift to the pool. I'm meeting a bunch of guys there."

"What time?"

"One-thirty."

"There is such a thing as the bus, you know. It has four wheels and a roof and normally goes in the right direction."

He looked stricken. "Thc bus?"

"I'm coming too." A rumpled Sean appeared, hovering above the bannister. His hair stood up in clumps and his face looked bruised from sleep.

"You're not invited," Nathan said.

"Who's going?"

"Never mind."

"I can come if I want to," Sean said, and began to descend the stairs slowly hanging on to the bannister.

"I don't want you to."

"Why not?"

"Because you're such an asshole."

I heard the bang of Sharon's footfalls on the upstairs landing.

"Stop right there," she said. Sean froze on the stairway. Nathan looked down at the floor.

"What is with the language?" she demanded.

"He is an asshole," Nathan muttered under his breath.

"I heard that." And before either of us knew what had happened, Sean had leapt over the bannister, launched himself on to Nathan and they began rolling around on the floor.

In one of those movie-like sequences, I dropped the paper and pushed myself off the couch while Sharon began to pound down the stairs. The coffee table had been overturned and a dish I'd always hated went crashing to the floor as the two boys thrashed about. On her way down, Sharon caught her foot and let loose with a piercing yell that brought the two boys to their senses enough so they sat up. She did a fine impression of a stuntwoman rolling down the stairs until she landed with a solid thump at the bottom. I made my way over to her. The boys looked red-faced and stricken with uncertainty.

I bent over her. "Sharon, are you okay?"

She was writhing in agony. "No, you damn fool, I'm not."

She clutched at her ankle and I cleverly assessed the problem therein. "Boys, get an ice pack from the freezer. Move." My tone seemed to jolt them out of their torpor and they scrambled off. Gingerly, I began to unlace Sharon's shoe.

"Oh good Christ, be careful, will ya?"

"Let's not be too harsh, darling. I am trying to help. Now just let me take a quick look." Slowly, I eased the shoe off her foot, then slid the demi-sock off as well. The ankle had begun to puff already and quickly discoloured. "Badly sprained at least, possibly broken, I pronounced."

"Oh thank you, doctor," and squeezed out tears of pain. "Those little bastards," she spat. "I'm going to kill them."

Having heard her, Nathan ran in quickly with two ice packs then skedaddled. "Don't worry about the lift," he said.

I applied the ice packs not too softly. She winced and gave me a murderous look. "We'll keep these on for a bit and then it's to the hospital for you. Better tell me what you want to take. I'm sure we'll be there for quite a while."

For some odd reason that I can't quite identify, it gave me a smug sense of pleasure to see Sharon in pain. Perhaps it was because she was an unsympathetic person. She preferred to move on and not get personally involved with others. When her employees started to tell her their personal problems, inevitably she'd say, "Too much information." That closed them off pretty quickly. And so people around her, her work mates and colleagues knew not to approach her on that level. I also knew that she hated the idea of sickness and being ill. She wasn't the nursemaid type. I had joked often enough that if I ever became incapacitated to any degree, she'd have me packed off to a nursing home before I knew what had hit me. So, to see her in discomfort, her injured ankle cradled in my lap as we sat across from each other in the hospital waiting area, pleased me.

"You're enjoying this," she said.

I looked up from the book I was reading, the new Le Carré. "What?"

"You're enjoying this."

"Oh yes, it's very good."

"I don't mean the book, you lummox. I mean, having me here like this. Seeing me at a disadvantage."

I smiled very carefully. "Well, it is unusual. And you do look so fetching in your workout togs."

Sharon tilted her head in acknowledgement, then turned to survey the sea of humanity about here. "Reminds me of the tenements back home." Indeed, she had grown up rough and poor in Belfast. After they emigrated when she was 12, her father Rory left them to seek his fortune playing in a country bar band. This left her mother, Felicity, with four kids to raise, Sharon and her three brothers. It hadn't been easy for them. But she'd left all that behind her in a past life. It's unlikely that she could even relate to it now, having spent the past 15 years forging her way up the corporate ladder and doing better and better each year. She'll be running the company soon, I thought. And why not? She was capable, no question. But did people respect her? Did they want to work for her and do their best? That was the only question in my mind. On some level, you have to like the people you work with and work for. That doesn't mean you need to know all the intimate details of their lives or hang out in the pub together three nights a week but having that ability to inspire respect made the difference in my opinion. It's hard to get people to work for you if they don't like you.

"You're a long way from that."

"I know. It seems like another lifetime. Well, this is the first time I've been back in a hospital since the boys were born."

I looked at her and felt a surge of tenderness. What a comedy of errors that had been. Before we left for the hospital, I called the doctor and found I couldn't rouse him from sleep. He kept snoring while the line was open and I couldn't hang up nor could I wake him. Must be drunk, the bastard I thought. And us with twins on the way. When we arrived at the Toronto General Hospital, it was chaos, five sets of twins had been birthed that same morning. We were the sixth. Nurses hustled about, hastily admitting the expectant parents, six women in varying degrees of discomfort, ranging from low moans to high-pitched shrieks, very unsettling for the would-be fathers, all of us looking as if we were about to pass out. One fellow did. He hit his head on the corner of a desk and opened a nasty cut to his temple. He had to be rushed off to be seen by a resident. Sharon looked and felt very ill. I had brought a bed pan with me in case she vomited, something she had been doing on a regular basis for the previous nine months. Why should this be any different? They shunted us from room to room. Sharon was given an epidural, had an intravenous in one arm, a blood pressure cuff on the other, and two fetal heart monitors strapped to her distended belly. And nobody could find the great, bloody Dr. Swann, the elderly patrician baby doc who was the best in the city we were told, who had the lowest Caesarian rate in the entire hospital. All I could think was, where the bloody hell was he? Well, true to his name, the old fart swanned in just moments before the babies came. Sharon had been prepped by the resident and the nurses. In the delivery room buzzed some fifteen people, not including me. I was shunted to the back like I was standing in a slow rising elevator and couldn't get out. Sharon and the action seemed very far away.

"That was something, wasn't it?" I replied thinking how quickly 15 years had passed.

Sharon shifted her weight awkwardly. "These chairs are bloody uncomfortable, aren't they? Listen love, do you think you could get me a water or something? It's awfully dry in here."

I patted her knee. "Sure thing."

The x-rays came back negative. Sharon was given an elaborate bandage, a set of crutches and told to stay off her ankle for a week. By the time she had hobbled out to the parking lot and settled herself in the passenger seat of the Navigator, Sharon had arranged a limousine service to ferry her to and from from work for as long as she needed it.

She snapped her cell phone shut and regarded me as I maneuvered the oversized vehicle through the suddenly too narrow streets of the city. Saturday was a shopping day and there was more traffic than I would have liked. We had arrived at the emergency department shortly before noon and it was now just shy of five o'clock. The shoppers poured into the streets to head home.

"I'm famished," she said. "Didn't have time for lunch."

"Why don't you phone home, see if the kids are there."

She nodded and pressed an exquisitely tapered finger and lacquered nail on the speed dial. "You don't feel like cooking tonight, do you?"

Sharon didn't cook, she had no aptitude or feel for it. I liked to cook and in addition to a host of other chores, all of the shopping and cooking fell to me. Through some shrewd negotiating and outright bribery, I'd managed to get Sean and Nathan to do most of the yard work, although I stopped at hedge trimming. God knows the carnage that might result in. It was scary enough to think about the two of them obtaining a driver's license in less than a year's time. Legalized homicide in my opinion. "No one's answering," she said.

"They could be listening to music. Nothing penetrates that."

"I don't know," she mused. "Sean seems to have a sixth sense about the phone. Sometimes, I think he can hear it in his sleep."

"That's only a result of limiting himself to four hours of chat a night."

Sharon looked down at her bandaged ankle and her bare foot, then wriggled her toes. "They put the damn thing on so tight. It's cutting off my circulation near enough."

"Is your foot all tingly?"

"Yes."

"Wriggle your toes."

"Oh, thank you, doctor."

"You're welcome. Standard therapy, you know. We'll adjust the bandage when we get home."

"Sure enough," she said, then switched on the radio to the oldies station. Elvis Presley singing, "Suspicious Minds" filled the interior. I decided to concentrate strictly on the driving. I didn't want to pulverize anyone or anything, after all.

I put Sharon's arm around my shoulder and helped her hobble up the front steps. Having her balance against me, I fumbled for the keys and only managed to drop them twice while she gave me an exasperated look, then unlocked the door. "The alarm's not on," she remarked.

We short-hopped into the living room where I deposited her on the couch. I got her foot elevated, propping it with a few pillows. "I'll see if they're here." I checked their rooms, then the basement and finally, the kitchen. There was a note, Gone to the movies, back around 11. It was in Nathan's hand but I assumed he wrote it for the both of them. "They're out," I said.

Sharon looked at the note. "Do you really think they've gone to the movies? Or are they making out with some girls, do you think?"

"I don't know. Let's give them the benefit of the doubt. You know Nathan has shown no interest in girls, at least not yet. Sean's a different story altogether."

"He is, isn't he? Let's hope he doesn't knock anyone up."

"They've had sex ed in school."

"Fat lot of good that'll do in the heat of the moment."

"Well. Shall we keep a bowl of condoms by the front door. Help yourself on your way out?"

Sharon thought about it. "Mightn't be a bad idea, at that," she concluded.

"You don't think we'll be encouraging them to be sexually active?"

"Well, they're going to do it anyway, whether we like it or not. Isn't it better to be open than have them sneaking around? Wouldn't you rather have them practicing safe sex than getting some poor lassie pregnant?"

"No," I said. "I want to be a grandfather before I'm forty."

Sharon fell back against the pillows. "Button up, will ya? You know what I think?"

"What?"

"I think you like to wind me up, that's what."

"So?"

"You're the only one who can do that. Now why is that, do you suppose?"

"You've forgotten about your brothers and your mother. I think they've got your number."

"Why don't we order some take-out? How about Chinese? It'll be just the two of us."

"Like a date?"

Sharon shaded her eyes. "Uh-huh."

I bent down to loosen the bandage. "Sure. Why not?"

"I'm worried about Sean."

I looked up in surprise. I was too but I didn't think my concerns extended to her. "And why is that?"

"He's just secretive in another way. I see too much of my brother in him. Never tellin' the truth, always sneakin' about thinkin' we'll never catch him out. Has the mind of a compulsive fool."

"Yes," I admitted. "That sounds a lot like Egan."

"And Sean," she said. I hadn't yet told Sharon about Sean's latest escapade. Apparently, he forged my signature on a permission form and told the office he'd be away the following week on a 'family trip'. The head secretary at the school became a little suspicious and called me at the office to confirm the story. I wondered what sort of family trip he'd had in mind and where this family might be travelling. This wasn't the first time Sean had pulled a stunt like this nor, I surmised, would it be the last. He was a devilish child who preyed on the good nature of those around him, especially his brother, who seemed willing to forgive him anything and follow along in the next antic, something that usually came back and bit him in the ass. "There's not much we can do, I suppose," she said and stretched her arms out behind her head.

"No," I agreed. "Why don't I go order?"

She eyed me with a small smile playing on her lips. "All right then."

The boys rolled in around eleven-thirty. Sharon had gone up to bed, or rather hobbled as I helped her up the stairs. I offered to help her undress but she told me that wasn't necessary, she hadn't become an invalid yet. Chastened, I beat a retreat back to the living room to read and wait up for them, the miscreants. I heard the fumbling at the door and then Nathan's dark head poked around the frame. From my vantage in the living room, I could see them clearly. The foyer was in darkness but I could see well enough.

"All clear," he whispered and stepped quietly inside, his sneakers scuffing but not squeaking along the floor. Sean breezed in after, unaware or not caring about the noise he made. He kicked the door shut.

"I need a drink," he said and made a beeline for the kitchen, his lean frame undulating in the semi-darkness. Nathan froze in the doorway as he glanced in my direction.

"Hi Dad."

"Have a good time?"

"How's Mom? Was she badly hurt?"

"Well you didn't stick around long enough to find out."

"Sorry about that." At least the kid had a conscience.

"What was that?" asked Sean, drinking from a tumbler.

"Your mother."

"Oh yeah, how is she?"

"Resting, thank you for asking."

Sean shrugged. "Yeah well, whatever. Uh, listen can you give me a couple bucks. We had to use our own money for the bus."

"No."

"Why not?"

"It was your choice to go to the movies. What it cost and how you got there was your problem, not mine."

He drained the glass. "Oh, thanks a lot. I'm going to watch TV." And he stalked off. Nathan hadn't moved.

"Is Mom really okay?" he asked.

I nodded. "Just a bad sprain, that's all but she'll be hobbling about for a week or two, so bear that in mind, all right? And the two of you might ask after her tomorrow or even get her a card or some flowers, that would be a nice gesture."

"Okay. Goodnight, Dad."

"Goodnight Nathan." I saw his dark shape melt away into the shadows of the hallway.

"Is that them?" Sharon asked, tipping her reading glasses down her nose so she could look up and over the lenses at me.

"Yes."

"Concerned for my welfare, are they?" she muttered, bitterness creeping into her voice. "What have I ever done to them except give them everything they wanted and more?"

This was a familiar refrain. I didn't want to encourage it. Rather, I began to change into my pajamas, well, a ripped T-shirt and a pair of old boxer shorts actually. Then I went about my exercises as solemnly as I could, knowing that Sharon was eyeballing me. She'd cut off the lament. I didn't want to talk to her because I would lose my concentration and when I went through the motions of doing crunches and push-ups, I needed very badly to concentrate or I'd collapse and never get beyond the first five or six. She always watched me with an amused expression on her face, an expression that communicated something like, who are you trying to kid? Still, I was attempting to keep middle-age and all that goes with it, at bay. I didn't think I was doing a terrible job.

"I don't think you listen to me anymore," she said and sighed. In reply, I grunted, my face about to burst from effort. I'd finished the 150 crunches and moved on to the push-ups, light blinked at the end of the tunnel, only 10 more to go.

"For God's sake, you sound like you're going to blow up."

"Thank you," I panted into the carpet, silently counting my blessings. I managed to make it through. I pushed back to my knees, face down, and breathed into the beige shag, that is, until I felt well enough to struggle to my feet. Sharon had pushed down the covers and I could see she wore only a silk teddy that had inched its way up her thighs. Lacking any self-control whatever, I felt myself stiffen almost instantly. She smiled at me.

"I want my pound of flesh," she said. I got into bed beside her. "Mind the ankle, won't ya?" I must admit, this had been a saving grace in our marriage. Whatever else may not be right, the sex remained pretty wonderful most of the time. And she always smelled good.

Sharon lay on her side, stark naked. We remained entangled under the covers. She stroked my face and I drifted into sleep, the heat of our actions slowly beginning to dissipate. "I was thinking, luv."

"Uh-huh."

"I was wondering about having another child."

My eyes popped open. I felt her thighs turn to steel effectively pinning me where I lay. God damn that personal trainer. "What? Are you insane?" I struggled, trying to pull back without success, feeling the semen leak out of me, microscopic traitors to the cause.

"No," she said in a low voice. "I just wanted to hold a baby again. I can't explain it really, it's just a feeling I've got. Men just don't understand it, I suppose."

"And don't want to," I retorted. "We've got children. We've done our bit to augment the population." My mind raced and thought about how much work a baby was, the sleepless nights, the changing, the feeding, the constant, never-ending list of tasks and chores, I wanted away from all of that. "You don't think we're a bit, uh, old, now?"

"Are you sayin I'm too old?"

"Well, it's just that, we're not 22 anymore. Personally, I don't think I've got the energy for a baby."

"Ach, you talk like you're a pensioner, Bernie. Lots of couples have children later in life. Sean and Nathan can help us out. They're old enough to assume some responsibility." I almost cackled out loud at that one.

"Sean and Nathan?" I exclaimed. "You've got to be joking. Getting them to put a way a dish is a major effort. Or putting the cap back on the salad dressing or picking up the clothes they've strewn about the floor. And you think they're responsible enough to help look after a baby? That's a laugh, that is."

"Don't underestimate them," she replied tartly. "Give them the responsibility and I think they'll run with it."

"Yes. In the opposite direction from a baby."

I was still pinned by those iron thighs and somehow the injured ankle didn't seem to be bothering her anymore. Perhaps it was the extra strength Tylenol with codeine she'd gobbled before bed. She put her hand on my face and squished my cheeks. I felt like a fish caught in a vise. "I want you to give some serious thought to this, luv. I mean it." Her face loomed very close to mine. I felt her hot breath.

She released my cheeks and I moved my mouth around to restore the feeling. "You're not, uh, I mean, you haven't... now, have you?"

Her green eyes widened. In the darkness, I swore I could see sparks flying off the flecks of gold in those captivating irises. "No, not yet. I didn't think that was quite right. You're entitled to your say, after all."

"Right. And then?"

"And then... I'll do what I like anyway, just as I always have."

Her thighs parted and I rolled on to my back, wilted and sticky. Inwardly, I groaned. There wouldn't be a moment's peace now, for years. Now I felt Ramon's pain right where it hurt, in the nuts. "Goodnight," I muttered. Sharon rolled over and fell asleep almost instantly. I marvelled at how she could do that but she had the knack for it. After this latest bombshell exploding my peaceful existence, smashing it to smithereens, I lay awake in the dark, imagining my life frittered away under an avalanche of stinky diapers and discarded wipes.

# 3

You might say that a swimming pool was a perfect place to loaf. After all, the water was warm, your body floated on an undulating current and your mind could drift wherever you or it wanted. And it was in this blissful state I put myself each and every morning. That is, when Hugo didn't kick me in the face with his wide leg sweeps or some other interloper didn't hog the lane or cause turbulence through sheer displacement. I tended to drift, literally and psychically, in the attempt to make the morning swim as pleasant as possible. There was something about getting wet in the morning. Most sane people found it rather repulsive and I was no exception.

Thus I drifted, floating up and down the lane, thinking the most tranquil and pleasant thoughts. I wanted to remove myself from the harsh realities I would face upon leaving the pool, purge all the poison and oppression I felt. Come out from under the pressures when I went to the office, distance myself from the latest load Sharon had plunked on my shoulders, forget about the stress of writing two novels at the same time and getting absolutely nowhere with either one. I imagined sun and sand and green fields, pleasant Vivaldi-like music wafting over undulating hills. That was it. I'd found paradise.

A sharp tug on my ankle jolted me out of this utopian reverie. I sputtered up and came face to face with an elderly woman in a yellow bathing cap. Even through my fogged-up goggles, I could tell she was upset about something, especially when she began to poke me in the chest.

"Ow."

"You have no right," she said with great indignation. "How dare you?"

What was she on about, I thought, the old biddy. "What do you mean?"

The old woman beckoned to the lifeguard, the pugnacious Maria, a dark-haired, tattooed girl with a wrestler's body, who took no crap from anyone. We stood in the shallow end and by now had attracted some attention from the other swimmers. Maria got down on her haunches, closer to our level. "This man," the old lady said and poked me again.

"Stop that."

"This man," she repeated. "Was peeing in the pool."

Maria's face pulled back in disgust. "That's ridiculous," I said. "I've been swimming here for years and I'd never do such a thing."

"Don't lie to me, young man. I saw you."

"Saw me? Can you even see anything let alone what you claim you saw underwater?"

Maria smirked a little then her face moved into an expression of studied concentration. "Ma'am, are you sure?"

"You're darn right I'm sure. I know pee when I see it. Didn't I raise four boys and believe me when I say I saw plenty of it above and below water."

Maria looked at me. "You'll have to come with me sir."

"What? Come with you where?"

"Into the office for a moment."

I gave the old biddy a dirty look, then hauled myself out of the pool, then stalked behind Maria into the alcove they called the office. She turned to face me. Her brown eyes turned to mud. I put my hands on my hips.

"Look," she said. "Do you have any sort of a, uh, problem?"

"Problem?" I wasn't cottoning to her question.

"You know, like a bladder problem?"

Now it was my turn to be indignant. "Are you insane? Of course I don't have a problem."

"Well, what's your explanation?"

"I have no idea. She's imagining things."

"She claims she saw something."

"That old biddy can claim she saw Martians for all I care but that doesn't make it true."

Maria chewed her lip for a moment. "Listen, do you mind if I smell your suit?"

"What?"

"I'd like you to remove your suit so I can smell it."

"You mean, take it off? Here?"

"Remove it in the change room. I'll give you a towel and you can hand it out to me."

"I don't think so."

"You're sure?"

"Yes." In the background I could hear the movement of the water as it slapped up against the sides of the pool. I could see the old woman had continued her routine.

Maria smirked again then picked up the phone. "Security," she said.

Well, that was it. The long and the short of it saw me banned from the pool for a month. They told me that if I had some sort of a problem, they understood but I should take steps to have it seen to. I felt humiliated and outraged, not to mention, the looks I got from some of the other regular morning swimmers. The old biddy sported a look of triumph on her wrinkly face that I wanted crush with a jackboot. Did I do it? I have no idea.

For the residents of Toronto, May 9th will be forever known as a day of infamy. The Maple Leafs lost the seventh game in the Stanley Cup playoffs to the New Jersey Devils, the Raptors were downed by the Philadelphia 76ers, also in the playoffs and the Blue Jays were humiliated again by the Oakland Athletics. And I was banned for a month because I peed in the pool. Allegedly. Naturally, I didn't tell Sharon any of this. She wouldn't be able to stand the public shame of it.

Mornings at the office were reserved for writing. I snuck in before everyone else. Like most magazines, the staff didn't roll in until nine-thirty or so and in Angela's case, her arrival depended entirely on what she was doing the evening before and with whom it was being done. Most days she appeared in immaculate form, not a frond or lash out of alignment. On occasion, however, we could tell by her demeanour, the secret, lascivious smile on her face, the puffiness in her eyes, that to the envy of all of us, she'd had a rollicking good time. I knew for a fact that both of her nipples were pierced. It's not what you're thinking, she actually told me, although the why of it was a bit embarrassing.

"Bernie?"

I looked up and Angela towered over my desk. The wooden clog-like things she wore added only four or five inches to her already lofty height.

"Hmm, yes?"

"I need to leave early today, okay?"

"I suppose so. Everything all right?"

She twisted her full lips, then shook her long blonde hair. "Well, if you must know, I have a bit of a problem."

"Oh?"

"Well, you know I've got my nipples pierced, right?"

My eyebrows almost shot off my head. They must have landed somewhere in the back of my cranium, upside down. "Uh, yes. Of course. Of course I do." And I cleared my throat.

"Well, one of the rings has cut through the skin a bit and it's infected. So I have to go see Derek and get it fixed."

"Derek?"

"Yes. He's the guy who does all of my piercings. He's the best in the city and he's the only one who can fix this." And she nodded down to her right boob. Angela had her stomach, tongue and ears pierced. She talked about her cheek or eyebrow next.

"I see. Derek."

"I've got an appointment for three. If that's okay."

"Uh, sure, I suppose. We don't want you to have any more problems. Down there, I mean."

"Derek's got to get this thing off me so it can heal properly and then I can have it re-done."

"Excellent. Uh, thanks for bringing this to my attention." As Sharon said, too much information. So off she went, Angela, to her nipple piercing removal appointment with Derek, the best in the city by reputation, of course.

I was still thinking of things related to piercings when Jessica came over to my desk. "Here are today's press releases," she said in her chirpiest tone and as I looked at her, I imagined her astride a small bulldozer forcing a mound of paper forward. I was amazed at her dexterity on the thing, not realizing she had any mechanical capability but she wheeled the dozer about like a trooper. As she approached my desk, the mound of paper grew and grew and grew until I thought I'd be trapped and suffocated by it. "Bernie?"

"Oh. What?" Snap out of it, I told myself.

"The press releases?"

"Yes, thanks."

She handed over a bulging folder and I set it on my desk. As she turned, I caught a look on her face that signalled concern. In any case, the first hour of my time was dedicated solely to writing before I'd let the intrusions of the day screw things up even more. Reluctantly, I opened up my email. There was a message from Charlotte: Well, she wrote. What about the opening on Friday night? Will I see you there? Whatever happened to letters and telegrams, I thought. Technology was so intrusive. I wrote back: I'll meet you there at 7:30. Taking the bull by the horns. And Sharon would have me by the balls if she found out. I don't think it was the Italians who invented the concept of vendetta, it was the Irish. Anything to take my mind off babies. I thought of calling Ramon and commiserating but I didn't want to hear from him and Nook right now. They'd just add to the pain.

I went round Roberto's desk to see how he was coming along with the layouts for our latest issue that was ten days late already. He was showing Angela the design of his new kitchen. It was up on the computer and the whole thing was really very clever what with side views and zoom ins and zoom outs and the three-dimensional perspective. It looked like a really nice kitchen. I too would have been proud to have such a kitchen in my home.

"Ahem," I said. Angela nudged Roberto who didn't respond but kept on zipping around the counters and cupboards. "The layouts. Are they done yet?"

"No," he replied.

"When are they going to be finished?"

"Soon."

"Can you be more specific?"

"Today. They'll be done today." Roberto hadn't turned away from the computer screen, just adjusted his glasses, sighed, closed the kitchen program reluctantly and punched up the magazine.

"They need to be done today. We're already late."

"I know, I know. Don't worry. It'll be done."

Angela had shrunk into her own corner, pretending that nothing was happening. Sometimes, I felt more married to Roberto than Sharon and I am sure that, on occasion, he felt the same way. I didn't doubt that his wife, Giovanna, would disagree. But I felt that this union had grown stale and I found myself getting irked by Roberto's habits and idiosyncrasies. The relationship, I feared was deteriorating. As a partner, however, the only way to see the back of him was to buy him out which I couldn't afford and indeed, wondered if it was worth it given the meagre earnings of the magazine at the end of the day. He could be remarkably obtuse at times. Roberto was born in Italy and came to Toronto when he as a boy. That meant that his English was spotty at best and his spelling atrocious. His work had to be checked and double-checked and checked again. And since we were in the word business, we couldn't afford any embarrassing mistakes. Like the time Margaret Atwood's name was misspelled as Elmwood or the banner headline on the cover one time: Harcourt's Brestsellers! And so on. Fortunately, the industry thought it was a gag as Harcourt had brought out a number of titles that could be categorized as "bodice rippers". That saved the day but fortune had smiled on us that one time. The others weren't so amusing.

Roberto was also remarkably forgetful and had to be reminded constantly about things. In fact, I often had to stand over him and direct, which I found increasingly fatiguing, not to mention, irritating. And messy. God knows how Giovanna could put up with him. Garbage everywhere, dropped anywhere, who needed trash bins? Not Roberto, the desk, the floor, the worktables, any surface would do. And I think the thing that bothered me most was the dishes. Lunch times, he often brought in pasta or pizza or veal that Giovanna had made the night before. Roberto would prepare his lunch in our small kitchen. That was fine but he left his dishes piled up in the sink. I refused to do them for him, even though I was tempted and they sat there until a thick, unguous grayish-green film, something resembling pond scum, enveloped them. And then finally, he'd give in, go to the sink, pull on a pair of latex gloves, after all, his hands needed to be protected, yet he could pour cement or roll out sod with no problem, and do the washing up. There were times when I wished I could clang him on the head with a garden shovel. And I dare say, he felt the same way about me.

"When you've got something, I want to see it right away."

"Sure. Sure."

"Advertisers aren't paying us to be late."

"Of course not." And then he'd sigh deeply as if his sanctimony had been violated and turned back to the work at hand, the work that paid his bills so he could afford to put in that new kitchen rather than moon over it on his computer screen. Roberto, a natural loafer par excellence.

I had made a date with Charlotte and the fact hadn't sunk in yet but I could feel a queasy stomach coming on. Immediately, I began to think of ways to get out of it. Blinding migraine, except I wasn't a headache person. Domestic emergency? Too contrived. Injured at the gym. Hmm, unless I'm on crutches, I don't think that'd work. Last minute deadline? Wouldn't take the entire evening as the showing didn't begin until 7:30. I was bereft of excuses at the moment. I called up a friend of mine, David Sugar, a lawyer, who was the emperor of excuses, a master of evasiveness. After all, wasn't that what lawyers were about?

"David."

"I'm not in."

"Yes you are, you answered the phone."

"Fine," he drawled. "Have it your way but that doesn't mean I'm agreeing with you."

"I need an excuse."

"You've come to the right place, Bernard. Excuses are my business. What sort of excuse?"

"Umm, the sort where you've accepted an invitation to something and now you don't want to go but you don't want to hurt the other person's feelings because they really, really want you to go. Got it?"

David breathed for a moment on the phone. "I think so. You accepted in a moment of weakness. So the excuse must be tactful but shouldn't have any lasting negative impact, is that right?"

"Yes, exactly. That's the sort of excuse I need."

David was tall and bony, all arms and legs. He spoke laconically which made his adversaries tend to underestimate him. He used that to his advantage in court. "How about, a school concert you forgot about?"

"Don't think so. My kids wouldn't be caught dead in a school concert let alone let us be seen attending one."

"Okay," he admitted. "A bit lame, I'd agree. Could there be a sudden business trip that's popped up?"

"No. I never go anywhere for business or anything else for that matter. We only fly on Sharon's points when we take vacation in the summer."

"There's always the 24-hour flu."

"This time of year? Unlikely."

"Sudden rash?"

"Nope. Don't think so."

"Put your back out lifting something heavy?"

"Get serious."

"Car accident?"

"Come on, David. This is well below your standard."

"I know," he replied ruefully. "To tell you the truth, I've been in a bit of a funk lately. Something just isn't right, you know?"

"Like what?"

"Like all this. If you'd called me up before, I'd have come up with a dozen plausible excuses just like that. You know, got to go to a stag for an old college chum, filling in as a DJ at a dance club, client dinner, planning a surprise party for a relative which was a surprise to me as well, any number of things, pulled into a last minute car rally, can't let the softball team down, whatever. It all seems to have slipped away for some reason."

"I wish I played softball," I said. "Well David, thanks anyway."

"Sure," he said, and put down the phone.

My mind was a blank and if David couldn't help me, well then, I suppose I was committed or more accurately, should be committed. I glanced at my watch. Lunch time. Well, it seemed as if I'd accomplished as little as possible since I'd rolled in at the usual time. Yesterday, Sharon had come home from a spa appointment I had given her for Valentine's day. Here it was the month of May and she had just got round to keeping the appointment. She looked flushed and relaxed, her face freshly made up.

"Have a good time?" I asked her.

"Wonderful," she said. "So relaxing." Then she unbuttoned the top of her blouse. "Come here."

"What?"

"Smell." And thrust her chest out. I leaned in and inhaled. "What do you smell?"

I was puzzled. "Garlic sausage," I said.

Sharon narrowed her eyes, giving me a less than friendly look. "That's what I had for lunch. I mean the fragrance."

I leaned in again. "Garlic sausage." Her lower lip began to tremble. "Honestly, that's all I can smell."

"You bastard," she spat. "Getting a compliment out of you is like pulling teeth." And she awkwardly stomped off, her face no longer fresh or relaxed, crutches squeaking on the tile floor.

She was right. I didn't often give compliments and it wasn't prudent. It wouldn't have hurt to say she'd smelled wonderful and fruity, like a tropical eggnog but I couldn't. I had to be honest instead. And look where it got me, in the doghouse. She'd sulk and stew for the whole afternoon, which she did. And as I reflected on this the following day, I felt pangs of guilt, particularly as I had been thinking about Charlotte too.

I worked on the summer reading issue. After all, what else do you cover in the summer time when smart people were away at cottages or hiking in the Alps or sipping wine in the south of France? For those dunces, myself included, who stayed at home in thc summer exploring what the city had to offer, that is, higher air pollution, clogged roads narrowed by construction and perky cultural festivals, it was a time to send your kids far away for as long as possible. And for that reason, I chose a scout camp in Northern Ontario. It was rugged, all male, and the focus was on self-reliance and discipline. They'd learn how to tie knots, start fires without matches and to sleep in trees. What's not to like? I knew that Nathan would love it and Sean would despise it but I figured it was good for the both of them and they had each other to rely on if they could ever stop fighting. More importantly, they'd be gone for an entire month. Yahoo. It was a much-needed break. They could be wearing.

I took a phone call.

"Hello?"

"Mr. Goldman?"

"Yes?"

"Jocelyn Bergamot, the principal from the school?"

She sounded as if she wasn't sure who she was. "Oh yes. How can I help you Ms. Bergamot?"

"It's about Sean. I think we should have a little chat."

"Chat?"

"Yes. A chat," she replied firmly. I hadn't been in school for years and even so, I felt a little intimidated by her tone.

"What about?"

"Sean's behaviour."

"I take it, it hasn't been good."

"You take it rightly. Shall we say around one?"

"Fine," I croaked and hung up the phone, thinking maybe I should consider boot camp instead.

The remainder of the morning passed uneventfully. I received a call from Jessica, who said she'd be in late because she had to rescue a cat that had got stuck up in a tree and it took her until 2:30 to coax it down and then she slept through her alarm. Fine. Angela called and said she'd was stuck out near the airport and was running an hour to an hour and a half late. Roberto called and said he had to wait for some guys he knew to deliver a load of sand. That left myself and the ever-graceful Ruth who stalked in, her lower lip thrust forward, her hair in a more tumbleweed state than usual.

"Ruth," I said by way of greeting. "How are you?"

She grunted in reply, dropped her plastic bag by her desk, sat down heavily and began rummaging around in it for something that seemed to take an inordinate amount of time to find. Finally, she pulled out a dime store package of tissues, dug one out and blew her nose heftily while I pretended not to notice. Not much of the tissue was left. The bulk of it had disintegrated. I reminded myself never to touch her phone.

As I scanned through my email, she hobbled over and dropped a large file folder on my desk. "Look through those, will you?"

"What am I looking for?"

"Names."

"What names?"

"Names you recognize."

"Why should I do that?"

She squinted at me, tried to read my mood for a moment, then huffed. "Forget it, then. I'll do it myself." And she grabbed the file folder from my desk, knocking several things on to the floor. She turned around nonchalantly and marched back to her own desk, leaving me to tidy up the mess. As I bent down to retrieve the papers, I asked myself why I'd hired her in the first place. To be truthful, I'd felt sorry for her. She seemed so eager to get hired and her references had been decent. Little did I know they'd all been written by her family and friends. After our first interview, she'd even sent me a nice card as a follow up which I thought had been very considerate. After I hired her, and mentioned the card, then saw her blank look, I realized she had forgotten all about it.

# 4

I arrived at Cedar Park High School right at one. The school had a good academic reputation. We had put our kids into an immersion program where, starting at age six, they spoke nothing but French. Over time, English was gradually introduced such that, by grade six, the day split fifty-fifty between the two languages. It had been a good decision giving them, in my opinion, a broader view of the world, greater insight into other cultures and customs, better job prospects and a jump on learning other languages from the same family. I tried to bear this in mind as I was shown into Ms. Bergamot's well-ordered office. She was a trim woman in her fifties with a helmet of greying hair, red glasses and a no-nonsense manner. She rose as I entered and I realized she stood barely five feet tall. Given some of the hulking teenagers I saw strutting the corridors, I gave her a great deal of credit.

"Mr. Goldman?" I nodded, my mouth had suddenly gone dry. Flashing back to my own misbehaviours in high school. "Take a seat."

"Thank you."

She settled herself in a leather chair that creaked slightly and smoothed her skirt over her thighs. "I'll come right to the point. I am worried about your son, Sean. We are seeing a worrisome pattern of behaviour."

"Oh? How so?" I inquired politely.

She gave me a look as if to say, you poor sod keeping your head buried in the sand and now it is my job to yank it out.

"Well, he has a habit of disappearing from classes."

"Disappearing?"

"Yes. For instance, his English teacher, Mrs. Praxis, told me that, on numerous occasions, Sean would ask to go to the bathroom and then he'd never come back. Usually, he'd be found wandering the halls or outside somewhere. And Mrs. Praxis isn't the only teacher to notice this sort of thing. To be honest, he has been observed on several occasions where he is staring off into space during class time, a blank expression on his face and the teacher has a time of it getting his attention. As if he wasn't there or he'd just blissed out, if you catch my meaning."

"I'm not sure I do."

She pressed her thin lips together. "I can only offer observations and clearly, Sean is your child and you must decide what to do."

"Yes."

"His academic work is in a downward spiral, are you aware of that?"

"Uh, no, I wasn't."

"He is in danger of losing his year. In fact, he's right on the borderline at this point."

"I see."

"He hasn't been doing his work, not turning in his assignments, his work when it's done is unorganized and he's not paying attention in class. Have you noticed any change in his behaviour at home?"

"No, not really."

"No change at all?" I shrugged. "Does he seem depressed to you?"

If anything, Sean was irrepressible, the opposite of depressed. We couldn't tone him down, he was always doing something, pulling some prank or other and it had been that way as long as I could remember. "Just the opposite, in fact."

"What about your wife?"

"What about her?"

"Is she around much? Does she travel a lot? Is he attached to her?"

"Well," I admitted. "My wife does travel and yes, Sean is attached to Sharon, much more than Nathan."

Ms. Bergamot nodded curtly.

"I thought so. In any case, I thought it important to bring this to your attention. He's also hanging around with a group that, frankly, is not the best influence on him. This group of boys is constantly in trouble and they all reinforce each other. And the results are not buoyant, I can assure you."

"What are the consequences?"

Ms. Bergamot pursed her lips. "Well, detentions don't seem to work. He just skips those and then gets more for skipping the first ones and it goes around in circles. I just can't fathom his attitude, Mr. Goldman."

"I'm not sure I can either."

"Ultimately, we're looking at retention."

"Retention?" I was thinking water or other fluids.

"We don't call it failure anymore. He'd be held back a grade."

"I see."

"And then there's this."

She reached behind her and picked up a piece of paper, then handed it to me. Here's what I read: Please excuse my son Sean from classes this week as we are away on a family trip. Sincerely, Bernard Goldman. "Is that your signature Mr. Goldman?"

"Uh no, it isn't Ms. Bergamot. Not even close."

"Didn't think so."

"He is enterprising though, wouldn't you say?" I was looking for a shred of something constructive.

"Oh yes. It's unfortunate that he doesn't put some creative energy into his school work."

"What do you want me to do?" I asked her.

Her small, brown eyes widened. "I think you should talk with him and see if he can't be straightened out. The school board employs a number of psychological consultants and you may wish to have him assessed."

"Assessed for what?"

"His state of mind, Mr. Goldman. He seems to me to be a troubled kid with no motivation to succeed. Quite the opposite, in fact."

"Otherwise?"

"His behaviour will hold him back. It will be an impediment to any success he may wish in the future, I'm convinced of that. We'll have to see how he finishes this term. Right now, he's borderline. Until we see his marks, I can't tell you whether he will go on to grade eleven. It's too bad he isn't more like his brother."

"Yes," I replied. "I'm sure he's had that rammed down his throat often enough."

Ms. Bergamot stood up, colour had flooded into her cheeks.

"Not from this office," she said indignantly, a sharpness in her tone.

I stood up as well and looked down towards her. "I didn't mean to imply anything, Ms. Bergamot." I was still holding the note. "May I keep this?"

"Certainly."

"It may be useful."

She put out her small, delicate hand. "Goodbye, Mr. Goldman."

I took it. Her grip was surprisingly firm. "Good day, Ms. Bergamot."

Although it was a beautiful day outside, I failed to notice. I'm not even sure how I got back to the office, what route I took, how many lights were red, what turns I made, suddenly, I was pulling into the parking lot and looking at Eric bloody Schwilden's gleaming Porsche. I picked up a handful of dirt and threw it at the windshield. When the car yelped back at me, I just about jumped out of my skin, then quickly walked toward the entrance before it had a chance to do it again. Jesus, even cars have feelings now.

Arriving home, I was surprised and concerned to discover an ambulance parked in the driveway. Sharon's Navigator was beside it. Panic flooded my chest, always think the worst, that way if you're lucky and it doesn't happen, you'll be relieved. If you're unlucky and it does, then at least you're already panicking and everything isn't quite as much of a shock.

I burst through the door and the first thing I saw was a stretcher in the foyer. "What's going on?" I called. "Sharon. Sharon. Are you here? Hello?"

Sharon appeared on the second-floor landing and bent slightly over the railing. She leaned on a wooden crutch. "Up here."

I bounded up the stairs. "What's going on? Is it the boys? Is one of them hurt? Did something happen?"

Sharon put a hand on my arm and gave me a wry look.

"Calm yourself, darlin', it's just my ma. She's had a tumble and broken her leg. Now the two of us are a real pair. Something about injuring legs in this family. So I thought it would be better if she moved in with us for a while."

The colour drained from my face. "What? I mean, uh, is she all right?"

"She's just getting set up right now. The ambulance people were very nice, so helpful they were."

"But...but..." Felicity and I did not get along well. I'd felt her sharp tongue lash my back on more than a few occasions and to have her settled in here all nice and cozy? "Surely a convalescent home is the best place, don't you think? With the facilities and resources, physiotherapists they have there?"

"Nice try but the doctor said it was okay. She'll be fine here."

"But who's going to look after her while we're away during the day?"

Sharon smiled then, a secret sort of smile that made me queasy and she gave me a look that had more than its share of wickedness in it.

A feeling of dread washed over me and for a moment I didn't want to believe it. I thought for a moment and wondered if this was to be the worst day in my life so far. I'd had plenty of those that counted but this revelation might just top them all. "Oh no. You don't mean…? Sharon, you can't. You can't do this to me. Please say it's not true. It isn't true, is it?"

Sharon wore a pink Anne Klein II outfit that featured a jacket and skirt. She shrugged her padded shoulders. "Come see for yourself."

Like a condemned man walking to the gallows, I stepped forward gingerly expecting the floor to open up and swallow me whole.

"Where is she?"

"Spare bedroom."

Each step seemed an eternity and yet I moved in a vacuum as if all the air and the sounds and the noise had been sucked out of the hall. The world was now muffled and as I leaned up against the doorframe, somehow I found the strength to crane my head around and survey the room. There lay Felicity, her leg in a cast and elevated on a steep set of pillows. Fussing and bustling around her in a starched get-up was Mrs. Sanchez, my sworn enemy for life. She glanced up and gave me a malevolent look.

" Señor Goldman," she acknowledged, then resumed the adjustment of the pillows under my mother-in-law's leg.

"Mrs. Sanchez," I replied, through clenched teeth.

"Well, you might ask how I'm doing?" barked Felicity.

I turned my attention to her. She hated not being the focal point of a room or conversation. "Of course, Felicity, how inconsiderate of me. And how are you feeling? How is the leg? Throbs, does it?"

"You'll be right well pleased, if it does, won't you? Well, they've put me on these wonderful painkillers and I can't feel a thing. Not even my face. It's lovely."

"Good. And I hope it stays that way." I glanced at Mrs. Sanchez and knew she was listening to what I was saying. There were those who could mask themselves, make themselves inconspicuous but Mrs. Sanchez wasn't one of them in my opinion. She wore her unbridled anger on the surface and it became evident very quickly what she liked and disliked. She hated me but worshiped the ground that Sharon walked on, would go through fire, plagues and pestilence for her, in fact. I was a minor inconvenience. And now the boys are older and more independent. When they were young, I worked from home and took care of them pretty much while Mrs. Sanchez was our housekeeper. The root of our problems began then. But it had been almost five years since Mrs. Sanchez had worked for us and she looked almost the same, except for some white streaks in her dark hair that was pulled back tautly in a severe bun. "Why don't you take a rest then, Felicity. Is there anything I can get for you?"

"Well, I'm not going anywhere, am I? I'll be lucky enough to make it to the loo in this state. Don't bother about me, Bernie, I'll be fine. Not that you ever did, mind but I've got the lovely Mrs. Sanchez here to look after me and she's just an angel, isn't she?"

I glanced at Mrs. Sanchez and thought I caught the subtle signs of a smirk. "Of course, whatever you say. Well, um, if you don't need anything, I'll stop in a bit later and see how you're doing." Felicity had her eyes closed now and I suppose she floated somewhere near the ceiling. Mrs. Sanchez still fussed with the sheets and blankets on the bed, smoothing them out, tucking the ends in so tightly, Felicity would remain pinned for life.

I found Sharon in the kitchen, her crutch leaning against the counter, leafing through the paper. She had her glasses on and I could see she scanned the financial pages. "Suppose I'd better get dinner started," I said.

Sharon looked up briefly. "Don't bother. Mrs. Sanchez has got a casserole going and a salad made. She'll take a plate up to Mum."

"You mean whenever she comes down from what she's on."

"Ach, she can always eat no matter what her state, haven't you learned that yet about your mother-in-law?"

"Apparently not. Although I do know she won't eat anything that is slippery or anything that is the colour green. And that eliminates a number of possibilities."

"Only about half the world's agricultural output I'd say," she replied mildly.

"Have you seen the boys?"

"In their rooms, I think."

Since Sharon was absorbed in the article she was reading on inflation rates, I took the opportunity to hunt down Sean. I found Nathan lying on his bed, headphones wrapped around his head, while he played one of those handheld video games. I could hear the music from the doorway to his room. I found a pair of socks lying on the floor and lobbed them over. He jumped.

Pulling off the headphones, he said, "Dad. Don't do that. You scared me."

"Sorry. Didn't think you'd hear me if I said anything. Do you know where your brother is?"

"I dunno. He's around somewhere. Did you look in his room?"

I made a face. "Yes."

"Then try downstairs."

"Right."

Nathan turned back to the music and the video game. The house was so damn big, Sean could be hiding out anywhere. He was very good at that. He could hide in a crack if need be. I remember once, when he was about ten, I searched the whole house for him and he'd been hiding at the top of the mattress and jammed himself between that and the box spring then covered himself up with the pillows. When he leapt out from under the pillows, I almost had a heart attack. Just looking at the pillows and the bed, you wouldn't have suspected there'd been a body under there. Once, he'd hidden in the dryer. I'd chewed him out for that one.

This time, however, he hadn't bothered to hide at all. I found him sprawled in front of the television in the basement.

"Hey," he said laconically.

I nodded. "Can you turn that down, please?"

"What?"

I spoke louder. "The television, turn it down please."

"Yeah, sure." He picked up the remote control and lowered the sound to just below supersonic level.

I removed a piece of paper from my pocket and unfolded it. "Do you know what this is?"

"Looks like paper."

"Bravo. But it's what's on the paper that is interesting." And I read: "Please excuse Sean from classes this week as he'll be on a family trip. Yours sincerely, Bernard Goldman. And there's a muddled looking signature that's supposed to be mine. The thing is, neither the note or the signature fooled anyone."

"Yeah."

"I had a little chat with Mrs. Bergamot today."

"She's an old biddy."

"Well, that old biddy influences whether you pass or fail. At the moment, it looks like you're falling off the rails. You're going to repeat your year."

"I don't think so. They can't fail me."

"Your marks say otherwise."

"I'm not failing any of my courses."

"Oh really? And what's with this leaving class and wandering the halls?"

"That's only in English. I can't stand Mrs. Praxis. She's a terrible teacher."

"And did you honestly think that you'd get away with this?" I held up the note. "You must think we are all exceedingly stupid."

Sean grinned. His face had become quite pimply and his voice had dropped an octave. "Something like that."

"You know. I may not be able to change your attitude but I don't have to condone or reward this kind of behaviour. You're grounded. For the week."

Sean jumped to his feet. "What for? I didn't do anything?"

To say I was stunned was an understatement. "You cut classes and wander the halls. You forge a note trying to pass it off as if it came from me, you are doing miserably in school and you call that nothing?"

"It is nothing because school is a waste of time. It's boring and I hate it. It sucks. It stinks. It's full of shit."

"Room please."

"No."

"Pardon?"

"I said no."

"Well, let's put it this way. If you don't go to your room by the time I count to three, you'll be looking at two weeks. And if you still don't go, I will physically put you there."

We were now about six inches apart and Sean, who was only slightly shorter than I, stared at me with what I could call unmitigated hatred. He held my look for a long moment, breathing noisily through his mouth, his chest heaved as if he was working himself up to something, then suddenly, he broke off and stalked away. I heard him stomp up the stairs and from the distant recesses, heard his door slam with tremendous force. Then I breathed a long sigh of relief. Ouch. I'd bluffed him again but we moved closer and closer to a physical and emotional precipice. I had no idea what to do about Sean who shouldered a "fuck-you" attitude about everything that he found unimportant, that excluded only the things he wanted to do when he wanted to do them. And Sharon was no help. She was away so often, either working late or travelling that when she appeared, she lavished the boys with stuff, whatever they wanted. "And why not?" she'd ask. "We can afford it." Naturally, she missed the point. The boys were being trained to expect things without having to lift a finger. And when it came to Sean, she just turned a blind eye. He'd always been her favourite and they shared that strange, mysterious bond that so many mothers and sons have between them. It was unbreakable, a solid laser beam of love.

I thought about the specific occasion that Mrs. Sanchez and I irrevocably parted not just affection-wise but civility as well. When the boys were young, I stayed home with them. I'd had an office set up and that's where I did my writing, in between taking them to and from school, going to the park, running errands, ferrying them to doctor's appointments, the dentist and other kids' houses. In Mrs. Sanchez's eyes, this sort of lifestyle, made me a wuss, less than the machismo standard she was used to. She'd had a rigid upbringing, did Mrs. Sanchez, where the men in her family had decent, honourable professions; plumbers, electricians, contractors, even a doctor or lawyer or two. Hanging around the house was not the accepted practice in her world and I contravened some sort of propriety as far as she was concerned, but I think it was really when I dumped a pot of melted chocolate on her head that she began to loathe me in earnest. Not that I did it on purpose, of course. To a certain extent, I have Sean to blame for that, even though he was only five at the time.

When I was young, my mother baked quite a bit. One of her favourite desserts was also one of the simplest. A pound of baking chocolate, a pound of peanut butter and a bag of mini-marshmallows. You melted the chocolate and peanut butter together in a pan over a low heat, then you set the pan aside for awhile. The marshmallows were spread out in a greased baking tin. Then you simply added the melted chocolate and peanut butter, stuck the tin in the fridge and let it cool. Once cooled, you simply cut the hardened mixture into squares and voila, a mind-blowing, calorific treat. The boys loved them and so did I, of course. Sean being Sean was prone to leaving his toys scattered about everywhere, especially the kitchen. We have ceramic tile in our kitchen and it is very slippery. Litter the tile with skittery toys with wheels and watch out, you're flat on your back in a millisecond. I carped at him to put his toys away but he'd leave a trail from his room down the stairs, into the living room, the dining room and yes, on that fateful day, the kitchen. Sharon had just bought the two of them a Hot Wheels set that featured racing cars and an elaborate track. Sean and Nathan had set the track up in the living room but they liked to shoot the cars along the ceramic tile because the cars would really move on the smooth surface.

Mrs. Sanchez had been working for us only a few months and our relations had lapsed into edgy but tolerable silences. She never spoke unless it was for some utilitarian need. "Do you require the linens changed today, Señor Goldman?" That sort of thing. It was awkward but I tried to ignore it as best I could. On that day, I had set the pan with the melted chocolate and peanut butter to cool and was searching through the cupboards, looking for the baking tin I normally used. Well, I couldn't find it anywhere and began pulling things out of the cupboards, fry pans, pots, colanders, steamers littered the floor. Mrs. Sanchez came in and stopped dead in her tracks, staring at the mess.

"What are you looking for? Perhaps I can help you?"

I described the tin to her and saw the flood of recognition wash over her stolid face. "I know where it is," she said finally. She pointed to the window sill. There, full of potting soil along with a newly planted dieffenbachia, sat my baking tin.

"You, you," I sputtered. "Used my favourite baking tin as a planter?" I was outraged and she seemed nonplussed.

"Yes," she said. "It was the right size and depth for it." Then she bent over and began to collect the pots and pans I'd strewn over the floor. Without thinking about what I was doing, I went to the stove and picked up the pan full of cooling chocolate and peanut butter. There was a bubbling cauldron in the pit of my stomach, seething at this flagrant violation of my sovereignty, this defilement of my authority in my own domicile. To be honest, I think I was momentarily insane and if I'd known that a simple baking tin could cause such an extreme reaction from someone normally as calm as me, I would have harrumphed or psshawed or made an equally derogatory response. But there was no one else to set me on the right path. And as I stepped forward without abandon bearing the offensive pan, the ball of my right foot landed squarely on one of the Hot Wheels that Sean had carelessly left on the kitchen floor. My foot shot out from under me like a naked tire on black ice and my weight went with it. My arms flew up and the pan left my grasp as I found myself temporarily airborne then flat on my back on the floor, landing with a cacophony of clatter, pings, bangs and bings as the pots and other cooking ware scattered. Poor Mrs. Sanchez, and I can say this now looking back on it, had been kneeling on the floor.

When I finally sat up and surveyed my surroundings, I saw to my horror and admittedly, perverse amusement, that my pan had landed rather neatly on her head and the melted chocolate and peanut butter mixture oozed its way down her vexed face, drooling down to her shoulders, splattering the front of her starched dress. She sat up, pawing at her eyes to clear some of the sludge. It was then that I did the unthinkable and the unforgivable. I'm afraid, I laughed. She looked such a sight that I couldn't help it. I'm sure I looked a complete fool as well, but whatever dignity Mrs. Sanchez had wanted to salvage, evaporated instantly. And it didn't help either that the two little hooligans had scampered in when they heard the commotion and seeing the mess, howled like little banshees, grabbing their sides and falling over on to the carpet. I was never forgiven. From that day forward, I was the sworn enemy and nothing could persuade or deter Mrs. Sanchez otherwise. And so it was, that over the years until her retirement, Mrs. Sanchez and I had many encounters and none had eased her view of me in the least, no matter how hard I tried to win her favour. Finally, I gave up. I'd done all that was humanly possible and didn't care anymore. So be it. Mrs. Sanchez would never think well of me and that was that. And now, Sharon had lured her out of "retirement".

As I sat at the dinner table that evening and watched as Sharon had her head buried in the financial pages and Sean and Nathan traded insults and threw food back and forth across the table, all the while watched over by the dour Mrs. Sanchez, I realized that family life is not all it is cracked up to be. No wonder I sought escape. They seemed oblivious to my observations, carrying on in their own bubbles as I fought to squelch the feelings of disappointment that welled up inside me. But what had I expected? I wasn't sure. Just something different, I suppose. Something that felt better, something more hopeful, something more joyful. And I knew that my bitterness was all wrapped up with the lack of success I had achieved in my own life and career. That I hadn't advanced beyond my father's reputation. That I was riding Sharon's coattails and there was something to Mrs. Sanchez's view of me as a wuss. Being stuck between all of the worlds that I inhabited, I came to realize that the only real one seemed to be that which existed in my own mind and everything outside was peripheral. How scary was that?

# 5

There were days that I dreaded going into the office. The only meaningful moments were those scant bubbles where I spent writing. But if someone should become even the slightest bit ambitious or God forbid, catch an early bus and arrive before they're due, the mood, the spell would be quashed. It could sour me for the whole day. I wasn't good at dealing with real flesh and blood first thing in the morning, not when I wanted to live inside this mental cocoon every day. Friday loomed closer and closer. The knot in my brain expanded to include my innards. Both Nook and Ramon had called during the week and I didn't return their messages. Seeing them on Saturday would be comeuppance enough. I had told Sharon that I would be late on Friday as I had a "book thing" to attend. I'm not even sure she acknowledged it.

"Mrs. Sanchez will be here looking after things," she said.

"Right."

I had dressed a little more carefully, which meant no wrinkled T-shirt or ripped jeans. "You look nice," she murmured, and then began to pack up her things into her gleaming, leather briefcase. She didn't need the crutch any more, just a tight bandage and a limp saw her off.

'Thanks." I kissed her on the cheek and inhaled her scent. It was very nice. I melted a little. "See you later then." Sharon and I rarely spoke during the day. She was just too busy, in meetings most of the time, or zooming off to another office or radio or television station to scare the bejeezus out of them. I watched her limp off and followed her to the door. I heard the roar of the Navigator's engine and turned away before she backed out of the driveway. I glanced at my watch. A little before seven-thirty. I put away my breakfast dishes, looked in on the boys to make sure they were less than comatose, brushed my teeth being careful not to dribble on my shirt, peed quickly, grabbed up my stuff and let myself out.

Although I felt distracted that morning, the writing went surprisingly well, smooth and almost effortless. The words seemed to fly out of my brain and some of the phrases seemed actually coherent. When Ruth huffed her way in, coughing spasmodically, I looked up in surprise. The time had blown by. For a short while, I had managed to push Charlotte to the back of my mind.

"Good morning, Ruth," I said.

She grunted in reply. "Hmmph."

I actually smiled then. I don't know why.

There were enough crises during the day to keep me busy. The bank called about some unusual transactions on our account and I assured them they were legitimate even though our account manager, a young woman by the name of Nadia, seemed skeptical. But I gave her the usual assurances and she accepted them readily enough. Jessica called in around ten that morning to say she'd overslept because she'd been up all night rescuing a sparrow that had fallen out of its nest, knocked itself senseless and had to be rushed to an all-night animal hospital on the outskirts of the city. I accepted her story at face value because it sounded too kooky not to be true and knowing her earnestness, I didn't doubt it for a second. She had two interviews scheduled for an article she was writing on self-publishing that I had to move around for her. Authors, even self-published ones, were often cranky first thing in the morning but still, I managed to carry off the change in times with only a limited amount of frustration and irritation.

Then Angela came in, her long face streaked with tears. She'd had a row with her latest boyfriend so she and Roberto huddled in the corner all morning. That meant, of course, nothing was being done on the design side of things as Roberto comforted the dear girl, whom, I thought could take care of herself very well. All she had to do was squeak even slightly in despair and Roberto appeared with a hanky. Sometimes, they cried together, Roberto being the emotional sort. It was a beautiful thing to see, in a film perhaps, but not a place of business. I would have to talk to him, of course, but I dreaded those sorts of things. Really, when it came to personal confrontation, I was a terrible coward. I hated having to criticize people to their faces. It was always much easier doing it behind their backs. But sometimes, the responsibilities of ownership lay too heavily on these broader shoulders and it was necessary to confront the truth, although I danced away from it as much as possible. So, from my vantage point across the large space we inhabited, I saw Roberto hand Angela a tissue, then take one himself and blow his nose forcefully.

The week ended satisfactorily. All of the major bills were paid that ensured another week of fruitful commerce, Angela had told her now ex-boyfriend to shove off and had laughed about it. Jessica marched in triumphantly after having saved one of nature's dear creatures and Ruth kept pretty much to herself the entire day. That is, she didn't pester me with annoying questions, which if she'd taken a moment to think through, would have discovered the answers on her own. But it was easier to just ask me than go through all of that rigamarole.

I'd taken a late lunch and didn't want dinner. I knew there'd be munchies at the gallery as there normally was for an opening. I drove downtown to the Queen Street West neighbourhood, home to bohemians and their galleries alike. The Rostov Gallery was one of the established ones, having been in business some 30 years, proprietor, Anna Rostov, a shrewd aficionado with a penchant for picking the up and coming artists and championing them. Everyone wanted to exhibit with her. Plus, she had a beautiful space to hang the pictures. I'd been to a number of shows she'd had over the years but nothing in recent memory. This show pushed a new artist known as DiCarlo, that was it. I couldn't tell if it was a last or first name and I suppose it didn't matter, really. His work was supposed to be quite startling and "super real", according to an article I'd read in the paper earlier in the week.

I parked the Saab on a side street and walked the block and a bit to the gallery entrance. My throat was very dry and my heart was doing its own syncopated rhythm. Art patrons crowded around the entrance. There was a great deal of black on both the men and women, heavy make-up on both the men and the women and bangs, you guessed it. The smoking crowd occupied the sidewalk. As I drew nearer and could see more clearly, I spotted Charlotte waiting outside, clutching a small bag to her bosom. She wore a simple, short but seamlessly fitted black dress with spaghetti straps and a silk shawl over her bare shoulders. She'd had her hair cut and recently styled and it looked very nice on her. I hadn't actually seen her since Christmas, almost five months earlier. She had a lovely figure and very, very nice legs.

"I almost didn't recognize you."

"Hello," she said and kissed me on the cheek. Her scent was beguiling, something vaguely tropical but not overwhelming.

"Been waiting long?" She shook her head. "Are you cold? Shall we go in?" She nodded and gave me a dazzling smile, then linked her arm through mine.

"I can't quite believe you're here."

"Neither can I," I said, but smiled back at her in case she got the wrong impression whatever the hell that was supposed to be.

She stopped and looked me up and down. "You're looking quite spiffy."

"Thank you." I had forgotten that Charlotte had only seen me dressed up. That is, tonight and the previous Christmas. I wondered what she'd think if she saw how I went to work each day, wrinkled T-shirts and soiled jeans. "Shall we?" We pushed through the smokers and itinerant drinkers and made our way into the Rostov Gallery. We picked up a program and signed in at the front desk, then began to wander. The opening had pulled good numbers as DiCarlo seemed to be making some waves in the art world and had received enough advance press to get people interested. A waiter came by and we each took a drink. I hadn't eaten, so I reminded myself to take it easy.

"Where shall we start?" asked Charlotte, wrinkling her nose. It was really a cute little nose and suited her small face that was framed rather nicely by her new hairdo. She still hadn't let go of my arm and I could feel the closeness of her presence, it was a kind of physical heat and I took a large gulp of the glass of white wine. I'm sure the crowded room had nothing to do with it.

We stood before the first canvas that was quite large, measuring at least seven by ten feet. A portrait of a young woman with her mouth open in what looked like rage or extreme despair. The canvas was entitled "Howl" and it couldn't have been more accurate.

"Goodness," exclaimed Charlotte. "How gruesome."

"Shit," I replied.

Charlotte turned to me, a little stunned. "What?"

"Shit," I repeated.

"You don't like it?"

"What? Oh no, it's not that. It's just that...see that tall fellow in the white suit over there?"

"Yes."

"That's my publisher, Julian de Groot."

"Oh."

"Right. Let's see if we can't make our way around so he doesn't see me." I was about to turn and head off when a long-fingered hand clapped itself onto my shoulder. I spun around.

"Julian," I exclaimed into the thin, greyish face and the yellow-toothed smile. "What are you doing here?"

"I was about to ask you the same thing, old boy."

"Uh yes, of course you were. Er, Charlotte, let me introduce you to Julian de Groot. Julian, this is Charlotte Ramsay. She's a colleague of Sharon's at Cablestar. We just bumped into each other. Isn't that right, Charlotte?"

"Hmm, yes." Charlotte murmured, then smiled into her drink.

"I didn't know you were an art lover," Julian said.

"Well, my mother was an artist Julian, you know that."

"Ah yes, of course, of course. But I haven't seen you at any of the other openings recently."

"Uh yes, well." My brain flew, trying to come up with something. "Actually," and I leaned in closer to him. Charlotte perked up as well. "I shouldn't be saying this, you know, but there's probably going to be a book deal out of this. I had it on good authority."

Julian reeled back. "Really? And nobody told me? Is it up for auction? Do you know what they're asking?"

I gave him a thin smile. "Actually, I don't. Nothing's been confirmed yet and in fact, it may just be a rumour but I came nonetheless to check it out."

Julian drained his drink. "Well, Bernard. It's a good thing I ran into you. I'm going to look into this right away." Then he swayed towards me. "And the manuscripts? Making progress, are you?"

"Of course. Every day. I'll have something to show you very soon."

He pointed a gnarly finger at me. "Promise?"

"Promise."

He wheezed a bit into his bony chest. "Good. I'm keeping you to it. Now then, "and he smacked his lips. "I must get another drink and see about this book business. Nice meeting you, Miss Ramsay."

"Likewise."

I watched Julian's narrow back part the crowd. He commandeered a waiter then went on a search and destroy mission amongst the crowd. I turned to Charlotte. "Do you think he bought it?"

"Bought what?"

"You know, the story."

"I don't know and I don't think it matters. He doesn't seem like the type who cares what other people do as long as he gets what he wants."

I chewed my lip for a moment. "Yes. I suppose you're right." And I downed the rest of my drink.

Charlotte put her hand on my arm. "Listen. It's crowded here and you're understandably nervous. Why not come back to my place for a drink. It's a lot quieter there."

"Um. Well. All right."

Charlotte tittered. "Don't sound so enthusiastic."

"Sorry."

"Come on then."

Charlotte had cabbed it over from her office, so we walked to where I had parked the Saab. As we were about to step off the curb to cross the street, a car swooped by, sending up a sheet of muddy water, spraying my pant legs.

"Damn." I glanced over at the car that had braked by the curb. It was a Porsche Targa. Eric Schwilden crawled out laconically then sauntered over.

"Sorry about that... oh, it's you Goldman." He turned to Charlotte. "And who is this lovely creature?" Charlotte stared at him. Schwilden was in Hugo Boss this evening. A languid blonde in a slinky Chanel get-up stood with her arms crossed behind him. I stared at him with all the malevolence I could muster. He glanced down at my trousers. "I'll pay for the cleaning, of course. And now, what's your name?"

"You'll never know," Charlotte said. And I don't know how she managed it, exactly but she went to step off the curb and somehow hooked her right leg behind his ankle and then with a quick swivelling of her hips bumped him. She caught him off-balance and I watched Schwilden teeter backward, his gleaming loafers scuffling on the cement, his arms windmilling behind him. Charlotte stood and viewed her handiwork with a look of admiration, then blew a puff of air at him and Schwilden, as if in a dream, or should I say a fantasy of mine, fell right on to his bum into the puddle he'd disturbed just moments earlier. The languid blonde looked on in horror, then her icy expression changed, actually disintegrated into laughter. Schwilden wore a shell-shocked look. Clearly, nothing like this had ever happened to him before. Charlotte gave him one last ironic smile, then took my arm and we proceeded across the street to find my car. I could hear the blonde shrieking with laughter now as Schwilden jumped up from the pavement and roared his indignation, rather impotently, I thought.

In the car, I turned to her. "Charlotte, that was marvellous but whatever possessed you to do that?"

She settled back and stretched as I started the engine. "I hate smug, overconfident men. They need to be taken down a peg or two."

One thing was certain, I was neither smug nor overconfident. "Where did you learn that trick?" I asked her, as I pulled out into the lightened traffic of early evening.

"Judo," she replied.

"Really?"

"Yes. I have a black belt, so you'd better watch it."

"Wow."

"It comes in handy, especially when I travel. There's nothing like a lone woman in a far-off land that gives courage to an ignorant and unsuspecting man."

"I see. But do you always travel alone?"

"Pretty much. I'm going to India next month."

"Sounds wonderful... but, uh, your husband doesn't go with you?" Charlotte had a phantom husband, at least that's what Sharon said. No one in the office had ever met him. She never brought him to any of the company functions.

"No. He hates to travel because he does so much for business. He'd much rather stay at home."

"I don't travel much either."

"I know. But you have other attributes."

I laughed nervously and tried to concentrate on my driving. "Uh, you'd better give me directions. I'm not really sure where I'm going." Charlotte pointed me to her address, an attractive row house on one of the prettier streets in the heart of the city. I pulled up opposite her door.

"Come on then," she said. "Let's have that drink."

"Will I meet your husband?"

Charlotte gave me a frank look, then laughed. "Good lord no. He's away with some work colleagues."

"Ah."

Charlotte let us in, turned on the lights and threw her wrap over a chair. I looked down at my mud-splattered trousers. "You can take those off, if you like and I can give them a scrubbing."

"No, no, that's okay. I'll just throw them in the laundry when I get home." I looked about. "Your place is lovely."

"Thank you." And indeed, it was. It was an older house and the original touches had been maintained, the wood trim and the mouldings that delineated the ceiling. The hardwood floors gave off a buttery glow and Charlotte had decorated (I assumed it was Charlotte) with a nice mix of the traditional and modern. That is, wingback chairs but a chrome and glass coffee table, but it all seemed to fit together. There were African masks and Indian silks adorning the walls. "I'll open some wine, shall I?"

"Yes," I replied. "Fine." I wondered what had led to all of this and I remembered it was something Charlotte had said to me at the Christmas party. We were talking about books and I had mentioned an Aldous Huxley I'd just finished, Chrome Yellow. Well, it turned out that Charlotte had loved that book. It and Antic Hay were among her favourites. Then, inexplicably, she had leaned in and whispered in my ear.

"I could speak with you forever," she had breathed. And it hit me like a jolt. At the time, I didn't know if she was serious or just putting me on. As our email correspondence had accelerated, I came to the conclusion that she had been serious.

She returned with a bottle, two glasses, a corkscrew and a rather lascivious smile. "I can't believe I've actually got you here," she said.

"Nor can I. Uh, do you want me to do that?"

"It's all right, I can manage." Deftly, she skewered the cork and had it out in flash. I could see the sinews in her arms and realized that judo must have served her well.

"How long have you been a black belt?"

She pursed her full lips as she poured out the wine. "Five or six years, I suppose. I go to the judoka three or four times a week."

"Really?"

"Yes, really," she confirmed. "Wine?" And she held out the glass, which I took from her. Our fingers touched and I felt like the glass would explode in my face.

I took a sip. "Suddenly it feels warm in here." I drained the glass and held it out for more. She poured, slowly and carefully.

"You look like you're working yourself up to something," she said.

"Do I?" And took another gulp of wine. I hadn't eaten since lunch and began to feel more than a little light-headed.

"I'll get some munchies. You must be famished," she said, standing up and smoothing her dress down her thighs. "I know I am."

"Great."

Charlotte disappeared into the kitchen and I heard her fussing about, opening drawers, the crinkling of plastic and the hacking of a knife against a board. I realized that I had been standing, and now swaying, since I'd arrived. I looked at her couch rather longingly and the thought crossed my mind, loafable moment. A perfectly inviting couch and what was I doing but hovering above it. In my lexicon, this made very little sense. I eased myself down, kicked off my shoes and lay back against the plump cushions and felt myself relax, melt actually into the fabric. With all of the worries I'd had during the week, skirmishes with suppliers, run-ins with that sleek cad, Schwilden, fretting about the evening with Charlotte, reeling from the bombshell that Sharon had dropped about wanting another child, dealing with the intrusion of Felicity and the glowering animosity of Mrs. Sanchez and then the deceit of Sean and his lack of interest or caring, no wonder I was exhausted. I closed my eyes, just for a moment, I told myself.

When I awoke it was dark and naturally I could not remember where I was or how I'd gotten there, eminently typical and perhaps, predictable. A single lamp flared in a corner of the room throwing long shadows everywhere else. I sat up and rubbed my face. My tongue felt like an inflated slab. The luminous dial of my watch read ten minutes shy of midnight. It was at this point, I felt dread ooze into my soul with the return of conscious thought. Oh my god. Charlotte. I looked around and saw no one. I found the bathroom, peed profusely, then doused my face in cold water. I dried off using a scented towel. Creeping out, I noticed a door slightly ajar and light spilling out weakly from the bottom crack. I knocked lightly.

"Hello?" I called.

"Come on in."

I pushed the door open and there was Charlotte all tucked up in bed reading a book. Her face was scrubbed and clean-looking and she wore a silk nighty sort of top that wasn't meant to hide any of her attributes.

"I fell asleep."

"I noticed."

"I am terribly, terribly sorry."

"Okay."

"Your couch was so inviting and I hadn't eaten and..."

"Not sleeping well, I gather."

"No."

She sighed. "It's for the best, I suppose."

"What are you reading?"

"Antic Hay."

"Ah." I nodded. There seemed to be something symbolic in that but I couldn't fathom what it was.

She gave me a wry look, then snuggled further under the covers. "Would you care to...?"

"Ah Charlotte. I feel such a cad. And you were so great with Schwilden and you looked so wonderful and look even better now..."

"So?"

"...and I probably need my head examined..."

"Yes?"

"...and it's not like I don't find you attractive, enormously attractive actually..."

"But you're not sure?"

"Right."

"I understand."

"Do you?"

"Yes, I do. You love Sharon."

"Yes but..."

"And you haven't worked out whether you're happy."

"Yes, that's true..."

"And you've never done this before."

"No, I never have."

"Neither have I."

"You haven't?"

She shook her head, then ran her fingers through her hair. I could see the outline of her full breasts and discern the point of her nipples. "Then you know how I feel."

"I think so."

"Perhaps we can try again."

"We might."

"Will you still email me? I'd hate to give that up."

"You know I will."

I was tempted to go to her and kiss her but instinct told me that if I came closer, penetrated that aura she appeared to create around her like a beckoning blanket, I might not ever be able to get out of there intact.

"Bye."

I drove home, cursing myself and thanking god for my good fortune, swinging between the two. The house was dark. Everyone appeared to be asleep. I crept into our room. Sharon had left my bedside lamp on and was curled up on her side. As I tip-toed toward the bathroom, she cleared her throat. She sat up, reached for her specs while flicking the bed lamp on.

"What happened to your trousers?" she asked. "Were you in a dust-up?"

"No. A chance encounter with a Porsche and a puddle."

"I see. How was the do, then?"

"Not bad. I ran into Julian."

"Julian?"

"Yes."

"What was he doing there?"

"Prowling the room for business, I expect. That's what Julian does best, isn't it?"

"I suppose." Sharon threw back the covers. "I've got to pee." And she practically knocked me out of the road.

"Hey!"

"Sorry. I really have to go."

I heard the tinkling from within as I hung up my jacket, unbuttoned my shirt, unbelted the offensive trousers and dropped them in the laundry bin. Sharon was just finishing up as I began to brush my teeth. She came up behind me, and barefoot she was perhaps an inch shorter. She snaked her arms around and dipped her fingers down the front of my undershorts. I spat toothpaste, missing the sink.

"What's going on?" And looked at her in the mirror. She was tousled and puffy from sleep but in a becoming way. I could feel the warmth of her and the probing of her fingers was pleasurable. And to be honest, the image of Charlotte in bed, her aftermath, had stayed with me.

"I've found something," she cooed. "Well come on. I'm awake now."

# 6

I know it sounds trite to say it but life is a diversion. My one true purpose was to find that perfect moment of ultimate relaxation and everything seemed determined to keep me from it. Work and home assuredly so. When I dragged myself into the coffee shop at the appointed time on Saturday morning, Nook and Ramon were already seated and drinking their various java concoctions. I had the bagels and the paper as usual but nothing felt normal that particular morning.

"What happened to you?" asked Nook, his eyes wide with alarm behind the wire-rims. Ramon too, looked on with great interest, even curiosity.

"Helluva week," I mumbled, dropped my chaff into a chair and went off to place an order. I felt exhausted. Sharon had kept me awake longer than I had wanted, she had felt uncharacteristically frisky and afterward, I couldn't sleep, tossing and turning, wallowing in my guilt. Thank god nothing untoward had happened. But what if I hadn't fallen asleep? I knew what I was doing, didn't I? We weren't in Charlotte's apartment to bake cookies and tell bedtime stories, were we? It struck me then that I hadn't noticed a single photograph of her husband. There were many of Charlotte on her various ramblings, Africa, India, Israel, Tuscany, Peru and so on, but none of him. He couldn't have been taking the pictures all the time, could he? I acquired my usual English Breakfast, without the lemon this time. I wanted the full tannin and caffeine hit, such as it was. No dilution this Saturday.

Wearily, I sat down. "Late night?" inquired Ramon, who then shot a knowing glance at Nook.

"Sort of." I sipped the tea and it felt like a searing blast furnace of a tonic roaring down my gullet. "Yow. Damn hot."

The two of them sat there. My friends, at least I could call them that, companion loafers, leisure seekers or for want of a derogatory term, fellow slackers, waited for me to speak. They held their tongues. I obliged them.

"Sharon wants another child."

Nook slapped the table and Ramon reared back in his chair.

"Whoa," they both said in synch.

"You're screwed," Ramon said and I grimaced at the poor attempt at irony.

"Thanks."

"Why?" asked Nook. "I thought you both were getting to a place where you were past that, didn't want any part of it."

"I guess that was just me," I replied glumly. "I really don't want to go back there. It's like putting your life on hold all over again. Uh, no offence Ramon. I mean, it's good to go there in the beginning, but not fifteen years later." Ramon shrugged, he wasn't bothered by it. He knew I wasn't myself. Clearly, I wasn't going to mention Charlotte. There were some things meant to be kept, even from male friends, even if we were chewing the fat in a locker room, I would have kept stumm all the same.

Nook took a sip of his mochaccino. "So, what brought this on?"

I looked up at the ceiling helplessly, then around the café where couples sat engaged in animated conversation or some singles peacefully read their newspapers, oblivious to my middle-aged angst. "I haven't a clue. She just felt ready for it. That's what she said."

"Maybe it's compensation for a lack of satisfaction at work," suggested Ramon, his dark brows furrowed in thought.

"Yes," Nook interjected. "Perhaps she's not fulfilled there any longer."

I mused on this. "It's possible. I mean, how much more money can she make and how many more people can she fire? She's been there and done that. Not only is she on this baby kick, but I've got her mother with us as well. She broke her leg in a fall."

"Ouch," said Ramon and winced. "The mother-in-law too. They'll gang up on you. They always do. When my mother-in-law comes over, I stay out of her way. I don't say anything unless I have to. It doesn't matter because whatever I say comes out wrong so I just shut up. And then my wife asks me why I never talk to her mother. I can't win."

"Well, Felicity and I have our ups and downs too. Mind you, she's on painkillers and floating so high that I could spit on her and she'd probably laugh at me."

"That won't last," Ramon said.

"So what are you going to do?" Nook asked. His expression was one of sincere concern and I appreciated it. Nook tended to be cerebral but there was a core of caring there. He tried to remain calm but I remember how wigged out he was when his wife became pregnant and how he practically fainted when her waters broke. She had to drive them to the hospital. The doctors in the emergency room gave him a sedative and when he came to, his daughter had been born. It wasn't his finest hour, he had admitted. All of those prenatal classes had been shot to hell.

"You really don't want another kid?" Ramon asked. I shook my head. "Why not?

"I'm not up to it," I replied. "My soul is sucked dry as it is. How do you think having a newborn at home is going to go down for me? I'm the guy. I made the deal. I have to be there and do everything. Sharon will take her four months maternity and voom, she's back in the office and there's mister nursemaid here. I just don't think I can do it again. I don't want to."

"What about a live-in nanny? You can afford it," Nook said, a little resentfully, I thought.

"Your life is different now too," Ramon pointed out. "Sharon can't expect that of you. You've got the magazine, an office to look after, employees who depend on you…"

I took another sip. The tea had cooled enough. "That's true."

"She can't expect you to just drop all of that," Nook added.

"Right." But I knew Sharon and they didn't. She could demand anything she pleased and always got it. It hadn't stopped her with me and it hadn't stopped her at work. If anything, each victory, encouraged her even more. She could be a monster when she wanted to be. And then there was the question mark called Charlotte. How did she fit into all of this? And what about her phantom husband?

"Any news on your end?" I asked Ramon. He shook his large, square, shaggy head. We all commiserated in silence, except for the sipping of hot drinks.

When I got home, Nathan wandered the hall in his boxers and a T-shirt.

"Why aren't you dressed? It's almost lunch time."

"So?" He gave me a heated look.

"What's the matter? What are you doing?"

Nathan looked down at his bare feet. Summer hadn't begun and already he was deeply tanned as if light had been absorbed through his clothing, even indoor light. "It's Sean. He takes all my stuff. He took my CDs, he took my pants, he took my socks, he took my damn textbook from school and he's taken my swim suit." He came up to me with a wild look on his face and grabbed the collar of my shirt. "I've had it, do you understand? I can't take anymore of this. I am going to kill him. From this day on, you will only have one son and it will be me. Okay? Okay?" he shouted.

"Don't get your knickers in a twist, Nathan. And let go of my shirt. I'll just go and put the bagels away and then we can discuss this, calmly and rationally, all right?"

"You bought bagels?" His face lit up.

"I always buy bagels. You know that."

"And they're fresh?"

"No. I bought stale bagels."

"Oh." His face fell.

"Only kidding."

He perked up. "I knew you were but I wanted to see if you thought you could fool me."

"Great plan," I said, putting my arm around him and leading him into the kitchen. "Let's have a bagel." Upstairs, I thought I heard Felicity talking to Mrs. Sanchez. "How's your Gran?"

"Much better, I think." But I could see he was really focusing on the bagels. When I opened the bag, the smell of fresh baking wafted out. "Mmm, smells good."

I put the kettle on for a cup of tea, removed the soy-based oleo from the fridge and cut him a bagel, slathered it, put it on a plate and plunked it down in front of him, where he sat at the counter. Half of it was gone by the time I turned away and then turned back again. Manners were not high on Nathan's list of priorities. A Goldman trait. My father and brother were the same way. My mother and I came from a more refined perspective, I liked to think. I let him eat and when he was done, sliced him another one, anything to keep his mouth occupied while I poured the boiling water from the kettle. Sharon was due home from her class at any time and I wondered vaguely where Sean had got to and I assumed he was in one of two places; sleeping or in the shower. His two favourite haunts and preoccupations, apart from tormenting his brother, of course.

Nathan sat at the counter, smacking his lips over the Sports section while I lingered over the news, when the phone rang. I never bothered to answer it because Sharon and I rarely got phone calls. Just the boys did. It didn't stop Nathan from lunging for the receiver, even though I hadn't twitched. He waggled a finger at me and grinned.

"Hello," he said, in his best basso profundo. "Yeah? Okay. Hang on." He banged the receiver on the counter. "It's for you, Dad."

I looked up surprised. This was a rarity. I put the receiver to my ear.

"Hello?"

A tinny, nasally voice came on the line. "This is Western Union with a telegram for Mr. Bernard Goldman. Is this Mr. Bernard Goldman?"

"It is."

"There is a message from a Mr. Isaac Goldman. The message reads as follows: Hello Son. Stop. Just wanted to let you know. Stop. We are coming home. Stop. Next weekend. Stop. See you then. Stop. Your father. Stop. Is there any reply, Mr. Goldman?"

"Uh no, thank you."

"A full replica of the text of this message will be mailed to you within twenty-four hours. Goodbye."

I hung up the phone, bewildered, more vermischt than I had been and I had been seriously confused. And now my father was returning home from Italy all of a sudden? What now?

As I stood at the counter perplexed, Nathan switched on the radio to a hip hop station, Sean emerged from some hole, belting out a rap song, Felicity hobbled down the stairs, aided by Mrs. Sanchez on one side and a cane on the other and I could hear the thump, thump on the wood. Sharon burst through the door, having returned from her personal training session at the gym. Around me seemed to be some sort of envelope and I stood in the middle of it. All of the sounds, the music, the rapping, the thumping, Sharon blathering, was thrown into a blender and came out as gibberish to my ears. I was helpless and rivetted to the spot, yet somehow protected and if I moved the fragile barrier, would evaporate, so I stood stock still. In all their cacophony, the others converged around me, acknowledging and greeting each other but somehow ignoring me as if I wasn't there, as if, somehow, I didn't exist. By making myself small, I'd disappeared from their collective view. The jabbering and blabbering continued, Mrs. Sanchez talked to Felicity while she got her settled in a chair, Sharon tried talking over the music and Sean's singing. That's what brought it all to an end, back into focus. Sharon had no patience for any of this and grew irritated quickly when she couldn't make herself heard or worse, draw anyone's attention.

"Turn the bloody thing off," she yelled at Nathan, then turned to Sean, "and you, put a sock in it, will ya?" Then she turned to her mother who put her hands up and clamped her jaw shut in mid-word while Mrs. Sanchez just bowed her head. And I wasn't talking, anyway. "I swear to the holy mother of god, like a pack of bleeding wallabies in heat, you are," she said to the assembled crowd.

"How do you know what wallabies in heat sound like?" Nathan asked, a reasonable question to his logical way of thinking.

"Don't question what I know or don't know," she declared. "Just have a bit of consideration, all right?" Nathan shrugged. The radio had been turned down low, Sean resorted to humming to himself and Felicity resorted to whispering to Mrs. Sanchez.

"Good workout?" I asked. Sharon turned to me in surprise.

"I didn't notice you standing there. You could have said something."

"Like what?"

"Like hello."

"Hello."

She put her hands on her hips and gave me a stare, setting her face like a mask. "Ach, don't be such a stupid bugger, Bernie."

"My father's coming home."

Her blue eyes widened. "What?"

"My father. Coming home."

"How do you know?"

"He sent a telegram."

"When?"

"Just now."

"What?"

"The telegram. I got it just now. They phoned."

Sharon looked exasperated. "When are they coming?"

"Next weekend."

Sharon absently chewed a fingernail. "It'll be good to see Catherine again."

"Yes, won't it." Catherine and I didn't get along. I thought she had hoodwinked my father and tricked him into marriage. But that was just my opinion.

"Wait a minute," Nathan broke in. "Zaidy's coming home?"

"That's what we've been saying," I said wearily.

"Cool," said Nathan. "We haven't seen him in so long. I wonder what he's gonna bring us from Italy."

"Don't expect anything," Sharon said. "He's not been there on a buying trip."

"We're his only grandchildren," Sean said. "And it is the duty of every grandparent to spoil their grandchildren. I think it's a law."

"And if it isn't, it should be," Nathan chimed in.

"Bugger off, the two of ya," Sharon said. Nathan and Sean exchanged looks, then together went to the fridge, pulled out some cheese, each grabbed a bagel, and without standing on ceremony like taking a plate, using a knife, and not bothering about where they dropped crumbs or pieces of cheese, began to eat and chew voraciously, leaving a visible litter as they trailed out of the kitchen, off to play video games, I suspected.

"So why're they coming home, do you think?"

"I've no idea, really. I thought they were there to stay."

Sharon glanced at the fridge herself. "I'm famished. A spot of lunch would do me well at the moment. Ma, what about you and you Mrs. Sanchez? Are you hungry at all? Let's all have a bite, shall we? Then we can gossip all we like."

"I like a good gossip," Felicity said, smiling like a tipsy bird while Mrs. Sanchez glanced my way, then solemnly nodded her agreement.

# 7

That Sunday afternoon, I lounged around watching baseball on television while intermittently doing the Sunday crossword and reading a book. I got up to pee. Normally, I don't pay a great deal of attention to bodily functions but lately that had gotten me into trouble and made me the object of some ridicule, at least as far as Eric Schwilden was concerned. I'd finished what I was doing and glanced cursorily down at the toilet bowl. Grape juice, I thought. Someone had spilled grape juice. But no one in the house drank grape juice. Sean and Nathan hadn't been in that habit since they were quite small and certainly not now. And it was then, with a sickening feeling, I realized that what I saw was not grape juice at all but blood and it oozed out of my member. The cold claw of fear seized my innards. How disconcerting to see blood flowing out of your privates. A sudden flush of panic and nausea swept over me. I steadied myself on the counter. I examined my undershorts and found some partially dried stains down the front. Oh my god. What did it mean? And could this be happening to me at the young age of 37? How many times had I heard about contemporaries who'd contracted terminal diseases and conditions, brain tumours, aneurysms, cancers, some of them younger than me? Snap out of it, I told myself. Carefully, I wiped around the toilet bowl. The oozing appeared to have stopped. I rinsed my face with cool water and stared at my suddenly pale face in the mirror. Breathe, I told myself. Breathe deeply. Stay calm. Try and relax. I needed to change. Somehow, I managed to find my way upstairs without anyone noticing anything. I felt like I'd been lit by a fluorescent marker and anyone who looked at me could tell. "Oh, blood in the urine, I see."

I changed then hid the afflicted undershorts at the bottom of the laundry bin.

The next day early, I managed to squeeze in to see my family doctor, a craggy-faced Pole with white blond hair and a ponderous manner. So plodding, in fact, that I found him funny but I admitted, he was very thorough. I looked across his cluttered desk.

"So. Blood in the urine," he repeated.

"Yes."

"Any symptoms?"

"Like?"

"Discomfort or a burning sensation when you are urinating."

"No."

"These stains. Where did you find them?"

"On my undershorts."

"In the front or the back?"

He'd confused me. "Sorry?"

"In the front or the back?" He caught my bewildered expression. Dr. Zolta stood up to demonstrate. "When I urinate, I sit down like this. And I do this because I know if I stand up it makes a mess. The only time I stand up is when I am in a public toilet, otherwise I sit. So now. These stains, were they in the front or the back?"

"The front?"

"You stand up?"

"Yes."

"Even when you are at home?"

"Yes."

"You don't make a mess?"

"I'm very careful," I said.

Dr. Zolta shrugged. "I don't want to worry about such things so I sit." He pursed his lips which were rather thin and girlish. "Now. Have you been eating beets by any chance?"

"No."

"Do you drink tomato juice?"

"No."

Zolta thought for a moment, and pulled at his face, then he brightened. "You had sex just before this happened?"

"No."

"Ah." He nodded. "Well then, I tell you what we will do. We will run some tests, blood and urine and then we will wait a month and run the tests again. We will see what the tests show. Sometimes, it may be a little early for these things and tests can show a false-positive, you understand what I am saying to you?"

"I think so."

"Good. If something happens, then you will call me."

"I shouldn't see a urologist?"

"For what? What do you expect him to do?"

"Examine me."

"Right," Dr. Zolta confirmed. "And then he will order these same tests. If we find something, then I will send you to the urologist. In the meantime, we wait."

"I hate to wait."

Zolta continued. "The least invasive procedure is the ultrasound where they will look inside you and see if there is any abnormality. Otherwise, it is the systolic where a tube is inserted inside…"

"I've heard about it," I said and felt a twinge in my groin.

"It's very uncomfortable," Zolta concluded. He sketched something on a pad, tore it off, then handed it to me. "Take this to the clinic downstairs on the sixth floor, room 620 and they will administer the test. Call me in three days and I will have the results. Okay?"

"Okay." I stood up, shook his hand and took the outstretched paper.

I went into the bathroom on the sixth floor armed with a small plastic container. The container was sealed and a square of adhesive with a bar code was stuck to the top. Unfortunately, I was wearing trousers with a button fly, just to complicate things, and positioning the container and the flow of urine required deft hands but I seemed to be managing it all right until, of course, the container filled up. Faced with the prospect of overflow dribbling on to my hand, I had to think quickly. Through the force of will, I staunched the flow momentarily, then bent down to place the container on the floor while holding myself in position. Bending down and holding were not natural actions for any male. Something had to give. That something was the container. I managed to set it down but nudged the silly thing with my toe and it overturned spilling its precious contents. But I've got more I thought. Great. The container had rolled behind the toilet tank and I had to inch my way over, keeping above the bowl in the ready position just in case and now my stopped bladder felt the pinch of damming in mid-spurt. Groping my way along, I just managed to reach the thing with my outstretched fingertips and it spun as I went for it. With a supreme effort, holding myself in a number of strategic areas, and with a final grunt, grasped the thing and hoisted it into position. Ah sweet relief. I had just enough left for a refill. I set the container down on top of the toilet tank, carefully, so it wouldn't slop or worse, roll off and re-buttoned my trousers. I looked around for the top. Nothing. I looked again. It must have fallen down a hole somewhere. So I crossed the hall very carefully leaving a puddle behind me, holding the sample gingerly and confronted the medical technician whose eyebrows shot up. A no-nonsense black woman who wore bright red lipstick and large hoop earrings.

"What'd you do? Swallow it?" She referred to the top, I presumed.

"Uh no, it just sort of disappeared."

"Hmm-mm," she replied as if she didn't believe that for a second. I held the thing out. "Just a second," she said and pulled on some latex gloves. She brought out another container, cracked the seal, took the one I held carefully, went to the sink and poured the one into the other, tossed the old one and sealed the new container tightly. "There, that's done." She stuck the specimen in a plastic pouch. "Now, have a seat and roll up your sleeve."

"Yes ma'am." I complied. She took three vials of blood, put labels on them and stuck them into the same pouch. She crooked a finger at me. "Now come with me," she said. She pointed me to a change room the size of a broom closet. "Remove all your clothes except your underwear and your shoes and socks. The gown there," and she indicated the hook, "closes in the back and the robe opens in the front. Got it?"

"Yes, ma'am."

"Stop calling me that. I 'm not your mother."

"Sorry."

"Just get changed."

"Yes…thank you," I gulped. As I tried to pull my trousers off, sandwiched in the little space, there was a knock on the door. I squeezed it open only to confront a middle-aged blonde beaming at me.

"I'm Nancy, your ultrasound technician."

"Hello."

"When you're ready, just come down to the end door and I'll see you there."

"Fine, uh, Nancy." And shut the door.

With the robe and gown flapping about my ankles, I sauntered down to Nancy's cubicle. "Come on in and close the door," she trilled. "Hang the robe up on the hook and lie down on the table." I hung up the robe and got up on the table. "Move further up, further, further, a bit further, a teensy weensy bit further but watch out not to... " I banged my head against the wall. "Not that far, sweetie." I grimaced at her. "Now pull your gown up to your chest and roll your undies down to your hips. That's it. Put your arms above your shoulders and move in a bit closer to the edge of the table. That's it. Comfy?"

"About as relaxing as a bed of nails," I muttered.

"Sorry. We are giving you a workout, aren't we?" I didn't bother to reply. "Now I've got to spread some of the goo on you and at first it will feel a bit warm but it will cool off quickly." She squeezed some of the stuff out of a tube and I must have yelled because she jumped back. "What was that for?"

"You said warm, not boiling."

"Whoops. Must have put the heat up a bit. It should be all right now." And she continued to spread the goo all over. It was lovely, like wallowing in a vat of petroleum jelly.

"Mr. Goldman, you'll have to stay as still as possible while I take these pictures, otherwise, this will take twice as long. No fidgeting, please." The problem was that I was ticklish and the apparatus she ran up and down my chest and abdomen hit all of my funny spots. That, and the fact that I was already tense, made every touch of the thing produce a peal of involuntary laughter.

"Stay still, Mr. Goldman and hold your breath when I tell you to. Now. Hold your breath please." I glanced over and Nancy seemed intent on her computer screen and I knew she was lining up the magic wand with certain of my vitals, kidneys, spleen, prostate, to get a shot for the doc to examine. Nancy peered closely at the screen, meanwhile I was rapidly running out of air. And it's interesting how you feel when that happens, suddenly light-headed, everything seems absurd and ridiculous, you lose all sense of proportion, even reason. And finally, you begin to choke and gag. I could feel my face drain of life as I felt my eyes roll over.

"Oh dear, sorry about that. Breathe now." I exhaled with a full whoosh. "Just breathe normally. It's just that sometimes it takes a while to get the focus right and if I don't do that, the picture won't be very clear and the ultrasound would have been a waste of time."

I began to relax as I realized that here, before me, hovered an opportunity that seemed so rare. Lying down during the day, not doing anything. The only thing that prevented it from being a perfect loafable moment was the fact that the business of the ultrasound made it unpleasant, sticky and a strain on my lungs. Nancy prodded me to breathe, then not breathe, breathe then pinch my nose and hold it until I was ready to burst, then breathe normally, as if that were possible after holding your breath for two minutes. Too bad. It had potential. Nancy stuffed a wad of paper towelling in my hand. "Use this to wipe off," she said. "There's more if you need it. Your doctor should have the results in about three days."

Three days? That meant Friday. Or Monday. Three more days of wondering. Three more days of uncertainty, of thinking that my body betrayed me from within. Apart from a desperate need to pee after all of that poking and prodding, I felt normal. I had no symptoms. And that worried me. If I had no symptoms, then it must be serious and of course, the only thing I could think about was cancer. I pictured Sharon a widow but then I speculated, likely not for long. She'd end up with Eric Schwilden, living in my house and he'd be best buddies with Sean and Nathan, because his maturity level was on a par with theirs. He'd let them drive his Porsche. Quickly, I'd be forgotten. After all, what had I done for them really? As I stepped out into the cool, spring air, I shook my head. That wouldn't happen. I tried to convince myself.

# 8

"Be positive," Hugo said, as he sank a two-pointer to put him up 19 to 4. In the last half dozen games with him, I don't think I'd scored more than 7 points a game. He'd noticed that I'd been more distracted than usual. "If you tell yourself nothing is wrong, it will be okay. Nothing to worry about."

Easy for you to say, I thought. At 87, what else could happen to him? I shot wide. Hugo sank the last basket. He'd been through the war, he'd had colon cancer and survived, he almost lost the sight in his right eye due to an industrial accident, so Hugo had suffered more than most and he was still upbeat. And still beating me at basketball. "I guess you're right," I said.

"Ah, come on. You are a young man not old like me. You have a lot to live for yet. Don't give up. What do you say to another game?"

"You think when I lose to you, it makes me feel better?"

"No, worse. But it makes me feel better. Why do you think I come here every morning? Do I have to get up? No, I'm retired. Do I need to exercise? I have an exercycle and a treadmill at home. So, what gets me going?" I shrugged. His beaky face broadened into a grin. "Beating you at basketball. It has done wonders for me. I even want to have sex with my wife again. Mind you, she is not that happy about it." And then he pivoted and sank a three-pointer. "I break the ice. Now, it's your turn."

I groaned inwardly. So now, I was saving the sex life of an octogenarian. I took the ball and shot. Missed. Hugo grinned at me with his new false teeth. We all have a role to play.

# 9

Frank Burgoyne chewed my ear off. A year ago, he'd written a blockbuster novel that had stayed on the bestseller lists for eons, or 27 weeks actually, before it dropped into remaindered oblivion. Born in Ireland, he wrote about his rough upbringing in Portadown but with pathos and humour. Especially the humour, dark, raucous and ribald, the humour sold the novel, that, on its own, was a fairly conventional coming-of-age tale. Images of his mother, left with six children, going down to the St. Vincent de Paul Society with a food chit and coming away only with a pig's head fomented pity and hilarity, particularly when Burgoyne described what happened to the head afterwards. Although it was a novel, clearly the events mirrored Burgoyne's own life closely and as more and more details emerged, well, you could say, it was strictly autobiographical. Thus, the expectation of the follow-up rose to giddying heights. The poor slob felt under tremendous pressure to do it again and pull a masterwork out of his bloody hat. Sharon had hated Burgoyne's novel because it promoted every stereotype imaginable, and I had to agree with her, but the sheer truth of it was that it was so damn funny. You laughed while you cried sort of thing. His new book followed the character of the older boy as he went off to school and chronicled his misadventures. A combination of Balthazar B. meets Trainspotting, if you catch my drift, Roddy Doyle notwithstanding.

Burgoyne had come to Toronto to read in its famous series down at the Harbour where all the major writers and the up-and-comers appeared. Before publishing this first tome, Burgoyne had spent most of his time driving a milk truck, which, he said, got him up early so he could get the most out of the day. Instead of heading off to the pub after work, he'd head home and have a go at the manuscript, then exhausted physically and mentally, hit the sack. I had met him a year earlier, the first time around and gave him a splash before most of the majors had picked up on him. Now famous and quite wealthy, he'd given up the milk business and was living the life of a gentleman scholar. He returned the favour in kind and truth be told, he was a decent sort, really.

I had him on the blower from New York where he huddled in his publisher's office with several PR flacks surrounding him. The new novel was called, Pretty Boy.

"What's with the title?" I asked him.

"What's wrong with it?" he wheezed back.

"Hmm, just wondering about the reference there, Frank. Is the character supposed to be handsome to that extent or is it satirical? Or is it a play on some known characters, real-lifers, like Pretty Boy Floyd?"

"Ah, just assume it's satirical then, would ya, Bernie? There's a good lad, eh?"

"What made you carry on with the same story, Frank?" I had a small tape machine plugged into the phone, so I had the luxury of not worrying about getting his remarks down verbatim and Ruth would not be left with the task of having to transcribe the tape, something she hated. So naturally, it made me happy to give it to her and wondered how I might prolong the interview. Frank's publicist ardently policed the time, 20 minutes only as Mr. Burgoyne had half a dozen interviews this morning, thank you very much, Mr. Goldman. No thank you, darling.

"Shite, Bernie. It's not the same story and you know that. But it is a continuation, like and I wanted to do that because the story was never finished, was it? I mean the Delaney's are seminal to Irish life, don't ya see? They're like Ireland herself, stepped on, prodded, brutalized and yet there's the nobility that emerges out of the blackness, ya know, they can hold their heads high in a way. It all comes down to dignity and how much of it you need to feel like a human bein', right? If a person has no dignity or it's taken away by the measures of a society like the Church or the government or whatever, then what have ya got? Not much, right? How can anyone function in a society if they haven't got their dignity? I mean it's bloody outrageous how people are treated, isn't it? So here you've got this family in dire straits, right? And somehow they fight their way through all of their troubles, there's no happy ending, they don't go off to Hollywood or fall in love or even beat the shite our of their tormentors. But it's the small things, eh, Bernie, that can make the difference in a life, yeah? Like buying a new pair of shoes, getting the girl you admire over the affections of a rival, having a full belly when you've been starving all yer life, those kinds of things which can perk up yer spirits and give ya some kind of hope that, perhaps, the world isn't entirely against ya and yous just might experience a little bit of success. And that's what Joey Delaney comes to find out. I mean he's gone to school and done all right and he's learned his catechisms and understands that the Church and the priests are a necessary evil, if ya know what I mean by that, but what truly has the poor bugger experienced of life? Nothin'. He doesn't know shite. He's been to but one dance, doesn't know how to act in company, is still a virgin at 17 and has never had a new suit of clothes. And he dares to dream a little bit. The dreams are small but comforting, yeah? To keep goin' to school, to meet a nice girl and take her out to a pub or a café and have a meal, ya know? Simple things, but when the story begins, to Joey these things seem terribly out of reach and he finds himself in a state of despair, a black hole of feeling that seems bottomless. Yet somehow, Bernie, he manages to find a sort of footbridge, like, marks in the desert that lead him, bit by bit to the oasis and with that journey, that process, he comes to understand himself and those around him and his bitterness and resentment drop away. It's at that point, he realizes he can get on with his life without any worries, he's got no burdens anymore and then he's got a chance at happiness and it's his to win or lose but at least he knows that. That nothin' from outside can take away that chance ever again. Am I makin' myself clear, Bernie?"

"Okay, now that we've finished talking about your life Frank, what about the book?"

He chuckled into the phone. "You're a bastard, do you know that? Hey listen, I've got to go, these publicists are givin' me dirty looks now. I'll have them send up my latest photo, okay? It's very handsome, the pic I mean. Not me, of course. Say hello to your lovely bride for me. I know she hates my work."

"She's her own person, what can I say?"

"You're a lucky shite all the same. Take care o'yerself, eh? I'll be up in a few months. We'll get together and hoist a few, right?"

"I'll look forward to it." I hung up, then clicked off the tape. I realized I liked Frank and, despite inevitable feelings of envy, wanted him to do well.

And that was a problem for someone in my position, struggling as I was with my own writing. Envy or loathing. That's what I brought to the party, didn't I? Either I envied the bastards I interviewed or I loathed the sods with very little in between but I genuinely liked Frank. He'd earned his success and he was a talented writer in my opinion. Besides the two of us were so different, there was no possible way one of us could poach from the other. And he was being coddled by the critics for the moment. But lord, how I knew how that could turn, and quickly. One moment, a hero and the next, yesterday's news. It was a brutal world so the smart and cunning among us leverage the good times and over the long haul, outlast the critics, take them with a grain of salt and keep on putting out good work. That was the nub of it, the ability to produce good work and in whose opinion? Always your own first, the others after and that seemed the best you could do. Frank rode high in media circles at the moment but that also meant a goodly number were waiting for him to fail and then they could nudge each other and send out those I told-you-so looks. Smug bastards they were. Not that I counted among their number of course. Like I said, I like Frank and I liked his books, both of them. In the lexicon of the moment, I should say the stories "resonated" with me.

Charlotte sent me a quick email: "Have you woken up yet?" I wasn't sure how to take that exactly. Woken up to what? To her? Or just physically woken up? I hated plays on words. They were so confusing and when you threw in communication between the sexes, it became uninterpretable, if that's even a word. Men trying to understand women and women trying to understand men was like deciphering some killer code, we operated on completely separate frequencies. I didn't know how to respond so I left it for the moment and hoped that Charlotte didn't interpret that as being rude or neglectful. I simply felt confused.

# 10

Sharon decided to accompany me to the airport to meet my father and his bride, Catherine. Arrival imminent at Pearson International Airport at 2:15 p.m. on Saturday afternoon. They flew Alitalia airlines. Surprised I was because this rendez-vous cut into her personal training time. But Sharon insisted we take the Navigator, the flying ship on wheels, she wanted them to ride in luxury and assumed they'd have plenty of luggage. She told the boys they couldn't come because there wouldn't be room for them. Nathan had stared at her in disbelief.

"In that boat? There's room enough for a tribe of Bushmen, a punk band, all of their equipment and the LA Lakers combined."

"Nevertheless," Sharon had sniffed. "Find something else to do."

Sean wasn't put off in the least. "Here Mom, can I have 5 bucks."

"What for?" I asked him.

"Why not?" he retorted as Sharon handed each of them a bill as I looked away in anger.

"Get yourself something at the mall but don't hang about with all of the other lazy sods, got it?"

"Yes mother," they trilled in unison, then set off, laughing and slapping each other on the back. I shook my head.

"What'd you do that for?"

"What?" she replied in a way that she thought made her sound absent-minded.

"They don't need any money."

"They don't?"

"No."

"Well, I just wanted them to do something out of the house and not bother Mrs. Sanchez and my mum while they were at it."

"You know they asked you because I would have said no."

"What of it?"

"It's the old ploy, Sharon. Divide and conquer. Split our feelings and play both ends against the middle and you fell for it."

She became indignant now, colour rising to her freckled face. "You're delusional. I did no such thing. I believe you've become senile at age 37."

I swallowed hard. This isn't how I wanted to start out before we went to pick up my father. That would be stressful enough.

"Fine. Forget about it. Let's just go, shall we?" I held the door for her. She sailed through it.

I'm always baffled as to why entire extended families congregate at the airport when meeting relatives. Wouldn't one or two or three or four do? Why bring 20 or 30 people, aunts, uncles, grandchildren, cousins twice removed? I understand that it's liberating to show support and solidarity, to demonstrate for the world that the person arriving from the old country is important but why bring the entire family tree to them? It was maddening when you were packed into a crowd, straining to see your party, anxiously watching the gate, checking the arrival times, looking at your watch and wondering how much the short term parking would cost. In the din of the arrivals area, the uncomfortable silence between Sharon and myself screamed in my ears. I kept telling myself she was wrong and I wasn't going to back down. I just hated the fact that our kids could weasel money and gifts out of her so easily without having to take responsibility for anything. She just didn't see it. She had the means, she thought, so why not let her loved ones take advantage of it? After all, she'd struggled in the early years, her family remained poor without any money and were denied the niceties that their schoolmates had. It was humiliating and Sharon had vowed never to let that happen to her again. I understood that but there was such a thing as appreciation and taking ownership, something our wayward teens didn't even remotely understand. So, Sharon stoked a foul mood because I'd confronted her. She fumed and soon smoke would pour out of her ears.

"I think I see them," I said.

"How can you see anything in this crowd? It's a bloody zoo," she said.

I had spotted my father's grizzled head but more than that, I knew his attitude when he walked, a haughty kind of posture, very erect and a bit stiff-legged that caused him to roll a bit, like standing on an undulating ship's deck. I craned to see through the glass into the customs and baggage area. The crowd closed in front of us and people milled around the carousels waiting for their luggage. A number of international flights must have come in because loads of people streamed through, toting bags and trunks of vast proportion, some new, many battered and scuffed and scarred from the rough passage of the handlers as they transferred the cargo from plane to airport and back again.

"It is them," I said. My father wore a light knit, black pullover and baggy jeans. He was deeply tanned and looked as if he'd lost quite a bit of weight. Catherine wore a loose sundress and sandals. No stockings.

"That's odd."

"What? What's odd?" Sharon asked me distractedly, harassed by the closeness of the crowd and the heat in the room. She fanned at her face.

I shook my head. "Nothing." I felt uncertain. I saw them at the carousel. My father grabbed for the bags, lunged actually, almost falling forward. A younger man next to him, pulled a large suitcase off the conveyor belt and set it down beside them. "She looks…?"

"What?" asked Sharon. "Looks what?"

I didn't answer. I couldn't. I froze. Shocked to the core. What could I do or say? Sharon hated it when people didn't answer her. She pulled on my unresponsive arm, then punched me. I looked away.

"What's up with you, Bernie. Answer me, will ya?" I just turned and looked, which silenced her right away. Something in my look, the intensity of my expression cut her off. Instead, she followed my gaze and focused on the entranceway to the terminal. We set our sights on the sliding doors. The triumphant travellers, sprung from customs then ejected into the waiting hordes, after marching down a specially cleared aisle that permitted overwhelmed relatives to rush up and hug and kiss them while others, also teary-eyed, snapped pictures.

We waited until they emerged, my father pushing the luggage cart. They hadn't brought much really but he struggled with it, nonetheless. Catherine stood beside him searching the faces, her hand resting on his shoulder looking wonderfully, gloriously, pregnant, before the world.

Sharon's eyes flamed into torches, her red hair blazed with colour and I could see the astonishment on her sun-dappled face. I don't think I had ever seen her stupefied.

I took Sharon's hand. It felt like leading a small child.

"Come on," I said. Catherine pointed to us as we approached and greeted us with a wide but fatigued smile, which even I had to admit, dazzled. Her face looked lightly browned and a ridge of freckles dotted the bridge of her nose and her tanned cheeks.

"Dad," I said and shook his hand. "Catherine." And gave her a light but unenergetic hug. Sharon made no effort to hide her surprise.

"Catherine. What happened to you?"

Catherine responded with a throaty laugh. I was vaguely aware of other travellers streaming about us, some muttering as we stopped the flow of traffic. "What do you think happened?" And she gave my father a wink. He grinned expansively like a schoolboy caught looking up a girl's dress. Sharon gaped at Catherine's extended belly.

"Come on," I said and went around behind the luggage cart. "We're blocking the road here."

"How are you son?" my father croaked as I began pushing the cart, navigating through the throngs of people.

"Fine, Dad. I'm fine. Really." I moved off at a brisk pace, weaving in and out, then looked behind me.

"Bernie." Sharon gave me an exasperated look. Leaving behind the elderly and the incapacitated, so I slowed before the exit.

"Sorry. I just wanted to get away from the hubbub."

"You must be exhausted," Sharon said to my father and Catherine.

"A little," Catherine admitted.

"I'm fine," my father said. "I slept on the plane."

"And snored the whole way," Catherine retorted. As we emerged from the terminal, waiting to cross to the covered parking, Catherine looked about. "What lovely weather. I am so glad to be back home."

"Is that why you came back?" Sharon asked. "Because…"

"…of the baby, yes."

I had to admit Catherine exuded a radiant aura. I mean, how old was she? Forty-four or five? A bit risky I would have thought.

"Come on," I said, when there was a break in the traffic. "We're just over here." I unloaded the luggage, unlocked the doors, returned the cart and redeemed the dollar coin. Whistling under my breath, I flipped it up into the air as I sauntered back to the Navigator, not wanting to imagine the scene inside. Sharon had helped Catherine and my father inside. All of that personal training had to be good for something. I got in and started the engine.

"Here we go," I said inanely, and then it occurred to me that I didn't know where we were going. "Where are we going?" My father had sold his house in the Annex, a lovely neighbourhood surrounding the University of Toronto. That had aggravated me as I had always pictured myself in that house, a three-story Victorian with a sweeping foyer, high ceiling, mounds of wood trim and a grape arbour in back. But my father had insisted and further insisted the money would be placed in trust for Sean and Nathan. I wondered if that would change now.

"We're going to Catherine's," Eph said.

"The tenants are out," Catherine added. Catherine had two grown children from her first marriage. Her daughter had graduated from university and was working in an architecture firm as a junior, while her son was studying second year law. They lived on their own.

"Why don't you come back to the house for a cup of tea, at least?" Sharon said. I think she hadn't had enough of staring at Catherine's girth. "Ma will be so happy to see you."

"Oh? Your mother's there?" I glanced in the rear view and saw Eph's quizzical look.

"She had a wee fall and has her leg up. She's staying with us while she recovers. I've got Mrs. Sanchez in to give us a hand."

"Ah, Mrs. Sanchez," Eph replied, knowingly. He was aware of some of my misadventures with her.

I merged on to the highway and wanted to concentrate on the driving. The traffic wasn't heavy but maneuvering such a large vehicle always required a dose of concentration.

"So, ah, when are you...?" Sharon was half-turned in her seat.

"Due?" Catherine replied archly. "In about six weeks. We just made it under the wire. Another few weeks and they wouldn't have let me on the plane. I've put on so much weight, I don't think I would have been able to hide my condition."

"And how do you feel, then?" My father and I let the women talk. Each of us had lapsed into silence. It was odd, really. In a way, I admired him. I mean, having a child at his age. How many men can claim that? Artistic men had children late in life, Charlie Chaplin, Picasso and so on. Not that my father travelled in the same sphere. Still, the analogy stuck. At the same time, I felt a bit betrayed. I hadn't wanted him to marry. I hadn't wanted him to marry Catherine. And now, I couldn't help but think whether my children would be deprived of something that I had assumed would be rightfully theirs. They would have an uncle or an aunt at least 15 years their junior. Birthright assumed biblical proportions and I couldn't help but think of the Old Testament story of Jacob and Esau and what a mess that made out of their domestic situation.

I pulled the Navigator into our driveway, then switched off the ignition.

"Here we are then," Sharon trilled. "Safe and sound everyone. Come on. Dad, I'm sure the boys are dying to see you." I pulled a face but said nothing. I went round and opened the door, helping Catherine ease her girth down the long first step. She smiled her thanks but didn't say anything, acutely conscious of my bristling disapproval.

"Dad," I said, and reached out my hand.

"I'm all right," he said irritably, and waved me away.

"We'll leave the luggage, shall we?" Sharon began to sound like a tour guide. Exit by the gift shop?

Before we could make it up the walk, the door burst open. Sean and Nathan appeared. "Zaidy!" they cried, their hands out but just as they got halfway down the walk, they stopped dead in their tracks and stared, open-mouthed at Catherine.

"Great," I muttered.

A short eon ticked-tocked.

"What's the matter boys? Haven't you seen a pregnant woman before?"

Sean looked at her, then at Eph. "Zaidy. Did you do that?"

Eph grinned. "Yup."

"Way to go, man." And Sean came and gave him a big hug.

Not to be outdone, Nathan followed and did the same. "I'm proud of you, man. Keeping up the family reputation. The Goldmans are supreme," he cried. And the two of them surrounded Eph, giving him the hug and fake cry routine.

"All right, you hoodlums. Let him go now. You've had your moment. Your star has shone, albeit briefly," I said.

"No, really, man I can't get over it. We can hold our heads up high, can't we Sean? Our Zaidy. What a guy. What a man. Awesome."

Despite the silliness of it, Eph laughed. "Knock it off you two. Let's go in. It's been a long flight and we're tired." But it would never end when or where it was supposed to, not with those two. They continued to cling to him, putting their heads down on his shoulder. Finally, I could see how exasperated he was and I pulled them off him.

"All right, that's enough. Now. Come on, Dad. Everything's a joke to them."

"So I see."

We managed to make it into the living room. Felicity sat upright in a wing-back chair with her leg up on the settee.

Her eyes lit up when we entered. "How nice to see you all," she chirped until her gaze fell on Catherine. "Oh my goodness. Whatever happened dear?"

"What do you mean?" Catherine asked, smiling.

"Well. You're...you're..."

"Pregnant. Yes." Catherine moved over to the sofa and eased herself down. "That's better."

"Why Ephraim," Felicity said, and waggled a finger at him.

"I think we'll have tea, Mrs. Sanchez," Sharon said. Mrs. Sanchez had been hovering by the doorway and she too, stared at Catherine. "Mrs. Sanchez?"

"What? Oh yes, Mrs. Right away."

"I'll have some too," Nathan said.

"Me too," Sean added.

Eph went and sat by Catherine. He held her hand. They exchanged looks that I could only describe as loving. Sharon glanced my way to see if I had noticed but I kept my expression neutral. Nathan squeezed in beside Eph and put an arm around his shoulder and gave him a bit of a shake. "So, Zaidy. Tell me, really. How are you doing? Tell the truth now. How was Italy? Was it great? Did you eat lots of pasta there? And pizza? What about the vino and the gelato? How was that?"

Eph shrank back from him a bit. "Your voice has changed," he replied.

"It's called puberty," Sean said.

"And we passed with flying colours. I don't have any zits but Sean's got tons of them."

"And that's all you associate with puberty?" My father asked.

"Pretty much," Nathan admitted. "That and shaving." Nathan sported a dark smudge above his lip.

"So I see," and Eph patted him on the knee.

"You must be tired," Felicity said. "Carrying such a weight and flying all that way, poor thing. You rest up now and a good cup of tea will help restore you."

"Yes," agreed Catherine. After all, what else could she say? There was an awkward silence until Mrs. Sanchez came rattling in with the tea things on a tray and set it down on the coffee table. She'd sliced some carrot cake and put out a plate of chocolate biscuits. I excused myself and went to the kitchen, ostensibly to cut up some lemon. I always took tea with lemon. So did my father. For some reason, Mrs. Sanchez never remembered or refused to acknowledge it. As I rooted through the fridge, my father came up behind me.

"Cripes," I yelped. "Don't do that."

"Sorry," he replied, and that wasn't something he said easily or often. We'd had our issues between us. I found the lemon and began slicing it up on the cutting board. "So, you enjoyed Italy then?" Eph hadn't been in Italy since he began the research for The Global View, his most famous book.

Characteristically, my father chose to ignore me. I felt his blue eyes boring in. "This doesn't change anything, you know."

"What? What doesn't change anything?"

"Don't be obtuse, Bernie. I'm on a short lead here. I'm jet-lagged and tired and I can see you've had a shock. Believe me, you couldn't have been more shocked than I was."

"It wasn't planned?"

"Of course not. It just happened."

"And you know about birth control, I suppose?"

"Don't be patronizing. Because of our collective ages, we just never thought about it."

"But there's a little bit of iron in the old steam engine yet?"

"Something like that," he muttered, looking quite pleased with himself.

"Oh please," I said. "You look like the cat that just licked the cream."

"Wasn't it, ate the canary?"

"Whatever."

He moved in a bit closer and with knife poised, I felt like moving back. He encroached on my space and that wasn't something the Goldmans did, certainly not lightly. "I meant what I said, you know. About it not changing anything.

Sean and Nathan will be looked after properly. They're still beneficiaries in my will."

"I'm not sure that's the point," I said.

"What is the point?"

Ah, he would ask that question. The pedantic side of him hadn't been fully subjugated while he'd been cavorting in Italy. "Well, for one thing, it's a little bizarre having a sibling suddenly at age 37, a half-brother or sister."

"Sister."

"What?"

"We're having a girl."

"Of course, Catherine was tested."

"Right."

"You could be happy for us," he growled. "Instead of sulking like a little boy."

"Oh, thanks for that. And you probably won't live to see your daughter finish kindergarten. Catherine will be raising a child on her own. And what if something happens to you? A stroke or something. She'll have to look after you and the kid."

"Well. You are full of good cheer. I'm glad I came in here to talk to you. You've just perked me right up after such a long journey and months apart."

"Yeah, well, sorry. I just said what was on my mind."

"If something happens to me, I'm planning on dropping of a heart attack. No lingering, all right?"

"As if you can control it."

"We'll see." He paused, then pursed his lips and continued to glare at me. "You might as well get it all off your chest."

"Excuse me?"

"Come on, Bernie. You're right about one thing, I am getting on and there's no point in beating around the bush. What else have you got? What else is bothering you?"

I cleared my throat then looked down at the glazy sheen on the sliced lemon. "Okay. What bothers me is seeing you so happy with Catherine and... well you weren't that way with Mom, were you?"

Eph took a deep breath, then let it out. He stared at me fiercely and I thought those blue eyes had frozen over, icy enough to skate on. Then he let all of the air out and suddenly, he seemed like a saggy old man. "It's just different, that's all. I loved your mother. And I've told you that a hundred times. But we weren't always happy together. I'm not going to sugar coat anything and tell you that we were rapturously in love with each other. We had an understanding, that close bond that forms when you've lived with someone for over 40 years. That's a long time. Longer than you live with anyone else, your parents, your children, hopefully," he added.

"I'm just uncomfortable with it."

"You resent me for it."

"Yeah, that's right. I do."

He nodded, then rocked back on his heels. "Okay. I'm glad you said something. You know, in the old days, this would have taken years to come out."

"Uh-huh."

"I'm not going to lose sleep over it, Bernie. I will do the right thing by you and the boys and your new little sister too. I don't shirk my responsibilities, you know that."

I didn't answer him. That would have kept us in the kitchen for hours, perhaps days, him and his responsibilities. As I carried the lemon into the living room, I thought about those responsibilities and how they didn't seem to apply to me and my younger brother, Harry, when we were growing up. It was only the work that mattered. And now, it doesn't matter enough.

Sharon's expression remained frozen as she sipped her tea and listened to Felicity natter on. Mrs. Sanchez hovered behind the sofa while Catherine's face drooped with fatigue.

"Ma, belt up will ya. Can't you see the poor girl's knackered? She's on the verge of passing out on the carpet."

"I am a little tired," Catherine admitted.

My father and I sat in low slung chairs that were excruciatingly uncomfortable, positioned directly opposite each other across the throw rug. It took a great deal of concentration to look at anything or anyone but him. I had just taken a sip of my tea.

"Bernie will drive you."

"But..." I protested, just about to reach for a piece of carrot cake. After all, I'd sweated off kilos that morning in the gym.

"Where do you want to go, exactly?" Sharon asked.

Eph stood up. He'd been balancing the tea cup on his knee. "We're staying at Catherine's for now. Until we decide what we want to do and where we wish to live."

"I don't think I've been there," I said.

"It's in Swansea," Catherine replied. Swansea. A neat little neighbourhood in the southwestern part of the city, an enclave of older, majestic homes that bordered a beautiful ravine. The area had a strong community association that prided itself on preservation. Avaricious developers had been kept out and the streets and homes had maintained their original charm. In doing so, property values had skyrocketed. I could understand why Catherine wouldn't want to let her house go.

"Nice," I said.

Eph took Catherine's arm. I couldn't tell who helped whom, the geriatric university professor or the younger but abdominally encumbered wife. Together, they said their goodbyes, Felicity waved at them and smiled from her perch, Mrs. Sanchez raised her hand in a grim farewell and suddenly Sean and Nathan came skidding around the corner, each of their heads wrapped in headphones as they infused cacophonic tympany into their brains. Once again, they went through the mock routine of hugging my father and telling him how proud they were. They made him high five them and slap hands like street musicians or local yokels at a pick-up basketball game. Eph took it all in stride, smiling indulgently at the antics of his teenaged grandsons. I wondered then what kind of father he'd be to his newborn child. Whether he'd fill in the blanks he'd left out when Harry and I were young. Would he diaper and feed? Walk the halls in the middle of the night? Take the baby out in the carriage? Go to the park and play? Would he? Could he? Was this his opportunity to finally get it right after all that had gone wrong earlier in our lives? Was he trying to make amends for what he hadn't done? My head spun as I picked up the keys to the Navigator. I was about to leave when Nathan grabbed me about the waist from behind, and Sean did the same to him, so we looked like a human chain wired to the front door.

I stood it for a moment but I could see my father and Catherine waiting outside.

"Don't leave," Nathan wailed, then pretended to cry.

"Let go, please."

"You can't leave us. When are you coming back?"

"Nathan, please."

"I won't let you leave." He buried his head into my side. Sean just laughed at it. Sharon stood with one hip cocked and a wry expression while Felicity had sunk back into her chair and was staring at the ceiling. I was about to peel Nathan's fingers off me, when I heard a sharp clap.

"Boys. Let your father go. The others are waiting for him." Mrs. Sanchez stood glaring at each of them in turn. Nathan released me but Sean, irrepressible as always, still held on, so the two of them shuffled off, still attached. "They are very high-spirited," Mrs. Sanchez pronounced. I rolled my eyes and walked out the door.

# 11

The trip to Catherine's home consisted of mumbled directions from my father. The two of them held hands in the middle seat and as I glanced occasionally in the rear-view mirror, they seemed absorbed in each other. The affection seemed genuine on both ends. It surprised me. I suppose it shouldn't have, as I'd suspected Catherine's motives from the beginning, but her pregnancy shed a new light on the subject. The two of them had known each other only several months before they'd been married but I suppose it was reasonable to expect that my father didn't have time to waste. If he was certain of his feelings and commitment and her commitment to him, why should he wait? That's the way he reasoned it out, I would have thought.

Catherine's house turned out to be a charming, three-bedroom bungalow on a spacious lot, backing the ravine, prime real estate in that area. The exterior had been re-done in stucco that gave it a California look. Someone had planted a lovely garden with tulips and roses and bags of impatiens hung over the railing of a generous front porch that wrapped around the side. The garage lay hidden around the back. I knew that Catherine had a senior position in human resources with a large petro-chemical firm, that meant she didn't fit the classic image of a gold digger. I would have been well-satisfied if she had. The realization that they genuinely cared for each other bit even more. Let's face it, I was jealous and I had no reason to be. But we know that human emotions rarely take a logical course, seeping into forbidden corners and crevices of the soul.

I helped them carry their bags. Catherine waddled up to the porch, fished about in her handbag, then bobbed up with a key. Before she could insert it into the lock, however, the door was flung open and a young girl in her early twenties stood on the threshold.

"Mum. You're home." She flung her arms about Catherine's neck.

"Hello Judith," Eph said.

"Hi Dad," Judith replied and came and embraced him as well. Dad? Then she stepped back and appraised her mother. "You really are big, oh my god." Finally, Judith glanced at me. "Oh, hello."

"Hi. I'm Bernie. Bernie Goldman…"

"The writer. Yes, I know. Pleased to meet you, Bernie." And she put out a hand which I took. She seemed too damned nice, too damned charming. I found myself smiling and actually liking her. She loomed as an attractive, younger version of her mother, taller and slimmer with auburn hair, brown eyes and a smattering of freckles across the bridge of her nose. "Come on in, everyone. I was just tidying up. The tenants left a bit of a mess."

I picked up the bags and stumbled after them into a spacious living room that extended into a dining area. The interior had been recently painted a pale gold colour. With the banks of windows in the front and along each side, the house filled with light. Damn it, I thought, I'm beginning to sound like a flack for Home and Garden. "Uh, where…?" I indicated the bags.

"Oh," said Catherine. "In the master bedroom Bernie. Thanks ever so much."

"I'll show you," Judith said, and led off up the stairwell to the side of the small foyer at the entrance. I found a large room with en suite, a canopied queen size bed and a fireplace. It was situated at the back of the house and the main window overlooked the back garden and further into the ravine. Judith must have opened the windows. The air smelled fresh and I felt a light breeze. Birds chirped in the yard.

"Nice," I said. "Very nice."

"I'll tell Mum. She'll be pleased that you think so." I set the bags down. Then she looked at me rather seriously. "I hope we will be friends, Bernie. Not just you but the two families, I mean, now that we will be sharing a sibling."

"This isn't a little weird for you?" I asked her.

Her face clouded for a moment but cleared just as quickly.

"She's happy. That's all I care about. She really loves your father."

"But she will be raising this child on her own. Surely you realize that."

"What do you mean? Your father's not going anywhere. And now that he's retired, he can devote a lot more time to the baby."

"But you don't expect that he'll actually do anything, do you? At his age? I mean, physically, it will be too much for him."

Judith smiled mysteriously and I found it irritating.

"Well, we'll just have to see, that's all. I don't think you should be resentful because he wasn't as involved in your life as much as you would have liked when you were young."

"He told you."

She shook her head.

"I'm not a dummy, you know. Don't you think I know what it's like, not to have a father around? I was only ten when my Dad left. Mum's raised children on her own before and she can do it again. This is a love child. I can see it in her face."

"You're young and you're optimistic."

"And you don't have to be so jaded. You're not that old." And we stared at each other rather intensely for a long while.

Finally, I shrugged, then grinned, sheepishly.

"Well," I said, then put out my hand. "Welcome to the family."

Her youthful face erupted into an expression of gratitude. She took my hand in the two of hers.

"Thanks. You too."

I returned home, deep in thought, vaguely aware of the route and the many hazards on the roadways of the city. I pulled into the driveway, then switched the Navigator off. Before I'd left, my father had cornered me on the front porch.

"Listen," he said. "When the time comes, I was wondering..."

"Yes?"

He scratched along his jaw line. His eyes were reddened from lack of sleep. "Well, you've been through this before, with the boys... I could use a little support, you know, down at the hospital."

"You're going into the delivery room?"

He nodded. "Catherine made me promise."

"And since you missed it the first two times..."

"It just wasn't done then. You know, it was very unusual in those days."

I patted his shoulder.

"No problem, Dad. Piece of cake."

I left him then, in a state of confusion and discomfort with the unknown. The birth of a baby was something he couldn't control. His towering intellect couldn't reason the pangs of labour into submission. Oh yes, I acted the cruel son, I know, but it felt good.

I barbecued chicken that evening and for once, our dinner together unfolded pleasantly. Sharon remained subdued but attentive and complimented me on the cooking. She even prepared the salad. We drank a pleasant white Sauvignon Blanc from New Zealand. Barbecuing without something to drink was just not on. The food tasted better when you cooked while drinking. The boys acted decently. They didn't throw anything, make stupid faces, imitate gluttonous cretins or make any rude remarks. Each of them ate a piece of chicken, took some salad, had a baked potato, grabbed a piece of watermelon and went outside to spit the seeds. Sharon and I exchanged glances.

"What's got into them?" she asked. "Oh, how tame the savage beast."

"I dunno. But I'm not gonna complain about it," I said. I felt pretty good overall. The shock of Catherine's pregnancy began to wane and I imagined my father as her labour coach. Now that was funny. Downing half a bottle of wine didn't hurt, either. Even Felicity's nattering didn't raise my hackles and Mrs. Sanchez had left for the day. The world or at least my small piece of it, appeared to be in alignment. I should have known better.

Sharon helped me tidy up and we took our tea in the backyard as the day began to cool but still, felt pleasant and warm.

Round about nine o'clock, she yawned, then gave a big stretch. "I'm going up. Are you coming?"

"It's only nine o'clock."

"I know. I think I'll read."

"I'll be along in a while."

"Don't be too long," she said, with some emphasis.

"It is Saturday night," I said.

"So?"

"Well, it's all right to stay up a little later, isn't it?"

"Not too late," she replied, then tapped the tip of my nose with her forefinger. Then oddly, she trailed the same finger over the edge of the chair and around the lip of the patio table as she went in. I watched her curiously. What the hell was that? I thought. It had been a strange day and everyone had been affected by it.

I read for about an hour until my head kept hitting my chest. Sean and Nathan were watching a movie downstairs. I popped my head in, told them I was going to bed and admonished not to stay up too late. They grunted their acknowledgement without the turn of a single head. Felicity had hobbled up to her room long before. She kept very odd hours, she did. In bed most nights by seven o'clock, then she sat up all hours of the night because she couldn't sleep. During the day, she had to watch her daytime trash talking TV shows and then the afternoon soaps, all cranked up at several thousand decibels. I stayed out of her way as much as I could.

Sharon lay in bed under the covers, her glasses perched on her nose, her red hair falling down about her shoulders. For a scant moment, I transposed Charlotte's figure on to Sharon's as she'd been lying in exactly the same pose when I'd last seen her. Inadvertently, I gasped. Sharon glanced quickly up. I gave her a weak grin and went into the bathroom to floss, brush my teeth and wash up. I was a dawdler. I'd always been that way since childhood. I don't know why it took so long but I'd stare at my face, pull at my cheeks, examine the pores on my nose, inspect my teeth and before I knew it, 20 minutes had elapsed.

"What're ya doin' in there? Reconstructive surgery?" Her peeved voice. I flushed, then emerged from the loo. She lay on the bed wearing nothing but a sly expression. Her honeyed skin had a sheen to it and a faint lemony smell wafted up. I stopped, startled. She had both hands on the bedpost above her head accentuating the fullness of her breasts. They heaved in a becoming way, the nipples taut and pointed, tinged with pink. Her tan lines had faded from the tanning bed she'd been frequenting but it gave her body a smooth, even texture. My jaw must have dropped several feet.

"Well?"

"Yes."

"Yes?"

"To anything," I replied. What could I say? I was an animal. Most men wallowed in bestiality when you thought about it. Our brains shut down and the primeval instincts took over. We became heated putty, malleable and pliant, rolled and pummelled into any shape desired then wedged into a crack or fissure somewhere. My undershorts felt uncomfortable suddenly. Her body glowed. I was mesmerized by the light. Sharon tugged them off me. I lay down beside her. We proceeded to engage in various forms of connubial bliss and blushingly, I must admit that went vocal, right until the end where her ankles somehow ended up wrapped about my neck. I made a move to disengage but to my dismay felt her thighs tighten.

"AAAcchhh!"

"Not yet," she said.

"W-What?"

"I can't move yet. I need to keep elevated a bit," she whispered, huskily.

"Sharon...?" Another male trait, the one that screamed survival kicked in automatically. Alarm flooded my brain. My libido hit the panic button. I went to move again but Sharon, thanks to those goddam personal training sessions, kept me pinned.

"Not yet, boyo." And she smiled at me sweetly, her irises still infused with the afterglow of love while a thin line of sweat beaded her upper lip. On the one hand, I wanted to dive in again except I realized that I'd been betrayed. Betrayed by my own lust and by her scheming. I resisted as she yawned and stretched, still holding me tight. "It'll only be a few minutes longer."

"I don't recall our having agreed to anything, do you?"

"I've decided, my darling. I want a child. I told you that and then when I saw Catherine..." The tenor of her voice rose a notch.

"Are you saying this is some sort of competition? She's having one so you've got to as well?"

"I'm at least six years younger and in much better shape."

"But, but..." I stammered. "We haven't discussed this. It isn't fair."

She released me then and I moved back on to my haunches and stared at her, lying happily on her back with her knees pulled to her chest, keeping her hips elevated. She didn't want the precious elixir to leak or run before it had a chance to do its job. I looked down at my produce, the emanations from my own body and labelled them, all 450,000 or so, traitor.

"I want this baby and that's all you need to know." And then she closed her eyes and went off into some dreamy state. The smile stayed put. I rolled off the bed, picked up my discarded undershorts and put them on. "Don't be upset," she whispered. "This will be our love child. It will make everything perfect between us. And think about it, we have built-in baby sitters with the boys."

Oh yes, I imagined Sean and Nathan coddling a wee baby. They'd make the cover of New Mother, each one of them. They'd treat it like a toy, more likely, or use it like a football, more to the point.

Wearily, I dragged myself around to my side of the bed and with a sagging heart, lay down. There would be no rest for me now, not for the next 20 years or so. As I closed my eyes, I saw the mischievous face of Charlotte laughing at me.

# 12

Short and dumpy characterized Mr. McWilly, a man who stretched his grey suit sideways. He wore a full moustache on his thin upper lip. His beady blue eyes chilled in the creepiest way. He looked like a leprechaun on steroids. McWilly spoke in a disquietingly quiet manner. I had to lean forward to strain to hear him. That seemed to be his intention, I'm sure, as it gave him an advantage over the listener. After all, McWilly knew what he was saying and unless you stretched yourself halfway across his desk, you were in the dark, auditorially speaking. Mr. McWilly functioned as my account manager at the bank and I could see he felt like an emperor at court without the requisite courtiers in attendance. But then he had me. And I was all ears. It paid to be all ears when your account manager, even an elfin one, spoke to you in earnest tones about fiscal responsibility. I noticed he was holding up a sheaf of documents and pointing to them with a pencil, or rather pointing to specific areas on the documents.

"Mr. Goldman, is that your signature?"

I peered at the paper. "Yes."

McWilly pointed. "And here."

"Yes."

He pointed again. "And here?"

"Yes, Mr. McWilly, you know that's my signature so why the charade?"

"No charade, Mr. Goldman," he murmured.

"Okay." But I wasn't appeased.

"And you know what this document is?"

I sighed wearily. "Yes."

"It is a loan document. Your signature is all over it which means you understand the terms of this document and agreed to abide by them to the letter..."

"Yes..."

"...to the letter," he repeated with some indignation thrown in for good measure.

"Okay. To the letter, yes."

"In the past three months, you have exceeded your limit no less than seven times."

"Uh-huh."

"Are you aware of that?"

"I am now."

"Don't be facetious, Mr. Goldman."

"Right. I'm sorry Mr. McWilly, I wasn't sure how many times we'd gone over the bar."

"Seven."

"Yes, seven."

"That is a lot in such a short period of time and the bank won't stand for it."

"No. I don't blame them."

He peered at me sharply to see if I was mocking him or being facetious again. He rubbed the bridge of his broad nose leaving a red mark.

"Publishing," he began as I finished it in my head, "is a risky business. The bank is not in the habit of assuming risk and what little risk is assumed, is normally secured risk. In this instance," and here he flapped the papers one more time, "we only had your personal guarantee. You wouldn't have received this loan if it hadn't been..."

"For my wife, because of her income. Yes, I am aware of that, Mr. McWilly."

"Mrs. Goldman earns a fabulous income," he admitted grudgingly, and stated in such a way that he wanted me to understand the he didn't think that I deserved it in the least. Ah, if he only knew. I could imagine him and Mrs. McWilly and all the little McWillys, short and stumpy like him, gnawing on hot dogs in the squat backyard of their stumpy house. For all I know, he lived in a manor home with a tall, aristocratic blond and drove a Rolls. From the condition of the suit, however, I'd say not. He cleared his throat. "You must live within your means, Mr. Goldman and it's up to you to determine how that occurs. The bank will not bail you out again. And if this pattern should continue, then we'll seriously consider calling in the loan. I hope I've made myself perfectly clear."

"As crystal, Mr. McWilly."

"You could ask your wife, of course."

I was in the process of rising from my seat and froze half-way. I placed my palms flat on his desk and leaned in so I was hovering over him and fixed him with a stern stare. "Would you, Mr. McWilly? Ask your wife for money?"

"Well," he smiled, uncertainly. "I'm not in that situation, am I?"

"That's not what I asked. Answer the question. Would you ever ask your wife for money?"

McWilly paled, then swallowed uncomfortably. "Well. No," he admitted.

"I thought so."

I left Mr. McWilly in his squat little office on a note of triumph, albeit a hollow one. It didn't solve my problems and I ran endless scenarios around in my mind as I trudged back to the underground parking lot beneath City Hall, where I'd left my car. It was a familiar conversation but when a person had to grovel before a stumpy little man in a worn grey suit, the pressure seemed worse. I couldn't ask Sharon for a bail-out and in fact, wouldn't. Stupid pride, I supposed. Ultimately, that would be throwing money at a sinking proposition. Magazines like Bookology weren't set up to make money, not realistically. They needed to be supported by some society or foundation or better yet, a wealthy benefactor, none of which existed to my knowledge in present day Toronto. And I'd been subsidizing the thing through my own personal line of credit as it was. Without that, we'd have been flat broke years ago and I would have closed up shop and that would have suited Sharon. She didn't understand what I was doing anyway but decided to indulge me. She hated my staff, thought my partner was a layabout and the magazine pointless. She only enjoyed the parties and receptions we'd been invited to, especially the ones for any Irish writers breezing through town. From a business perspective, if we'd been a subsidiary of Cablestar, she'd have cut us down years ago. I wouldn't have blamed her. There was no business case here, no way to turn a decent profit. I took home maybe 35K a year if I was lucky and struggled with my own writing while having the worries and stresses of running an ailing business that bogged me down even more.

"Why don't you just stay home and write?" Sharon had asked on more than one occasion. "I'll support you. You know I will." And I suppose that's what it came down to, in essence. Unadulterated male vanity. I was still conventional enough, still macho to the point where I couldn't stomach being supported by my wife, whether she made a "fabulous" salary or not. I had my dignity and I counted it out, day by day, as the creditors kept on calling and the dollar coins slipped through my fingers into the coffers of someone else. In my heart of hearts, beyond any notion of logic, into the ether of pure, concentrated instinct, I knew that Bookology had some worth. I didn't know how to value it or why I felt that way, I just did, and so I kept going against all the odds while my friends like Nook and Ramon progressed in their careers and were duly rewarded financially, along with the prestige that accompanied position. As for me, I had nowhere to go and the prestige was more imagined than real. But I had my pride and I had my dignity.

It was with those productive thoughts in mind that I navigated through the maze of the underground lot under City Hall (the best parking deal downtown) and drove idly back to the office. If I couldn't loaf for real, at least I could pretend while the day radiated bright and warm, I had the windows rolled down so I could feel the fine breeze on my face and I had a Mozart tape seeping through the aging speakers in my creaking car. The music blared loud enough that a few people turned their heads as I drove along. One or two, pretty young things actually, whooped and waved at me. Mozart, you sexy old devil, you. Still had the stuff. The love juice flowing through. I laughed out loud because it seemed so outrageous. Here I was at my age putting my cojones on the line against my 78-year-old father to see who came out on top. I knew Sharon, and she could become a woman possessed. Once she got her mind on something, she'd never rest until it was done immediately. I knew that I had many breathtakingly exhaustive evenings ahead of me while she and I engaged in carnal pursuits until she got what she wanted. I'd suffer at her hands, treated as no more than some sort of object, some mechanical device that delivered the sputum of life. I'm sure she'd cleared the racks of our local pharmacy of all the home pregnancy tests she could find and would burn through them just like she'd burn through me eventually. And admittedly, this didn't embody an act of joy. Bringing a child into the world was bloody hard work and high time society acknowledged the sacrifice that men made to uncork the spigot of life. Father's Day, a secondary event in my opinion, should also commemorate the upfront effort required by males to become fathers in the first place. But that, of course, was only my opinion.

In my mind, all of those delicious loafable moments, real or imagined, were pushed farther and farther away. I couldn't stretch out far enough to pull even one of them back. And if I heard it from one, I heard it from everybody.

"You're screwed," croaked Ruth, after she'd wrung it out of me, then begged off for a cigarette, "poor bastard," she muttered under her breath. She had no children of her own and had been divorced for a few decades.

"You're screwed," said Nook, after setting his coffee cup down on the table, scrutinizing me carefully to see if I was cracking up or not.

"Yup, definitely screwed," agreed Ramon, and he and Nook exchanged glances. "And I thought I had it bad," he added, then shook his shaggy head slowly.

"Looks like you're screwed. Literally," Charlotte wrote in her latest email and then went silent. Perhaps not a wise move to discuss with her, considering how Charlotte had become entangled in my mental and emotional anguish in such a way that I couldn't really unravel how I felt about anyone or anything. The opinions ran four to zip at this point, not in my favour. I decided to email my brother-in-law, Egon, who resided with my Israeli cousin in Jerusalem. He sojourned as a painter who hadn't quite learned to tame his wild ways but at least he'd managed to harness his demons and pour that energy into his work.

Egon wrote back: Ah, to be an uncle again, Bern, I think it's grand, really I do. But I've no conception of children myself. I don't mean, by the way, that I don't know how they're brought into the world, I had that figured by the time I was 10 or 11 and Polly Devlin dropped her knickers...but what's involved in it all? How do ya find the time, man? And what happens when you want to go off to the pub and get hammered? Who's lookin after the kids? I don't think I could handle it. I'm barely responsible for myself. So, yeah, it looks like your screwed, laddie. We all know Sharon when she puts her mind to it. A team of overexcited pack animals couldn't budge her. Dina says hello, by the way. Write soon, will ya. Egon.

All of that did a lot to cheer me up. Sharon didn't buy into my loafable moments because that wasn't her nature and I hadn't told her about this indulgence of mine. We all need to keep some secrets from our close loved ones and this was mine, my personal quest, the hidden journey to fulfillment.

Don't get me wrong, I liked babies, I really did. They were cute and cuddly and so totally dependent on you. They didn't talk back or swear, at least, not until they were two or three and it felt joyful watching them grow, develop and evolve. I didn't mind the trips to the park and the power walks with the stroller. I didn't even mind changing diapers or bottle feeding or washing bibs or sterilizing bottles or car seats and schlepping half a warehouse with you each time you stepped out the door. I didn't mind the months of no sex during pregnancy although I had to admit that Sharon became even more attractive as her breasts swelled along with her belly. She simply glowed, I had to admit, at least, that's how I remember it some 15 years earlier. No, none of that bothered me. I knew it would be easier this time around with only one to take care of and all the help we could expect with Felicity and Mrs. Sanchez and even the other two, the knuckleheads pitching in. And we certainly had the room and could fix up a lovely nursery. No, it wasn't any of that really.

I just didn't want to start over. Having a baby now felt like starting over again and I don't mean in the sense of renewal but more like stepping backward and rehashing something you'd already done. Been there, done that, let's move on. But maternal and competitive instincts were a powerful combination and coupled with the weakness of my will, my lack of resistance to Sharon and her attentions, I knew I was doomed. What to do? What to do? I could plead impotence but it was a wee bit late for that, especially after the other night.

"So, am I screwed or what?"

Hugo smiled at me, a humorous gleam in his gray eyes.

"Nah," he spat. "You should be happy. There is a beautiful wife and you get to make lots of love with her and you will have a baby. This is joy, not depression. What's the matter with you? You are a young man. If you are not interested, then let me sleep with your wife and I will be very happy to give her a child. I'll still be around to look after it too." And he pounded his smooth chest with a gnarled fist. We were sitting in the dry sauna at the community centre. Again, I had taken on the Romanian rowing champion and had been beaten into the ground. My self-esteem plummeted to a low ebb.

"Don't listen to all those others. They don't have a good attitude. Be positive," he shouted. "Always be positive. This is how I operate my life and it has worked for me all these 87 years. How else could I have gotten through the war? Witnessed the deaths of my parents and my sister and her husband and her child? How else could I have killed all those Nazi bastards, not knowing if I was going to live or die from one moment to the next? Believe me, that gives you a different perspective on life. You cherish every moment because it is a moment you might not have had. I was lucky, I know that. Plenty of my comrades are still buried in the fields and furrows of Russia."

"So you're saying, I should embrace this?"

Hugo nodded his graying head, the wattles of his neck shook.

"Of course," he roared. "What's not to enjoy?"

"But I don't want another child."

"Accept it. Look at it as a positive development."

"I'm trying."

"Try harder."

"I don't look at you beating me at 21 as a positive development."

Hugo smiled slyly. "That's funny. I do."

There it was, literally in front of me. My own dick was the instrument of my undoing but I needed to look at it positively, as Hugo suggested. Man's primordial need to procreate had taken over. I, Neanderthal Man, screwed to survive. That made it seem so much better.

# 13

Eph and I met for coffee at Starbuck's. He sipped a decaf latté while I had the regular tea with lemon. He wanted me to help him buy a computer. He'd never needed one before but he wanted one for the baby. I told him it was a bit premature. Why not wait until, the kid is able to read at least? Then buy the computer but he said he could use it for his own work too. And so could Catherine. Work? They were both retired, for god's sake.

"How's your work coming?" he asked me.

"What work?" I wasn't sure if he meant the work I did on the magazine or my own writing or the work it took to keep things going at home.

"The only work. Your writing, of course."

"Oh that. Okay, I guess. I get an hour or so in most mornings."

"You don't sound very sure."

"No, not really."

"What does de Groot say?"

"He wants to see a draft as soon as I can get it done."

"A draft of what?"

I looked at my father and sometimes I honestly thought he was going batty. "Of the manuscript."

"Which manuscript?"

"Well. There are two."

"You're writing two books?"

"Going back and forth is more like it."

"And how's it going, which was my first question."

"Okay, I guess. I'm making some progress. I'm just not ready to release it to de Groot just yet."

"Well, he can wait."

He said it with some emphasis. I knew he didn't care for de Groot and he wasn't shy about showing it. And that was that. I looked around the café. There were always very interesting looking people in places like this, I'm not sure why exactly. Maybe they just liked to be seen. A young girl with a rose in her hair. A fellow dressed all in black talking to a tall blonde dressed all in white. Interesting and distracting. I couldn't quite fathom the allure of such places, yet I frequented them myself.

The silence between us blossomed. There was always a barrier to climb over, it seemed. Things used to be a lot worse. When I wrote about *The Global View*, we'd had a few things out that cleared some of the air but even when you went through a cathartic-like experience, not all restrictions fell away. We still struggled to deal with each other and I didn't think that was going to change. I mean, how did you talk to your geriatric father about the baby he was about to have or why your own wife was competing with his in the baby department? Figure that one out.

"How much do you want to spend?"

His brows jerked up and for a moment, he looked puzzled, then the fog cleared and the blue eyes went bright and sunny.

"About three thousand, give or take. I don't need all the fancy gizmos."

"But you'll want to surf the Net, play games and have reading programs and the like. ECE stuff."

"What?"

"Early childhood education," I explained.

"Right," he answered gruffly, as if he had known all along.

"Was this an accident?"

"Buying a computer?"

"You know what I mean."

He grunted, then sipped his decaf. "Sort of."

"Go on." He ran a gnarled hand through his gray hair that he'd combed back in waves from his forehead. His deep tan became him, making his eyes shine like blue beacons.

"Well, late last summer, about a month after we'd moved and settled in the flat in Siena, we were sitting on the terrace looking out at the view. It was a beautiful evening and we'd just finished dinner. We'd managed to hire a splendid cook. Her name was Paolina and she cooked like a dream and to be honest

I felt like I was living in one. A new home, a new wife, it didn't quite seem real somehow…"

"And it happened so quickly," I added.

He gave me a sour look, then continued.

"I was very content sitting there, enjoying the warm evening and the light breeze, content to be there with Catherine and satisfied for once with the choices I had made. And I felt like this was my greatest accomplishment and I hadn't even done anything, just gone along with the flow of events…"

"You mean it was all done for you."

"…look," he said, with a note of anger creeping into his voice, "if you're going to keep interrupting, what's the point? You want to know something and I am trying my damnedest to answer you."

"Sorry. Go on, please. I won't interrupt again," I replied, the soul of contrition.

He glared at me for a long moment, then wet his lips.

"She, Catherine, kept giving me these looks. There was something in her expression, something different, something I hadn't seen before and I found it a bit disturbing. I asked if something was bothering her and she shook her head, pursed her lips and began to cry these huge rolling tears."

"Women will do that to get what they want."

"Don't be such a cynic, Bernie. That used to be me, but not anymore." I sighed at his naiveté but left it alone for the moment. "She looked up at me, her face all tear-streaked and said, "You're going to think I'm crazy." "What? What, I said. What could it possibly be?" "I want a child, she said. I want your child." I know this is hard for you to imagine, Bernie, but for a moment I was stunned."

"And how did you respond?"

"I told her that I didn't think I could give her a child. After all, it had been so long. I'd been a widower for a long while and I didn't know if there were any, uh, bullets left in the gun."

"Apt metaphor," I said.

"Yes, well, I thought you'd appreciate it, of all people."

"So, now we know that you weren't firing blanks."

"Precisely. And I can say it gave me a certain sense of satisfaction, even pride."

"And you weren't concerned for her well-being, not to mention the child?"

"Don't be ridiculous, of course I was and am. I know that Catherine is beyond the normal age of motherhood and that the child would have to be monitored carefully. After all the tests, we decided that if there were any abnormalities, she'd have a therapeutic abortion and we'd never consider it again. That would have been an unrealistic strain on the both of us."

"Raising a child with a handicap."

"A healthy child will be taxing enough, I'm sure."

"And how long did this whole thing take? To get her pregnant, I mean."

"I was surprised. Not long at all. Two months, not even."

Oh great, I thought. Not only was I competing in a virility contest with my father but there was a time limit too. "That's fairly quick."

"Catherine was ready," he said. "Boy, was she ready."

"Okay, Dad."

"It was quite a rapturous experience. I don't think I'd…"

"You know what? I really don't want to hear any details, okay? Okay?" I said louder.

"Fine," he said, and drained his cup. Although I detected a slight smirk in his expression. That air of superiority to which I'd been subjected all my life. Screw the damn computer, I thought.

# 14

We had been working on a special project with the federal government. The Culture Ministry agreed to sponsor a special issue of *Bookology* that featured only Canadian books and authors, all six of them. Along with it was a French issue that focused on Francophone writers and books. With the additional funding, we increased our distribution and newsstand presence. This was a big deal for us. It meant, that for once, an issue was paid for in its entirety and it came with publicity giving us more profile in the industry. I had worked on that deal for almost a year before it finally came to pass.

The work energized me while many, many details small and large demanded capable managing. One of the requirements stipulated the issue run a letter from the culture czar, the woman who functioned as the government minister in that department. A compromise but a relatively small sacrifice, in my opinion, when compared to the return we received. We were still allowed to sell advertising in the issue and since all of our costs were covered upfront, the ads provided extra gravy. Money in the bank. Provided it all went according to plan, of course. Attention to detail was not Roberto's strong suit. Not mine either but I possessed more diligent skills. The Minister's letter, like all letters, required a signature. The signature appeared on a separate piece of paper. It had been shot separately for film and then would be dropped into the allotted space on the page, above the Minister's name and title. That's what was supposed to happen.

The production of the issue took six long months of hard work where every fact, every detail had to be vetted, verified and approved by 12 layers of government bureaucrats. It was bloody well excruciating and slow, painfully slow, but we had made progress and after that time elapsed, the issue was finally ready to go to print. I don't know how many times I asked Roberto about the damn signature and he sloughed me off, shrugging in his Italian way and saying it had been taken care of. So many details, so many opportunities for disaster.

I celebrated quietly at my desk, taking some moments to relax and not think about anything, pushing all of the looming stresses thrown at me into the background, when I received a phone call. It was production supervisor, the one who was overseeing the printing of the magazine.

Ruth took the call. I looked up expectantly. "It's someone from the printer. He says it's urgent."

"Hello?"

"Mr. Goldman?"

"Yes?"

"Dick Wanderly here, from Two-tone Press?"

"Right. How are you?"

"Fine. We have a problem."

"Oh?"

Wanderly cleared his throat and his voice went a little higher.

"One of our pressmen noticed something about the issue. The problem's on page three, you know the letter?"

"What about it?"

"The signature is missing."

"What?"

"The signature. It's not there."

"The signature," I repeated tonelessly as my mouth went dry and I could feel my heart palpitate in my chest.

"Uh, Mr. Goldman. We've got the issue on press now so time is of the essence. What do you want us to do?"

"We can't run it without the signature."

"Then we'll have to pull the job from the press and re-run it and that's going to be expensive. I can't hold things up here. It's my head if I do."

"How much?"

"I uh, don't know."

"When will you know?"

"Give me a few minutes and I'll call you back."

"Fine. Do that."

Roberto sat with his feet up on his desk, talking on the phone. We all have our limits and I think I had just crashed into mine. I became the racer, spinning out of control, cartwheeling end to end on the tarmac, metal sheared, tires bouncing, springs and bumpers flying, glass shattered. I'd had it. I banged my hand down on the phone and Roberto looked up in surprise, his jaw dropping. I grabbed his shirt and pulled.

"The signature," I screamed. "How many times did I ask you about the fucking signature?"

"What, what, do you mean?" he asked.

"It's not there. The magazine is sitting on the press and the signature isn't there. Where the fuck is it?"

"I sent it. I'm sure I sent it."

"You couldn't have. Or else it would be there. I'm sick of this. Sick of the whole thing. Busting my ass for what?" I let him go then and his shirt sprang back into place with the marks of my fingers still impressed on the fabric. I'll say one thing, I scared the shit out of him as he backed away from me, thinking I was going to do something crazy. Angela just stared at us, frozen to the spot, her long-fingered, nail-lacquered hands hovering above the keyboard of her computer. I think I actually reached out for his neck and he flinched away from me as I imagined how wonderful it would be to sink my bones into that overabundant flesh and squeeze until Roberto's eyes popped out of his head. He, however, had been saved by the phone.

"It's that guy again," Ruth drawled. "Mr. Panic."

I gave Roberto a final malevolent stare and turned toward the nearest phone.

"Yeah," I barked.

"Mr. Goldman? Uh, Wanderly here."

"Got a price?"

"Yes, uh, I told you it would be expensive."

"How much?" I began to feel like Jonah Jameson. All I needed was a cigar stub, a clean white shirt, a loosely knotted tie and a brush cut.

"Uh, $7500."

When he mentioned the sum, I reeled back a bit, then shot a fast glance over at Roberto, who hadn't even twitched.

"All right. Do it. We'll get you the signature." And before Wanderly could sputter an answer, I slammed the phone down in its cradle.

"Find the damn signature and get it the hell out of here and to the printer, pronto." Nothing happened. No one budged.

"Now," I yelled and that galvanized them to action as Roberto started thumbing through folders stacked on his desk and Angela began sifting through miscellaneous photos, layouts, proofs etc., piled on one of the tables. "Once you've found the damn thing, you're going to drive it out there."

"Of course," he agreed, as if it was the most reasonable request possible. Two-tone Press was forty minutes out of town where most of the printers had built warehouses, and the real estate had remained cheap and plentiful.

"Assuming, of course, you still know how to drive." His eyes and face took on a wounded look but I didn't care. Angela turned and dropped her jaw even further in astonishment.

"That's a little harsh, isn't it?" she asked.

"Have you got $7500 on you?"

"Well. No."

"Then we'll leave it at harsh. A small price to pay."

I scanned Roberto's disheveled desk. Something caught my eye. I reached into a pile of documents and pulled out the sheaf of paper with the culture czar's signature in different styles and various thicknesses of ink. I held it up practically pushing it into Roberto's face as he now looked dismayed and aghast, his thick face undulating from one expression to the other and back again.

"Take it and go," I said, and laid it carefully back on the table.

"Oh jeez, Louise," Angela exhorted. Jessica had been sitting quietly, throughout the entire ordeal, trying to concentrate on her work, focusing inwardly, only blocking out all external factors, like shouts and screams and arguments that might have broken her fragile nature, her delicate psyche. I found that she needed continual support or she didn't have the confidence in herself I felt she should. She was a very bright and capable young woman but she remained fixated on her computer screen while Ruth couldn't get enough.

"This is better than the soaps," she wheezed. "Keep it going."

"Oh, be quiet, you," I snapped.

Ruth swivelled back away from me in a snit.

"If you're going to be that way," she muttered.

"I am." And repeated it. "I am." It had almost become an anthem and while it played, Roberto hustled about, found an envelope for the signature, looked for his car keys, grabbed his glasses and the case to go with them and scurried out, his eyes flicking out at me nervously. He kept his distance I noticed as he went by, just in case I lashed out at him. For what? Spite? What good would that do? Would it restore the lost money? Or save the project I'd spent a year working on? Maybe. But was that enough? The small feeling of satisfaction I'd had, turned to bile. I needed to vent it.

After Roberto had left, everyone remained in their spots, immobilized.

"It's okay," I said. "I'm not going to eat anyone else today. You can relax and get on with whatever you were doing."

"Whew," Angela said, as much to herself as anyone. "That was something."

I turned away. Well, that had thrown all of my planning out the window. Now what?

I went down to the parking lot to cool off. The wind blew swirls of dust across the tarmac. Marked off by a rusted chain-link fence, the perimeter overlooked a train track. The land on which the parking lot stood was actually owned by the rail company and they leased it back to my landlord, who built the lot to squeeze more cash out of his real estate. The track became a favourite walking trail for local residents, mainly dog walkers. At night, crack heads and dopers who frequented the neighbourhood turned it into a party place. The sun hung high in the sky. I shielded my eyes and squinted across the track toward the adjacent building, a six-story cinder block affair. That's when I heard the clickety-clack of expensive heels scuffing along the surface of the cement. I sensed who it was.

"What's the matter, Goldman? Pee down your front again?"

It had been over 30 years since I'd hit anyone in anger. At age four, my father of all people, gave me a pep talk about the little boy who lived across the park from us. He bullied me constantly. My father told me to stand up to him. He showed me how to assume a boxer's stance, how to weave and jab, how to throw a punch. Eph had learned a few things while growing up in a tough area where he'd been the token intellectual among Italians, Portuguese and other Jews, not willing to show their intelligence on the outside. One day, I saw this kid, Donny, from across the park. My mother was watering her garden. She heard a yelp and saw me galloping across the field, my right fist windmilling like a dervish. I galloped across the dewy grass, letting go with a coyote yell, Donny frozen in my sights, not knowing the ultimate outcome. I came up to him and without missing a beat, my underhanded fist caught him on the jaw as the bottom end of my manufactured windmill came whistling up. The force of the blow and the momentum I achieved literally lifted Donny off his feet, where he fell back hard on his rump. In an instant, he began to cry, then ran home to his mama. His parents complained to mine but nothing came of it and

Donny never bothered me again. Little Donny came to mind as, infused with rage, my fist hardened, knotted with blood and sinew as I turned in one fluid motion and brought my fist up without thought or hesitation. It connected with Eric Schwilden's smirking jaw and I knew I had got all of it. I felt the clanging vibration from my knuckles jolting down my arm into my shoulder like an electric pulse along the heavy muscles of my back. I saw Schwilden open his eyes in panicked surprise as his head snapped upward and like little Donny all those years ago, he left his feet and sprawled backwards into the dirt and mud that had dried in the crevices of the cement. Slowly he raised his head, moaning heavily. I could see a deep bruise purpling his jawline as his eyes glazed over. He tried shaking some consciousness into them, then gave up and flopped on to his back, lifting his knees to the sky. I stood there and watched him for a moment and didn't utter a word. I waited until I could see that he appeared to be all right, that he wasn't unconscious or seriously concussed. He'd have a nice reminder on his face and would have to get his Hugo Boss suit dry-cleaned. For me, it had been a purging of the soul. I didn't expect that I'd be hearing any more taunts from Schwilden again. I turned and walked through the light swirls of air, then gained the stairs that led to my office. Schwilden had been lucky. No one had been around to witness his humiliation. Upstairs in the bathroom, I filled the sink with cold water and soaked my hand in it. It would be sore but I didn't think I'd mind it, not this time.

# 15

"Do you think it's okay for a man to cry?" I asked. We sat in our usual Saturday morning grouping with our papers and our mugs in BoBo's café. Ramon looked startled and Nook blinked quickly a few times behind his rimless specs.

"You mean, when a guy's in acute physical pain?" Ramon asked, hoping that was the right answer. I shook my head slowly. "Oh, I see." And he chewed on his thumb.

"It is possible to cry on the inside," Nook interjected. He sought to tame his unruly emotions raging within through yoga and meditation. He had achieved placid, outer calm but what turmoil did it mask? We may never see it but that didn't mean no rip tide swirled and eddied inside, slapping up on the jetty of his psyche, now did it?

Ramon laid his left hand on my right forearm. For a small man, his hands were large, the fingers thick and powerful.

"Something happen?"

He gave me an inquiring look that surprised me with its tenderness. Ramon's normal expression tended to a scowl. He had a heavy brow that made him look surly, even ferocious.

"Nothing too far out of the ordinary," I replied. Then, I told them about my father and Catherine and her pregnancy, Sharon's attitude, what was happening generally at work and the latest kerfuffle. Once again, I didn't mention anything about Charlotte or another work-related incident. We had won a contract from a large telecommunications company that wanted to associate itself with literary issues. I had convinced them that we could design a fantastic Website for them. And I was right. We could, eventually. The project lagged five and a half months overdue and the worst part of it was, we'd been paid for the damn thing because the client wanted to use the money out of the previous year's budget. I had an angry message from the client demanding to know what they had been paying for. So what would any self-respecting publisher do? I lied, of course. I told the client that our main designer, Roberto, and the only man who had the vision and creative spark for the job, had been off for several months on stress leave. Due to the nature of this malady, it was impossible to predict when he would be back or if it was worthwhile to bring someone else in. Being a small firm, naturally, these decisions were of paramount importance. Bring in a senior designer only for a few weeks before they've even got their feet wet? Or wait it out and hope that Roberto recovered sufficiently and within a reasonable time. I felt remiss, I admitted, in not laying out the situation but in truth had no idea how long the illness would last and had hoped it would be over sooner than later. I begged forgiveness and generally prostrated myself before the client. I then related that Roberto had recently recovered and was now applying himself full time on the project and that completion was expected shortly.

"Wow," said Ramon. "If all that happened to me, I'd want to cry too." Nook nodded his agreement.

"So?" Nook asked. "Did you?"

I gave him a long, reflective look, then sighed.

"Not yet," I replied. "But I'm working up to it."

When I returned home with the bagels and the paper, I found Sharon looking at swatches she'd spread out on the coffee table in the living room. Felicity read a book with her leg propped up. Mrs. Sanchez was nowhere in sight, thankfully.

I dropped the bagels on to the kitchen counter and brought the paper with me into the living room. "What's that?"

"They're swatches, of course."

"I know what they are. What are they for?"

She concentrated on the colours and the fabrics. Some home decorating magazines lay open at her feet. "I'm thinking of re-doing a few rooms, that's all. Nothing for you to be concerned about, is there?"

I settled into the wingback chair opposite her.

"No, of course not."

I tried to take a neutral tone. These discussions rarely bore fruit and if it turned into an argument, it would be one I'd never win.

"If memory serves me, didn't we re-decorate about 18 months ago?"

Sharon bit her lip, then sucked on an orange thumbnail. "We?"

"You."

"Yes. And your point being…?"

"No point. I just wanted to see if my memory was accurate, or not," I added.

"You know my daughter never lets the grass grow under her feet. She's restless. Always was and that hasn't changed a bit, even if she's not a young girl any longer."

"Thanks Ma."

"I'm just speakin' the truth as I know it."

"How's the leg, Felicity? Any better at all?"

I should at least carry on the pretense of being the solicitous son-in-law.

"Better, thanks for asking," she replied. "Though I think you're asking because it's expected not because you really care at all." She nodded to herself like a righteous pigeon and tucked her chin into her neck.

I poked my nose into the paper.

"Of course, I care. After all, I'm the only son-in-law you'll ever have."

"That's what I get for only having one daughter," she said. "And it wasn't for lack of trying. I had two miscarriages before Sharon was born. And I was told that at least one of them was a girl."

She removed a linen hanky from her sleeve, blew her nose prodigiously, then stuffed it away from view.

"Oh Ma, belt up, will ya? How many times?" Sharon said, shaking her head and the tips of her hair brushed her shoulder blades. I thought about Eric Schwilden sprawled in the dirt and smiled.

"What are you smiling about? Have a secret, do you?" Sharon looked at me quizzically. "The cat swallowed the canary, did it? Or is it the nip you're on?"

"I don't know what you're on about," I replied, then smiled again, not being able to help myself. Rather, I fussed with the paper.

"Where are the boys?"

"They're about someplace," Sharon replied, idly still looking at me. "You are looking awfully pleased with yourself. Something must have happened. Come on, out with it."

"I don't know what you're referring to."

"I think you do. I know you too well, Bernard Goldman. These last 15 years have given me a little bit of insight into your soul and your state of mind."

"Well, I don't have anything to share. How about some lunch?"

"Change the subject why don't ya?"

"I'm hungry. Anyone else want something?"

"I'll have a sandwich and a wee cup of tea, thank you," Felicity said. None of her shows were airing, so she was forced to read. Food became a wonderful distraction.

I was about to turn away when something caught my eye. Sharon had her elbows pressed down on a magazine layout and those being my particular specialty, rarely escaped my attention. "What's that?"

"What?" She looked up at me and blinked innocently through her specs.

"That. That. What you are reading. Where you've got your elbows."

She lifted her elbows and looked at them as if seeing them for the very first time. "I honestly don't know what you're on about, Bernie. Really."

I snatched the magazine away from her and saw what lay underneath. A catalogue. Not just any catalogue but one for baby clothes.

"This," I said, triumphantly holding my prize to the ceiling. "What do you think you are doing with this?"

"I was looking at it, you silly sod, what else?" Sharon remained nonplussed, even amused.

I threw the catalogue down on the table where it created a breeze that riffled the pages of the other magazines strewn about as if a ghost had crossed our threshold.

"Let's get this straight, shall we?"

I was on a truth mission. I'd had it with obfuscation.

"I don't want another baby, do you understand? I don't want another baby. I don't want another baby. I don't want another baby…" I may have begun stamping my feet, balling my fists and screwing up my face to cry. I'm really not sure.

"I can see why," Felicity said tartly, turning to look rather pointedly at Sharon. "You've already got one, haven't you?"

I was about to offer a nasty rejoinder when the doorbell rang.

"Who the hell can that be?" I muttered and stalked to the door. I flung it open and saw two uniformed policemen on my step. They looked a bit awkward and intimidated by the size of the doorway alone, not to mention the rest of the place.

"Mr. Goldman?" asked the burly, dark-haired one. The other one was older and chewed placidly on a stick of gum.

"Yes?" I was profoundly puzzled at this point.

"Mr. Bernard Goldman?"

"Yes, twice."

Then the older one who rocked on his heels, looked me up and down and said, "Don't look like a criminal, do he?" His buddy shrugged. "You're gonna have to come to the station with us, sir. There's been a complaint."

"Complaint?"

"Yes sir. Allegation of assault."

"Assault?" By this point, I could only stupidly repeat what they were saying. "Am I under arrest?"

"Not yet," the gum-chewing cop said. "But you need to come with us to answer some questions."

"I see." Although I didn't at all. Then Sharon stormed up and as she did, the two policemen reared back a bit. Sharon was quite a sight when she was in full fury.

"What's going on?" she demanded. "What do they want?"

"They want me to go to the police station."

"Why?" she asked, then turned to them. "My husband hasn't done anything ya fools. He's not a criminal."

"Ma'am," the younger one began but his wiser partner stepped in front.

"There's been a complaint, Mrs. Goldman. Of assault and we need to have your husband come with us to answer some questions."

Knowledge and understanding then came flooding into my being and I lit up with recognition. Sharon turned on me. "Bernie, did you assault someone?"

"Er, not exactly," and tried to make twitchy faces toward the policemen. After all, I didn't want to incriminate myself.

"What do ya mean, boyo? Speak up, will ya?"

"Well, there was an incident."

"An incident?"

"Yes. With Eric Schwilden. In the parking lot," I added.

"And what happened?" The cops followed this exchange with interest. After all, Sharon might save them a lot of time and work.

"Well, he said something."

"What did he say?"

"Something rather crude."

"Crude?" Sharon bit her lip and mulled that over for a second. Her glasses drooped on her short, pointed nose. Then her face brightened. "Was it about me, then?"

Not one to lose an opportunity such as this and stoke the affections of my wife, of course, I lied about it. Two fibs in one day. No telling where this was going or where I'd end up.

"Naturally. Why else would we have had an, an altercation at all?"

Sharon beamed at me, then turned to the policemen. "You can take him now, officers."

"Right," said the older one, while the other looked just puzzled.

I stepped down from the landing on to the ceramic tiled porch. "Uh Sharon?"

"Yes, darling?" She was about to turn and close the door.

"You might want to call Julian. I'm sure he'll know how to deal with this. Uh, which precinct are we going to, officer?"

"The 54$^{th}$," replied the younger one.

"Got that?" Sharon nodded.

"This is very exciting," she said and actually giggled. "Wait until I tell them at the office that my husband was arrested while defending my honour. They'll hardly believe it."

"I hardly believe it myself," I murmured. "Bye darling. Don't forget to call, Julian, will you?" She answered by slamming the door, too far gone in her rapture of the moment.

The policemen stared at me as if I were a strange species.

"I know. I know, officers but this is the life I live."

"You don't mind my saying," the younger one interjected. "But your wife is a real looker."

"She is, she is at that." As I headed down the drive with each of the policemen hemming me in on either side, Sean and Nathan rode up on their bikes. They'd been playing basketball. For a moment, they stopped and gaped and we stood in tableau.

"Dad," Nathan exclaimed. "What's going on?"

"I'm being arrested."

Sean perked up. "Arrested? Wow. Way too cool. Did you kill someone?"

"No."

"Rob a bank?"

"No."

"Run over a drunk on the road with your car?"

"No."

"Steal money from the company."

"No."

The older cop gave me a nudge. "Sir?"

"Uh, look, boys. I'm glad to see that you are concerned about my welfare but I think I've got to go now."

The policemen nodded at Sean and Nathan and grabbing my elbows led me to the squad car. They pushed my head down as I maneuvered into the back seat, I could never figure out why they did that. It wasn't as if I'd hit my head and I wasn't handcuffed. Anyway, I heard the faint chant of "Attica, Attica." Sean. He'd dismounted from his bike and left it lying in the drive while Nathan still had a leg over his. Sean waved his arms, pumping a fist into the air, chanting louder now. Dog walkers and passersby stopped and gaped. Nathan joined in. As the squad car pulled away, I heard faintly the whisper of their voices, Attica, Attica, Attica. I wished fervently this had been a movie.

"You don't mind my saying, but you got a strange family," the younger cop said over his shoulder. The back seats of squad cars were not meant for comfort. No leg room at all, no seat belts and I was separated by bulletproof plexiglass from the officers in front. They spoke through a small window.

"Thanks. Appreciate it."

"Don't mention it. Nice house ya got."

"Yes. It is." And that was it until they parked outside of the station. The young cop came around and opened the door for me. He didn't clamp his mitt down on my head, thankfully and I managed to stumble out on my own.

"Not much leg room there, huh?" He grinned as he said it, enjoying my discomfort.

"No."

They took me in past the front desk and sat me down in what I guessed was an interview room. "Wait here, sir," said the older cop and then, without another glance, they left, closing the door behind them. An exceedingly dingy and bare room, just a rickety table and four plastic chairs. Green chairs. Everything else was off-white or had been white once but over the years, too many cigarettes, cups of coffee and sweaty palms had left their marks of distinction. As I sat there, examining my fingertips, the door burst open. I looked up. A tall, fellow with hair down over his ears and a thick grey moustache, entered. His cheeks looked weather beaten as if he stood on exposed corners a lot and he ran to fat. I saw the beginnings of a gut lifting over his belt.

"Mr. Goldman, I'm Detective Spezza."

"Hi." It hit me then that the detective bore an interesting resemblance to Carl Perkins, the musician. I must have been staring at him because he sighed and said, "Go on, say it."

"You look like Carl Perkins."

He grinned, the moustache inching up his cheeks. "Now we've got that out of the way, let's get to business, shall we?"

"You don't like looking like Carl Perkins?"

"No, I didn't say that."

"Because if that was the case, you could always get a hair cut and shave your moustache."

"I don't mind looking like Carl Perkins."

"But you seemed a bit annoyed by it."

"No, not at all. I just expected it, that's all."

"Okay. Carl Perkins was a fine musician."

"I'm aware of that," Spezza said. "Now then, why don't we get to it."

"To what?"

"The reason you are here, Mr. Goldman. There's been a complaint."

"By who?"

"Whom."

"Okay, by whom?"

"I think you know the answer to that one, Mr. Goldman."

"Please enlighten me, Detective."

Spezza looked down at the notepad he'd removed from his inside jacket pocket. The jacket looked as if it had come from the same era as Carl Perkins in his prime. I guess there wasn't much of a clothing budget on a cop's salary.

"A Mr. Eric Schwilden."

"What's the nature of the complaint exactly."

Spezza rubbed his jaw. It was red from where he'd shaved that morning. "Mr. Schwilden claims you hit him in the jaw. According to him, it was an unprovoked attack."

"Unprovoked?"

"That's what he says, yes?"

"I see. That's interesting."

"What do you say?"

"Am I being charged with anything?" Spezza shrugged. "What if I say nothing happened? It would be my word against his, wouldn't it?"

Spezza looked at me in the way that those with a lot of street experience looked, pitying and disgusted at once. He cleared his throat and smiled. "You could try but Mr. Schwilden has a broken jaw and that needs to be explained..." And then he hesitated and looked down at the surface of the table.

"You were saying?"

He looked up at me and smiled again, this time it was more of a predatory look. "...and you would need to explain the marks on the knuckles of your right hand, the puffiness and bruising, all consistent with having hit something or someone with some force."

"There could be any number of explanations," I replied, less sure of myself now.

"Try me."

"Well, I could have closed the car door on my hand. I've certainly done that before."

"Then we'd see a line of bruising likely. I don't see that here."

"Speculation on your part, detective."

"Perhaps."

"Mr. Schwilden could have slipped and fallen and been too embarrassed to admit it."

Spezza shrugged. For a tall man, he had very narrow shoulders. "The officers heard your wife ask you if it had something to do with her. Did it?"

"Well, uh, between you and me, I was trying to make her feel good, you know, put a few points in the plus column."

"Having some troubles are you, at home, I mean?"

"No, nothing of the sort."

"She cheating on you, Mr. Goldman?"

"Absolutely not and I resent the implication."

"Maybe she's been seeing this guy Schwilden? I've seen it happen dozens of times before and often in these cases, the husband's the last to know."

"Schwilden is a playboy from what I gather but there is nothing between him and my wife. Besides, I hardly know the guy. I bump into him in the hall. His parking spot is beside mine. And that's it. That's the extent of our relationship."

"Do you like him? Schwilden, I mean."

"Not particularly."

"Why?"

"He's just very smug, that's all. Thinks he's got it over everyone else. So, I think he rubs a lot of people the wrong way."

"Including you."

"I just said so, didn't I?"

"Ever been in trouble with the law, Mr. Goldman?"

"No."

"So, you're not admitting to anything?"

"Do you have any witnesses, Detective, who saw anything?"

Spezza pursed his lips, then grimaced. "Not at this point."

"Then I'd like to leave if I may."

"In a few minutes."

"Then I'd like to confer with my lawyer. I think that's my right." And just then, as if on cue, the door was flung open and a man I recognized from his picture in the paper, strode in and banged his briefcase down on the table.

"What are you going to do, Spezza, strip search him next?" he boomed.

"Hello Manny."

Manny Rappoport slipped a neatly manicured hand into his coat pocket where it emerged with a card that he handed to me.

"Manny Rappoport, attorney-at-law and I am representing Mr. Goldman."

"Hello," I said.

Manny Rappoport was one of the most famous and respected criminal lawyers in the country. "Julian sent you?"

Rappoport nodded his jowly head.

"That he did."

Brusquely, he turned back to Detective Spezza.

"I've had a look at the complaint. No evidence of any kind and no witnesses. The complainant's word against my client's. You've got nothing and I'm here to insist you let him go immediately."

"Stop the grandstanding will you, counselor? Fine, we'll bounce him for now but this won't be the end of this I can assure you."

"We'll see," said Rappoport. He picked up his briefcase, beckoned to me, then nodded at Spezza.

"Tootles."

Spezza laughed in spite of himself, then shook his head, made a note in his book, then sighed and rose as Manny Rappoport escorted me out the door.

"What'd you hit him for?" We stood in the street about a block up from the police station. I shrugged, not wanting to admit anything.

"You did hit him, didn't you?"

"Yeah."

"Why?

"He said something insulting and I was having a very bad day, so without thinking I just swung around and he was there. My fist connected with his jaw perfectly. He went flying, my hand went numb and I left him flat on his back in the parking lot of our building. He parks his Porsche beside my car."

"What did he say that got you upset enough to clobber him, if you don't mind me asking?"

Squirm time. "He asked me if I'd peed myself again."

"Peed yourself? What does that mean?"

I swallowed a few times feeling very dry suddenly.

"Well, I had spilled something on to my pants some weeks ago and Schwilden saw me in the bathroom using the hand dryer to dry them out. Right away, he started making a big deal out of it. Saying that I'd peed myself, that sort of thing. So when he came up behind me that day and said something in that snooty tone, I didn't even think, I just reacted."

We had moved to a Starbucks just further along Eglinton Avenue. Rappoport sipped a latté. I had my usual tea.

"You said you were having a bad day. What was that all about?"

I explained the circumstances to him, piling one incident on top of he other as he listened gravely, inclined his head from time to time, all the while making notes. After I finished, he drained his cup and banged it down on the table.

"I always like doing that," he said with a wide grin. "It sounds like a gavel. I feel like everyone should be on their feet just like court."

"What do you think will happen?"

"Well, it sounds like this Schwilden character isn't the type just to drop it. It also sounds like he's a pain in the ass and will keep after Spezza to do something about this. On the other hand, it seems like a private matter between two individuals, both of whom, I assume, have no criminal record but certainly we'll check on that. What does he do, this Schwilden guy?"

"He's a partner in a software development firm. He dresses well, likes the flash and dates seriously attractive women."

"Well you never know," Rappoport said. "A private complaint like this, no witnesses yet, thank god. You could plead to a misdemeanour and get a fine and some community service or you could make a deal and pay him off. That would be up to you. You don't want this thing dragging on. It could get very expensive and lead you nowhere. I'm assuming that Mr. Schwilden will be hiring an attorney and we'll see what they have to say when the time comes. Meanwhile, Bernie, I'd stay away from Schwilden. No contact. If you meet in the toilet or the hall, just nod politely but say nothing. And do nothing to provoke him. Is that understood?"

"I suppose."

I gave Rappoport my contact information and then wrote him a cheque for a thousand dollars. The first installment on his fee. Then the portly lawyer checked his watch, tapped the face and said," Gotta run. I've got my usual tennis game at three. Been doing it for almost 30-years and haven't missed yet." He got up, almost knocking the table over, stuck out his plump hand which I took and found the palm surprisingly firm. Tennis calluses.

"I'll be in touch."

"Thank you."

He waved at me like he swatted at something, then barrelled out of the café.

I decided to take the subway home. I could have asked Sharon to pick me up but I wanted some time to myself and think a little bit. I walked the few blocks east along Eglinton to the subway stop at Yonge. From there I went one stop north to Lawrence then grabbed a bus west to our neighbourhood. It took fifteen, twenty minutes at most. Sharon would have cringed at taking the bus, consorting with the common folk, even though that's where she came from herself. There were tired-looking women lugging shopping bags, saddled with the domestic chores and few resources behind them. Kids headed to the mall or the movies, seniors on outings, neatly dressed men and women going off to their retail jobs and me, potential felon and convicted criminal. It gave me a surreal feeling that I could run afoul of the criminal justice system because of an impulsive act. One that, I thought smugly, had delivered an enormous amount of satisfaction and until the screws were turned, seemed worth it. I lay my ahead against the window and promptly fell asleep. When I awoke, I found myself at the other end of the line. I glanced at my watch. I'd been asleep for half an hour. This time, I took a cab.

# 16

"This is how you turn it on," I said and pushed a button on the keyboard. My father sat in his chair with wide eyes, that is, as wide as he could open them given their saggy countenance. I heard the familiar ding as the motor began to whir and the monitor flashed awake.

"Not much is happening," he grumbled.

"Be patient," I advised, not one of his virtues. "It takes a while to warm up, to boot up that is."

"Okay. If you say so."

I think he hated being subservient in any way and in particular, subservient to me as we sat in front of his gleaming $3000 Macintosh computer. He'd gone for the top of the line reasoning that someone, not him necessarily, would get good use out of it. Catherine's daughter or even Sean and Nathan, although they already had their own computers at home. Who knows, eventually, this new entry into the world, this unborn being would be the recipient of such technological largesse?

Over the next hour, I showed him the basics; how to use the mouse, what icons represented, how to double click programs, how to get on the Internet, how to start up and shut off the computer. Then he could practice until the next time. We sat in Catherine's study, a pleasant room that faced out on to the yard where early sun streamed in. Older furniture occupied the room, chairs fitted to the bodies that had occupied them opposite a small, love seat. I suppose that originally, it had been a family room, albeit a small one but as her children grew and moved out, Catherine had converted it to its present use.

I looked up. She balanced a tray full of tea things that rattled as she made to set them down. I won't say that Eph leapt up but he hurried to his feet to take it from her.

"Here, let me. You shouldn't be doing that."

Catherine smiled Madonna-like.

"It's all right. I can still function a little bit. And carrying a tray is still within my powers you know. You worry like a mother hen. I'm fine."

Eph shrugged at me, something he would never have done in a past life. "Here you go son." He handed me a mug of tea with a slice of lemon, the way I liked it. "Bickie?" he asked.

"What?"

"Bickie. Biscuit?" He held up a plate. I shook my head. "I'll indulge," he said.

Bickie? What the hell was that about? The dad I knew would never have engaged in such soft talk. Not the hardheaded intellectual I grew up with, not the Eph Goldman who duelled verbally with some of the greatest thinkers of the past 50 years. Good grief. He had turned to mush in his old age, yet I smiled indulgently.

"How's the pupil getting on?" Catherine asked. "He's not used to being in that position."

"Just fine," I replied, as sweet as pie.

"He's not being a cantankerous old bear?"

"Not at all," I said, beginning to feel my stomach churn as I sipped the tart tea.

"Were you a cantankerous bear?" she asked turning to my father and taking hold of his chin and giving it a wag like you'd hold the muzzle of a pet dog.

Eph smiled but removed her hand just the same, albeit gently.

"I was on my best behaviour," he said.

I drained the mug and stood up.

"I'd best be going then. I promised I'd be home for lunch."

I'd made no such promise and to tell the truth, no one gave a damn whether I showed up for lunch on a Sunday or not. Everyone headed off doing their own things. Sean and Nathan had gone to the movies. Sharon was out shopping. Felicity watched her shows broadcasting to the entire neighbourhood, so I wasn't expected anywhere really. That's when I decided to phone Charlotte.

# 17

I drove from Swansea to the Yonge and St. Clair area, a high-toned district with upscale shops, swanky offices, expensive yet small houses and pricey condos. Charlotte and her husband lived just south of St. Clair and east of Yonge on one of the nicer and quieter streets. I parked near the old cinemas that were due to be torn down and looked for a phone booth. I didn't have a cell phone, hated them, in fact. I could never punch the buttons properly, they were too small and the ringing scared the crap out of me, particularly when I didn't know where the ringing came from. And I didn't want to keep in touch with people, to be frank. I'd rather have control over who got in touch, and when and how rather than be at the beck of anyone at anytime. It just seemed a ridiculous notion.

The day turned streaky, alternating sun and cloud with a nice breeze. Cool when the sun was cloaked but altogether pleasant, with very little humidity. That's what I liked about Toronto, the diverse weather. One day it could feel like Manilla, the next, Yellowknife.

"Hello?"

"Charlotte?"

"Yes?"

"It's me. Bernie."

"Bernie. What are you doing?"

"Calling you up."

"Whatever for?"

"To see if you were free."

"What? Now?"

"I guess." How definitive was that. "Are you alone?"

"As a matter of fact, I am."

"Where's...?"

"Off playing golf actually. A stupid game that I have no time for."

"Well," I commiserated. "It's not a bad way to spend an afternoon."

"I suppose so." She sounded irritated. "Did you want to come up?"

"I'm not sure."

"Where are you?"

"In the area. Phone booth by the old Hollywood."

"You're two minutes away."

"Right. Listen, why don't we go for a drink or a snack or something?"

"All right." Did I hear disappointment in her voice?

"What's around here?"

"Let's meet at Rosie's, it's a little bistro just off Yonge."

"Good. How do I get there?"

Charlotte gave me directions and it turned out to be a two-block walk. She said it would take her about fifteen minutes to get ready. I walked the two blocks and found that Rosie's had a nice little patio in the back, sheltered and separated from the street by some sort of retaining wall, giving it a lovely feeling of privacy in the heart of the city. I ordered an iced tea. On my way down, I'd picked up the Sunday paper and began working on the crossword while waiting for Charlotte. The young waitress was an aficionado of piercing. I counted seven pieces of metal protruding from various orifices but she seemed pleasant and had a lovely smile, what I could see of it.

Not ten minutes later, Charlotte came bouncing in. She'd poured herself into a little sundress that was both sleeveless and backless. It seemed to be held up by a strap that hooked over her neck like an apron and zipped up the back. If it didn't fit just so, the thing would have ridden straight up or fallen right off. But Charlotte had chosen well and it hung just the way it was supposed to. Her legs were bare, smooth and gleaming. I could see she'd been tanning either at a salon or some self-action ointment. The colour seemed too even to be entirely natural but it gave her a healthy glow and when she smiled her teeth came at me on high-beam. I stood up, almost knocking the table over. I heard a few titters. Since this had been an unplanned encounter, I was wearing khaki shorts, and a worn crew neck T-shirt and comfortable but unstylish walking shoes. I mean, it was Sunday afternoon after all and I hadn't anticipated going out anywhere. I didn't feel I had to dress for my father.

"Hello," she said, breathlessly.

I kissed her on the cheek. "You look sensational."

"Thank you."

She smoothed her dress under her as she sat down and I tried not to look at her heaving bosom. "What a nice surprise, you calling me up. I mean, I just didn't expect it."

"It was a bit impulsive, I have to admit." Our pierced waitress bustled up.

"Can I get you something to drink, Ma'am?" she asked, snapping gum at us.

"I'll have a wine spritzer. Thanks." Charlotte eyed the girl suspiciously for a moment.

The waitress grinned. "Sure thing." Then she moved off to clear an adjacent table.

Charlotte leaned in and it was all I could do to keep my eyes on her face. "You don't think she'll spit in it, do you?" she hissed.

"Why do you think she'd do that?"

Charlotte's brow furrowed for a moment. "I don't know. Sign of contempt for the bourgeoisie perhaps?"

"Is that what you are?"

"We, darling, we."

"We are?"

"That's who hangs out here, didn't you know?"

"I guess not."

I slurped some of my iced tea. That was distraction enough until the waitress plunked the spritzer down on the table.

"Were you going to have anything to eat?" she asked.

"Give us a few minutes," Charlotte replied.

"Sure thing." And she slipped off again.

Charlotte lifted her glass. "Well. What should we drink to?"

"Uh, how about pleasant interludes?"

"Pleasant interludes it is."

We clinked glasses and I smiled at her, guiltily.

"You look like you've been caught with your pants down," she said, running her tongue over her lips so they glistened. She had a distracting habit of pressing her elbows together.

"I do feel that way," I admitted.

"I don't think I've ever met such a moral man, Bernie. How do you survive in this world? I know half a dozen men who'd be paying the cheque right now and trying to get me back to their bedroom or mine."

The sun went out of my life momentarily but I made a good recovery I believe. "I am my father's son and having just spent the morning at his new house, showing him how to use a computer, not that it's relevant to what you're saying, his influence has scarred me forever."

"But I thought your father had an affair?"

"How did you know that?"

"I read your book, silly."

"Oh. You did. Well, that was a long time ago. Anyway, he claims that my mother was frigid and he'd been drinking, which was unusual for him and he'd been enchanted by a young American woman travelling on her own and…"

"…the rest is popular prose. So, what happened to you?"

I stared into my half-drained glass rather miserably.

"I don't even know why you're interested to tell the truth."

"I don't know, either. You're perfectly hopeless. I don't think I'll ever get you into bed."

"Charlotte, I…"

"You feel guilty, I know."

"Yes, but…"

"And you have a lot at stake…"

"No question but…"

"And you take your responsibilities very seriously…"

"No argument there…"

"And you think the world will change…"

I stopped there. "Won't it?"

She placed her hand over mine. The palm radiated warmth and felt smooth and comforting. She caressed my knuckles with her fingertips.

"Some things might change. Your perspective, perhaps."

"That might not be a bad thing," I admitted.

Charlotte's hand on mine grew still and she fixed me with a gaze, her left eyebrow arched. "So?"

I glanced down the curved face of her cheek, down the fine line of her elegant neck where I could see her pulse throb and followed along to the smooth skin that swelled up, then down, slightly up and over the front of her sun dress. The question hung and I felt as if my entire existence, my entire future depended on my reply. My gaze then travelled steadily upward until I met her dark eyes that seemed to deepen into inky pools. I wanted to fall in and be swallowed up. I glanced at our young waitress who sensed something was up as if the metal studs and rings coming out of her were antennae and she'd picked up our signals.

"Cheque please."

Charlotte broke into a broad grin that pushed her features straight up, lit like a Christmas tree.

We walked hand in hand back to her flat that wasn't more than three minutes away on a small side street called Rosehill. Aptly named, I thought, as the city had planted rose bushes along the perimeter of the street, touching on the sidewalks. They were now in full bloom, as it was May, and the effect came on lush and intoxicating. Just like the scent Charlotte wore, just like Charlotte herself and I wondered if I was drowning in my own sea of despair. I pushed that thought and all others aside for the moment. I felt her electric presence, lightning bolts ran up and down my veins, my body tingled from head to toe, I felt flush and heated, throat dry and a bit raw. We drew abreast of her door and she fumbled with the keys finally wrenching them out of her purse.

"Stupid things," she muttered. "Far too big and clunky."

Charlotte pushed on the latch and the door swung open. We stepped inside. She dropped her purse and, in an instant, we were on each other, entangled in the sort of embrace you never forget, chest pressing, hip hugging, hand spreading as if each of us would be consumed by the other. Intoxicating. I felt as drunk as I'll ever be. Somehow, the front of her sun dress came down and I looked at her full breasts barely held in by some sort of strapless cup holder. The tops of her nipples clearly visible. We had pressed against the door and slid over to the wall as she had one leg wrapped around me and pulled my pelvis to her. I realized there wasn't much to that dress and wondered how women had the nerve to go out in public so scantily clad. That took a lot of confidence, I thought. I sank my face into her cleavage and felt them expand like balloons gasping for air. And then suddenly, the little dress slid down her curvaceous hips, over a pair of smooth thighs and lay in a neat little pile on the floor. Charlotte now wore the teeniest pair of thong briefs and this brassiere cup thing. I marvelled at how it stayed up.

She stepped back and posed. "You like?"

I nodded. "Fantastic." I reached out and touched her. "How does that thing stay on? It's a marvel of engineering."

"Now there's a line," and she gave a guttural laugh and I could see she was flushed from her bosom up into her face.

"That would get me every time."

She unhooked it from the back and it too joined the little dress on the floor.

"Your turn," she said and grabbed my belt buckle and pulled. Her fingers were deft and strong. In a trice, she had me unbuttoned and unzipped and slid her hand into my briefs, feeling her way.

"Mmmm, nice," she said. I lapsed into some kind of trance until she came closer and we embraced again. This time, she pressed harder, rubbing herself up and down against me.

"We need to lie down," she commented, matter-of-factly.

"Yes," I breathed. "We do."

We managed to keep each other excited for just the right length of time until neither of us could stand it anymore. When she came the first time, Charlotte gasped and held her breath until I thought she would explode. When she came the second time, she whimpered and whinnied rather noisily. The third time we came together and she uttered a moan deep and low down in her throat that then built and rose in pitch and tone until she crescendoed like a soprano who'd lost all control and verged on shrieking. I, on the other hand, didn't make a peep.

"Oh my God," she said, between pants of air, her breasts heaving, nipples erect and darkened.

"That was amazing." Then she looked at me. "You were awfully quiet, though."

"How could you tell?" I asked, then laughed.

She gave me a baby slap on the cheek. "I was enjoying myself. I really let go with you. That almost never happens."

"Really?"

"Yes, really."

We were still connected and it was a pleasant feeling. I made no move to disengage. She still held me in her. "I don't want you to go. Not just yet." Her thighs tightened around me.

And then I woke up. I didn't know where I was at first but sat up groggily and looked about. Charlotte was nowhere to be found.

"Have a good nap?" Sharon asked and looked at me with concern. "You were knackered."

"How long have I been sleeping?"

"About two hours. I thought you needed it after all you've been through so I left you alone."

"Where are the boys?" I felt slack-limbed and listless.

"Out playing tennis, I think. May I join you?" I could see I was lying on our bed. Sharon stretched out beside me and snuggled close. Having woken from such an erotically vivid dream about Charlotte, one part of my anatomy had remained alert. Like a heat seeking missile, Sharon went right to the spot.

She pressed against me. "What's this then?"

"What?"

She gave me a bump with her pelvis. "This."

"What this."

It was like getting forechecked. She'd really put some spring into it.

"This, ya bloody git."

"Oh that," I said. "Nothing."

"Nothing my arse."

"If you say so."

Sharon could see I was playing with her and her mood and tone softened. I'd kept my eyes closed while all this unfolded but I opened them now. She placed her face close to mine and I felt the warmth of her breath.

"Am I ugly to you now, is that it? Too old for a roll in the sack?"

"Of course not. You haven't changed since we met. Only become more beautiful, more attractive. I am the envy of my peers and that bastard Schwilden too. I think they all want to get into your knickers."

She smiled at me radiantly. "Well, so far luv, you're the only one I'll let in. So how about it, big boy? Show me what you've got."

With a display of resigned reluctance, I unzipped my trousers.

"Come on," she said. "Let's get under the covers." She drew off her top and unhooked her skirt so that she sported only her bra and panties. She slid under the blankets, then blinked at me. When I didn't jump right away, she beckoned with her head. "Jump in, it's lovely."

And that's what I did. We made merry until Felicity called up looking for her tea, then the boys banged their way in, having returned from the tennis courts several blocks from our house.

"You can't fall asleep again," Sharon murmured.

"Just watch me."

"You won't sleep tonight."

"Who said I was going to get up at all."

"Ach, don't be daft, Bernie." She sat up and flung the covers off. We were both naked and the air she stirred up blew cool on my exposed skin.

"Party pooper."

"That's right, mister. And don't you forget it."

After all these years, I still loved watching her dress and undress. It remained a privilege for a man to see such efficiency, which, when observed in the boudoir, came erotically charged. I especially liked the way she put on pantyhose, like pulling on elastic pants, difficult to do with a sense of style, but somehow, Sharon managed it. She started with her left leg first, propping it up on the chair and rolling the material deftly up to mid-thigh, slid into the other leg and did the same easily and smoothly. They always seemed to fit just so. She slipped on her panties, had her bra fastened in a flash, then jumped into a pair of charcoal sweat pants and a tank top and shoved her feet into a pair of rubber flip-flops. Somehow, she managed to look slightly tousled but sophisticated and elegant all at once. Her sculpted cheeks had the flushed afterglow, the residual effect of erotic exertion and a smile played on her full lips. Her red hair, down to her shoulders, nicely tousled. She did a quick check in the mirror.

"Ach, bed head. I'd better fix that right quick." And she darted into the bathroom, leaving me lying on my own. I began to drift off again when a pillow smacked me rudely in the face.

"You'll not fall asleep now. It's dinner time. Do you want to go out or order something in?

"Let's stay in. Can I eat here?"

"Don't be daft and get crumbs all mixed up in our bed? Not bloody likely. Come on then." And she gave my arm a tug. I resisted so she tugged harder. I went totally limp and she put one foot on the mattress and heaved until I slid onto the floor and she'd fallen on her bum, laughing, lips pulled back from her large teeth in a wide smile.

"You bugger you."

Why, oh why was I dreaming of Charlotte?

# 18

When I arrived at work the next morning, the tall version of Carl Perkins, was sitting in his unmarked cruiser, drinking coffee and smoking a cigarette. After I had parked my car, I noticed Schwilden hadn't arrived yet, and walked the length of the lot toward him. Detective Spezza stepped out. I saw he was actually sporting black, hand-tooled cowboy boots. He was wearing a jacket, jeans and a turtleneck. In this weather.

"Detective. Where's your guitar?"

"Mr. Goldman."

He ground the cigarette stub out with his heel and tossed the Styrofoam cup on to the pavement.

"Isn't that littering?" I asked.

He looked at me laconically, his face slack, his eyes drooping.

"So, arrest me."

"Did you want something?" He shrugged and didn't say anything. "You just like hanging out in parking lots? You're thinking of moving into the area? Maybe it's a career change. I don't think I'd recommend magazine publishing. The pay stinks."

"Show me where it happened," he said.

"What happened?"

"The, uh, altercation."

"What altercation?"

"You know."

"I'm not sure I do."

"Schwilden's got a broken jaw. It's going to be wired shut for awhile and he's gotta eat through a tube."

Picturing that in my mind, I said, "That is unfortunate."

"You're saying nothing happened?"

"I'm saying that, before I say anything to you, I must have my lawyer present." Spezza's jaw clenched and his face darkened less than subtlely. "Surely, you have better things to do, Detective. This was a private dispute, nothing more, nothing less."

"Schwilden made it public."

Now it was my turn to shrug. Spezza rubbed his square jaw, feeling for spots he'd missed while shaving that morning or last night.

"Listen, I'll level with you. I don't like this anymore than you do. And yes, I have better things to do with my time. But Schwilden's got an uncle who's a judge and the way things work is that I have to conduct a thorough investigation here. The guy's old man and his brother are howling for blood."

"So, it's gotten political now."

"Something like that."

"I'm sorry to hear that."

Spezza nodded, then spat at my feet. "Yeah. Me too. But they're looking for results. You're all I've got, Mr. Goldman." Then he turned and got into the cruiser, slamming the door. I watched him through the windshield as he turned the ignition, gunned the engine, then peeled out of the parking lot, missing my toes by less than a foot. That's what they call intimidation, I suppose. Sighing, I walked into the building. It was a great start to the week.

When I walked into the office, I found Jessica, my assistant, had arrived before me. She normally showed up well after nine. It took her time to pull herself together in the morning. At work, her demeanour was both professional and diligent and that's all I really cared about. Except this time she sat at her desk, crying. She turned away as I came in, shielding her face. I looked at her, went over to my desk, put down my bag and my computer. Clearly, this was something I couldn't ignore even if I wanted to.

"Do you want to talk about it?" I asked. She looked at me, her long, narrow face streaked with tears. "When you're ready. Do you want a drink of water or a cup of coffee?" She shook her head, then grabbed a handful of tissues from a box on her desk and blew lustily. I could see the physical effort she was making to become composed. Jessica was a pretty girl when her face stayed neutral but when her expression changed, even when she smiled, the façade cracked.

Her most becoming look remained neutrality but, I surmised not so wisely, that didn't mean emotions didn't roil within, sometimes turbulently.

"I'm just not feeling well," she gasped. "I need to take some time off and I hope you understand. Here," she said and thrust a piece of paper at me. I looked at it. A doctor's note stating that Jessica was ill and required at least several weeks off for recuperation but gave no clue as to the root of the problem.

"That's fine, Jessica, really. Take all the time you need. I think the important thing is for you to feel better, however long that takes."

"I'll understand if you want to replace me."

She blew her nose again.

"Oh no, no. Why don't we see how things go. I mean, is there anything I can do for you? Anything you need?" She shook her head. "All right then. Well. Why don't you go home and try to take it easy and call me next week and let me know how you're getting on. Why don't we do that?"

"Okay."

I took her arm and helped her up.

"Will you be all right to drive? Do you want a cab?"

"No, I think I'll be fine," she said, and indeed seemed calmer than a moment ago.

At the door, I said, "Is there anything you want to tell me? Is there something else I can do to help you?"

"I don't think so."

"All right then. You take it easy."

Then came that façade-cracking smile and, holding herself stiffly, I watched her march down the hall, the heels of her clunky shoes causing an echo. Empty. Exactly how I felt.

When Roberto strolled in, I briefed him on the Jessica situation and he nodded, then spoke out. "She's on anti-depressants."

"What?"

"She's depressed."

"How do you know that?"

"She told me."

"When?"

He shrugged his broad shoulders, shoulders that were accustomed to digging out basements, re-fitting bathtubs, laying down cement. "A couple of months ago."

"Why didn't you say anything?"

"What for?"

"Because I might have needed to know."

"Did you?"

"Not until now. Did she say why?"

He shrugged. "Something about this boyfriend and how he did a number on her, then he broke up with her, but now he won't leave her alone and, even though they're not back together, they see each other every day and she doesn't know what to think about the relationship and where it's going…that sort of thing."

"Oh thanks," I said and gave him a sour look.

"What?"

"Nothing, nothing," I muttered angrily to myself and walked back to my desk. Yeah, Monday mornings were a blast.

I stood in the lunch line on the main floor of our building A local caterer ran a small café. Fingers plucked at my shirtsleeve and I turned around to face a young woman I had seen around, a very attractive young woman at that. She stood medium height with shoulder length blonde hair and luminous green eyes. She wore a peach coloured business suit that offset her pale complexion nicely. I noticed her shoes matched the suit. She blinked at me through chic spectacles that seemed to make her eyes even larger. Her full lips were parted slightly. She worked for Schwilden's company, marketing or something. We nodded to each other in the hall.

"Mr. Goldman?" She seemed nervous and looked around her.

"Bernie. Please." The line edged forward. And I put out my hand. She took it and I was surprised. Her palms felt a bit sweaty. As if reading my thoughts, she pulled her hand away quickly.

"Uh, Caroline Brooker. Listen, can we talk?" she asked. "Over there?" She indicated a table in the far corner of the room.

"Sure." And I stepped out of line. "Go ahead," I said to the person behind her. The guy, one of the workmen in the area, nodded gratefully.

"Suits me, Bud." And then he eyed the young woman with undisguised pleasure.

I took Caroline by the elbow and led her to the table. Ever the gentleman, I pulled out her chair. "Thank you."

"You're welcome." I sat opposite her a bit warily, I admit. "How can I help?"

She folded her hands in front of her, then folded them again. "I'm sorry. I'm a bit nervous." She glanced around the room again then leaned forward and whispered. "I shouldn't be seen talking to you."

"Oh? Why is that?"

"You know, because of the incident."

"What incident?"

"The one where you punched Eric in the jaw. That one?" She arched her brow and smiled, showing a set of even white teeth. Her parents had spared no expense on braces, I saw.

"Yeah, well. I've heard that rumour too."

"It's more than a rumour. Eric came into the office with his jaw all wired up."

"An unfortunate accident, I'm sure."

"Did you know the police were in our office, questioning all the employees?"

"No," I admitted. "I didn't."

"They were looking for witnesses."

"Did they find any?"

Her expression changed to a frown. "Not yet."

"Not yet?" I repeated, feeling rather stupid.

She had sat back in her seat but leaned forward again. "Here's the thing." And now she was really whispering. "I saw you."

"Saw me…?"

"Saw you hit him."

"Okay."

"I had left something in my car and went down to get it. I had just rounded the corner of the building when I saw you swing around and hit him. It was awesome. I mean, he really went flying, didn't he?"

"If you say so."

She bit her lip. "For some reason, I stepped back around the corner and peeked. When I saw you coming my way, I scooted."

"Why are you telling me this?"

She began to knead her hands together in a worrying fashion.

"Listen, Eric is my employer but in my book, the guy's a creep. He's hit on every woman in the office, more than once."

"So why work there?"

"Because it's a good job in an exciting industry and the company's doing really well. I mean, he is a bright man."

"I see."

"But I am looking around. Anyway, I wanted to ask you. There's a rumour going around that he said something about your wife. Is that true?"

"There was an incident at one of the parties he threw. That was before I got to know him a little better. I brought my wife with me."

"I know," she said. "I was there."

"So you can understand my feelings."

"Yes, yes I can." She sat back in the chair, her padded shoulders slumping a little bit. "You know, I don't think I've ever gone out with a guy who'd do that for me. In fact, I don't even think I know anybody who'd consider it." She looked up at me then. "I admire that, I really do. Don't worry, Mr. Goldman, your secret is safe with me." And she stuck out her hand. "I just wanted to…"

I took it again, still a bit sweaty. "To check me out?"

She nodded. "Kind of, but I'm glad I did." She glanced around the room again, then withdrew her hand. "I'd better go. I wouldn't want anyone to get the wrong impression, you know."

"I know."

She stood up and smoothed her skirt over her hips, then smiled at me like she was looking at a baby photo. "Bye."

"Bye." I let her walk away, then sat for a moment before joining the lunch line again. By the time I got to the front, the chicken pot pie was gone. I had really been looking forward to it. I settled for a soup and a sandwich instead. When I took my tray back up to the office, I saw Roberto gobbling up chicken pot pie and smacking his lips.

# 19

“Twenty-one,” called Hugo with delight, crinkling up his leathery, weather-beaten face. I had scored eleven, a personal high for me. I retrieved the ball and passed it to Hugo, who bounced it awkwardly. I don’t think he could do anything else with it but shoot. He certainly couldn’t run, let alone dribble. But then what did I want with a guy who was turning eighty-seven? I stood looking at him uncertainly. He grinned, no I’d say, beamed back.

“I’m going to the pool. Do you want to come too?”

I sagged a bit more. “Can’t. I’m still banned.”

He waved a gnarled fist in the air, then turned around and threw the ball toward the cage where they were all kept and hit it neatly with a thud. The ball wedged inside the cage and didn’t bounce out. He turned back to me.

“It will be okay, trust me.”

I stared at him for a moment thinking that he’d come up with another way to humiliate me but then, how much worse could it get? I was already the laughingstock of the gym. I saw the smiles and the looks, heard the whispers, felt the finger-pointing. So what did it matter if I got snookered? It would just consolidate my considerable reputation. Actually, I felt like going into the sauna, locking the door behind me and going to sleep. Maintaining a consecutive losing streak in Twenty-one was exhausting.

“Okay,” I said and went with him into the locker room to get changed.

We marched down the draughty corridor to the pool together. Hugo tottered a bit as he walked. He sported an impressive zig-zag scar through his left knee. It looked like a badly drawn lightning bolt. When I asked him about it once, muttered something about a, “Bayonet”, and left it at that. Morbidly, I hungered for the details but hadn’t the nerve to ask him, not yet.

The same lifeguard who had banned me was on duty. She scowled when I poked my head around the corner of the showers before stepping on the pool deck.

"I will take care of it," said Hugo, nonchalantly as he breezed by and strode up to her. She eyed me uneasily. He leaned down towards her. I couldn't hear what he said but within moments, they began laughing. Hugo beckoned.

"No funny stuff," she spat as I walked past her. I turned to give her a piece of my mind but Hugo yanked my arm.

"You wanted in and now you're in," he hissed and pushed me toward the edge. The tiled deck was slippery and with Hugo's bit of force, I lost my balance and cartwheeled into the water. The lady already paddling about in the lane stood up indignantly in the shallow end and began to bleat. I went to apologize, to remonstrate, to no avail, she squawked to the lifeguard, who rolled her eyes in her head. I could read her thoughts. You've only been here 30 seconds and already you're causing trouble. I decided to go about my business. I submerged under water, pushed off from the wall and swam as far as I could, holding my breath, surfaced, and began moving fluidly with powerful strokes. It felt good. It had been a long time, longer than I remember having been away from the water, and to me, on this morning, it felt redemptive and rejuvenating. I don't know what happened above the surface but below I heard nothing and kept to myself moving regularly and smoothly, harder and harder, until I'd exhausted and expunged all the evil from my system. Hugo was no dummy. A basketball shark maybe but no fool when it came to human nature. He bobbed under the water and floated up again, moving his arms and legs like a frog, a royal amphibian as he commanded the water to push him forward. And it did. It didn't dare not to.

That evening, we had a rare, civilized meal together. Sharon came home on time, the boys had been out playing basketball but put their plans on hold over the supper hour. Felicity decided to stay in her room and Mrs. Sanchez had left for the day. I arrived home just after five, to find Sean and Nathan sprawled in the living room watching a re-run of Star Trek, the original series. It had never been off the air but for some reason the two of them had just discovered it and thought it was a pretty cool show, although the special effects, according to Sean, were "really cheesy". They found it hard to believe that I watched it when I was in junior high school. "You had television then?" Nathan asked. "Don't fool with me, Bernie. You're fooling with me." Lately, he had begun using my first name while Sean referred to me simply as, the father. The father wants him to do this. The father wants him to go here and so on. I'd been objectified in his own mind and trivialized too, I imagined. That way, he wouldn't have to relate to me on such a personal basis, especially when I got in his face about something. I'd be just another authority figure to him.

I'd had the foresight that morning to remove some skinless chicken breasts from the freezer and defrost them. I fired up the barbeque, opened a dry Chilean Riesling I liked, rolled some potatoes in foil, shucked the sweet corn and had the salad tossed by the time Sharon walked through the door at six, looking a bit haggard and puffy around the eyes, but otherwise in command of her presence.

"Ach, I'm buggered," she said as she dropped her briefcase, her computer, her phone and her keys by the front door. I brought out a glass of wine that I thrust into her hands, gave her a kiss on the lips and a pat on her well-muscled bum. She looked at me with open eyes.

"You're a life saver, you are. Cheers." And sipped the wine. "Hmm. Very nice. What's going on?"

"I'm just about to throw some chicken on the barbie. Everything else is done."

"Where're the boys?"

"Watching Star Trek."

Sharon smiled and gave me the Vulcan salute. "Let me get changed and I'll be down in a minute. How's mum?"

"Haven't heard a peep out of her," I admitted, and headed back into the kitchen while Sharon mounted the stairs to our bedroom.

I topped up my glass, then stepped out onto the deck where the barbecue chuffed away.

Using the tongs, I'd received last Father's day, I dropped the chicken on to the grill and watched it sizzle and hiss. I'd made up some of my special basting sauce, the like of which could never be reproduced. That's because I had no idea what went into it until I looked in the cupboard and the fridge and saw what ingredients we had in place. For a moment, I felt at peace. I closed the lid and let the smoke rise up. I watched a pair of wrens charge around the yard. Sitting on the back fence was a blue jay. I heard cardinals and orioles in the trees. The tall bushes rustled full of sparrows and a trio of blackbirds perched on the phone lines, waiting for the right moment to swoop down and steal something from the smaller birds. My own living, cackling aviary. They watched me curiously, hoping I had something for them. The sky burned bright. I looked up at the clouds in the distance, wisps of smoke more like it. Far in the distance, two jets criss-crossed leaving a long and intricate vapour trail etched against the glowing horizon. As I flipped the breasts over, it occurred to me that this might be as close to paradise on earth as I would get. For a time, I felt proud, proud to be a husband and a father both.

Later that evening, as I prepped for bed, I took a look at the wall chart Sharon had done up on her computer and hung on the bathroom door. It tracked our sexual progress, how many times, and the dates marked. Her moments of ovulation were marked in red with exclamation marks. So far this week, we'd had sex seven times. I suppose most men would be envious of that. A beautiful wife etc. etc. Frankly, I was exhausted. Mentally and emotionally bled dry. It surprised me that I could even manage an erection but the thing had a mind of its own and sprang to attention on command. Sharon was a general after all, leading her troops daily into battle. She knew how to motivate, cajole, intimidate and order them around to get what she wanted. So why should it be any different at home? Similar technique but vastly different execution. I hoped. After I emerged from the loo, having flossed, brushed, washed, powdered, peed and lathered on face cream, I saw her, stretched out on the bed entirely naked. Her lithe, tanned and moderately freckled body had a buttery glow. She'd placed a pillow under her hips and angled herself toward the bathroom door.

"JESUS!" I exclaimed.

She laughed low in her throat. "Is that a good Jesus or not?"

"What are you wearing?"

"Not much if you'd notice."

"I meant on your skin."

"Just a bit of cocoa butter, that's all."

"Oh."

"Want to touch?"

As if pulled in by a tractor beam, I felt myself dragged toward the bed. As I drew closer, I could smell the cocoa that seemed to rise off her skin, infusing the air with an intoxicating scent. She watched me through heavy-lidded eyes. "Where's the pineapple punch and the luau?"

"You're not funny," she said, smiling nonetheless.

"I know."

"Come closer." I went a bit closer. "Closer still. I can't reach you from here."

"You really want this child a lot, don't you?" She nodded. "You're working hard for it. Trying to make it happen." She nodded again, then reached out her hand. I took it and now she was the tractor beam pulling me toward her heaving breasts and glistening belly.

"This doesn't have to be a chore, you know," she whispered. "I'd like to make this as enjoyable as possible." I lay down beside her and she turned off the bed lamp. Amen to that.

# 20

That Saturday, Ramon announced to Nook and myself that his wife was pregnant. After the initial shocked silence, where the lull in the conversation hung between us, he said it again in case we hadn't heard him the first time.

"We're going to have a baby."

I shook his hand vigorously. Some of his mochaccino slopped on to the table. "Congratulations, buddy. This is great news."

Nook put his hand up and he and Ramon slapped palms. Not very convincing. They were the least likely pair to do something like that. They both looked away in embarrassment.

"How far along?" I asked.

"Just three months now." He furrowed his thick brow and brought the mug to his lips and took a slow sip. A thin line of whipped cream stuck to his lower lip.

"What's the matter?" Nook asked. He could be quite intuitive in his own cerebral way.

Ramon breathed out heavily through his nostrils, causing them to flare like a horse after a quick canter. He leaned back in his chair and held himself rigidly, palms flat on the table and his elbows locked.

"I don't know if I'll be seeing you guys for awhile."

"What do you mean?" I could see he didn't want to answer me. He worked his tongue around his mouth, then proceeded to chew on his lip before answering.

"Luisa wants me to stay with her, you know. She's had morning sickness and hasn't been feeling too good. She says she's feeling needy, like she wants me to take care of her."

"Oh." I glanced at Nook and I saw the surprise on his face.

"But this is just an hour on Saturday morning," he said, trying to make light of it. "What's the harm in that, Ramon?" Ramon didn't answer, merely shook his head.

"I can understand it," I said. "This is your first baby and she wants you with her and to experience as much of it as possible. I mean, I did that with Sharon."

"It was easier for you," Ramon said. "You were working from home."

"That's true."

"She made it clear to me that she was very serious about this. I've got to be there for her."

"But you are, aren't you?" Nook asked him.

"I think so but the way she puts it, now I'm not so sure. It's like I'm selfish for coming here. Like I want to get away from her."

"But you do," I said. "We all do. Right? Isn't that the point?"

Nook nodded. "Yes. Yes, it is."

"What about her? Doesn't she go out with her girlfriends?"

"That's different."

"How is it different?" I asked him.

"I don't know. It just is. Besides, it doesn't happen that often. It's not like a regular thing with her. Maybe every couple of weeks."

"Isn't that a double standard," Nook prompted gently. He didn't want to raise any hackles. He knew Ramon could be volatile.

"She doesn't see it that way," he replied. "Look. She's in this fragile state right now. All her hormones are changing and firing and misfiring, who knows? She's not being very rational. It's just raw emotion and how am I supposed to deal with that?" He picked up the mug and drained it, then set it back on the table. "I've got to go." He pushed his chair back and stood up. He grabbed his paper and stuck it under his left armpit. "Listen, I'll see you guys around, okay?"

"Sure," I said.

"I'll call you," Nook said.

Ramon nodded but didn't say anything. He looked tight-lipped and tense. It was one of the moments when you thought about the choices you'd made and whether they were the right ones. Even though there might be no way back. Even though you loved your wife and were sure to love the child about to come into your world. But it didn't mean that doubts wouldn't linger. A pregnancy tested a relationship, I thought. Maybe that's what I feared more than coping with a newborn. Could that be it? Ramon dragged himself out of the café, his thick, muscular body, sagging. Nook and I exchanged looks but didn't say anything.

Two days later, I received a call from my lawyer.

"Schwilden is suing you for a million dollars," he said. "I think you'd better come down to the office." How could I say no?

Manny Rappoport's office couldn't be found in one of the glittering towers downtown. He owned a small building on an exclusive side street, ironically called Toronto Street. I parked the Saab in a parking lot that advertised cheap rates for just three and a half bucks a quarter hour with a twenty-five dollar maximum. After that, I could stay all day if I wanted. What a deal. As I rode the elevator to the fourth floor, I savoured my gratitude. The elevator had mirrored walls and I made a quick study of my face. Haggard. Dark circles under the eyes. Not a pretty picture. I began to look more and more like Eph. And that wasn't a pretty picture, either. How might I end up looking like my father as I grew older but, in Sharon, I saw no resemblance to her mother at all? Don't think I wasn't grateful. The elevator doors opened to reveal a sumptuous lobby with thick carpeting and sweeping oak panelling. A smartly dressed receptionist in an expensive suit sat at the Cadillac of desks wearing a headset. She smiled brightly at me as I took the two steps from the elevator before I collided with the mothership she commanded.

"I'm here to see Manny Rappoport. Bernard Goldman."

The receptionist smiled and then murmured into her headset. I didn't even hear what she said. "Just have a seat, Mr. Goldman. Mr. Rappoport will be right with you. Is there anything I can get for you in the meantime? Coffee? Tea? Water?"

A pair of sunglasses, I thought. "No, thank you. I'm fine."

The couches were covered in burnished leather and looked as if a bum had never touched the surface. All of the de rigeur magazines were spread artfully on a side table along with The Globe & Mail, The Wall Street Journal, Barron's, The Law Review and The Times of London. I considered sitting down when a middle-aged woman, whose bearing and look screamed "no nonsense", came around the corner.

"Mr. Goldman?"

"Yes?"

She put out her hand which I took and shook it once, then returned it to her. "I'm Carol Waldman, Mr. Rappoport's assistant. Please come with me."

"Uh, thanks."

We marched down a long corridor and I swore my ankles disappeared. It was rough going for a bit. At the end of the hall, stood a doorway. On either side of the corridor, we passed the offices of other lawyers, juniors I assumed, all engaged in some activity. Each office was buttressed by cubicles where the administrative staff hid themselves away. Carol Waldman opened the door and we entered an antechamber with a desk. This, I took it, was her office; that placed her in the stratosphere above the other admin types. Opposite the first door was a second. She led me to it, rapped once sharply, then went through. This room appeared to be roughly the size of a doubled racquetball court. High ceiling speckled with oval portholes, a new twist on skylights. Two walls consisted of floor to ceiling windows. At the far end, that you could scope with a pair of binoculars, a huge semi-circular desk hovered, the aircraft carrier of the species. Manny wore shirtsleeves. He too, sported a headset which, upon our entrance, he ripped off and dropped, leaving a clump of hair standing out on the side of his head. As we marched toward him, he stood up. It was then that I noticed a dark-haired woman seated opposite him. She too, stood as we approached. As we drew closer, I could see she was rather exotic looking, below medium height but powerfully built, with muscular thighs and calves. She had a broadly angled face and thick dark hair swept off her face and down to her shoulders. Her skirt was quite short and the heels of her shoes quite high.

"Bernie. Good to see you," bawled Manny. "I'd like you to meet Gloria Martinez, one of my colleagues."

"Mr. Goldman." Gloria took my hand and almost crushed it in her grip. I blanched but managed a weak smile.

"Ms. Martinez. A pleasure."

"Sit, sit," said Manny and he gestured broadly.

"Does anyone need anything?" Carol asked.

"Bernie? Want something? A drink. A nosh? Anything?"

"No thanks."

"Gloria?"

"I'm fine." And she loosed a dazzling smile. Ouch.

"I'll have a coffee, please Carol. Thank you."

Carol withdrew.

Manny remained on his feet. Despite its size, the office almost seemed a bit too small for him. He was a large man who bristled with nervous energy. A bear on uppers.

"I've brought Gloria in, Bernie, because she is going to take over your case. The good news is this: the police couldn't make a case for a criminal charge to stick, so that's been dropped. The bad news is this civil thing. I handle the criminal end while Gloria's specialty is civil cases. So you're in good hands with her. She's the best or I wouldn't have hired her."

Gloria looked as if she had heard this hundreds of times before.

"We thought we should go over the facts to plan the best strategy," Gloria said. She had a well-modulated voice that inflected upward slightly. There was the slightest hint of an accent.

"Okay."

Manny looked up as Carol wheeled in a cart full of coffee things that included a silver urn, china cups, an array of English biscuits. She filled a cup, added cream, no sugar and handed the cup, then the biscuits over to Manny. She then moved the cart to the side and left the room without having said a word.

Gloria stood up. She stood just over five feet tall but the heels accentuated her muscular figure. "Why don't we move to my office?" She indicated a door behind Manny's desk. Manny started pawing through a stack of files and slurping coffee.

"If you need anything, just holler," he said and as we left, we vanished from his consciousness too. The back door led into an antechamber that, in turn, led into another office, one not as large or as sumptuous as Manny's but in the scheme of things, grandiose. Gloria led me to a leather couch.

"Have a seat, Bernie." She went behind her desk, a rectangular one fashioned out of a burnished mahogany veneer. She rooted around in a drawer for a moment, pulled out a file folder wadded with papers, a notepad and a pen. Then she sat opposite me in an armchair that she pulled closer to the coffee table. "Now then," she intoned. "Have you ever been involved in a civil suit before?" I shook my head. "Well, that's a good thing. Who wants to be when it comes right down to it? No one right? Let me describe the process to you in a general way. The system here is set up to compel parties to settle. Only when there is a complete breakdown in communication, does a civil case go to court. Close to 95% are settled before then. So really what we're talking about is a process of negotiation."

"What are we negotiating about?"

"Money, it's always money. The only time you go to court is if you are convinced beyond a shadow of a doubt that you can win. Because if you don't, it is very, very expensive."

"How expensive?"

"Between now and the time you went to trial, it might cost you $25,000 to $30,000 conservatively. That's not including the cost of the trial itself which could add another $10,000 to $15,000. If the plaintiff, that's Schwilden, should get any sort of a judgement at all, he would also get a portion of his court costs and legal fees covered and that could add another $30,000 on top of that, not to mention any interest assigned depending on the judge's view at the time. So you're looking at $80,000 to $90,000 potentially."

"Wow."

Gloria nodded her raven-maned head. "Wow is right. That's why the best way to go is to negotiate a deal. Cut your losses, get the guy out of your life as quickly as possible. That's always my first recommendation but ultimately of course, it's up to you. You may decide to take your chances in court."

"I might at that."

Gloria crossed her legs and I heard the friction of her panty hose as one thigh eased over the other. "Let's look at the facts. You guys were in the parking lot. Schwilden said something to you. You hit him. Pretty straight forward so far."

"I guess."

"The good thing is there were no witnesses."

I thought of my encounter in the cafeteria the other day. "Right."

"But the guy went to the hospital with a broken jaw. So, how do we explain that?" I shrugged. "And according to the police report, a Detective Spezza, noticed you had swollen knuckles on your right hand. What's your explanation for that?"

"Caught in a car door?"

Gloria smiled. "Pretty lame, Bernie. They could probably dredge up some expert who would testify the bruising would be different or you'd have a different type of injury and so on. Spezza will be called and he might qualify as an expert or at least, an informed witness who has seen a lot of bruised and swollen knuckles from fights over the 22 years he's spent on the force. We can discredit him. After all, he's not a doctor, but a jury would likely find him credible. There's still a healthy respect for the police in this country."

"So, you're saying what, exactly?" I cleared my throat a few times. It felt tight and raw.

"Well, let's look at it this way. You haven't denied you were with Schwilden in the parking lot. One of the constables overheard you say something about an altercation. Okay, that's hearsay but the standard for the burden of proof in a civil case is much looser than in a criminal trial. This cop also heard your wife exclaim how wonderful it was that you were defending her honour and you didn't disagree, did you?"

I looked down at the offensive hand and set of knuckles that went with it.

"Uh no, I didn't. I thought it would impress her, you know? It's very out of character for me. I'm not a violent person. In fact, Schwilden's the first guy I've ever really hit like that."

"Well you did a good job by the looks of things. We'll check out his medical records, just in case. Mr. Schwilden might have been exaggerating the extent of his injuries."

"I thought his jaw was wired shut."

"So he says. It wouldn't be the first time a scam was pulled in this sort of situation."

"So, where does that leave us, exactly?"

Gloria sighed, then shifted in her seat. I could see that her blouse was filled out nicely, then told myself to stop it immediately and concentrate on the task at hand. But then I thought, what of it? Aren't I allowed to admire an attractive woman? I loved women. I much preferred their company to men, in fact. It was just great to be around them, especially when they were dressed up and looking good and smelling good too. It was intoxicating. I couldn't get enough of it.

"Focus Bernie."

"What?"

"You were having some sort of conversation with yourself. Your lips were moving."

I smiled weakly. "I do that a lot. Sorry."

Gloria nodded and a lock of raven hair fell across her forehead. She flipped it out of the way. Her nails were long and very red. No rings, I noticed. "That's okay. It was kind of cute, actually." I think then I blushed. "Anyway. I describe this whole process as death by a thousand cuts and that's what it is. The further you go, the more expensive it gets and you have to decide whether a moral victory if one is even in the offing, is worth it."

"So you are suggesting?"

"Make him an offer. Get him out of your life as quickly as possible."

"I see."

"I hope you do. Not many clients are inclined to take my advice and they usually end up paying for it in the end. My time is quite valuable."

"Out of curiosity, what do you charge?"

"Four hundred and seventy-five dollars an hour."

I let out a low whistle, then inadvertently checked my watch.

Gloria reached across the table and touched my wrist.

"Don't worry. The first hour is free."

"Ah. Great."

Gloria shuffled through some papers in the folder, then settled on something for a moment. "We'll check Schwilden out too, of course. His financials, family, background, his business. It pays to be thorough. You never know. There might be something we can use as we um, negotiate." Then she looked up at me. "Does he know anything about you? Your background, I mean?"

"I'm not sure what you're getting at?"

"He's met your wife?"

"At a party once, yes."

"And did something happen?"

"Well. He did try to hit on her but Sharon told him to stuff it in no uncertain terms and then we left. So there wasn't much to it, really."

"Do you think it's possible he knows something about your family?"

"Like what?"

"Well, how wealthy your family is, for instance."

I rubbed my chin and tried to look pensive.

"I don't know. Look, I mean, Sharon does very well but I don't think I would call us wealthy by any means. I'm certainly not. I've got less than $5000 in a savings account and about $20,000 put away for retirement."

"That's it?"

"Yup."

Gloria shook her head, pondering I supposed, the stupidity of some men. "Well, I wasn't talking about Sharon actually."

"Well, who did you mean then?"

"Your father."

"My father?" As if I had more than one. "What about him?"

Gloria then began to look a bit uncomfortable. She crossed, then re-crossed her legs tugging at her skirt. "I'm sorry, I assumed that you knew. I am your father's lawyer. He didn't tell you?"

I shook my head and stared into my lap. "He doesn't tell me much."

"Well, you could say I'm your family lawyer and my job is to look out for your best interests. That includes all of you, Harry included."

"So what about my father?"

"Well. He's a very wealthy man and in part, with thanks to you."

"Sorry?" Now I was really confused. "We're talking about Eph Goldman here?"

"That's right. Eph Goldman, your father."

"Define wealthy."

"Well, he is a millionaire many times over. And when I say, many times, I mean many times. I don't think you appreciate how well The Global View has sold over the past 40 years. That's a long time for one book to be a bestseller and your father negotiated a pretty shrewd deal with the publisher. When they went out of business in 1966, all rights reverted back to him."

Skepticism reared its ugly head. "My father is a millionaire?" I saw him in his torn tennis shoes and baggy jeans so worn they the seat lit up like a beacon.

Gloria nodded emphatically. "We're talking serious money here, Bernie. He's also made some very solid investments."

"And what did you say before, something about my influence?"

"Right. After you wrote the biography some five years ago, sales of The Global View jumped forty percent that first year and have been steady at ten to fifteen percent increases year over year since then.

"I've increased his sales by almost one hundred percent because of my biography?"

Gloria licked her lips, then smiled. I saw her tongue dart between strong white teeth. "That's right, Bernie. His income is over $1 million a year just on that alone, not to mention his pensions, investment income and royalties from his other books which, although relatively small by comparison, do add up collectively to a tidy sum."

"I don't believe this."

"And then there's the house."

"What about it?" My father sold his three-story Victorian near the University before he and Catherine moved to Italy. I loved that house and was bitter about his selling it.

"He netted $1.75 million on that deal."

"What?"

"Oh yes. A valuable piece of property, Bernie. A 3500 square foot, three story, detached home on a 60 by 140 lot in the heart of the city, including a garage, private drive and a solarium."

"Oh." I was pretty ignorant about these things. Once again, I felt like I'd been had by him. A feeling growing increasingly familiar.

"That's what I meant about Schwilden knowing anything about you. If he smells money, he might grab hold of your ankle and hang on for dear life. He might be difficult to kick away."

"I see."

"And then there's his counsel. A fellow by the name of Grusinski, Walter. The man's an attack animal. Known in the business for his ruthless doggedness, excuse the pun. If he smells the cash, he'll be tough to shake off too."

"And the bottom line?"

"Offer him enough to go away."

"For instance?"

Gloria shrugged. "Fifty thousand. Seventy-five? Something substantial."

"I haven't got that kind of money."

"Your father has."

"I wouldn't ask him."

"Why not call it a down payment on your inheritance?"

"And bequeath it to Schwilden?"

"He might get a lot more if you don't."

"I wouldn't ask him for the money. Besides, he's got other priorities now," I mumbled into my shirt.

"Bernie." Her tone stung, to get my attention, I guessed. My teachers used that tone all through school when I day-dreamed or stared out the window. My mother had used it too.

"Yeah." I raised my head and looked at her.

Something had softened in her eyes, her expression. Sympathy perhaps? "You're talking about his new family, of course," she said crisply. "I think it's fair to say that there is plenty to go around and everyone is provided for amply. Trust me on that. Now, you could do a couple of things. You could ask your father…" Gloria paused as I continued to shake my head. "…or not. You might position it as a loan against funds that would be coming your way in any case."

"Don't think so."

"What about your wife? Could you borrow the money from her?"

"I don't know. I'll have to speak to her."

"Do that, in case you want to make an offer. I don't want to be too quick with it because that will make Grusinski suspicious. So, I think it's better to string it out a little bit. The paperwork grinds on anyway. There are papers and motions to file, we have to deal with the master of the court who controls the case load. The courts have this fast track system now for civil cases. You can't delay and delay like in the old days. They try to get the parties together quickly and get it resolved. Saves court time and the government money."

"How fast is fast?"

"Mmm, six to nine months, something like that. Before, it could take two to three years before something like this might get heard. We could be in discoveries in less than four months if all the parties cooperate. You see, the system is really set up to benefit the plaintiff. And it came out of situations where individuals with few resources were suing companies for one thing or another. The companies could stretch things out and delay which got to be very costly for the small guys. So the court decided that wasn't fair. They don't take into account that the defendants could be small and vulnerable too. The change in policy just doesn't work both ways. It tends to be one or the other. So the deck is already stacked against you. I've had clients who were completely innocent of any wrongdoing…"

"Implying that I'm not?"

"…don't get testy, Bernie…and they settled anyway because of all the hassle and the potential expense. It may not be the greatest system but that's what we've got to work with and it's the best we can do for now. Okay?"

She stood up and held up her hand. I took it. "Thanks. I guess."

"Don't worry. These things happen and you can't beat yourself up about it." She released my hand. I looked down at her.

"I'll keep in touch with you, of course. Please speak to Sharon about the funds. It could come in handy and may be the best way out."

"All right." I turned to go and headed to the door. Gloria caught me by the shoulder.

"It's that one." And she pointed to another door.

"Oh."

I got as far as the door handle. "And Bernie?"

I looked over my shoulder at her. "Uh-huh?"

"You don't have to worry about my fee. It's already taken care of." Then she turned her attention to another file as the phone rang on her desk. I left her then and found myself in a long corridor. I turned to the right and kept on going.

# 21

To take my mind off things, I began interviewing for a summer intern. The fact that Jessica had exiled herself for some vague period of time, didn't make the task any easier. Ruth might have helped, I suppose. But Ruth being Ruth, she just snorted and shook her head giving me a look as if I might actually be demented. I don't know why I tolerated her. She was irritable, unsociable, arrogant, reeked of coffee and nicotine and was eccentric but I found myself drawn to such characters. God save us from the efficient and the organized. I had four interviews that day and six the next. More than enough. After all, the work was pretty mundane and not very challenging. Pulling press releases out of the slush pile and writing them up. Sorting through the books we received, classifying them for review. Looking for news briefs and phoning the relevant parties and checking the facts that included the correct spelling of their names. I posted a job description on the local University Web site. Within two hours, I received 30 resumes sent electronically, one by fax. They poured in. Weren't there any decent jobs out there? By the end of that day, I called the university and told them to pull the posting. It had gotten out of hand. Why would so many bright young people want to work in an office for eight bucks an hour? I didn't really understand it.

Of the first four, three were Asian and one Russian. All good students who scored in the mid-three range on their GPAs. Impressive, given that English was not their first language, not a one. Doesn't speak well of native-born Canadians, does it? Of the four, two were outstanding, quick, enthusiastic, personable, organized and efficient. Their names flew to the top of the pile. After the first four interviews, however, I felt exhausted and decided to call it a day even though the clock had just ticked past four. Roberto stared into his computer screen, studiously avoiding me. Ever since the blow-up about the missing signature, that, in turn, led to the incident with Schwilden, Roberto assumed the model of studiousness. Whether he's accomplishing anything is another story. But now at least, he knows what needs to be done since I'd put it on a schedule and handed it to him. I didn't want to think about the interviews tomorrow. With a wave and a nod, I said goodbye.

"Skulking out early," Ruth muttered and I could imagine the cigarette stuck between her lips as her jaw jutted outward, contemptuously.

"No skulking. Striding," I said and gave her a wink. She winced in reply, and waved her hand in front of her face as if clearing out the stink of a bad joke.

"See you tomorrow."

"Don't count on it," she said.

I had to laugh. That was utterly Ruth. In the parking lot, I noticed Schwilden's car beside mine. I'd contemplated getting something new but then I didn't want him to think I had the wherewithal, so in the end, I decided to nurse the old Saab along for a while, at least until this thing ended. Not only was his car in its spot, but Schwilden occupied it. The driver's door hung open with a highly polished loafer planted on the tarmac. A Hugo Boss pant leg jutted out from under the door. Schwilden slumped back in the driver's seat. Some low and lazy music spilled out of the speakers while a furious cloud of smoke billowed out of him. Definitely not tobacco. I leaned across the door and peeked in. He noticed me but didn't bother to turn his head. I saw a flicker in his eyes. His glossy hair combed back from his forehead. He looked like he hadn't shaved in a few days.

"What do you want Goldman?" He slurred.

"Nothing."

"Haven't you done enough damage?"

"Apparently not."

"I should wring your bloody neck."

"I see the wires have been removed."

"You pusillanimous bastard."

"Watching Monty Python again, Schwilden?"

"Fuck off."

"That's not tobacco you're inhaling."

He turned in his seat and looked at me contemptuously. "It's recreational only."

"I've heard that one before."

"I'm sure you have. I just said it." Then he smirked. "You are going to pay big time for what you did. I will wipe you out, do you understand? You won't have a penny. Nothing. I will take your business and your home and who knows, maybe your wife too."

"Your egomania has run amok, Schwilden. I hear there are pills for that sort of thing. Failing that, there's always surgery."

"Don't make me laugh," he said in a tired voice. It oozed with exhaustion.

"You don't look good, Schwilden. You look haggard and even a bit unkempt. Stress, is it? The business world got to you?"

"Fuck off," he snarled.

"Hmm, you're running out of dialogue, I see. Too bad. Your brain matter is leaking out of your nostrils." Then I walked to my car, opened the door and climbed in.

Before I could make my getaway, Schwilden half fell out, half climbed out of the Porsche. "I am going to bury you, Goldman. Just you wait and see." He panted and spittle formed at the corners of his mouth. He looked crazed not suave and sophisticated. I slammed the door, turned the key in the ignition and backed out of the parking lot as he glared at me. I could feel his wild-eyed stare bore into the back of my neck.

I arrived home to find Mrs. Sanchez dusting the furniture. Her heavy-lidded eyes acknowledged me but nothing more.

"Is Mrs. Goldman home yet?"

She shook her head and that was the best answer I'd get out of her. I poked my head into Felicity's room. She was watching one of those family court shows, the one with the female judge and the grating voice. A dispenser of TV justice. She could tell who told the truth, merely by looking at them. She saw into their souls, she said.

"Hello Felicity." No reaction. "Hello Felicity," I said, a little louder. Still no reaction. "Felicity," I yelled.

"Oh, I didn't see you there, Bernard." Her eyes bugged wide. I'd startled her. She picked up the remote and turned the volume down a tad.

"How are you?"

"Very well, thank you. How are you? I'm just watching my show, Family Court. A mother and her daughter are fighting over money. The mother loaned the daughter a thousand dollars and now she wants it back. The daughter says it was a gift. Can you imagine it? Mothers and daughters fighting over money like that?"

"No, I can't. It's unthinkable."

She wagged a finger at me. "I think you're having me on, you."

"Not at all. You and Sharon wouldn't fight over money, would you?"

"Of course not."

"Good," I said, and wondered what she might think if she knew I was going to ask her daughter for $50,000. I closed the door. As soon as it shut, I heard the volume swell. I changed my clothes, not that what I'd been wearing was formal in any way. I rarely wore business attire except when I attended some function or other. I slipped into a pair of jeans and a t-shirt and pulled on my walking shoes.

In the kitchen, I dialed Sharon's mobile number. I got her voice message. I left a message, then tried her office number and got another voice message. I left the same message on that line as well. I felt like pasta and began hauling out the pots I needed. I'd made up some sauce some weeks before and had stashed it in the freezer. I put the container in the micro and set it to defrost. That would save some time. I filled the large pot with water and set it on the burner, then went to the fridge, pulled out the fixings for a salad and a bottle of wine. I uncorked the wine and poured myself a healthy glass full, then turned back to the counter and the salad.

"What's shaking, Pop?" I turned and saw that Sean had the glass to his lips.

"Don't even think about it." He moved his top lip lower down on the rim and tilted the glass. His lip sat about a millimetre from the wine. I reached out and pulled the glass from him. A little slopped on the floor.

"Now look what you've done. You've made a mess," Sean said. "You better clean it up before Mrs. Sanchez sees and gives you a spanking."

"Watch what you say, boyo. She'll hear you."

Sean shrugged, then grinned. "So, how was your day?" He clapped his hand on my shoulder, just as I was about to slice into a green pepper. I straightened up.

"Fine. You?"

"Just fine too."

"Did you go to school today?"

"Yes. Of course I did."

"Did you do anything there?"

"Not really. There was a fight in the schoolyard at lunchtime, though." And he started swinging his arms around in a mock fight.

"They were so bad. Neither of them landed any punches. It was stupid. I could have taken both of them."

"Why would you want to?"

"I dunno. Because it would be fun."

"Fun to hit people?"

"Yeah, Pops. Don't you know, we're all hoodlums?" I was about to reply when he turned around. "See ya. Call me when dinner's ready. I have a date with the all-important Nintendo." And he disappeared. So much for father-son communication. And that was a positive encounter.

The micro beeped. I dumped the partially defrosted sauce into a pan and turned the heat up. It began to sizzle. The phone rang.

"Hey." It was Nathan.

"Where are you?"

"I'm at Beano's."

"And?"

"We're playing basketball. What time's dinner?" I checked my watch. It was five-thirty.

"Six o'clock. Be here."

"I'm not sure."

"You can meet Beano afterward."

"Can he come for dinner?"

"Does he like spaghetti?"

"I'll check." There was a muffled conversation. "No, it's okay. See you at six." Then he hung up. Well, at least he called. I picked up the phone again to try Sharon when I noticed the beeping. A message. Sharon wondered where everyone was and said she was on her way. ETA about 20 minutes. While the sauce defrosted and the water began to boil, I set the table. Felicity hated pasta so I doubted she'd be joining us. Perhaps that's why I made it in the first place.

When Sharon checked in, banging the front door with her bag, computer and briefcase, we were all set to go. Nathan arrived about a minute before and washed up. Sean slouched up against the kitchen counter. I'd sent Felicity a ready-made microwavable dinner with Mrs. Sanchez who gave me a disapproving look but I knew Felicity wouldn't mind. She liked that sort of thing. Mrs. Sanchez made certain that Felicity was squared away then took her leave for the evening. By the time Sharon had hung up her jacket, I'd poured wine, served steaming pasta and pulled hot garlic bread out of the oven.

"Wow. What's this?"

"This," I said. "is dinner."

"Let me get changed then. It smells really good. I won't be a minute." She kicked off her high heels and went prancing up the stairs. I called the boys to the table. They'd been hovering anyway. I didn't need to flush them out of dark corners like usual. Sharon changed into a T-shirt and tight jeans with a pair of flip-flops on her feet. Her toenails were peach-coloured I noticed. I couldn't think of when she had painted them but they matched her fingers. Again, the dinner went well, our own small corner of domestic bliss. The boys were attentive, even polite. They ate well and even cleared their plates, rinsed them off and put them away in the dishwasher. Sharon and I exchanged looks.

"What's got into them?" she asked after they'd left.

I shrugged. "I don't know. I honestly don't know."

"Could it be Mrs. Sanchez?"

"Could be..." I was loathe to pay Mrs. Sanchez a compliment but certainly things seemed better organized since she'd been here and she worked a good turn with Felicity as well.

"You don't want to admit it," Sharon said, draining her second glass of wine. Her lips glistened from the liquid. "Mmm, that's decent wine, that."

"It's a new Australian I thought I'd try. Very reasonably priced too."

She pushed her glass forward. "Top me up, would you?" I poured her half a glass more and saw that she pouted.

"You're a working girl and you can't afford a thick head in the morning, can you? All those divisions you've got to keep in line, right?"

"I suppose." She toyed with the glass, running a slim finger around the rim. It made an eerie, droning sound. I grimaced.

"Sorry. You saw the lawyer this morning?"

"Uh-huh."

"And? What did they recommend?"

"A settlement."

"A settlement? Why?"

"Because, as she said it, this is a death by a thousand cuts. And it just gets more expensive the longer it goes. It doesn't matter if you are innocent or guilty, just pay up and get it out of the way. Gloria asked me how much money I could put up."

"What did you tell her?"

"That I had virtually nothing."

"And she said?"

"To ask you."

Sharon raised her eyebrows. Her cheeks were pink from the wine she'd drunk. She toyed with her fork. "She did, did she? And did she have a figure in mind?"

"$50,000 to $75,000."

Sharon didn't flinch. "It's yours if you want it."

Now it was my turn to flush. I looked away, then down at my empty plate. I'd eaten with gusto, finishing everything. Now, it felt like a lump in my abdomen. "Thank you, I appreciate it. It's nice to know that it's there as an option."

"Is this woman good?"

"I believe so."

"Then what reason would you have to doubt her?"

"No reason." I described my encounter with Schwilden earlier.

"Maybe he has other problems as well. Ones we're not privy to."

"That'd be nice."

"Which means he may go for the quick out. And then it's done with."

"Right. Just the way you like it."

"No point belabouring anything is there? It doesn't make sense. Find the solution and get on with it. Make it part of history."

"Is that how you do it for Cablestar?"

"Yes, of course. What other way is there, Bernie?"

"The compassionate way. The humane way."

"That doesn't work in business, my darling. Not really."

"That's sad," I intoned.

"It is a bit", Sharon said, looking down at her plate. "I'm thinking about having more? Is there any left?"

"Yes, there is." I got up and took her plate and served her a new portion. And that was that. It had been dealt with in her mind. Put the offer on the table. It lay there waiting for me pick it up. And I wasn't sure what I wanted.

I slept fitfully that night.

# 22

Early the next morning, Hugo reeled off 8 baskets in a row.

"You are good for my ego. You give me the energy to carry on. I owe my life to you."

"I think you're exaggerating just a bit," I said, standing at the foul line, still trying to break the ice. I bounced the ball several times, feeling the spring off the floor. I looked at the back side of the rim and aimed, focusing on the arc of the ball. It went in with a swoosh.

"Nice shot," Hugo muttered grudgingly, conceding the point.

"Thanks. It may be the only one I get."

"I would like to think so." I shot again and got it in, some sort of record for me. Hugo's bushy grey eyebrows shot up in surprise. To his delight, I missed the next one. We played on and as usual I lost but I managed to sink nine shots, better than I'd done in a while. After sinking the winning basket, Hugo grabbed the ball, holding on to it. "Things must be going well for you. I haven't seen you shoot this well in a long time. You seem relaxed."

"I'm being sued for a million dollars."

Hugo stopped mid-court and stared at me. "You have nothing left to lose?"

"Something like that," I admitted.

"Be positive. If you think in the positive sense, nothing will happen. This is what I tell myself and it has worked for me throughout my entire life."

"If you say so."

"You know I do. You can defeat anything if you put your mind to it but that is what you must do. Don't just say it, do it, whatever it is. You must have the willpower."

"All right, Anthony Robbins. Let's get to the pool, okay? How's that for positive?"

Hugo smiled. "Okay." He knew not to challenge me in the pool. At his age, I'd be lucky to get out of bed, let alone shoot hoops and swim, among other things. Like he told me he and his wife had sex every day. He attributed that to the fact his wife was 15 years younger and she needed to keep up with him. "And I don't use any stimulants," he proudly declared.

"So...?" We were walking down the long corridor toward the pool. He had a white towel wrapped around his waist. Once he'd shown up naked just to get a rise out of the lifeguard who laughed and threw him a spare bathing suit from the Lost and Found. So, Hugo could prance around naked and it would be fine while I committed an alleged act and had been banned for a month. Go figure. I couldn't.

At the office, I put in an uninterrupted hour, working on the manuscripts. Baby steps but progress nonetheless. I felt unusually pleased.

Then I got Jessica on the phone to see how she was doing.

"Not very well," she said, her voice quavery.

"Well...What does that mean? What can you tell me?"

"I'm just on this medication and, and I had stopped taking it, which was a big mistake, and now it will take some time for it to be effective and it has been bothering my stomach and...I'm sorry, really sorry. If you feel you need to find someone else, I'll understand, it's just that right now, I feel like I'm losing my mind..."

"I see. Um, why don't you take some more time and when you're feeling better, just give me a call, all right?"

"You're being very understanding."

"It's okay, Jessica. I just want you to feel better and come back when you are ready. Let's give it another week, all right?"

"Okay."

"Good. I'll speak to you in a week then." I hung up the phone as Ruth wheezed her way in. "Morning," she said, and hacked for several moments before regaining her breath.

"I don't suppose there's any point...?"

She turned and looked at me malevolently. "None, so don't even try."

"Okay." A long-time divorcée who had no children, Ruth's ex-husband had been head of a brokerage and escaped to New York City years before. I believe she survived on her alimony payments. It certainly wasn't the salary I paid her that covered her expenses. Her indulgences comprised the symphony, taking free walking tours, offered by the city's heritage society, and eating out, usually on her own, I gathered.

I hired a Russian student, Maria Ouspenskaya, who had emigrated five years earlier. She studied psychology at the University of Toronto. Her English was perfect, very precise but she spoke in clipped tones. Despite English being her second language and she spoke little if anything when she came over, Maria maintained a 3.7 grade point average at school. Impressive. She was a tall girl with light brown hair wound up on top of her head, a pert nose and dimples. She wore ultra thick glasses that magnified her grey eyes such that they seemed almost luminous and a little scary. I started her on Jessica's work, setting her on the growing slush pile of press releases that had piled up as publicity assistants sent them out with abandon from the book publishers. If nothing else, *Bookology*, functioned as a receptacle for industry puffery. Maria mobilized quickly. She set out her approach to organization. At least she had one.

"First, I make lists," she said. "And then I will categorize them for you ranking in order of importance. I will give them to you in a folder and you can decide, which you like, which you wish to run in the next issue. Is that acceptable?"

I stared at her for a moment and then found my tongue. "Yes, perfectly."

"I shall start immediately." And that's what she did, quickly sorting through the papers on Jessica's desk. I left her to it, feeling that I had made a good decision.

Maria had shown up a little before nine. I checked my watch, then verified it with the time on my computer, about nine-thirty and Roberto hadn't shown his face yet. His routine dictated rolling in between 9:30 and 10 a.m., taking a leisurely lunch, where he sat, eating at his desk playing video games. It was a rare day indeed when he didn't have to leave early, running an errand for his mother or mother-in-law, picking up his kids from the sitter, meeting his wife at the subway station or the best one, taking his wife to have her legs waxed, somewhere out of town. Not that there weren't places to have it done in town but for some reason, she had to go out of town for this delicate medical procedure. Strange as it may seem, Roberto, when he got around to it, actually did good work and although clients fumed about the delays and tardiness, they were usually delighted with the results. All of which placed before me a perplexing dilemma. Roberto was a partner, albeit in a minority position, but a partner nonetheless. It became no simple matter to shed one of those. You couldn't actually fire a partner. I suppose you could but then they still owned a piece of the business. Without a reasonable buy-out, that I couldn't afford anyway, I was screwed. That's why I tolerated Roberto's annoying idiosyncrasies over the years. But it was getting to be too much. My blow-up the other day, a harbinger, a tiny warning light blinking in my head.

As I watched warning lights blinking off and on, I thought about the evening before. When I'd come up to bed, Sharon was sprawled on top of the blankets in a fetching little outfit, micro-sized really that looked like it had come from the Victoria's Secret catalogue. Her skin had that glow from some balm or oil she'd smoothed on. The cups of the bra barely covered her nipples and as I looked at her, she rolled on to her side so I could get a good look at her taut buttocks.

"You like?" she cooed.

"It's okay."

Propping her head on an elbow, she crooked a finger at me drawing me in like a magnet. "You're not one to spare a compliment, are you?"

"No." As I was drawn forward, I glanced over my shoulder at the "screw" chart stuck to the bathroom door. Sharon marked all the score days with an "X". There had been four so far this week. I stood in front of the bed. She sat up and put her feet on the floor. I looked down at her as she stroked my thighs, then unzipped my fly. "Easy there."

"Don't worry, darling. I'll be gentle."

"Okay."

She took a good look and a firm grip. "So, this is what 50 grand buys me?"

I felt glum. "I suppose so."

"Well then." Sharon lay back on the bed. She slid her panties down her legs, then flipped them away with a toe. I watched them crumple on to the floor. She slipped a pillow under her buttocks and put her knees up. She ran her hands up and the inside of her legs. "It will have to do, I suppose."

I felt charged and exhausted at the same time. My body obeyed its internal and external commands.

# 23

"Where's Ramon?" I dropped the bag of bagels on the adjacent seat and unfolded the paper before sitting down.

Nook looked glum. "He's not coming."

"Why not?"

"You know..."

"Is he sick?"

"No."

"Well then?"

"Luisa needs him. She's not feeling well."

"Oh, that." I took a look at the headlines. "Can you believe these damn gas prices?"

"Yes, that. And yes, I can," he replied testily. The mochaccino sat untouched in front of him.

"Something wrong?" Nook shrugged. "Are you ticked about this?"

"Maybe." Typical guy response, no commitment, no emotional outlay. Nook adjusted his glasses, resettling them on his nose.

"He'll be back."

"Sure."

I settled back in my chair, then looked up at the board, checking the prices. I should know it by now but could never remember the cost of the damn tea. "You know, it's not like we do a helluva lot."

"I know."

"We really don't hang out much together, maybe do dinner twice a year, so..."

"So what?"

"So...nothing."

I realized I strayed into dangerous territory here. After all, it had taken me quite some time to find a support group, a compact if you will, of those who pursued the same goals: peace, serenity and the opportunity to do nothing for as long as possible. There weren't many of us, that is, those willing to admit to it in this driven world we inhabited. Ramon's absence could put a serious dent in our confidence, that this goal could be successfully achieved. That it could be undermined by day-to-day affairs. What was the point of having a mission if it was so easily derailed? I thought about this and other things as I glanced at Nook, seemingly calm, yet turbulence brewed behind those flashing lenses.

"We'll get him back," I said. Nook nodded and that's as far as we went that day.

The sounds of Beethoven's Fifth rang out. The tones were muffled. Nook reached down into his leather carry-all and pulled out his phone. He put it to his ear listening, then handed it across the table.

"It's for you."

"What?" I was startled but took the miniature handset reluctantly. "Hello?"

"Bernie? Gloria Martinez, how are you?"

"Gloria? How did you find me?"

"I called your wife. She gave me the number."

"Unusual working on a Saturday, isn't it?"

"Not really, par for the course, actually."

"What's going on then?"

"Just thought I should let you know, that Schwilden has come in with an offer to settle."

"Oh? What is it?"

"He'll take two hundred thousand. Wants a certified cheque a week Monday."

For some reason, I felt my heart quicken. "That's generous of him."

"I take it, you're not prepared to cut him a cheque," she said, in a flat tone.

"Hmm, don't think so."

She chuckled on the other end. "I had a feeling you wouldn't."

"What's your read?"

Gloria cleared her throat. "Looks like an attempt at a quick score. They have nothing to lose. If you go for it, they get the money with no muss or fuss. Could mean he's open to a more reasonable deal. This is only the first shot across the bow. Or it could mean he's got some other reason not to go through the legal motions."

"Such as?"

"I'm not sure. We're still trying to dig into his financials. There might be some clues there. When I get something, I'll let you know. In the meantime, I'll draft up a reply and fax it to your office for Monday morning."

"Sounds good. Thanks Gloria.

"Have a good weekend, Bernie. Order a latté for me."

I handed the phone back to Nook. "My lawyer," I said. His expression read cynicism.

"Whatever," he replied, then grinned. "You've got your own situation."

"That I have."

It wasn't a successful Saturday morning by any elastic measure.

When I arrived home, Sharon, as usual, had departed to the gym. Felicity was sunning herself in the backyard. I found my father waiting for me in the kitchen. I dropped the bagels on the counter.

"Hi Eph. What are you doing here?"

"Can't a father visit his son and his grandchildren?" He looked at me, warily girding himself in case I acted in an unexpected way.

"Sure. Want a drink or something? Tea. Lemonade. OJ. Milk. Coffee. You name it."

"Lemonade sounds promising," he said, drily.

I took the container out of the fridge and poured two glasses. "Bagel? I don't have cream cheese, just low-fat soya-based margarine. But they're fresh."

"No thanks."

He perched on a stool and had his elbows propped up on the counter. He was wearing a pair of khaki shorts, sandals and an overly long T-shirt. His face was lightly tanned and I could see white lines undercoating the creases on his forehead, where the sun didn't penetrate. He sipped the lemonade and smacked his lips. "Very good. Tasty."

"Glad you like it. What's going on?"

"Nothing much."

"No labour pains yet?"

"False labour once. It was a little unsettling." I noticed a pager on his belt.

"You've joined the modern world, I see."

He laughed at that, a full-throated guffaw.

"Right. First the computer and now this." And he patted his side near the pager. "I can't get away. Catherine can track me wherever I go. It's a bit unsettling."

"You've never been monitored before."

"No," he admitted. "I haven't. I could come and go as I pleased."

I left that one alone. No point in dredging up the bones of the past.

"Well, it's not so bad, really."

"But you don't have a cell phone or a pager?"

"No, I don't. I'm never far enough away. I go to the office and then I come home. Occasionally, there are meetings but I leave numbers where I can be reached. To tell the truth, if I was talking on a cell phone while driving, I'd probably kill someone. So it's not a good idea."

"Not if you put it that way."

"It is that way." Without knowing it, I had raised my voice. "Sorry."

He waved my apology off.

"I was concerned about you. You've had your share of troubles lately."

"I don't think about that too much. Gloria Martinez seems very capable." I hesitated, then sputtered on. "I wanted to thank you for that."

"She's a wonderful lawyer and person too. I have peace of mind knowing she will take good care of you." He drained his lemonade, smacking his lips. "That was good. Listen, Gloria mentioned a few things to you, uh, about my estate."

"Yes."

"I wanted you to know."

"Okay. But you have other priorities now, a new family."

"There's enough to take care of everyone. Catherine and I have discussed it and she agrees."

"Who knew *The Global View* would do so well?"

"I owe my life to it. It has been a wonderful boon," he said, scratching under his chin where the wattles grew. Liver spots formed on the backs of his hands. "And its legacy will continue helping our family to grow and prosper for many years to come. At least, that's my hope."

Then Sean and Nathan burst in. They whirled about the island like two dervishes chasing their tails, stopped at the fridge, grabbed the lemonade, poured two glasses recklessly, left the container on the counter and were on their way.

"Hi Zaidy," they called.

"What's shaking?" Sean asked, and put out his hand. Surprisingly, Eph slapped it, then laughed. Then they were gone. The whole incident lasted seconds.

"Are you sure about that?" I asked wryly.

"They've got energy," he said. "They make me laugh. I don't begrudge their youth, their exuberance, Bernie. They're pretty good kids, I think."

"Our future is in their hands. Will they do the right thing?"

"Did we?" Eph responded. "I sometimes wonder. What is our legacy?"

"Well, we know what yours is."

"And yours too. You've published one very successful book and there will be more."

"How can you be so sure when I can't?"

Eph shrugged. "Call it the grizzled optimism of an old man. I believe in new things now. I have hope for the future. My life has made surprising turns and unexpected twists. Two years ago, if someone had told me that I would remarry and father a child, I would have said they were nuts. I would have said they belong in the loony bin."

I sat on the stool opposite him. "Yeah, I guess you're right about that. Who would have figured? You know my friend Ramon?" Eph nodded. "He's having a baby too."

"So what's wrong with that? You make it sound like it's a tragedy."

I shrugged. "Well, I guess it's his wife's attitude. She's not giving the guy any breathing room at all. He's suffocating, for god's sake."

"Meaning he can't go out with the boys?"

"Well. Yeah."

My father put out a gnarled finger. "Going out with the boys is highly overrated."

"When did you ever go out with the boys?"

"A few times. In my younger days before you and Harry were born. To tell the truth, it was incredibly boring. We didn't know what to say to each other. What to talk about. Instead, we fell back on work or women. Sports didn't even interest us. It was pathetic really."

"So why do it?"

"For a break, I suppose. The need for some adult male companionship."

"But you and mom were just newly married. Don't tell me you were tired of each other so quickly."

"No, we weren't but I didn't want that to happen, either. I guess I went out because of that fear it could happen. A little separation didn't seem like such a bad thing. And remember, this was in the Fifties, hardly the age of enlightenment when it came to relationships."

"You think things are better now?"

"Hallo, boys." Sharon breezed in. Her cheeks were slightly flushed, giving her a radiant glow that seemed to emanate through her shoulder length red hair. Her tall figure moved with purpose and power. She gave Eph a peck on the cheek and kissed me on the lips which she held a bit. I peeked at my father over her shoulder.

Eph grinned. "I know they are."

Sharon broke away. "How's Catherine? Is anything stirring yet?"

"Not yet. Soon, we hope. You'll get a call from me. It could be in the middle of the night."

Sharon waved her hand. "Och, don't worry about it. Bernie's glad to do his bit, aren't ya, darlin?"

"Of course."

"I'm famished. What have we got that's good for eating?"

"Bagels. Tuna. Low-fat turkey, low-fat cheese, low-fat yogurt, low-fat chocolate." Sharon turned to me in surprise. "Sorry. Got carried away. No chocolate."

Eph stood up and rubbed the palms of his hands along his shanks as if to stimulate the flow of blood through them. "I'd better be going."

"So soon?" Sharon turned to him with her arms full of lunch things. "I just got home."

"I know but I promised Catherine I wouldn't be long. It's hard for her to get about now. She needs me and to be honest, it's nice to be needed again."

I bit my tongue. Sharon glanced at me. She dumped her lunch things on the counter. "Oh Eph, that's so sweet, it really is. Funny, your son never says such things to me now."

"But he's thinking them. I know my son, Sharon. Don't ever doubt that, will you?" And he patted her on the arm. "I'll find my own way out." With a wave he was gone. Sharon and I looked at each other.

"He's gotten quite sentimental in his old age," she said.

"So it would seem."

"Do you think he's afraid of dying?"

I was startled. Sharon had this capacity to ask blunt questions and expect equally honest answers. "I think everyone's afraid of dying. Why should Eph be any different?"

Sharon buttered a bagel. "There you go, answering a question with a question. Just give me the answer, will ya?"

This annoyed me but I answered her. "Okay. Yes, I think he's afraid of dying. Right now he has a great deal to live for."

Sharon had cut herself a piece of cheese and nibbled on it. "I think you're right. For once." Then she turned back and busied herself with the bagel. "I'm putting the tea on, you want some?"

I nodded. "Sure."

"Where's Ma?"

"Out in the back doing her sun bunny routine."

Sharon glared at me. "At least she's getting up and about now. That's a good thing. She won't be here much longer if that's what's bothering you."

"If it is," I replied. "It would only be one of a thousand things."

"Is that so? And what else is on your mind, then?"

"Nothing. Everything." I was taking a risk and knew it. Normally, Sharon would blow air in and out of her cheeks until her face ballooned up and her lovely blue eyes cracked like ice and her fists were balled at her sides, but today she surprised me. Normally, it didn't take much for me to wind her up.

She smiled at me rather sweetly. "It's too nice a day to get upset. Besides, I'm famished. The boys around?"

"Somewhere," I admitted, grudgingly.

# 24

That evening the screw chart remained unblemished. Sharon blamed fatigue and lack of mood, all of her sexy things were in the wash and she felt sore from her workout.

"Whoa," I said. "You don't need any excuses. There's nothing wrong with just going to sleep."

"But I feel as if I've lost my resolve. It's not like me to back off so easily."

"Don't beat yourself up over it. There's nothing wrong with a bit of a break now, is there?"

We lay in the dark on top of the blankets. Despite the air conditioning, the house felt warm, or perhaps I felt that way after the nightly exercise ritual where I did a 150 crunches and 30 push-ups. I lay on the floor at the end of the bed out of Sharon's sight. Over time, she had gotten used to the routine and paid me no mind. It's only when one of the kids burst in, without knocking, that it got to be a problem. Why did I feel like retiring from life itself?

"What's the matter with him?" Sean peered at me intently, then pulled his face apart, rubberizing it. I didn't even blink.

"I don't know. Bern. Bernie, snap out of it." Nathan began snapping his fingers in front of my face.

"Stop that," Sharon barked. "It's annoying me. Now leave your father alone. He's under a great deal of strain. Something you two hooligans wouldn't know anything about. Your biggest decision is whether to put on a pair of clean knickers or not."

"Wooohhh." Sean gasped, and grabbed at his throat as if he were gagging.

"Clean?" asked Nathan, as if hearing it for the first time. "No wonder I have so many pairs in my dresser." He turned his attention back to me, waving his palms in the air like a swami. "Come on, Bernie. You've been in a trance but when I fart you will come out of it. One. Two. Three."

"Nathan!" Sharon screeched.

"Relax Mom. I wasn't really going to do it."

But then a vituperative noise was heard. "But I was," said his brother, which set the two of them laughing their faces off.

"Go on, get out of here, you swine." Sharon swatted at them with the newspaper. It was an easy task for them to sidestep her while they were bent over with laughter.

I watched the entire display dispassionately, as if I were sitting in a theatre or had just turned on the tube. Who were these people? Two gangly hyenas, one dark, one fair being chased about the bedroom by a tall redhead, her eyes blazing, her hair swinging, the look of fury on her. Were they mine? God help me. I think maybe I'd had it. There was nothing left inside but a scooped-out cavity.

After Sharon had beaten them off, she came up to me with a concerned expression. But I knew her. She was thinking how this setback might affect her. "Are you depressed, is that it? Shall we engage a head doctor to take a look?"

"No. I don't want a shrink."

"What then?"

"I don't know. I think I need to get away for a while."

"Get away? To where?"

"I don't know. Somewhere. I need to relax and not have to think or be annoyed or frustrated or angry, that's all."

"Is that what you are?"

"Yes."

"And is it my fault?"

I avoided eye contact. "No, it's more to do with me than you."

"Look at me and say it."

I did as asked and it wasn't a cakewalk. "It's not you."

"I'm pressuring you with the baby."

"It's one more thing," I admitted glumly.

"Do you want to make a baby with me?"

Something, a vise, gripped my throat. "Well, I enjoy the effort we put into it."

"That's not what I'm asking."

"I know. I, uh, don't know how I feel. I really don't. That's as honest as I can be."

The expression on her face became pinched and tight. It hadn't occurred to her that I might not share her feelings, that the pretense she saw wasn't one at all.

"I'm sorry, Sharon. I just haven't come to terms with it yet, that's all. And it's not as if I haven't got other things on my mind."

Something maternal awoke in her and she pulled my head down to her heaving bosom. "I know. But I think you will love any child we have. I know you think the pair of them are louts but I know you love them all the same just as I do. Am I right?"

I gave a muffled reply, deadened by the material of her cotton top.

"Yes."

What else was there to say, after all? Then I was released and cool air surrounded me.

"Let's just go to sleep then." Sharon got up to go to the loo.

"Okay." I became the acquiescent baby, sucking my thumb for peace. Sharon kissed the top of my head, then left the room.

Nathan slid back in. He peered at me curiously, then lunged forward stopping inches from my face. "How you doing, Poppy?"

"Go away. And step back, Your breath smells."

"Oh, Poppy. You're so cruel." And he began to fake tears.

"Just go away Nathan, I mean it. I'm not in the mood for this." He went to put his arms around me and I shrank back but he persisted and a flush of anger rose from the depths. I pushed him and he stumbled back.

"Listen to me," I hissed. "When I say I don't want to be bothered, I mean it." He looked at me in surprise, shock and hurt mixed into his expression. Then came the exaggerated tears.

"I'm so hurt. How could you do this to me?" And before I could rise from the bed, he had backed out of the room, giving me a sly grin. I was annoyed and ashamed both.

# 25

I knew a rustic place perfect for a getaway. I resolved to take an extra long weekend. Given that it was May and early in the season, I gave the Valhalla Lodge nestled in the Haliburton Highlands, a call. Perhaps the name should have been the tip-off but I dreamed of well-ordered cabins, sitting on an elegant hillside, overlooking a sparkling lake. I thought of peace and tranquillity. I'd take my computer and spend the mornings writing. Vacancies awaited. The heavy season would begin on the Victoria Day weekend, a week later. Thus marked the official beginning of summer, the commencement of cottaging and generally hanging out. Breakfast and dinner came included and as I recalled thinking back before I was married, the meals seemed quite palatable then. The same fellow, Jurgen Traut, remained the proprietor, he and his wife, Ilse. I was looking forward to it.

What if I decided to stay the entire summer? Wouldn't that be grand and glorious? Yes, and expensive too, given what Traut charged for rentals. A quick calculation told me, it would run about $8000 for the season. So, a long weekend it was. I wouldn't even tell Nook and Ramon. I just wouldn't show up and leave them wondering what had happened to me. The secret pleasure of it gave me chills.

That Sunday evening, we lay in bed. Sharon read an Irish novel, her glasses perched on the end of her nose. I lay on my back with the light on my side off. I pretended to sleep. "What are you smiling about?"

I cracked an eyelid. "I wasn't smiling."

"Yes, you were. A very contented smile too."

"Was it? I had no idea I was smiling at all."

"You're thinking secret thoughts again. As usual."

"What do you mean?"

"I mean, you're always thinking things but it shows plainly on your face. I see a guilty pleasure there, I do."

"Well, there's nothing to hide. I've booked a long weekend away."

"Where are you off to then?"

"A little hideaway in Haliburton. That's all. Just four days."

Sharon snorted. "Four days of bliss it sounds like."

I sighed. "Peace and tranquillity."

"You think so? You'll be hearing the birds screeching and the squirrels chattering and the frogs croaking and the peace, as you think of it, will be shattered. Even crickets get on your nerves."

"That's not true. I love the outdoors."

Sharon snorted again. "Through a picture window, you mean."

"You don't know what you're talking about."

"Hah."

"You don't."

"Double hah."

"Well, we'll see, Missus Smarty-pants."

Sharon dropped the book into her lap.

"Smarty-pants, is it? Couldn't you have toned it down a little? I'm really wounded I am."

"Ah, forget about it."

I pulled the sheets up to my chin and rolled on my side away from her. She laughed softly under breath, then picked up the novel and resumed reading. Sharon could be a real pain in the ass sometimes.

I dreaded Sunday evenings. Beginning mid-afternoon, a lump formed in my gut, my heart began an asyncopated rhythm and I felt edgier and more irritable. By the time I turned in, I felt angry and depressed, smacked around by hopelessness. That I wasn't getting anywhere, that the business wouldn't get ahead, that my next book would flop. So many details, the bloody minutiae of work life. I hated it with a zeal and passion found only in missionaries. There was no use talking to me and Sharon didn't try. All in anticipation of what was to happen.

I woke up the next morning and dressed in the dark as I normally do, went to the community centre, lost to Hugo in 21, hit the pool, and by the time I returned home around 7:30 a.m., I actually felt pretty good, even optimistic. I arrived at the office and my spirits registered neutral if not marginally buoyant. And this week, I had something to look forward to; a short week and a long weekend away in Haliburton by myself. Blessed solitude. The days stretched out ahead of me but I didn't mind because I knew that if I knuckled down, they would fall one by one until it was time to go. And I was right. The week slid by blissfully uneventfully, one of those rare times when events took place as they should without cock-ups or confusion and the worker bees buzzed along on a true trajectory. Even Roberto seemed focused. I couldn't believe my luck. Late Thursday afternoon, my thoughts strayed to Charlotte. I pushed her image away. She strayed back into view. Another push. She floated back, bobbing like a cork before me. The ideal loafing I envisioned didn't just connect to the physical side of things but the mental as well. From an early age, I knew that I lived primarily in my head. That I experienced the most acute feelings in my mind and imagination. I remember my mother querying me at the dinner table; 'Who are you talking to?' When I hadn't uttered a sound. I recall saying, no one, I hadn't been speaking to a soul. And my mother, in her wisdom, would smile and tell me she saw a lively conversation going on in my head. And it has always been thus. I could submerge mentally, drift off, then suddenly snap back to the present. This mental bliss formed a significant part of the loafing experience.

So, I conjured Charlotte in my head, re-lived that erotic dream I had about her and drifted off for a time in a sensual reverie. I may have felt my fingers move on the keyboard. I couldn't be sure. A moment or two later, I jolted back to consciousness, only to feel Ruth's contemptuous stare. She harrumphed and turned back to her desk, muttering, 'sleeping on the job, again'.

I left three pages of notes for Roberto and the staff. Jessica's return became imminent, due to re-start the following week, having recovered from whatever mental anguish had ailed her. The Russian summer student I hired, seemed to be doing well, keeping the paperwork manageable at least. I hadn't glanced at any of it and didn't have a clue. That would be for Jessica to sort out on her return with Maria's help. I was off until Tuesday, treating myself to four whole days away, completely and utterly alone. For once, I didn't mind packing and loading up the car. I took writing pads and my computer and books and magazines I hadn't got to as of yet. And a camera. I hoped for decent weather. It would be nice to see the lake, get out on a canoe and dog the shoreline, peeping in at how others lived.

That Friday, Sharon left for work while I ate breakfast. I wrote out the contact information for her in case she needed me for something and stuck it to the fridge. The boys had just pulled themselves out of bed.

"So you're really going huh, Pops?" Sean asked.

"That's right. Abandoning your children and family," said Nathan. "How could you be so cruel."

"Don't forget to pack your lunches, will you? And Sean, there's a form I signed and you have to take it back to the office."

"Where's my form?" Nathan demanded.

"I don't know. Did you have one?"

"No."

"Well, then?"

"I should have had one. What's it for anyway?"

"It's a detention form if you must know, Nathan."

His face fell a bit. "Oh. No wonder I don't have one."

"Oh shut up, browner boy. So I got a couple of detentions," Sean sneered and lashed out at him, just missing his face.

"Just get ready for school, the pair of you." The blood went up a bit but I told myself to calm it down, that soon, I would be free and clear. For four days at least.

Hugo made some noises of disappointment when I told him the morning before I'd be away. He sucked on his teeth and pulled on his cheeks and sighed deeply. He'd have to find someone else to slaughter at 21. But he smiled at me bravely.

"I understand. You need some solitude, yes? You have been under too much stress. This is not good. It is the way to die young. Me, I put it out of my mind at my young age. I think about the girls I used to know and that relaxes me. Think positive. You can control anything you want with your mind, Bernie." And he tapped his forehead with a thick finger. Then he turned, threw the ball up and sunk the basket. "Twenty-one. You lose. Again."

I wasn't angry or irritated. I slapped him on the back and together, we went to the locker room to get changed.

I began loading up the Saab. Taking a look at it, I hoped the car would make the three-hour drive to the Haliburton Highlands. Some of the roads were a bit rough. Perhaps it was time for something new. I packed warm and light clothes, not knowing what to expect in terms of weather. I preferred warm days and cool nights, ideal for relaxing and sleeping. I had no illusions about the water temperature but packed a swimsuit just the same. I might just brave it. Mrs. Sanchez was dusting in the living room as I carried my bags out to the car. She didn't glance up. I'd have to stop in the village of Haliburton to pick up a few things. The Valhalla didn't serve lunch. The cabin I'd selected sat on the perimeter of the grounds, farthest away from the main cluster grouped around the lodge itself, the tennis courts and in-ground pool. I threw my raincoat into the boot, just in case. Weather systems blew in and out with great frequency in the spring. I slammed the lid closed, then climbed the stairs to the house and sat on the stoop. The boys tumbled out, backpacks secured, caps on, wearing those extra long baggy shorts the kids liked today. I stood up.

"See you guys." Nathan put his hand up and I slapped it. Sean did the same thing but pulled it away at the last second, then pointed and grinned, saying I couldn't outfox him and shouldn't try.

"Have a good time, Pops," he said.

I nodded. "Be good for your mother. Don't drive her crazy."

They stopped and stared at me with expressions of wonder.

"Don't get too lonely up in the wilderness, Bernie," Nathan said. "Remember, we're only a phone call away. Do they have phones up there?"

"Yes."

"You see. Even if they didn't you could drive to a pay phone. They have pay phones up there?"

"Yes. And houses and pizza parlours and doughnut shops and all the comforts of modern life."

"Television?" Sean asked.

"Yup."

"They can't have Nintendo," Nathan said decisively. "It's impossible."

"Go on guys. You'll be late for school." I indulged them as they each gave me a mock hug and feigned tears, their standard performance. As I watched them trudge off to the bus stop, however, I noticed how tall they were getting. A study in contrasts, Nathan so dark and evenly tanned. His brother, so white and blotched red by the sun. Never letting up, they tried to trip each other, jostling and shoving back and forth. Nathan ran up ahead. Sean whipped a stone at his feet. I was about to call out but it was just horseplay. Settle down, I told myself. This is the beginning of relaxation. So I smiled instead.

# 26

I followed along the 401, the main artery across the top end of the city. Heading east put me in the opposite direction of most of the traffic flow. Although the volume stayed fairly heavy, it kept moving. I was grateful for that. I didn't want to start off bumper to bumper in a jam. It would be 35 minutes at least before I turned off and headed due north.

The secondary roads remained lightly travelled as I headed north toward Haliburton. I followed a windy circuitous route that meandered through the hills with roads blasted through walls of granite and pre-Cambrian rock. The fabled Canadian shield in all its glory, glittering like rusted metal in the hazy sun, filtered through the weak cloud cover.

Outside of Minden, I stopped at a local favourite, Kawartha Dairies, for an ice cream sundae. This would do in lieu of lunch. I'd had a decent breakfast. I don't know if the ice cream tasted better than any other but it was made locally and took me back to my youth when I'd spent my summers here at camp. Ten years of wood cabins, bad food, engorged mosquito bites, punishing sun, frightening storms and camaraderie amongst pimply, squeaky-voiced cabin mates. I'd see the same kids year after year, although we'd have no contact after the summer, we'd pick up where we left off a year earlier. We graduated to staff as well. I worked at Hinterland Camp for four summers, first as a counselor and then on sailing. I'd taken to sailing rather well and earned my level 3 rating which was pretty good at the time. But I'd had little opportunity since. Still, all those memories came rushing back. And the girls, how wonderful they were, tanned and fit in their skimpy bikinis, driving all the boys wild, speculation running as to who you might end up with by summer's end. I felt like I lived it again as I spooned up the sundae while sitting at a battle-scarred picnic table that had better days behind it. After the sundae, I shivered. It felt a bit cooler up here with a biting wind blowing through the jack pines and evergreens. I bought myself a tea to go and got back in the Saab. Just up the road I spotted the turn-off. South Kashagawigamog Road. Windy and curvy, like driving on a roller coaster track, standard for the roads in this area but it gave a kind of sick thrill at the same time. I felt the ice cream congealing like a lump in my gut. I passed cottages that looked like mansions and rustic resorts that had seen better days. About 10 kilometres in, I found the entrance and turned in the driveway parking beside a red pick-up truck. I stepped out, stretched, then took a quick look. The office appeared right in front of me. Built on a gentle sloping hill, the view from the lodge, allowed you to see clear down to the water. To the right lay a grass tennis court with a basketball net inside the court. Straight ahead, encased by a chain link fence, stood the heated pool. I looked beyond to the beach that stretched several hundred feet. To the left bobbed a rubberized dock made of recycled tires with three motorboats and a rowboat tranquilly moored. I heard the water gently lapping the sides. Pulled up on the beach half a dozen canoes had been stacked. I stared across the lake at what I knew was the Wigamog Inn, famous in these parts and formerly an exclusive playground for the aristocratic and newly wealthy. Now, of course, anyone could book it and they'd be welcomed with their credit cards. No one was about. Apart from a lone boat at the far end of the bay and the chirping of birds, I heard nothing. It was beautifully, blissfully tranquil. I felt my flesh melt into my bones. Bloody marvellous. I couldn't wait to get started and do absolutely nothing.

I opened the door to the office. Deserted. A buzzer sat on the pine desk. I pressed it. A door at the back opened and a thin, man with fading hair and piercing blue eyes came out, smiling.

"Yes? May I help you please?" I detected an accent. I glanced at a card tray on the counter. Jurgen Traut, proprietor. German.

"Reservation for Goldman."

The fellow's eyes lit up. "Ah yes, Mr. Goldman, of course. Did you have a good trip up?"

"Fine. Thank you."

"You've been here before?"

"In Haliburton yes."

"But not here at the Valhalla?"

"No."

"Do you mind if I ask you how you found out about us. It helps when we decide where to put our money. Advertising you know."

"I found you on the Internet, actually. The Resorts Ontario Web site."

Traut pursed his thin lips. "Ah, very good. Thank you. Um, your cabin is not ready yet."

"Oh?" I glanced at my watch. It was quarter of two.

"Our policy is between two and three for check-in."

"Yes, I know but..." I turned and looked out the window. There were two other cars besides mine in the parking lot. "...you don't seem terribly busy at the moment."

"Ah yes. Well, this is our transition day you see. Give us half an hour, all right, and check back with me here. In the meantime, may I have your credit card please?" I handed it over and he ran it through the machine. "We'll just get that recorded, just so. I will take a $250 deposit and then we will settle up finally when you leave." He placed a placard on the menu. "Would you select your evening meal please? We prefer to have guests pre-order. It helps the chef when deciding the portions, you see."

I examined the placard. I had a choice of fish, baked salmon in this case, roast lamb or a vegetarian dish. "What's the vegetarian dish?"

Traut looked up from his paperwork. "I don't know. But then I never do. Something healthy I expect." And he flashed a brief grin.

"Salmon then."

"Will you be having wine with dinner?"

"Probably."

"If you order your own bottle, it will be cheaper for you."

"I won't drink a whole bottle."

"Don't worry about it. We put it away for you and you can finish it another night. All right then." He snatched the placard back. "I will let the chef know. In the meantime, I will show you on the map where your cabin is." He pointed to a diagram affixed to the wall and showed me the Valkyrie, the name of the cabin. It boasted a direct lake view.

"It is one of our latest with all of the modern conveniences. I'm sure you will find it to your liking."

"I'm sure I will," I replied.

"Good. Well, take a walk and I see you in half an hour."

Jurgen Traut rose from his chair and disappeared into the back. I took a walk.

Half an hour later I returned, only to be told to have a short stroll, ten minutes would do. I took a stroll. It remained lovely and very tranquil down by the shore. The water lapped gently up on the sand. There wasn't much muck or goo you saw on lakes nowadays, just the usual film of oil leaking from the motorboats and the normal flotsam that came in on the tide. No dead fish or poisonous scum that I could see. The wind had come up and I saw half a dozen boardsailors and a catamaran, picking up the breeze. Something in my bones melted into my ankles. I took a deep breath. No point in getting aggravated over anything up here. I picked up the key from a contrite Mr. Traut and drove down to the cabin. It was two cabins actually in one with separate entrances for each. I entered an enclosed kind of foyer adjacent to a small deck with two Muskoka chairs left there. You could have cocktails or a beer and some munchies while gazing at the view. Inside, the cabin was quite nicely done. A large bedroom and queen-sized bed, small efficiency kitchen and a large bathroom with shower and jacuzzi. The compact living room had a television that received six channels. That seemed fine. I didn't care about television. The only things I'd want to see were the news and a ball game. The way the Blue Jays had been playing lately, I wasn't even sure about that. I emptied my bags and threw the clothes into the dresser drawers, hung up the few shirts I had brought with me, then decided to take a towel down to the beach and read for awhile.

I saw a couple of lanky teenagers playing tennis while a few families splashed around down by the pool, little kids huddled under towels held closely by their mothers. One or two braver ones waded into the water by the shore while making sand castles, again under the eagle eyes of the mothers. No Dads in sight that I could see. Probably out fishing, that was supposed to be good in the lake. Plentiful bass in the right spots, of course and further out, lake trout and white fish. I pulled a plastic chair out from under a tree and planted it in the sand. I kicked off my shoes, threw the towel over the back of the chair and sat down to read the latest by Roddy Doyle, one of my favourite contemporary writers. I'd never interviewed him but had his books reviewed in *Bookology.*

The balance of the afternoon passed comfortably and I even managed to snooze off and on. By four o'clock the beach and pool were deserted. Time for the little ones to be bathed before dinner. The program I had received from Traut, suggested that those without children take the later dinner seating at seven o'clock. That left time for a proper nap, a shower and a drink before dinner. Perfect. The boardsailors had gone back to shore and the catamaran had disappeared, it's sails luffing somewhere on dry land.

I awoke shortly before six o'clock feeling groggy and decided it was time to bring my head around in the shower. Before stepping out, I turned on the cold just to scare me into bright consciousness. It worked. I was towelling off when I heard a knock on the door. I thought that perhaps Traut had forgotten to give me something. Cursing under my breath, I wrapped one towel around my waist and put the other over my shoulders. When I pulled it open, I was in for a shock.

"Hallo darling." She hovered, bright-faced and expectant.

"Good God. Charlotte, what are you doing here? How did you know where I was?"

Her face pouted. "Aren't you going to ask me in?"

"What? Oh, of course. Come in." I stepped away from the door. Charlotte looked me up and down as I backed away.

"Uh, just out of the shower actually. So, you were saying?"

Charlotte took a quick stroll around. She wore exaggerated heels, banana coloured pedal pushers and a sleeveless linen white top. "You emailed me. Don't you remember?"

"Well...no, er yes...I ...be honest, I really don't remember, sorry. ..."

"I wanted to surprise you."

I nodded vigorously. "Well, you did. You absolutely did." By this time, she'd made her way over to the bedroom.

"It's a marvellously big bed, isn't it?" She smiled, brightly.

"Uh yes, yes, it is." Given my clumsy surprise, even embarrassment, I didn't notice that the knot in the towel around my waist had loosened and as Charlotte turned to face me, it dropped to the floor as her eyebrows shot up and her mouth went open.

I looked down. "Oh my God..." And reached down to pick it up, bending over as Charlotte came toward me, giggling hysterically.

"You naughty, naughty boy..."

And that's how Sharon found us. She too, thought it would be a great surprise. Instead, the tables turned...on all of us. I was just bending over when she came through the door. Charlotte hovered above me and Sharon caught us in a terrified tableau.

"Sharon." I straightened, pulling the towel to me but of course, she'd seen me naked oodles of times. "I think I can explain."

In reply, she arched an eyebrow and cocked a heel. The colour had gone from her cheeks. Suddenly, she looked ashen.

"This had better be good."

"Uh, I think Charlotte was just leaving, weren't you Charlotte?"

Charlotte glared at me for a moment, then acquiesced. "Yes, I suppose I was." And gave me a withering glance before drawing herself up. She stood before Sharon. "You'll have my resignation on your desk first thing Monday."

"Fine," Sharon said, through tight lips and looked away.

Charlotte shrugged, gave me one last look, then left the cabin.

A roaring silence shrieked between us. I cleared my throat.

"I know how this looks but honestly she just dropped in out of the blue. I had no idea she was coming here and I had just gotten out of the shower and answered the door with this towel wrapped around me, thinking it was the chap from the lodge asking about something and there she was. And then there you were. Nothing happened or was going to happen, I swear to God. This took me by surprise as much as you? Say, it's just about dinner time. Are you hungry?"

I realized I clutched the towel so tightly it dug into my waist. Sharon strode up to me kicking her heels, her jaw thrust forward. She brought her right hand back and I watched mesmerized as it swung forward palm flat out. She really put her shoulder to it. All those workouts and personal training sessions had paid off. My head reeled from the blow. At the same time, I felt my cheek on fire, stinging from the slap, not to mention the sound of it that rung in my head.

"You must think I'm a bloody fool," she hissed and turned to the door. After touching the knob, she paused, " Your things will be packed and waiting for you when you get back to the city."

In that moment's hesitation, I thought I had a chance to recapture her but I was too stunned to react, to realize the opportunity no matter how slight. Not hearing my voice, she pulled the door and left. I sank to my knees and wondered what had happened. Had I dreamed it? Another internal conversation or fantasy I'd concocted?

I awoke in the dark, sprawled on the floor still clad in the towel. I heard a light but insistent rapping on the door. For a moment, I thought it was Sharon. She'd come back. But when I flung the door open, I saw Traut standing there looking at me strangely.

"We missed you at dinner," he said. "I thought something might have happened?"

"Uh, I feel asleep. Sorry about that. Been a long day."

"I see." And he nodded to show me that, yes indeed, he had seen the comings and goings. "And your visitors found their way, did they?"

"Ah yes, thank you, yes, they did."

"Didn't stay very long, did they?

'No, they didn't." And I really wanted him to go away. Such an irritating man.

It was then that I realized he was holding something. A tray.

"What's that?"

"The cook sent me down with something. It would be a pity to have it go to waste, yes?"

"Of course. Too kind, really."

"I'll just put it down here, shall I?" and he moved past me into the room and set the tray down on the small table that had been provided. The cabin had a cozy nook designed for two.

"I've also brought you this."

From the inside pocket of his light jacket, he removed a bottle of white wine. "I thought you could use it. There's a corkscrew in the drawer there." Then, Traut withdrew. "Goodnight Mr. Goldman. We'll see you in the morning at breakfast."

And he was gone before I could smile weakly in agreement. The smell of the food raised my appetite. I pulled on a T-shirt and a pair of shorts. The condemned man and his last meal. At least the bottle of wine seemed decent. I had two glasses.

# 27

The tranquil weekend transpired as anything but. I stayed on because I had no place to go. I also decided that, rather than wilt away, I should throw myself into the life of the place, such as it was. I met two other couples on vacation. Fred and Rita hailed from Hamilton. Fred was a teacher and Rita was a nurse. Then I met Joe and Madeleine from Belleville. A couple in their fifties with four grown children, Madeleine had persuaded Joe to take a break from his job as a site supervisor for a large construction outfit. They seemed like nice people, conservative, bewildered by the big city and the fast pace of life. Joe wore white socks with his sandals. Fred and Rita were an anomaly, a mixed-race couple in their mid-forties. They had three girls, teenagers who looked like Fred. Rita had very pale, milky white skin and very light blonde hair, along with a benevolent smile and a gentle manner. I took to them both immediately. We played volleyball and cards and tennis. We rented a motorboat on the Sunday and went around the lake together. I drove at first, then we took turns so everyone could feel in control, even Rita and Madeleine. It felt very pleasant as I needed to mask my anguish and keep from thinking about what had happened.

At night, I paced the floors, unable to sleep. Sunday morning, I missed breakfast. I fell asleep close to dawn after pacing all evening. When I showed up at the tail end of it, I was chided by the rest. We'd taken to sharing a table. Check out was Monday morning. I went around and shook hands with everyone, even Traut, who had remained a risible presence in the background watching everything with an alert eye. That was his business I supposed and what else was there to do up there anyway? We exchanged addresses and phone numbers and vowed to phone, to drop by. They must have wondered what I was doing on my own but they never questioned and made me feel welcome. I hadn't been lonely just miserable.

I drove back to the city, not knowing what to expect.

I stood on the threshold, bags in hand, and rang the doorbell. My father answered. He gave me a rueful look, a sour expression I knew too well.

"Don't say anything," I said as he stepped back. I picked up the bags and struggled inside banging the doorframe. Catherine, having heard the commotion, waddled in from somewhere.

"Hello Catherine."

I saw sympathy in her eyes. I must have looked bedraggled. That's how I felt. "Oh, Bernie. I am so sorry." My father stared at his feet. Catherine nudged him.

"He told me not to say anything," he replied testily.

"Where shall I…?"

Catherine turned on a weak smile. She looked ready to burst. "Up the stairs, second door on the right."

"Thank you for letting me stay."

I turned and struggled with the bags. I'd gone half a dozen steps when I put the bags down and faced them. They'd remained in place watching me.

"I just want to say…nothing happened. I did nothing wrong. It's all been a terrible misunderstanding." My father still said nothing but looked at his gnarled toes, wriggling in his sandals. Catherine nodded in agreement. I picked up the bags and continued my trudge up the stairs. I found the room and dropped the bags inside, then slumped down on the bed. After a moment, I looked up to see Catherine's daughter staring at me from the doorway. She came into the room, sat down on the bed and put an arm around me like I was a buddy in arms.

"Don't worry," she said. "I got kicked out of the house tons of times."

I snorted, then laughed. "That makes me feel better."

"Really?"

"No."

"Oh."

"Different reasons."

"Yeah sure. I was running around with boys until all hours and smoking dope. I don't think that's your situation, is it?"

"The boy-girl part maybe."

"Did you…?"

"No, I didn't."

"But you were thinking about it?"

"That doesn't count."

"Why not?" she asked indignantly.

"Because nothing happened. And nothing was going to happen. It was all just a mistake. A stupid, lousy mistake."

"Well, we all make mistakes."

I gritted my teeth. "Yup. Listen, if you don't mind, I'd like to get settled in a bit."

She stood up. "Sure. I just wanted to say, don't sweat it, that's all. It'll work out."

"Yeah," I replied, wondering how much the average divorce cost in this country. At least, I'd be entitled to spousal support, if I wanted it.

They both got me on the phone. "Dad," Nathan said. "What'd you do to Mom?"

"Yeah," Sean chimed in. "What'd you do?"

"I didn't do anything. Not really."

"Well how come she's crying all the time?"

"Mom's crying?"

"Yeah," Sean said. "She's crying."

"Stop repeating what I'm saying, butthead." Nathan took this seriously while, as usual, Sean thought it was a joke.

"You're the butthead."

"Guys. Enough, okay?"

"Anyway," Nathan continued. "She's not even going into work."

"Mom's taking time off work?" That was pretty serious. "Wow."

"I don't remember her ever staying home, even when she was sick."

"Yeah," Sean said. "Even when she sprained her ankle."

"And Gran says she'll scalp you alive if you ever show your face here again."

"Of course she would," I replied, drily.

"And I'd stay away from Mrs. Sanchez too," Nathan said, earnestly. "She's got this look on her face. When Gran mentioned your name, she broke a dish with her hands."

"What kind of dish?"

"One of those serving platters, you know, the ones that have different animals. This was the one with the chicken."

"That was my favourite one," I cried. "She broke it with her hands? Really?"

"Yeah, like she's the Incredible Hulk or somethin'." Sean laughed. "It was pretty funny. No one was laughing 'cept me though."

"So Dad," Nathan cut in. "When are you coming home?"

"I don't know."

"Why?"

"Why what?"

"Don't you know?"

"Guys, listen. I don't know when I'll be coming home. It could be a while."

"Well, how long's that?"

"I really couldn't say."

'But Mom's really upset and we don't know what to do."

"Just be good to her. Be considerate. Don't fight and goof around. Don't cause her any extra grief, okay?"

"Yeah sure."

"Sean?"

"Yeah?"

"Well?"

"Well what? Sorry, I wasn't listening, I was watching TV."

I sighed, a long drawn out one. The sigh of the workingman, as Felicity might say. "Don't give your mother any grief, okay Sean?"

"Yeah, whatever." He began to sound indignant.

"When are we going to see you?" Nathan asked.

"Uh, I don't know. I guess I'll have to wait until Mom and I are speaking again to figure that out."

"Well how long's that going to take?"

"Nathan, I can't give you an answer, okay? I just can't. Listen you guys, I really mean it about helping Mom out. Do your best for her."

"Sure," said Nathan.

"Right," echoed Sean but I could tell he was distracted by something. It could have been a song on the radio, something on his computer or a CD on the stereo, a commercial on television. It didn't take much. It wasn't as if he was being overtly cruel. Sean was just spectacularly self-absorbed. He could only take an interest in something or someone if they noticed him first.

"Okay guys, I gotta go. Give me a call in a day or so, let me know what's going on."

"We even have to make our own lunches," Sean said, as if he'd just remembered that it bothered him.

"That's not such a bad thing. Bye guys."

"Bye Dad," Nathan said.

"Bye Bernie," Sean said and I could almost hear his laughter. I hung up the phone and then looked at it as if deciding whether it was friend or foe.

# 28

"What are you doing?" I asked. Ruth was about to light a cigarette in the office. Her face assumed a puzzled aspect, then snapped back into focus.

"My mistake. I was daydreaming."

"I'll say."

I walked into the office and put my bag down. I was in no mood for eccentricities or frivolities of any sort.

"It won't happen again."

I thought I heard her hiss behind my back. When I turned, she was calmly typing away at her computer.

I settled in to check my email. A note from Charlotte: I'm so sorry. I don't know what to say. Please forgive me. C. I must have emailed her in some trans-hallucinatory state and of course, didn't remember. I don't even recall what I had written and now, of course, it was too late. Messed up, big time.

Fifteen minutes later, Jessica showed up. She gave me a weak smile that cracked her face open. Smiling wasn't for her. Nor laughing. Upon reflection, however, I asked myself whether I'd actually heard her laugh and the answer was no. I don't think she did well with joviality. Her life had a much darker aspect to it.

"Jessica. How are you feeling?"

She came around her desk.

"Much better, thank you. The medication seems to be working." I saw Ruth cast a disgusted glance over her shoulder then shake her head to herself.

"Well, good. That is good news. I, uh, left a pile of things on your desk there. We also have this girl in for the summer, a student, Maria, who has been helping out with some of your things. She should be in shortly and then you two can see what needs to be done."

"Okay. I'm sorry about taking the time off." And she began to pull at her knuckles. A nervous gesture. "I hope it wasn't...I hope I didn't..."

"Don't worry about it. It's been fine." With all that had been going on, I barely noticed but I didn't want to tell her that. She took everything so seriously.

"I'm glad you're back, Jessica. Things now feel a bit more normal around here."

Again, she gave me the cracked smile, one of relief. "I'm glad."

She busied herself with the pile of papers I'd left on her desk. One thing for certain, she remained a focused and diligent worker.

"Say your prayers," I muttered. Jessica looked up, startled.

"Uh, just something I was reading," I said, by way of reassurance. Ruth glanced back, taking a longer look this time, then snorted.

I read through a fax from Gloria Martinez. Marked both confidential and urgent, meant that everyone in the office had read it. Gobshites as Rory, Sharon's estranged father might say. I missed the old bugger even though I'd only met him a few times. He had a carefree manner that I knew radiated immaturity but he'd done as he pleased and seemed happy about it. Now retired on a decent pension, having worked as a pipefitter all these years. He'd remarried a woman of his own age with property and they seemed well-suited to each other. On occasional Saturday nights, he could be found playing in country bars. His new wife, Lillian, had kept a tight rein on him since that had got him into trouble with Felicity. Living the bar life, drinking, smoking, fighting and carousing too much. With his good looks and velvety voice, Rory became a magnet for the ladies as they were for him. It didn't take much to know that belied unadulterated trouble. No wonder the word trouble and troubadour are similar.

Earlier that morning, when I informed Hugo about what happened over the weekend, he looked at me and said: "I feel sorry for you. You didn't even get to enjoy sex with the other girl." Then he sunk the last basket for 21. I hung my head. Double-whammy.

I looked over Gloria's fax. Legalese for informing Schwilden's lawyers that in no uncertain terms would we be paying them 200K and they could take that to the bank. Odd, how it took an entire letter to say just that. I shoved the letter into a file I'd started for my legal difficulties along with the documents that had been served on me.

Ruth picked up the phone. "Your father," she called.

"Hello?"

"Hi son."

"Dad."

"Didn't hear you leave this morning."

"Well, you know I'm up and out early. I had to leave earlier to get to the gym at my usual time."

"I heard you. I was up."

"I'm sorry. I hope I didn't wake you."

"No. I'm usually up. I haven't slept well in years. I don't want to keep you but I just wanted to know if you were going to be home for supper."

"What?"

"Are you going to be home for supper?" he repeated slowly and carefully.

"I don't know. I guess I haven't given it much thought. I suppose so. At least, I don't have any other plans at the moment."

"Good. Be here by six. I like to eat early and Catherine has to stick to a schedule."

"I see."

"Oh and by the way, you didn't make your bed this morning."

"I, uh,..." What could I say? He was right. I didn't make the bed because I wasn't used to doing that. Sharon was normally in it, slumbering away.

"Sorry. I'll remember tomorrow."

"That's the ticket. This will all work out well, I'm sure."

"Well, I'm sure too," I replied, with a brightness I didn't feel.

"Wonderful. See you tonight. We're having chicken. Bye." He hung up the phone before I could answer and I slumped down in my chair just a bit further. Fortunately, we were on deadline with our chockablock summer issue and I spent most of the day reviewing printer's proofs and talking with Jessica about planning the fall issue. That and organizing the myriad of details involved with getting a magazine out the door. Inevitably things went astray. We'd get frantic calls from the production supervisor who'd be searching for an Ad or tell us some of the film hadn't been supplied. I would ask why they didn't notice it before. They'd reply that it remained our job to count the number of pages of film before it came to them. And of course, that was Roberto's job. I concluded that he simply couldn't count. I refused to do it myself. I wasn't going to start doing his job too, in addition to everything else I had to do. Down there lay the road to insanity.

Sometimes, when things appear to be at their bleakest, there can be a shining moment. I received a call while I pored over the proofs.

"Mr. Goldman?"

"Yes?"

"Frances Schwartz of NLT."

"NLT?"

"New Living Television."

"Oh, right. Of course. NLT."

"I have a proposition for you."

"I'm married." When there was dead silence on the other end, I said, "Sorry. Poor joke."

"Don't worry about it," and I could hear amusement in her voice. "We are putting together a show. A book show and I'd like to talk to you about it."

"A television show about books?"

"Right. We thought there could be an interesting tie-in with Bookology, great name by the way, we really love that. I know this is short notice but I was wondering if you were free for dinner this evening." I glanced at my watch. It was two-fifteen. Late notice was right. Why the rush?

"When were you thinking of airing this show Frances?"

"In September."

"I can see why you're in a hurry."

"How about Porretta at seven? Do you know it?"

"Yes, of course." Only one of the hottest joints in town. I'd been at a publishing party there recently.

"My treat, naturally."

"All right. See you then."

"Rightio." And she rung off. Rightio? TV people were a strange breed indeed.

# 29

The working day ended, more or less but I kept on. After all, I had a date and there wasn't time to go home in between. Fortunately, I kept a change of shirt and shower things, toothbrush and toothpaste in the office, just in case something came along. I realized how useful this was when these book launches kept cropping up and I began accepting invitations. After that it became incessant. I had become more judicious now and only attended a few. Mostly pretty boring affairs except to the author of course. I'd been thrilled with my own but de Groot had done it in style and billed me for half the cost. At least, that's what the royalty statement I received from him indicated. If I had known, I might have chosen the local deli and beer on tap rather than the sumptuous lounge he had chosen. Having my father there helped with the publicity of course. de Groot knew how to get the press out. All of this predated *Bookology*, fortunately. Otherwise, I may have been in the position of having to cover my own book launch and review.

Porretta's seemed in full swing by the time I got there a few minutes before seven. The waiting area was jammed and the noise in the place had gone several decibels above the DEW line. I pushed my way to the front where a trim little man in a dark blue suit directed traffic. I asked for Frances Schwartz and he looked up at me, then nodded.

"Just one moment sir and I will show you to her table." Then he conferred with several of the wait staff, sending them scurrying in different directions. "If you'll follow me." Porretta's boasted all leather bankettes and rectangular tables, swing lighting that set a halogen glow on the faces of the diners and ceramic tile flooring. The tile also extended to the walls where great swirls of blue and green fitted together like a giant jigsaw puzzle. It felt like staring at the bottom of a swimming pool from inside the water only you stayed dry. The waiters (only male waiters worked there) wore black tuxedo pants, crisp white shirts and pale, yellow vests. I followed the fellow's well-tailored back and neatly trimmed hair until he halted at a table occupied by a slim young woman in white slacks, a silk blouse and a shapeless jacket. Her hair was dyed blonde and she looked as if she just rolled out of bed, but I figured it was a deliberately stylized look. She smiled as I approached and stood up to shake my hand. She couldn't have been more than five foot two. A large gust could have blown her over. But her handshake came on firm and the smile genuine. The maitre d' bowed slightly then took his leave.

"Frances Schwartz. Nice to meet you Mr. Goldman."

"Likewise." We sat. "Been waiting long?"

She shook her head. "Just a couple of minutes. I made a few calls."

"How can you hear?"

"I just stay focused that's all. A little practice and you're there. What are you drinking?"

"Oh, white wine or a beer will be fine. What about you?"

"I'm drinking vodka." And she hoisted her glass. "I need it after a long day."

"Is television that bad?"

"Well, it's probably no more stressful than publishing. It's just that the stakes appear higher because it's such a public medium. When something screws up, everybody and their brother knows about it." She ran a slim finger around her glass. "The salmon is very good here and so is the rack of lamb. I've always enjoyed the fresh pasta too."

"You eat here a lot."

"Practically live here. Another thing about television, it doesn't allow you much of a personal life."

"You don't sound as if you regret it."

"Well, we all make choices in our lives. If I hadn't wanted to be in television, I would have made other choices."

"Too true."

"You made a choice to get involved in publishing."

"True again."

She sat back and levelled me with her gray eyes. "I am a bit curious though. You published a very successful book. Why do this? Why not keep on writing?"

"Well, I am still writing. My publisher is salivating over what I am working on and keeps pestering me to show him some pages. I haven't yet."

"And *Bookology*?" The waiter came over and I ordered a beer, one of the local microbreweries I favored.

"It was a kind of misguided stopgap sort of a thing, I guess. I wasn't sure what I'd be doing after I wrote *Spinning Out of Time*. It was an exhaustive process for both personal and professional reasons…"

"I can imagine writing about a living parent wouldn't be easy."

"No, it's not. I had a little bit of money. Sales were going well…"

"It was on the bestseller list for 12 weeks as I recall…"

"Yes, that's right. Not bad for a first book. And the expectation was that I'd keep churning them out. Other biographies were offered to me but I wasn't interested. I really wanted to work on something new but wasn't at all sure what that might be. And then I had the idea for *Bookology* and the rest, as they say, is history."

The waiter brought my beer. We decided to order up. I took the salmon while Frances went for the rack of lamb. The discreet waiter departed once again. I took a gulp. It tasted good. "So, what are you working on now."

"Two manuscripts actually. Sort of going back and forth between them."

"Oh, like Dickens."

I snorted.

"Hardly. Give me two percent of what he had and I'd be sublimely happy. So, no, just undecided. One story is about a guy who loses his memory in an accident and when he comes to his senses after being in a coma, discovers he can recreate anyone's voice, male or female. When I say recreate, I mean he can duplicate the sound, inflection, tone so that, if you closed your eyes, you'd swear it was the actual person."

"Sounds a bit spooky"

"It is, creepy even."

"And the other story?"

I paused, then rubbed my jaw and took another gulp of the beer. It was good. "More of a war story. It's about a Jewish warrior, a guy who grows up in Poland but is determined never to be a victim. He fights his way through two wars across Europe and Russia, falls in love, searches for his family, then eventually ends up in Canada. It has a surprise ending. I know because I wrote that part of it first."

"They both sound intriguing."

"Well, I have to finish them first and then polish, revise and edit before either will be ready for showing. It will be some time yet. In the meanwhile, I have the magazine and other things to occupy my time."

"Such as?"

"Family mostly. My father has just moved back from Italy with his second wife and they are expecting a child any day now."

Frances reared back in her seat. A little vodka sloshed over the rim. "Wow. How old is he now?"

"Seventy-eight."

She raised her glass. "Well, here's to him." And she took a slug.

"Right."

I tipped the beer and let it go for a moment. I was thinking about having another. When I lowered the bottle, my line of sight took in the far side of the room and there I spotted Sharon in animated conversation with a dark-haired stranger. She looked terrific but then when didn't she? I choked on the beer and came up sputtering.

"Are you all right?" Genuine concern clouded those unusual eyes.

I nodded. "Fine. I'll be fine," I croaked. I wheezed. She looked concerned. "I'll be right back."

I took an instant dislike, even loathing to the guy. As I approached the table, hackles went up on the back of my neck. Sharon saw me but it was too late. I gave her a peck on the cheek.

"Darling, I didn't know you were going to be here." Her eyes widened and she forced a grim smile. I turned to her companion. "Bernie Goldman." And put out my hand. To his credit, the fellow stood up. Damned if he wasn't tall and well-built. My dislike grew by the milli-second. He smiled and his perfectly even white teeth shone out of his gob. I saw dimples that women would fawn over. His hair was thick and expertly cut. He had just enough of a tan. Armani suit, I noticed. "Sharon's husband." The fellow continued to smile as he took my hand and I felt a callused palm and a solid grip.

"Bill Haley," he responded.

"Where are the Comets?" I quipped, knowing he'd heard it a thousand times or more but he seemed a good sport and chuckled.

"I get that all the time." And then he resumed his seat and gazed appreciatively at Sharon.

"What are you doing here?" she asked me.

"Having dinner. And you?"

She ignored my question. "I thought you were seeing Eph tonight?"

Oh my God. "Eph." I smacked my forehead. "I forgot to call him. He'll be hopping. I'll call him later. So, is this a work thing or…?"

"Bill works for our subsidiary in Dallas."

"Ah."

"He's a senior programming executive. Now you didn't answer my question. What are you doing here apart from having dinner?" Sharon had a haughty way about her that rubbed many people the wrong way. But that's one of the things I liked about her. Her imperiousness.

"I'm having a discussion about doing something in television."

Sharon's carefully honed eyebrows shot up. "Really?"

"What sort of discussion?" Haley asked.

"A show about books apparently."

"What's the connection?"

"Bernie publishes a magazine, *Bookology*. It's all about books."

"I see. Who's the producer?"

"NLT." Haley shook his head. Sharon drew a blank. "New Living Television?"

Haley nodded. "Must be one of the new channels. Well, good luck with it."

"Thanks. I intend to." And there was nothing more to say. I turned to Sharon and bent down to kiss her cheek again. She could hardly shrink away but she did manage to pinch me behind the knee. "See you at home darling."

Sharon smiled graciously, but there was an intensity behind it that belied her lack of pleasure at my appearance. "Of course. Don't be late."

"Nice to meet you Bill." And for good measure I shook his hand again, then turned and walked away from the table gritting my teeth.

"Who was that?" Frances asked me.

"My wife, Sharon. She works for Cablestar."

"And the hunk?"

"A guy she works with from Dallas."

"I'd watch him. He reeks of danger."

"Thanks," I replied, glumly.

"Your wife is gorgeous."

"I know."

"You don't sound too enthusiastic."

"We're not speaking to each other actually. Had a bit of a tiff on the weekend."

"Some tiff."

"Yeah, well..."

"We're talking to Cablestar about coming on as an investor."

"Well, good luck with it." I drained the beer then grabbed a piece of bread. I realized I was feeling pangs of jealousy and then I looked at Frances and saw the wheels spinning around. "Forget it," I said.

"What?"

"You know perfectly well."

"Know what?"

"Having me involved with you would help with Cablestar's investment potential. Believe me, Sharon is about as cold-hearted as it gets when it comes down to dollars and cents. I doubt whether I'd have any influence at all. Just the opposite, in fact, given our recent relations."

"I wasn't suggesting anything of the kind, Bernie." But her look said otherwise.

"Okay." Just then the waiter brought our food and I dug in just for something to do and end the conversation and the direction it was taking. "Tell me about the show. This salmon is very good by the way."

"I knew it." Frances dabbed at her lips with her napkin. "The premise of the show is to be out there with it, kind of edgy where we go into an author's environment, follow them around, see where they hang out, where they drink, relax, that sort of thing. We're going to do panels, we're going to do readings, we're going to cover the tough topics, not shy away from the grit, you know?"

I forked some salmon into my mouth. "No, I don't."

Frances laughed. "I know. I'm not sure either to tell the truth. We'll be using a new digital video format that can go virtually anywhere in the palm of your hand. The idea is to give the show a little more relevance and immediacy."

"What do you want from me?"

"We are thinking about you as host."

"You can't be serious."

"Why not? You've got a professional acting background..."

"How did you know that?"

"We do our homework you know. We may be shooting on a shoestring but we're still professional. You are also good looking and quite charming and I think the camera will take to you."

"I'm more of a behind-the-scenes type actually."

"Maybe it's time to get out in the open, lay yourself on the line a bit."

"I do that every day."

"I'm sure you do."

And as she continued her pitch, I thought about what I was facing. We were about to go into print with the "blockbuster" summer reading issue. The printer demanded payment for an overdue invoice before the presses would roll. I couldn't blame him for that. Meanwhile, payroll loomed, I was three months behind in the rent and one of our computers had gone on the fritz. Not to mention, I had to put some money aside for postage, so we could mail the magazine out once it was printed. Sharon and I were in limbo and if I needed a financial bail-out, not that I'd ever asked her for money for the magazine but in any case, that would be out of the question under the circumstances. And I felt that my father was already doing more than enough for me on account of the law suit.

"How much did you say this gig paid?" Frances looked a bit startled. I'd interrupted her thoughts.

"Uh, about $3000 an episode, give or take."

"And how many episodes are there?"

"Fifty-two. We'd be running two new shows a week then bicycle them through the schedule."

"That's $156,000 a year."

"Right. But then there's no fancy schmancy stuff. You know, no limo, no private dressing room, all that jazz. Plus you'll have to do a lot of your own research and we expect you'll be able to pull in a lot of the interviews on the basis of your contacts. We figure you can open a lot of doors for the show and the channel too."

"What's the show called?"

"Well, *Bookology* naturally. If that's okay with you."

I leaned back in my chair and smiled. "I always knew that was a good title. Catchy."

"It is." Her face clouded momentarily. "Listen, there are no guarantees, okay? We have to do a test with you before a final decision is made."

"What the hey..." And I shrugged. "Listen, what kind of time commitment is there on this thing?"

"We'll be shooting two shows back to back on Saturday, if that works for you. So that will be a full day. Other than that, we'll have a couple of production meetings, one hour max, during the week."

"Just out of curiosity, how is this thing paying for itself?"

Frances wiped her plate clean with a piece of bread.

"Well, it's pretty straightforward actually. The channel gets five cents a subscriber based on how many subscribers there are for each of the cable systems that carry us. Right now, we've signed up with the two majors that, between them have, 2.5 million subscribers. That gives us ready made cash flow of $125,000 per month or $1.5 million a year. That's just seed money. In the case of *Bookology*, we have a sponsor for the entire show."

"Really? And who might that be?" She mentioned a name and I grimaced. A large discount retailer trying to horn in on the book business and every other business going in the retail market.

"I know, I know," she replied. "But they asked for you specifically."

"They asked for me?"

"Yep. And they're kicking in $500,000 to make the show go. So, any advertising we rack up is gravy."

"And you can make a channel work for such a small amount of money?"

She wiped her lips with her napkin, then crumpled it up on the table. "Well, it's all incremental like anything. We'll start off broadcasting maybe 16 hours a day and we'll have maybe half a dozen original shows. The rest will be licensed from other programmers or re-runs of old author interviews. We'll make it work. But *Bookology* is being positioned as our flagship show so there'll be a certain amount of publicity that goes along with that. We may require you to do appearances and show up at book launches, that sort of thing."

"I do that anyway."

"We'd heard you were a tough ticket."

"I've gotten a little more discriminating, that's all. You can't go to all of these things, it'd be insane. There's one practically every night."

"I know. You may have to do some stand-ups at these things. I mean, if you're there anyway. We also want to tie in the entertainment industry too. You know, movies based on books, adaptations, television tie-ins, that sort of thing."

"What about issues?"

"What sort of issues?"

"Like literacy. Encouraging people to read. Pushing our own books and authors in the school system so they get read by kids. Those sorts of issues."

"Perfect. That's what we want. Lots of ideas. We need you to put your personality on the show. Make it your own."

"I haven't got much personality."

"I don't think that's true, Bernie. So, what do you say? Willing to give it a go?"

I shrugged. "Why not? It's not every day I get offered 156K."

She stuck out her hand. I took it. Her handshake was powerful. It reminded me of Sharon. "Don't worry. We'll make you work for it. That's a promise." Before I took my hand away, I gave her my thoughtful look. She picked it up. "Something's up already, I see."

"I was just wondering... about the sponsor. Will there be any editorial interference? What if they don't like a particular topic? What if we do something on predatory pricing at the retail level and they're part of that story? Will they let it go or clamp down?" I gave her her hand back.

"I don't know. I have to be honest. We'll just have to see what comes up. That's the best answer I can give you. We do try and protect the editorial independence of all our shows but we have to be practical too."

"Okay. Play it by ear."

"Exactly." She signalled to the waiter who brought the bill. She handed over her credit card without even examining the tab.

"Sorry, but it's been a long day and I am a little tired. I know what you're thinking but I've eaten here often enough that I can practically calculate the bill to the penny. And I'm rarely wrong."

"I understand."

The waiter returned her card and she slipped it into her wallet which disappeared into her purse. Then she stood up.

"I'll call you in a day or two to set up the tryout. I think this is going to work out well. It was a pleasure meeting you. Stay and have a coffee, if you like." We shook hands again. "You won't mind being a media star, will you?"

"I don't know. We'll have to see."

Frances laughed. "Spoken like a true Libra."

I was impressed as I watched her walk out of the restaurant. Then I turned and saw Sharon and "commander" Bill, laughing together.

The light was on in the living room when I attempted to open Catherine's front door as quietly as possible. The stupid thing had a creak in it that would wake the dead. Didn't matter anyway. Eph sat reading. His head bobbed up immediately and his eyes narrowed into slits of rebuke.

"I'm sorry. I forgot to call."

He pursed his lips. The skin around his mouth tightened, then he blew out and nodded curtly as if agreeing with something he'd decided earlier on. All without my involvement, of course. "Sometimes I forget you're a grown man..."

"Well, I, uh..." He held up a hand, silencing me. I clammed up.

"...but then your behaviour belies your immaturity..."

"I'm sorry I didn't call. Honestly, something interesting came up at the last second and it just took over and I just forgot. Sorry."

"Nathan called. He wanted to know when you were coming home. He said that Sharon's been crying a lot."

"You could have fooled me," I said.

"What do you mean?"

"I mean, she was out on a date."

"How do you know that?"

I must admit he looked rather shrunken, sitting in the wingback chair but he still had a presence. I didn't trifle. "I saw her." I tossed my jacket over the back of a chair and sat down opposite him on the loveseat. "Listen, I don't like this, you know? I suppose it would be a moot point to observe that my marriage isn't perfect."

"No marriage ever is."

"Earlier this afternoon I got a call. It was from a woman who works for one of those new television channels. They're starting a book channel and they want me to host a show they're doing. She asked me if I could meet her for dinner. We met at Porretta's at seven and that's where I spotted Sharon in her tête à tête."

"I see." He'd remained motionless and expressionless, the layman's idea of a shrink.

"The type of guy I guess you'd call a hunk. Tall, athletic, good hair, white teeth, steely forelocks." He didn't bite at my feeble joke. "She said it was work but it didn't feel like it to me."

"Maybe that's all it was."

"I don't think so."

"Perhaps she felt entitled after your escapade."

"Goddammit, it wasn't an escapade. It was a bloody coincidence, that's all. A mistake."

"You never invited the girl?"

"No, I did not. And thanks for taking my side on this."

He showed a few teeth, those that weren't hooked to a bridge. "You're welcome." He paused and cleared his throat. The book was set aside. "I have to wonder, however..."

Oh no, here it came. That famous rumination. The noggin of supreme repute was being activated. "What?"

"How did she know how to find you in the first place? It is rather curious."

"I must have mentioned it to her."

"Mentioned?"

"In an email. I have no recollection of sending it but apparently, that's what happened." Eph's bushy brows had gone up and stayed up. He was waiting for an explanation. "We correspond from time to time, that's all."

"And?"

"And nothing. It's harmless, that's what it is. Nothing more."

"How did it start?"

"We met at the Cablestar Christmas party a couple of years ago and struck up a conversation. Charlotte is a very intelligent, warm woman with a wide range of interests and we just connected. We had a lot in common."

"That's it?"

"Just about. We began to correspond. Gradually it emerged her marriage was not the best. Her husband travelled a great deal. They spent less and less time together. No children and I guess she was looking for some companionship."

"And you?"

"The same," I admitted. "Sharon is very focused on her work. It consumes her. She works long hours, has had very little to do with the kids and I guess we've just been drifting a little bit, that's all. But it's nothing serious. We've gone through episodes here and there and we've always got back on track."

"You've been derailed this time," he said, drily.

"Yeah. Thanks for that. I don't know what Charlotte was thinking, honestly, I don't. I really wanted a break away, that's all. I just wanted to be on my own and relax, not have to think about anything or anyone, just get away from all the stress and write a little bit. Recharge and come back refreshed hopefully. And then, out of the blue, she showed up."

"And then Sharon."

"Right."

"Maybe she wanted to make it up to you."

"Who? Sharon?"

Eph nodded. "No slouch in the brains department, you know. Maybe she saw an opportunity for the two of you and took it, thinking it would be a lovely surprise."

"It was that all right." I leaned in a little closer. "I want you to know I have been faithful to her our entire marriage. I haven't strayed once nor have I been tempted. But I have to admit, I've been lonely like I've needed a friend and Charlotte filled that need for me. I never consciously expected it would get out of hand. I truly like Charlotte. And whether you believe it or not, I truly love Sharon."

Then Eph did an extraordinary thing. He patted me on the knee. "I know you do. Anyone can see it. That's why I knew she was the right one for you, even though I felt you were both too young. But the two of you made a believer out of me. And then the boys came along and I thought it was the best thing that could happen. I'd never seen you so purposeful. It was a balm."

"A bomb?"

"B-A-L-M," he enunciated whistling through his teeth.

"Ah, got it." I sighed. "Well, I'm glad we've had this little chat. You're ready to toss me out on my ear, I suppose. I forget to call about dinner, I don't make my bed, I'm being sued, my business is a mess, my personal life is a mess. It doesn't get much better than this."

"I need you as my personal labour coach. After all, you've been through it and I haven't. So, there's some time yet to make all the adjustments."

So, he'll honour my contract until the delivery and then I get traded to another team, I thought. Not like the good old days. No such thing as a lifetime deal anymore.

"Perfect. I don't suppose you think even this is a little odd?"

"What is?"

"My 78-year-old father asking me to be his labour coach? You're not the one having the baby, by the way. That would be Catherine."

"Some days it just feels like I am. Catherine's okay with this. She's had children before, after all. I want you there for me, someone to lean on."

I sighed. "I hope I can be of some use. I don't know what I'll be able to do, truthfully."

"Just being there will be a help."

I watched him for a moment in silence. His eyes flitted and his lips twitched. "Something else bothering you?"

He hemmed and hawed a bit, then broke into what I would describe as a foolish grin. As foolish as I'd ever seen on him. "This, uh, situation...it's a difficult adjustment."

"What situation? Or I should say, what other situation?"

"Sex."

"What about it?"

"The lack of it."

Something drained out of my face. It could have been blood. "Oh."

I wanted to slap that stupid grin off him. "It's just that I'm finding it harder than I thought going without. Funny, I don't remember that when you and Harry were born."

"You were too busy working to think about it." There was a hint of sarcasm in my tone but I don't think he picked up on it.

"Hmm, probably. I just want her to have that baby so we can get back to normal."

"Nothing is normal after having a baby."

"Well, it will be for me. I'm going to enjoy this immensely."

"Good. That's good to hear. By the way, you have to wait six weeks after the birth before resuming normal relations you know."

"Six weeks? I'm not sure if I can wait six weeks."

"You may have no choice."

"I think Catherine feels the same way. She can't wait to have sex again."

"Really?"

"Yes. We both miss it. A lot."

I feigned a yawn. Anything to get me out of this conversation. "Okay Casanova, I'm beat."

"I'm going to stay and up read for a bit."

"You should get your rest. You'll need it once the baby comes."

"That much I do remember. Between you and Harry, there wasn't much time to catch up on anything. One of you cried all night and the other cried all day. It was a perfect combination."

"Yeah, we planned it that way. Goodnight, Eph. And I am sorry about the dinner."

"That's okay. We'll have something to pick at for the next few days. It won't go to waste." I began to climb the stairs to my room. "Bernie?"

"Yeah."

"You might want to do something with the kids. I think they're missing you."

"Really?"

"Really."

"Even Sean?"

"You'd be surprised."

"Well, maybe we'll grab dinner and a show this weekend." Eph grunted. His idea of a get together was a philosophy lecture or a museum tour. I stripped off my clothes and took the time to hang them up, washed, brushed, then fell into bed, knowing the alarm would buzz all too soon.

# 30

The next morning, I scored maybe two baskets. Hugo gloated. I think I added a decade to his life. But I was barely awake and felt as if I hadn't slept at all which was close to the truth. He pointed to my eyes.

"The last time I saw bags like that, my wife was playing mah-jong with her friends."

"Ha. Ha. I'm just a little tired. I got to bed late last night."

He threw the ball down in disgust. "Ach, there's no point in playing anymore. There's no challenge."

"Since when have I ever been a challenge?"

"Let's go for a swim," he said abruptly and began to totter toward the locker room. I followed, like the guileless victim I knew myself to be.

I hadn't told Roberto about my new living arrangements. Not yet anyway. He was my partner and when it came down to it, a very decent guy, just easily distracted. He surprised me that morning and showed up early. I looked at him and he shrugged sheepishly as if he'd been caught playing hooky. I gave him the abbreviated version and he seemed genuinely upset. Being Italian and knowing the value he placed on family, I could see he hated to hear about this happening to anyone, especially someone he knew fairly well.

"I am sorry for your trouble," he said, and hung his head.

"Thank you."

"I hope you and Sharon work things out. You seemed to have a good marriage. And the children of course, they will suffer if this continues."

"Yeah."

"You need a cooling off period and then you can talk it out. This helps I think, you know? When Giovanna and I have a fight, it gets very hot very quickly.

And then it is done. We make up and things get back to normal. But always I remember never to say something you can't take back. Something hurtful that deeply wounds because then it will fester in her heart. That's when you know you are in trouble."

"I guess." He sighed as if he'd lost his best friend, then patted me on the back. "It will pass." And then he made his way to his desk and turned on his computer.

I thought about the TV deal and what it could mean to our bottom line. That alone could finance close to 50% of our operations and that meant we had a shot at being profitable for the first time. The financial situation was a confusing one. We couldn't get a bank loan or a business line of credit. No bank would touch us. However, in the past few years, I'd managed to accumulate some five different lines of credit that I juggled back and forth using one to pay the other but I was getting lost, trying to keep track of it all. Positive cash flow was required. It seemed every time I opened a bank account, I was offered a personal line of credit which I always took. And since I took it, I used it. I had also convinced Sharon to secure part of the house with a line as well. The house is mortgage free thanks to Sharon's "fabulous" salary. The account manager seemed so pleased we were securing part of our house, she threw in an unsecured line for the heck of it. Over time, whenever an application came in the door, I'd fill it out for the heck of it and send it in. For some reason, they were always approved and I'd managed to amass a fair amount of credit. On the down side, it didn't reflect well on my personal credit history because it demonstrated a huge amount of debt and liability. That, in turn, meant, a bank wouldn't touch us corporately because they always judged small businesses on the owner's credit history and debt level.

I explained until I was blue in the face that I needed these lines of credit to run my business but the bankers always looked at me sadly as if I had been misguided or damaged at birth. I also explained that, with corporate financing, I could retire these personal debts since they were business related. But no, it always came down to, don't call us. The irony being, of course, that the same banks were more than willing to see me mired in personal debt and had no trouble handing out personal lines of credit like they were candy. I tried endlessly to figure out a way to get out from under this paper tower I'd built. It threatened to cave in on my head. Such was the world of small-time publishing and big time corporate finance.

Frances Schwartz called. My TV tryout lay two days hence. She'd be sending over a draft of the script for me to peruse so I had some familiarity with it before going on camera. I admit that I missed my own house and bed. I missed sleeping with Sharon. Not just the sex but the closeness of a warm, perfumed body nearby, was comforting. I'd always felt that the two of us together formed a unit and we could face just about anything. And now, split asunder, I just didn't know. I felt a greater lack of confidence than ever before. Maybe this was a test to see if I could be self-reliant. Perhaps, I'd end up in a better place, be a stronger person? Then why did I feel so discombobulated? So miserable, if the truth be known? And hearing about my father's physical needs didn't help any. I should be grateful that he's still able and willing. That boded well for me when I got to that stage. But still, it was unsettling to hear it for the first time.

Later that morning when I went to the loo, I passed Schwilden in the hall. He gave me a sardonic look but said nothing. We passed each warily, but in silence. I sensed a grim humour in his eyes as if he were thinking about a joke only he would understand. He turned into his unit. Nicely turned out in Hugo Boss as usual. But I noticed too, dark circles under the eyes, a tightening of the skin along the cheekbones and frown lines that hadn't been visible before. A fleeting impression only and I didn't give it a great deal of thought. After all, I had my own issues to deal with, his lawsuit being one.

Ruth answered the phone, put the caller on hold and called out:

"Your shyster on line one."

Annoyed, I picked it up. "Nice manner your receptionist has," Gloria Martinez said.

"I apologize for Ruth. She must have woken up on the wrong side this a.m."

"Not just this morning, I assure you Bernie. I hope I'm not disturbing you?"

"Uh no, not really."

"I just wanted to let you know they've dropped their offer to settle by $25,000. They're looking for $175,000 but it can be spread over two years."

"Great. That is generous of them."

"You speak sarcastically I'm assuming."

"You assume correctly."

"I thought you might respond that way but I have to run it by you anyway. Listen Bernie, I did explain about this fast track system now?"

"Briefly."

"Well, the gist of it is this. The courts are trying to settle these cases more quickly. They're not allowing the defendants to drag them out like in the past. All of the case numbers go into a pool and a bunch are picked randomly to go fast track. Well, our number came up."

"Great," I said with weak enthusiasm, then paused. "I don't think much of their offer."

"Neither do I. So, I will draft up a reply and send you a draft first for approval. Meanwhile, in the next few weeks, we'll need to get together to prepare for the arbitration."

"When will that be?"

"I'm not sure. We are given a list of names of arbiters and we get to pick the ones we want and submit that to the Master of the court. He then selects one of the names on the list unless both sides are in agreement. Then you have to cough up $500 bucks which is the fee for three hours work"

"That's not bad."

"No, it's not. A lot of lawyers are specializing in arbitration now. It's relatively easy and there's not a lot of paperwork and the hours are yours. So, it's not bad at all."

"Well, you'll keep me posted."

"I will. And when this is over, I'll treat you to dinner and a few drinks. How's that?" Her voice took on a sultry hue.

"Well Gloria, that's a wonderful offer. I'll look forward to that."

"You can tell me all about the world of publishing."

"Sure."

She rang off. Was I being hustled by my lawyer?

I received the "script" Frances Schwartz sent over by a particularly surly courier. He just growled at me, thrust the package in front of my nose and the waybill, huffing impatiently while I signed. He snatched it from my hand and strode out as if he had better things to do. Well, excuse me.

It seemed obvious that Roberto had blabbed to everyone about my current domestic problem. Jessica looked at me with sympathy and even patted my hand which came as a shock since there'd been no physical contact between us at all. Ruth sneered at me with a "serves you right" kind of look that made me wonder why I was the object of such enmity. All I had done was give her a job when few would and keep her employed when most wouldn't. Is that why I was subject to such contempt? I could feel their eyes following me about the office. I was tempted to seek refuge in the bathroom, but then I might run into Schwilden and who knows what would happen then?

To avoid the obvious interest I generated, I grabbed the script and went downstairs to the café for a cup of tea so I could read in peace. Except music blared and a few video monitors had been set up with some promotional bumpf running on a continual loop that distracted and annoyed me. Well, I had a cup of tea anyway. After reading for a few moments, I realized my demeanour had taken a fall. The "script" was lousy, silly, clichéd, artificially forced in its cheeriness and full of schtick. And that was the best I could say about it. I thought the text should exude a dry sort of wit that had a bit of an edge. I think that was the sort of thing book lovers would find appealing and attract that younger audience everyone wanted. In the 200-channel universe, you had to do something to stand out, I reasoned. Apart from going on air naked which some were doing anyway, how else might you attract attention? Why not appeal to their intelligence and sense of humour? You might say I knew nothing about broadcasting, and that was true, but then the content of *Bookology* was deliberately designed to be provocative, within the realm of good writing and detailed research, of course. If this show bore our name, my name, then it should reflect the same attributes, shouldn't it? I don't know with whom I was arguing exactly but tussled mentally. When I heard some giggling, I looked up and saw two young women covering their mouths and glancing at me, then away again. We traded looks back and forth for a moment. Finally, I got up and approached.

"What's so funny?" I asked. I was in a combative mood.

One was blond and the other brunette.

"We don't mean to be rude," the blonde said. "But you looked so funny. Like you were having this deep conversation with yourself. We could almost tell what you were thinking."

"It was kind of neat actually," chimed in her companion. "First you'd say something and then you'd answer it like you didn't agree with the first thing, but you didn't say a word. And you didn't have to."

"So you found it entertaining?" They both nodded and giggled. "What if I told you there was a channel on cable that is being devoted to just this sort of thing? Hidden conversations we're calling it? I was just rehearsing."

"Really?" exclaimed the brunette. "That is so cool."

"What channel?" asked her friend. "When is it going to be on? Is it like a psychic kind of thing?"

I tapped my temple. "I'll have to get back to you on those details." I went back to my table to continue my conversation, wondering if it was so obvious and did I do that all the time in my work environment without realizing? How embarrassing.

That evening I came home on time for dinner, only to discover everyone had gone out. My father had been considerate enough to leave a note on the fridge. They were visiting friends for dinner but they'd left some leftover chicken. I wasn't terribly hungry and rooted around for a drink. I found a single beer, alone and forgotten in the vegetable crisper. Reluctantly, I pulled out the chicken and the fixings for a small salad as I drank the beer. Catherine's kitchen was rather small, not like mine at home. Limited counter space, more of a working kitchen really with just enough room for a small table and two chairs. Most of the eating went on in the dining room. It was a cozy house but I felt caged. As I tossed the salad and looked for some palatable dressing, the phone rang. I debated about answering it. After all, it wasn't my house and it was doubtful the call was for me anyway. But its insistent tone encouraged me.

"Hello," I said, wearily.

"Who was she?" Sharon.

"Who was who?"

"That woman."

"What woman?" I was tired and confused. Yesterday seemed a long time ago. "And hello to you too by the way."

"At Porretta's."

"Oh. Right. Just a business thing, that's all. I'm trying out for a new television show. Besides which, you are asking me to believe that guy you were with was strictly business?"

"Of course, it was," she replied haughtily as if I had the right to question her, not in the least. "I'd forgotten he was flying in and had made the commitment."

"Whatever. Why are you calling? Just to harangue me?"

"That's right." And she abruptly hung up. I heard the dial tone buzzing in my ear and hung up with a small sense of satisfaction. A modicum only, but being satisfied didn't solve the problem, just made me feel a bit better and only temporarily. The phone rang again. Aha, I thought.

"Dad?"

"Oh. Hi Nathan. What's up?"

"When are you coming home?"

"I'm not sure. When your mother forgives me."

"What did you do?"

"It's complicated."

"Tell me."

"She thought I was seeing someone else."

"Were you?"

"No."

"Then how did she get that idea."

"I told you, it's complicated."

"Come on, tell me." And his voice took on that strident tone. "I need to know."

I tried to figure quickly what the right balance between knowledge and information should be in this instance and became flummoxed. "I'll explain it to you later."

"Bernie. Tell me now."

"Don't call me, Bernie. I'm your father."

"You won't be unless you get your ass back to this house."

"Oh, that's nice. You're going to disown me is that it?"

"That's right. You've got it."

"Forget it. I disown you first."

"You can't do that."

"I just did."

"It doesn't happen that way," he insisted.

"Well, how does it happen, smart guy?"

"I don't know. But I don't think it's like that."

"Listen, you guys want to do dinner and a show this weekend?"

"Sure. There's new kung-fu movie I'd like to see."

"Well, clear your schedule. We'll do it Saturday. I'll pick you up around four. Tell your brother, okay?"

"Yeah. Bye."

Kung-fu movie? Yeah, I suppose I could get into that. It'll be kicks.

# 31

The morning of the audition, I awoke remarkably clear-headed. I knew things were going well when I scored 16 points in 21. Hugo looked at me in surprise, even awe as I sunk six baskets in a row from all angles. Normally, I could hit from the free throw line and from the right side. On the left I was hopeless. I don't know why.

"What is going on with you?" Hugo asked me. "You must have had good sex last night, huh?"

I shrugged, trying to make a joke of it. "I wish."

"Ah, come on. A young fellow like you. The sex should always be good."

"I suppose so."

Hugo tossed the ball up in the air a few times, then over to me. "Let's go again. See what you can do."

The second game I went a point better. Hugo looked even more surprised, almost stunned as we went neck and neck. At one point, we were tied at 15 each.

"You are starting to worry me," he said. "If there was one thing I could count on, it was beating you in 21. Other than that, nothing was for sure. You know what I'm saying?" I nodded solemnly. "I can't be sure I will be able to take a piss or a good shit or have an erection. I don't know if I will be able to get out of bed, I might have a heart attack at my young age. But I always knew I could beat you, Bernie Goldman, in 21. And now you have shaken my faith a little bit. Ach, well, it serves me right for taking things for granted." Then he pivoted and pushed the ball into the air and watched with a smile of satisfaction as it swished through the hoop. "But then, the hard-fought victories are always the best, yes?"

"If you say so."

He clapped me hard on the back. "I do say so, Bernie, I do." and I wasn't at all certain if he was referring to a simple game or something else from his past.

Nonetheless, I remained fairly buoyant as I bounced into the office that morning humming a Bach concerto I'd heard on the radio. Nobody else was in. I switched off the alarm, amazed that I remembered the code, dumped my bag in a chair, flipped on my computer, then plugged in the kettle. I was on after lunch, around two pm at the studio, Dead Snake Video, down on Bleecker Street, in the city's south end.

I had worked or rather re-worked the "script" yesterday and last evening, re-jigging it while attempting to watch a British cop show on public television. Afterward, there was an interview show with writers that I had frequently watched but never paid attention to except when someone had been on that interested me. I had been on the show once when the producers were doing a retrospective on the most popular Canadian writers. I had been called in as a sort of expert to give some feedback on a survey we'd run in one of the issues of *Bookology*. Wild hair, had been one popular reason for being one of the chosen as well as a surplus of profanity for another. Solid reasons both, I thought, each as valid as the other. Of course, the television audience ate it up but the host seemed amused, wanting the meatier stuff. "Well, there are the stories and the quality of the writing, I suppose," I had offered and been given a fleeting smile for my troubles. The fellow had switched to someone else after that, asking them all the questions I could have answered with my eyes closed, my ears plugged and my mouth full of marbles. Some people really are peevish, aren't they? Well, if I got this gig, I wouldn't play it that way at all. I'd determined that it should be fun and entertaining. I also knew that I had better contacts than virtually anyone else and that the publicists who sent us review copies would twist the arms of all their star clients to get them on the show. We had a double whammy, a TV vehicle and a well-respected national magazine that was sent to booksellers as well as the general public. I wouldn't say titles were picked up as a result of what we said but I'd be confident in saying we had some influence with the book buyers from the public and the trade. Now that I'd stoked my ego, I was ready to conquer the medium of mediocrity. After all, I could be just as mediocre as the best of them, couldn't I?

The video studio had formerly been a factory now converted with the entrance through the loading dock. You climbed a set of metal stairs on to a ramp. At the back of the loading dock, stood a moveable wall held in place by a metal clamp. When you flicked one arm of the clamp the wall opened up like a big door. In fact, that's what it was. Frances met me on the loading dock. When she tugged on the "door", a buzzing hive unfolded beyond. Technicians scurried about pulling cables, hanging lights, moving the studio cameras into position. Three women worked on dressing the set, giving it a comfy yet modern look and feel. A set of steel bookcases in the background looked like they'd been forged out of some burnished metal, a low black lacquered coffee table and two sling back chairs. Off to the right, a counter had been positioned along with several stools made up to look like a bar. That's appropriate, I thought, since most writers I knew felt very at home in bars.

"Wow," I exclaimed. "The place is humming."

"It's always hectic," Frances said. "It wouldn't be normal otherwise. Let me introduce you to our director. Vince, Vince," she called. A lean, dark-haired man looked up. He'd been in a small group huddled around one of the cameras. He put his finger up as if to say, just a minute, then ducked his head down again. "Camera shots."

"What?"

"They're going over the shots," she repeated.

I felt nervous, and my stomach buzzed. Consequently, I'd had little to eat, a piece of fruit and some bottled water but I could feel the flow of adrenaline coursing through me. It's just a performance, I told myself, like most things are. The difference is, you will be talking into a camera and somewhere on the other side thousands of people will be watching. Otherwise, there's no difference. You know what that's like. You've done it all before.

"Sorry about that," the dark-haired man said. He put out his hand. "Vince Brassard."

"Bernie Goldman." His grip was firm and his palms callused. Maybe he still pulled his own cables?

"Good to meet you, Bernie. How are you feeling? Are you up for this?" Vince revealed a tight smile and a set of jagged teeth that gave him a wolfish look.

"Absolutely."

"Good." He slapped me on the back. "That's good. Look, I've got to get back to the crew and finish setting up. We'll call you in a few minutes, okay?"

"Sure." He nodded at Frances and headed back to the huddle.

"He seems capable," I remarked.

"Vince is a very talented director. He started off in commercials. He's in great demand. We were lucky to get him He's only 27, you know." Frances sighed, as if life had been unfair to her. I put her in her early thirties at most. Twenty-seven now seemed a long way off. The boys would have been just five then.

I touched Frances on the arm. She turned her attention from the hubbub and looked up at me. "Listen, I took the liberty, I mean, I hope you don't mind, of making a few amendments to the script."

"You changed the script?" There was a slight flare to her nostrils.

"Right."

"But they've cued it up already."

"Pardon?"

"On the teleprompter. So you won't fluff your lines."

"Well, I guess I'll have to wing it a bit then. Do you think that will be a problem?"

Frances' face turned inward into a frown.

"I don't know actually. We'll have to see. You're asserting your independence, I see."

I shrugged. "I'm a writer but also an editor too. It's in the blood, I suppose."

She patted me on the arm.

"Well, we're not interested in the status quo, are we? If we want to be successful, we'll have to be provocative. Right?"

"I couldn't agree more."

"So, we'll see what you've got."

"Uh-huh," I replied with more confidence than I felt.

"Why don't we get you into make-up?" she suggested. "You're looking a bit shiny."

Vince stood behind one of the cameras. His voice came out of the dark, like I imagined God's might, except this voice seemed a bit higher-pitched. "Move around the set and get comfortable with it, Bernie, okay? I want you to get your bearings. We can't have you wandering, I'm afraid, during the take. It's better if you're stationary but there is a definite perimeter that's been set up." I wandered around the set as he suggested, more to get the jitters out than anything else. I could feel my throat constricting and I opened my mouth and swallowed that ended in a yawn. It was a relaxation technique I had learned years ago. Yawning increased the flow of oxygen as well as opening up and relaxing the throat. If your throat stayed tight, you'd dry up and squeak instead of talk.

"We want you on the stool front and centre."

"Uh Vince, could we try something a little bit different? Something that might help set the tone a bit for the future?"

"Like what?" came the voice, a bit skeptical now and clearly annoyed.

"Well, something like this." I went to the back of the set and removed my jacket and set it on top of the faux counter. I hadn't really done this with any regularity since high school but I'd practiced the day before. Facing the wall, I went up on my hands, legs perfectly straight and walked into the light, talking as I went. "Welcome to *Bookology*, the show about books that will literally turn this delightful topic on its head." I came out of the handstand, sat on the stool and, with as much energy as I could muster, smiled out into the darkness.

"Books invented sex and violence. There isn't a topic invented by humans that hasn't been written about in a book. I invite you all to come and explore with me the provocative, stimulating, exciting world of books on this show. You will see the authors you admire and perhaps the ones you despise, talk meaningfully about their work. We'll go out to book signings, book stores, out into the streets where writing and writers dwell. We'll bring the world of the imagination to you. All you have to do is sit back and enjoy it. Or is it? Part of the format of this show includes audience participation. You will have the opportunity to speak directly with your favourite authors and for those of you who are online, you can follow along by logging on to our Website at www.bookology.com. Stick around, we have a demanding and stimulating show for you." Then I rose from the stool and stepped toward the back of the set. I paused for a moment, grabbed a glass of water that was sitting on the counter and took a large gulp. A few drops ran off my chin. I retraced my steps and shaded my eyes against the light. "Well, what did you think?" There had been complete silence.

"Lenny," said Vince. "Did you get that on tape."

"Yup," came the reply from the fellow I supposed was Lenny.

"Let's take a look."

Frances emerged out of the darkness with a pensive smile.

"Well, that was different."

"Uh-huh."

"I didn't know you were so athletic."

"I'm not really. I was just pretty good in gymnastics in high school. It had the desired effect, I think. We don't want a show just for eggheads, do we? We want to popularize it a bit, right?"

She bit her lip. "Mmm, possibly. Why don't we take a look?"

A group of people, Vince in the centre, huddled around a monitor. It was quite astonishing, really, seeing your image on a screen. I didn't think it looked or sounded like me at all. Yet when I gazed about, there wasn't anyone else who fit the bill. The group viewed the intro in silence. After a pregnant pause, Vince said, "Right. Let's do it again."

"What? Why again?"

"Camera angle was off and your mike slipped a bit. If you're going to do a gymnastics routine, we need to anchor it a bit more securely, okay? Come on people, time is money."

In all, we redid the opening another five times. I am convinced it happened that way to teach me a lesson. That Vince wanted me to know that I wasn't to take any liberties without his say-so or at least, at his suggestion. At one point after Take Three, he asked sarcastically, "what's next, cartwheels?" The crew burst out in laughter. So, of course, I had to oblige them to a round of applause I might add. After the fifth time, my arms went wobbly and my breathing laboured.

"Sheila," Vince called, "Touch him up a bit, will you? If we get any more glare, I'll have to pass out sunglasses."

The make-up lady applied a powder puff to my face.

"There you go, lovey," she said. "Now you won't blind anyone." They were all cards in this business.

The camera followed me as if I were right side up and then flipped around when I landed on my feet. Afterward, Vince took me by the elbow and walked me away from the milling crowd.

"That was a pretty cute idea you had there."

"Thanks," I replied, obviously pleased with myself, but I had misread him.

His grip tightened. "Do that again and I will throttle you personally, get it? You want to try out new ideas? Fine. But you go through me, understand? And if you don't, I will do everything in my power to make you look like a complete idiot and embarrass you in front of thousands of people, some of whom may be your friends and relatives. Do we understand each other?"

I stared at him, this kid barely out of short pants, and wondered where that came from. "I think we do, yes." Egotistical bastard, I thought.

Vince relaxed, even managed a flicker of a smile.

"Good. You don't know how cutthroat this business is. I've got to stay on top and if I don't, there are five hundred guys waiting to take my place."

"Wouldn't it work better for you and me too, if we collaborated rather began in an antagonistic way."

He waved at the air.

"Oh, I agree completely but I have to let you know where I'm coming from, right? Anyway, I think you did pretty well, I mean, not bad for an amateur. I think we got something we can use, you know, show the big boys and let them make a decision."

"I'm so glad."

He nodded and walked briskly back to his production team who still huddled around one of the monitors laughing at something or other. Frances came up looking flushed. She looked over her shoulder.

"What did Vince want?"

"Oh, just to congratulate me on a job well done, or so he said."

She put her hands on her hips, that made her look a bit schoolmarmish, if you could say that about a young woman dressed in black stretch pants and patent leather boots.

"Is that what he said? Really?"

"Really."

"You don't have to cover for him, you know. I know how paranoid he can be. He's pissed off because he didn't think of your little stunt. And why would he? No one knew you could walk on your hands."

"I'd almost forgotten about it too. It's been so long."

"Well, it was a pretty neat trick. It really got everyone's attention, I can tell you, but let's not push it too far. Before you know it, Vince will have you crossing Yonge Street on a tightrope while interviewing Salman Rushdie."

"That could be a challenge. I happen to know he is a tough interview," I replied.

"Don't be so damn smug."

"I am not, believe me, I am not. Smugness is not me. I've taken too many shots for that."

"You don't look battered and bruised."

"Kind of you to say so." Then I glanced at my watch.

"Is that a hint?"

"I should get back to the office. God knows what's been going on these past few hours."

"Probably not much," she said.

"That's what I'm afraid of."

Frances walked me to the door.

"Thanks for coming down. I think you impressed everyone."

"Oh, I don't know about that."

"Don't be so modest. Anyway, we'll talk it over with the money guys and get back to you. I think you've got the production team on your side and that counts for a lot, believe me. They seemed pretty stimulated today. Give us a couple of days to get back to you."

"You're trying out others?"

She nodded. "A few. But I'd give you a better than even chance at this point." Frances touched my arm, then giving me a secret little smile I couldn't interpret, backed away, cupping her hand as she went.

# 32

I unlocked my car and was about to start the engine when a Porsche pulled into the parking lot and a sleek-looking fellow, who greatly resembled Eric Schwilden, climbed out. He didn't glance in my direction but I'm sure I recognized the suit, the hair, the cocky swaggering gait as he disappeared inside the studio. Typical of him, he took up two parking spots. Thoughtfully, I started the engine, then drove slowly away.

I felt elated and a bit dirty at the same time. I couldn't get over the feeling I'd prostituted myself. As if I needed or wanted more time commitments. At this rate, I'd never get either book finished nor attain the peace and tranquillity I sought. My loafability quotient dropped daily. I'd been seduced by the money, I admit. The money would bail out the magazine and put us both on the map in a way. Profile could never hurt, I supposed, except when you tried to get things done and got away from them at the same time. Does that make any sense? And then I had to wonder, appearing on channel 77 in a 500-channel universe, does that constitute fame?

Saturday morning, I had a quick nosh with Nook. Ramon was still AWOL and neither of us had heard from him. By now, Nook knew fully of my situation. He'd sussed it out when I didn't have the bag of bagels with me. Catherine didn't like bagels, can you imagine? I knew there was a reason we didn't get along. My father had to watch his cholesterol and could only eat one or two a week at most. I really bought them for the boys who gobbled them up like cookies.

"It isn't the high holidays," Nook said.

"I know."

"So, did you forget where the bakery was?"

"No."

"So?"

"I'm living with my Dad. Temporarily."

I had never seen Nook look shocked. On his face it just didn't go but this was as close as I'd ever seen. His eyebrows shot up and his mouth dropped. And then, of course, I explained the whole thing to him and to his credit he didn't pass judgement.

"That's rough," he said.

"Yeah."

"I'm sure you'll patch it up. The two of you are so sympatico."

"That sounds like Ramon."

"I know. That's why I said it but it's also true, you are. I can't imagine you or Sharon with anyone else."

"That's a good thing. I just don't know how to make a start, break the ice."

"Why don't you send her flowers?"

"Flowers?"

Nook nodded, then blew on his mochaccino.

"Women like flowers. It couldn't hurt to send some, could it?"

"I suppose not. I've got nothing to lose, anyway. Actually, I could bring flowers. I'm picking up the boys for dinner and a movie tonight."

"Seems like an ideal opportunity," Nook said quietly. "Why not use it?"

"I don't even know if I'll see Sharon."

"Doesn't matter. As long as she knows they're from you."

On my way over to the house, I stopped in at Denby's, a flower shop that had been around for eons and picked up a dozen long-stemmed roses. Carrying them under my arm, I admit I felt my pulse quicken and a dryness in my throat as I approached my own door. It seemed so strange to have been away. It had been barely two weeks and yet seemed like a lifetime.

Nathan flung open the door. "Bernie!" he screamed and flung his arms around me.

"Hi Nate," I said, in a muffled tone. "Hey, hey, watch the flowers." Sean hovered in the background.

"'Lo Dad," he intoned, and he slapped my palm.

"Are those for me?" Nathan asked. I made a face. "Okay, Bernie, now don't get upset. I was just joking. Do you want me to stick those in some water for you?"

"Is Mom here?" Nathan shook his head and Sean just shrugged. "Oh well. Sure, why don't you do that? Find a nice vase and put them on the dining room table."

I stood on the threshold and looked around. Everything was as it always had been except shiny and clean, spotless. Not a pillow out of place. I saw Mrs. Sanchez in the living room. She looked up and stared at me briefly, with extreme malevolence, I might add. Thinking what had I done to Sharon to upset her so. And whatever happened, it was obviously my fault. I nodded to her and she turned away disappearing into the kitchen. So much for my charm. Sean slouched against the wall, hands in his pockets.

"So, what's shaking?" he asked.

I shrugged. "Oh, you know, the usual. Work, living with your Zaidy, waiting for your step-buby to give birth, that sort of thing."

Sean grinned. "Yeah, that's kind of cool. Good to know the Goldman's still have the juice at that age. Way to go Zaidy." He raised his fists in the air.

"You've got a future," I said. "In the fertility industry. Never forget that."

He cocked a finger at me. "Don't worry, I won't." And then he laughed softly to himself, enjoying the joke.

A study in contrasts, these two. As we were driving to the theatre in the car, Sean piped up. "So, Pops, you gonna make it up with Mom or what?"

I considered the question. He stared at me intently with a bit of a smirk on his face. He was visible in the rear view, positioned so he could admire himself. "I hope to. Just so you both know, I love Mom very much. This is all painful."

"You gonna apologize?"

"I don't know."

Nathan followed this exchange silently.

"I wouldn't."

"Wouldn't what?"

"Apologize. Not to a girl anyway."

"What?"

"You heard me," he insisted.

"Where's this coming from?"

"You just don't apologize to women," he said.

"Why not?"

"'Cause they'll walk all over you, that's why," he replied and shrugged his shoulders as if everybody knew that. "Come on, Pops. Get in the groove."

"What if you were wrong?"

"So?"

"You still wouldn't apologize? Not even if what happened was your fault?"

"Probably not. It's a pride thing."

"Pride? Stupidity more like it. Where did you learn this shit? From your friends. From television?"

"Everybody knows it. So, you gonna apologize or what?"

I kept my eyes on the road while considering his question.

"It's not that simple."

"Why not?" Nathan looked at me as if daring me to give some sort of an excuse.

"It was circumstances, a misunderstanding, that's why. I need to convince Mom it was all a mistake and she misunderstood. I need to tell her how much I miss her and how I hate not being at home."

I found the parking lot, pulled into the entrance and grabbed a ticket. Everything was automated these days, including the parking lot. I'd have to pay at a machine on the way out. The film we came to see was a remake of the cult classic, Planet of the Apes. The kids had been talking about it for months and it had opened the week before. I anticipated a large line but when I saw it extended around the block, my heart sank. We got a place in line, then I went to buy the tickets. Thank god, this was one of the old movie theatres that had extra capacity seating and a big screen. The theatre, the Fairmont, held at least 2000 people, possibly more. They'd want popcorn and drinks though. I fretted about getting decent seats.

Half an hour later, we began to move. Inside, I made a beeline for the balcony and we managed to snag three seats in the second row. Not bad. Then I took the food and drink orders and went to fight the hordes. Was this the deal for weekend Dads? This activity took another 20 minutes before I stumbled back to our seats in the dark, just as the first trailer came up.

"Psst. Dad. Up here." I noticed Nathan's yellow baseball cap. It turned out to be the only distinguishing feature that I could make out in the dark. I sat down with a sigh and handed round the treats.

"Thanks Pops," said Sean then shoved a handful of popcorn into his mouth a fist at a time. I began to wonder whose child he actually was.

I loved the theatre, its size, the sweep of its lines, the presence of the screen and the upgraded sound system. The audio seemed to be talking directly into your ears. Absolutely no chance I'd be able to slide down in my seat and slip into unconsciousness for a while. The film track boomed, full of shrieks, grunts and the beating of chests. A macho type film, full of fantasy, perfect for two in the midst of early adolescence. I endured it but I experienced no enjoyment, seeing none of the cleverness or intrigue I'd discovered in the original. But then I celebrated nostalgia rather than the actual modern-day qualities injected into cinema today, with its special effects and prosthetics. The whole thing just seemed silly to me. But Sean and Nathan burbled excitedly, when, some two hours later, the lights finally came up and we saw drink containers and popcorn boxes littering the floor. I blinked, then smiled at the two of them. Nathan stretched while Sean jumped onto his seat and did a monkey dance. I looked around nervously as other patrons pointed and laughed. I spotted an usher making his way quickly up the aisle.

"Okay Sean, get off the seat now." I pulled him down.

"What'd you do that for?"

"You were wrecking the seat and the management here doesn't appreciate it." I pointed to the usher who had stopped mid-way and stared at us unblinking, arms crossed while patrons flowed around him. His biceps bulged under his short sleeve knit shirt.

"Who cares, Pops? You think they'll throw us in jail?"

"Let's go."

We followed the crowd in silence until they led us out into the early evening light.

"Where'd you park?" Nathan asked, always concerned about those details.

"Just down the street but the restaurant we're going to is just a couple of blocks over."

The three of us trudged along in silence for a few moments but silence wasn't Sean's forte and he stuck his foot out in front of Nathan who stumbled.

"You asshole." Nathan pushed him and Sean pushed back and before I knew it, they were grappling on the sidewalk. I forced myself between them.

"Stop it, you fools." I glared at Sean. "What'd you start for? Can't you even walk down the street without causing a problem?"

He grinned at me. "Apparently not, Pops. What're you going to do about it? Ground me?" I felt like grabbing him by the throat and lifting him in the air. Well, perhaps, the ape movie had affected me, after all. But I was annoyed in the extreme.

"We'll see about that. Now cut the crap or I'm dropping you off home." As I turned to continue, Nathan delivered a short, quick jab to the meat of Sean's shoulder. Sean was about to retaliate when I turned back and he stopped, shoving his hands in his pockets. "And that goes for you too. Both of you."

We continued on and I suddenly realized this was their normality. Their dynamic. Sean instigated. Nathan responded. They mixed it up. One or both got hurt. Until the next time. It never changed and it never stopped. Except Sean became more and more unpleasant, less and less likable.

I took them to Pisarro's, a family-run Italian restaurant that served good food at decent rates, not cheap but decent. They catered to families and prided themselves on astoundingly swift and efficient service. Over the course of a meal, you might be served by six or seven different staff and they really hustled. The boys ordered individual pizzas, Hawaiian for Sean and pepperoni double cheese for Nathan, I had a small Caesar salad, pasta and seafood in a garlic sauce and a beer. A local microbrewery I favoured, Sleeman's. The two were slightly more subdued but not much and amused themselves by grabbing bread off each other's plate. I started to stand up when simultaneously they each shoved the remaining morsels into their mouths and stared down, looking ashamed. It was a brilliant act and despite my irritation, I laughed. That broke the ice. To emphasize the point, I reached under the table, grabbed each of their hands by the wrist and squeezed. They grimaced. "That's enough all right? Behave yourselves and I might even buy you ice cream after. But you must be good little boys." I released them and they rubbed their wrists but Sean grinned insolently.

"Nice grip, Pops," he said.

They behaved themselves reasonably well after that but nothing had changed since they were small. The interaction remained depressingly the same. A sign of affection, I supposed. Although remarkably different in looks and temperament, they were about as close as you can get. They had a special relationship I didn't understand entirely.

We walked back to the car. The boys took turns swinging on lamp posts. I bought them an ice cream from a gelato place and we sat outside as they ate. I told myself I was watching my weight and refrained. Nathan leaned into me and put his arm on my shoulder. This made me nervous. He was a messy eater and I figured I'd be wearing the rich fudge chocolate down my shirt. Gently, I eased him off.

"Until you finish your ice cream," I said. Sean behaved the same way with Sharon. Whenever we went anywhere, he'd be draped all over her. Sharon only tolerated this behaviour from him. I had permission to put my arm around her lightly but lean in with my weight? Never. She was more affectionate with Sean, possibly because he looked the Irishman in the family, appealing to something deep inside her. I'd didn't want to psychoanalyze it but then, Sean could get her goat faster than anyone else too. Apart from Felicity, of course.

"How's your Gran doing?"

"Good," Nathan said, grinning with chocolate all over his teeth and lips. "She's walking with a cane."

"Yeah. She whacked me with it too," Sean added.

"And why'd she do that?"

"'Cause I farted at the table." And this brought the two of them into paroxysms of laughter. I had to admit, it was pretty funny. That was my problem with Sean. In so many ways he was perverse but could be comical too. And he enjoyed this perverseness, took such pleasure in it, that I found it difficult to take as seriously as I should.

I checked my watch. Getting on nine. I hurried them up and we made it back to the car with no incidents. They stayed quiet on the way, until I pulled up into the driveway. Sharon's Navigator hunkered there.

"Bye Dad," Nathan said, and he gave me a hug. "Thanks for the dinner and show."

"Yo Pops," and Sean gave me his hand like a brother. "Thanks a bunch." They popped out of the car and scrambled up the walk. Nathan let them in with his key. Sean had probably lost his. They talked to each other, oblivious of everything and everyone else. The door slammed. It was an odd and empty feeling to be shut out of your own home, where your children were growing up. Where you'd taken walks or gone to the park and read the paper. I felt a grumble of sadness in my belly.

I drove home listening to a jazz station on the radio.

When I came through the door, Eph was waiting for me. He had a worried look on his face.

"It's time," he said.

"What? Now?" Eph nodded. "Where's Catherine?"

"Upstairs."

"Is she okay?"

"I think so?"

I looked closely at his face. He was frightened. "It's okay, Dad. She'll be fine. What's she doing?"

"Throwing a few things together."

"Okay."

I went up the stairs. "Catherine?"

"In here."

I located her in the obvious place. Her bedroom. She was stuffing things into an overnight bag. "You okay?"

"Apart from feeling like I've been kicked by a horse, you mean?"

"Yeah. Apart from that."

"Wonderful." And then she doubled over as the colour drained from her face. "Oh Shit, it's a live one all right."

"How far apart?"

"About four minutes."

I went to the bed and took the overnight bag and her small suitcase. "We'd better get going then, don't you think?"

She nodded, then tried to lift her head up. "Christ, I'm tired already." She managed to straighten up finally. "All right. Let's get this baby out of here."

I had to smile.

"After you."

She squeezed by me and her extended belly brushed my hip. Despite her obvious discomfort, I noticed an amused glint in her eye. At the top of the stairs, I called down. "Eph. Are you ready? Catherine's coming down now." There came a weak, muffled reply. Catherine used the banister, going down by the same foot, step by step. Eph met us at the bottom, looking very pale. His breathing came fast and shallow. "Are you okay?" He turned to me and nodded once attempting a ghoul's version of a grin. "All right then." I looked from one to the other. I didn't know who was in worse shape.

"Let's get to the hospital before something drastic happens."

"You mean, you don't want to deliver this baby in the car?" Catherine laughed, then flinched with pain.

"Only if I have to."

"Lock the door darling," Catherine said, gently.

"Yes, of course." My father reached into his pocket with his keys. "Have you got everything?" He turned to her in a patronly way. Catherine nodded. "I can't quite believe this is happening," he said to the air.

"You'll get used to it. Again," I replied. I carried the bags to my car and stowed them away in the trunk. I held the door for my father and then for Catherine who needed to sit in the front. It was awkward getting in the back of a two-door and Eph strained himself, squeezing in.

We drove to the hospital in silence punctuated by Catherine's groans and my father's murmurings of concern, although I wasn't entirely certain who they were for. I turned on the classical station to help ease the tension. It played Berlioz, not a terrific mood lifter. At that time of night and on a weekend, it took no more than 12 minutes to get to The Eastern Hospital, where Catherine was admitted right away. I parked temporarily in the circle drive normally reserved for ambulances and helped her out. "I'll bring the bags," I said. Eph went right to her side and took her left arm. We helped her inside where a nurse behind a plexiglass divider looked up at us, expectantly. Immediately, she stood up and came around. "How far apart, dear?" she said to Catherine.

"About three minutes now," I replied.

The nurse gave me a look. "Are you the husband."

I hesitated. Then Eph spoke up. "No, I am. The husband." The nurse looked him up and down. He'd forgotten to put shoes on and was wearing his carpet slippers. His bony ankles stuck out at the bottom of an old pair of chinos that were threadbare and far too short. He looked like a rumpled escapee from a retirement home. "Well, good for you," the nurse retorted. I could see Catherine was about to say something when her face erupted into a spasm of pain.

"Come on, dear. Let's get you settled, then we'll get the paperwork sorted out." She walked her around the plexiglass enclosure and through a set of double doors.

"You better go with her, Dad. I'll just park the car."

He nodded at me wearily, then smiled.

"Thanks for being here, Bernie. This is all a little overwhelming."

"Well, it'll soon get boring probably."

"You think so?"

I shrugged. "I don't know, Dad. I've only been through this once and that was fifteen years ago. I'll be back in a minute." I left him and walked to the car. I'd left the flashers on. The parking lot was around the corner, one of those high rise, automated municipal lots. Fortunately, I found a spot on the first floor. The maximum rate topped $25 and I had no doubt that I'd reach it in no time.

When I returned to the lobby, I spotted Sharon. My heart jumped and my throat dried. I wanted to run and throw my arms around her. She looked up as I came through the doors. She looked flushed and her hair was tousled. She was wearing a long, tan raincoat, brown velour slacks, a cream pullover and sensible suede shoes with no socks.

"Hello."

"I came as soon as I heard," she said.

"Who called you?"

"Why Eph, of course," and she looked at me in surprise. He must have called while I was upstairs helping Catherine.

"Boys okay?"

"Yes, they had a good time at the movie. That was good of you to take them."

I was getting frustrated. Here we'd known each other for 17 years and we were talking like strangers. "Well, it was a blast for me, too," I replied.

A smile flickered across her face briefly. "And thank you for the flowers. They are lovely." Her tone was clipped, her jaws tense. I saw circles under her eyes. It seemed to me that we were crazy for being apart but I couldn't say it. I thought it but when I opened my mouth, it went dry.

"You're welcome." And then I indicated the doorway leading to the bowels of the hospital. "Shall we?" I touched her on the elbow, she didn't flinch but for a scant moment, looked grateful. I found myself wanting her, a tremendous ache throbbing within me. I'd always wanted her. I just couldn't account for my moral lapse.

Catherine sat in a wheel chair. My father held her hand. She had one hand on her belly and looked uncomfortable. Her things were piled in a second wheelchair. Sharon rushed up to her and gave her a hug.

"How're you feeling?"

Catherine looked at her and shook her head. "Like hell."

"I got you into this."

Catherine squeezed Sharon's hand. "I know. Thank you."

"And what about you, Eph? Are you coping?" And she put her arm around him.

He nodded. "I have no choice."

An orderly came around the corner holding a clipboard. "Mrs. Goldman?"

Sharon and Catherine answered together. "Yes?" The orderly looked confused. Catherine put up her hand. "I'm the pregnant one."

"Ah yes, of course." The orderly was young with a brush cut and a goatee. "I'm just going to take you down to the birthing area now. How are you feeling?"

"Like I'm going to have a baby," Catherine said.

"Well, that's good," replied the orderly. "Better than gallstones or appendicitis."

"If you say so." We followed behind.

"Trust me."

The orderly moved quickly. We struggled to keep up, especially Eph. His frailty really hit home to me and I could see he felt uncomfortable in a hospital, the associations bothered him.

At breakneck speed, the orderly wheeled Catherine into one of the birthing rooms. A nurse came over with a gown and helped her change. Her clothes and purse were put into a locker and then she climbed into the birthing chair, a reclining sort of contraption that provided some measure of comfort while allowing gravity to do its work. Some Chopin filled the room suddenly. Eph sat opposite her while two nurses bustled in. One took her temperature and blood pressure while the other hooked her up to a fetal monitor. Due to her age, Catherine was automatically placed in the high-risk category.

"Blood and pulse look good, a wee bit high but nothing to worry about," said the one. We could hear the pinging of the monitor.

"Baby sounds good too," said the other. "Heart rate is steady and strong. Don't think there's anything to worry about. Try to relax for a bit. Do you think you'll be wanting anything for pain?"

"I don't know," panted Catherine who was going through her breathing exercises.

"Well you have a little bit of time, Mrs. Goldman. If the pain becomes too unbearable, let us know and we'll arrange it for you. Do you have other children?"

Catherine nodded, blowing out through her lips. "Two others, a boy and a girl, all grown up now."

"Good for you wanting to do this again, hon," said the first one. "I wouldn't in a million years but then my husband's a slob and does nothing around the house."

"You can say that again," said the second one.

"Hey," said the first.

"Well, you said it."

The first nurse looked sheepishly at us, then smiled.

"You relax now, Mrs. Goldman. If you need anything, you just holler. One of the doctors will be in soon to see how you're getting on, okay?" And then the two nurses left, carrying on a heated discussion between them.

Some two hours later, Catherine descended into the throes of labour. I occupied one side with Eph and Sharon taking the other. We stood no more than two feet apart. I held Catherine's hand because she almost cracked Eph's bones. He hung off my shoulder. I don't know who was sweating more, Catherine or Eph. Sharon patted her face with a damp cloth murmuring to her in what I assumed was Irish. When the contractions came, Catherine arched her back, squeezed her eyes shut and bellowed lustily. The veins on her forehead popped out and her neck swelled with blood. Not once did she curse Eph out. I was impressed.

"Come on, Catherine," I said. "Breathe. Breathe." And went into the breathing routine I remembered from pre-natal class all those years ago. Sharon looked at me and smirked.

"Oh, can it, you two," Catherine said. "I'm the one in labour."

Just then the doctor bustled in. A young oriental man with a smooth complexion. He looked absurdly young. "Mrs. Goldman," he said. "How are you feeling?"

"Shitty, Dr. Lee, just plain shitty."

The young doctor bent over and examined her via a mirror placed at her feet. "About six centimetres dilated, I'd say. Not long now, it's starting to move fast. When you feel your next contraction, I want you to push very hard, okay? Each contraction, push as hard as you can."

"I'll try."

As she went into her next contraction, Sharon and I and even Eph egged her on. "Push, push, push." Until I thought her eyes would pop from the strain.

"Good. Good," said Dr. Lee. "Now rest and try again." He and the nurse knelt at Catherine's feet in a plush looking device that looked like an ergonomic pew. It even had rollers on it. Dr. Lee stood up. "I'm going to tilt your chair back a little bit so I can get a better view, okay?" Catherine nodded, oblivious to all else but her internal discomfort and very real pain. She went through several more contractions, looking exhausted after each one, pale and limp. "Almost there now. I can see the head." Another nurse wheeled in the warming unit and a glass bassinet. Catherine grabbed the bars on the sides of the birthing chair and thrust her hips upward.

"No more sex," she shrieked. "I swear to God, no more sex." The doctor and the nurse chortled. I guess they'd heard it all. I glanced at Eph. He looked stricken.

"I don't think she means it," I whispered.

"I sure as hell do," Catherine yelled. "Oh god, I sure as hell do. Come on, baby, come on."

Sharon leaned over and glanced down. "I can see it, Catherine. It's coming. The baby's coming."

"One more should do it," Dr. Lee said. "Ready Catherine? This is it, the last one. Big push now. Come on. Push, push, push." Catherine grunted and groaned like an animal making guttural noises while foraging in the brush. I thought she sounded like a bear growling at an enemy.

"That's it," Sharon cried. "I can see the baby." Catherine collapsed backward panting and gasping for air, her now empty belly heaving.

"Thank God," she exclaimed.

Dr. Lee and the nurse took the child and quickly suctioned out its mouth. I saw the bloodied bottom and heard the slap, then the small whinny-like sound, a lamb whimpering for its ewe. "It's a girl," exclaimed the nurse. "A beautiful baby girl."

"A girl," breathed Catherine. "How lovely."

"Would you like to cut the umbilical cord," Dr. Lee asked Eph, as he was removing the afterbirth and dumping it in a metal tray. Eph keeled over.

"Dad."

I was still holding Catherine's hand. He'd just crumpled on the spot. I managed to pick him up. He'd gone completely limp, it felt like holding soggy spaghetti.

"Put his head between his knees," ordered Dr. Lee as he snipped the cord and tied it into a tight little knot then wrapped some rubber tubing around the end. I pulled over a chair.

"Is he all right? Eph? Speak to me, darling." Catherine looked exhausted, frantic and immobilized.

"He'll be fine," said Dr. Lee. "Happens all the time."

I maneuvered Eph on to the chair, then pushed on his back, forcing his head down. A moment later he came to.

"Whaaa. What happened?"

"You passed out."

"Oh no." He rubbed his face with his palms. "What a weeny."

"You're not a weeny," Catherine said. "We have a new daughter, darling." The baby was now wrapped in a blanket and the nurse placed her in Catherine's arms. "Come look, before they have to take her away. I helped Eph to his feet. He wobbled a bit but he made it. He leaned down and kissed Catherine's damp cheek, then touched the baby's hands with his finger. The child grabbed hold making little grunting noises.

"Oh my God. This is unbelievable. I, I, …" And tears splashed down his cheeks. I glanced at Sharon and her eyes filled. I didn't feel like crying but it was moving. I gave my father a hug.

"Thanks Bernie."

"Don't be silly."

"And you too Sharon." He reached out for her and she came around the chair. They hugged. Sharon laughed through her tears. The nurse took the baby from Catherine and placed her under the warmer.

"I'm going to take her up to the ward now. We need to run the standard tests. You will see her in a little while."

Dr. Lee shook hands all around. "Good job. Good job, everyone. Congratulations, you two. All the best. Catherine, you'll see your pediatrician within two weeks, okay?"

Catherine nodded. Her hair was tousled and her face pale but I thought that I'd never seen her look so attractive. Her lids fluttered then closed. Eph hunched in a chair at her bedside. I glanced at my watch. Just gone two o'clock in the morning.

"Dad?" He glanced up at me, startled. "You should get some rest too. Why don't I drive you home now?"

He shook his head. "I want to stay with Catherine. I'll rest later."

"You look terribly knackered," Sharon said.

"I'll recover. Go on you two. Get home and get some sleep. At his words, I thought about which home I'd be going to. Certainly not my own. I glanced at Sharon. She looked down at her toes.

"Where are you parked?" I asked her. She told me.

"I'll walk you."

I gave my Dad a hug.

"Bye Eph. I'll speak to you later on, then," Sharon said. "All right?" He nodded wearily but smiled through his fatigue.

From the doorway, I said, "Call me and let know what room you'll be in." He waved his hand in response.

I took Sharon by the elbow and we walked stiffly down the corridor. A sickly green light made atmosphere seem positively ghoulish.

"I must look a mess."

"A bit frazzled, but otherwise pretty good."

She touched her hair lightly. "Oh thanks," she said.

I held the door for her and she brushed by me. I could smell her perfume and for an instant my knees buckled.

"Are you all right?" she asked me.

"Fine. No problem."

We walked the deserted street in silence, the heels of our shoes clopping on the sidewalk. I felt unbearably tense and suddenly miserable. We rode the elevator up to parking level three and I saw the Navigator sitting on its own like a beast waiting to be awakened at its master's bidding. Sharon had her keys out and pressed the unlock button on the wireless remote. The vehicle beeped or barked, echoing off the concrete interior. We were standing at the driver's door now.

"Well," she said. "That was something."

"Yes, it was."

"Well. Goodnight then."

"Goodnight."

I hesitated and wanted to say something, call her name but she had the door open and stepped inside, slamming it. She looked at me through the glass expectantly for a moment but I froze, just looking at her, feeling this pain in my heart. Then the motor turned over, she put it in gear and with a little wave, moved off. I watched it disappear, then trudged down three levels to my car.

I resolved to sleep late the next morning but the phone rang. When I looked at the clock, it read seven-thirty and I groaned. Who would be calling me at such an ungodly hour on a Sunday?

"Dad, what happened?"

"Nathan. What are you doing calling so early?"

"Mom's still asleep. Tell me Bernie. What's going on. Did Catherine have the baby?"

"Uh-huh."

"She did? She had the baby?"

"Right."

"She had the baby?"

"Nathan, for god's sake. Yes, she had the baby. It came out of her. It is no longer in her, okay?"

"Hey, you don't have to be sarcastic. I mean, be nice, Bernie."

"I'm only working on a few hours sleep here, get the hint?"

"What hint would that be?"

"Okay. She had the baby, she's fine, Zaidy is fine. We, including me, are a little tired right now."

"Can I go see it?

I shrugged. "I don't know. I suppose so. She probably won't be in hospital long. I wouldn't be surprised if she came home tomorrow actually."

"Will you take me?"

"I don't know. Maybe. Right now, I want to go back to sleep, all right? I'll call you later, Nathan. And whatever you do, don't wake up your mother. She'll snap your head off. You know how she likes to sleep."

"Okay, okay. But what am I going to do until then? I mean, I feel like I've got so much energy right now."

"Run around the block a few times."

"Good idea. I'll do that." And he hung up. I stared at the phone, then set it back in its cradle.

I tried to fall back asleep but it no dice. Instead, I hauled myself out of bed and shaved, then took a shower.

I had breakfast, drank some tea and read the paper. But I felt restless. I decided to go back to the hospital around noon if I didn't hear from my Dad. I'd pick Nathan up on the way.

Sean was out shooting pool with some of his buddies, a laudable Sunday activity. Nathan and I prowled the corridor of the maternity wing. We went to the baby display first, the room where all babies slept in their glass bassinets. We looked for the one marked Goldman. I pointed to it through the glass. Nathan tapped on the window that, in turn, caused some sort of chain reaction. First one cried, then the next picked it up like a signal and within seconds the room echoed with the plaintive wails of crying babies. A nurse sitting in a rocking chair glanced up at us and smiled. I thought she'd be annoyed but she surprised me. I smiled back. I suppose she thought I was the father of a newborn not the half-brother of one or that my fifteen-year-old son had come to visit his aunt.

"Oh my gosh," Nathan exclaimed. "We'd better get out of here."

"Don't sweat it. Babies cry all the time. Don't you want to see your new auntie?"

"Yeah, I guess so. Where's Zaidy?"

"I don't know. With Catherine I would guess."

Nathan pressed his face to the glass. "They're so small. Is that a stupid thing to say?"

"Yeah, it is."

"Come on, Bernie. I don't become a nephew every day, you know."

"You're right. The trauma of it."

"And you're not a half-brother every day, either."

"Not unless your Zaidy gets busy but let's assume it's unlikely to happen again."

"Don't be so scientific, Bernie. Be happy. This is a blessed event," he said in that voice of his that sounded like Bullwinkle J. Moose. I touched his upper lip. He swatted my hand away. "Don't."

"I just wanted to see if it was dirt."

"Ha. Ha. You're getting humorous in your old age."

"I know, a barrel of laughs. Shall we look for their room?" We ventured to the nurse's station, where we were directed to Catherine's room. I put my finger to my lips, tapped lightly on the door and poked my head in. Catherine and Eph were lying on the bed together fast asleep. I don't know how two people could fit on such a narrow cot and still look comfortable.

Nathan tapped my shoulder He spoke in an exaggerated whisper.

"Why don't we leave them a note? We'll go back and see Auntie again on the way out."

I looked back at the two of them. They looked so relaxed and peaceful, I was loathe to disturb them. I nodded my agreement.

"You got a pen and paper?"

"No."

"Okay. Why don't you go back to the nurse's station and get some?"

"Why don't you?"

"Because I asked you."

"Not good enough."

"Oh, come on, Nate. It was your suggestion."

"I'll do it for a buck."

"No."

"Fifty cents."

"No."

"A quarter."

"No."

"Why do I have to do it?"

I rolled my eyes. "Because I asked you to, that's why." And started off on my own. Nathan followed me.

"Hey, I'll do it, okay? Can't you take a joke, Bernie?"

I put my hands on my hips. "I guess not." We secured the pen and paper. I let Nathan write the note. He placed it quietly and carefully on the side stand beside the bed. Catherine began to stir but she didn't wake. We swung by the baby display one more time.

"Is that red hair, I see?"

"Could be."

"She looks awfully cute but a little beat up, maybe."

"Most babies look like that at first."

"Did I look like that?"

"You were worse. Your head was so misshapen it looked like it'd been used for a football and both your eyes were black. Within a month, that had cleared up and you turned just plain ugly."

"Thanks for that, Bernie. I'm glad that I know how you felt back then."

"Well, you cleared the canal for your brother. He came out pink and rosy and totally unblemished."

Nathan snorted. "Nothing's changed."

I flicked his skinny bicep. "How about going for a chocolate croissant?"

Nathan's dark face lit up. "Sounds great. Can I have two?"

"We'll see." There's a little bit of the kid in all of us, even a fifteen-year-old. I took him to my local café. He was in seventh heaven.

"Can I have a chocolate latté too?"

"Why not?"

# 33

I sat at my desk Monday morning. The time read eight-thirty as I tried to work on one of the books I had in progress when Ruth walked in.

"Good morning. What brings you here so early?"

She growled at me, then set about getting herself organized, pulling her arms out of her raincoat, setting her bag down, rummaging through it for something she needed, glaring at the pile of papers on her desk, among other things. "Okay. I'll leave you alone now." And went back to my work. Within a moment, the phone rang.

"I have some bad news and some good news," said Frances, my erstwhile producer.

"Oh?"

"Which do you want first?" She sounded almost smug.

Thinking about the miracle of birth and how lovely my new half-sister was, I said, "Give me the bad. I can take it."

"We're going with someone else as the host of the show."

"Oh. I see." I can't say I wasn't disappointed but a bit relieved too. It just wasn't me. "Who are you going with, if you don't mind me asking?"

"V. S. Singh. Do you know him?"

"Yes. Yes, I do."

"We thought he had all the qualities we were looking for actually. Witty, urbane, edgy, funny and very natural on camera. That's not to say you weren't of course. I don't mean to imply that but he just had a sort of presence that we found very compelling."

"That's okay, Frances. I'm not insulted. I'm a bit relieved actually. I don't think I could have pulled it off anyway. And V. S. is an inspired choice. He's everything you say he is and more."

"Well. I'm glad you think so."

"I do. Now if that's the bad, what's the good?"

"The good news is that we want to hire you or your firm to do our research, hook us up with authors, give us the background and so on, the sort of thing you do for the magazine anyway."

"I see. More of a background role."

"Exactly. That pays $4000 an episode for that service by the way. And I've been authorized to also to offer you $50,000 for the rights to the name, *Bookology*."

I worked the numbers out quickly in my head. Thirty-eight episodes times four grand came out to 152 grand a year plus the 50 Gs, made the take 205K for the year, a tidy sum that could help out our bottom line significantly. Now I'm a media whore, I thought. But I was more than willing to take the money before.

"Seventy-five," I said.

"Excuse me?"

"Seventy-five for the rights and we've got a deal."

"Bernie, Bernie, we thought you'd pull something like this. Fortunately, I've been authorized to go that high."

"Good. Have you got a contract or something?"

"I certainly do."

"Send it over."

"I'll have it in the courier bag first thing."

"When do we start?"

"Right away. We haven't got much time as you know. You'll have to set up a meeting with our story editor and writer. They'll work out the details of what we'll be needing over the next couple of months."

"I can do the work here?"

"Sure. Just get us what we need, okay?"

"Done."

"You're happy now?"

"I am. I'm quite happy actually."

"Good. I hoped you would be. I think this is going to be a great relationship, don't you?"

"I have every expectation it will be."

Frances laughed into the phone. "Spoken like a true Libra."

"How did you know I was a Libra."

"Bernie," she said with that don't underestimate me tone.

"Okay, okay."

"Call me when you get the contract or if you have any questions about it, okay?"

"You got it."

"Bye." And she hung up.

For the first time in years, I actually began to feel as if I had gainful employment. I hoped Jessica would get a kick out of this too. I worried about Roberto, though. It meant even less time to supervise him.

After a decent lunch that day, I was still riding high from the contract offer. The courier had just dropped off said contract and I'd gone through it quickly once. It looked like a decent deal upfront. Frances' company was new and I had no idea about their finances but she'd included a copy of the sponsor agreement and from what I could tell, all of the expenses including mine appeared to be covered. They'd signed on for two years, after which, the sponsorship agreement was subject to renewal.

Well, I wafted through the ether. Then I received a call from the school ordering me down there immediately to deal with a grave situation that had arisen. The caller assured me, that both Nathan and Sean were all right and safe but something serious had come up, nonetheless. I glanced at my watch. The secretary who'd phoned had been infuriatingly vague. Just that the principal demanded my presence in her office at once. It fell just short of three o'clock. Oh well, an early day.

When I was shown into the principal's office by the anxious secretary, I was shocked and surprised to see Sharon seated there. Sean slumped sullenly in his seat. He looked as if he'd slide off the chair and disappear into a crack.

"Sit up, young man," the principal barked. I don't know how but even in the way he sat up, he looked insolent with a half-sneer on his face.

"Mrs. Bergamot," I said. "Nice to see you again, I think." We shook hands curtly. I glanced at Sharon. She'd never been to a school meeting before. This had to be serious. Blotches of colour spotted her cheeks. She appeared both nervous and flustered, two un-Sharon-like characteristics. Mrs. Bergamot, though diminutive, appeared imposing and no-nonsense.

"I'm sorry to have called you both down here but there has been an incident involving your son, Sean and another boy." Sean looked at his feet.

"Sean?" I said. He didn't look up.

"What happened, please?" Sharon said.

Mrs. Bergamot harrumphed. "We're still trying to get to the bottom of it, actually. Neither of them is talking. I will say that we found the other boy stuffed into a locker and bleeding rather profusely from the nose."

"What?" Sharon looked as if she was going to gag, her face turned pale and sickly.

"Sharon, are you okay?"

She nodded. "I, I just need a drink of water, that's all."

Mrs. Bergamot got up. "Of course." She strode briskly to the door, poked her head out and said something. I glanced back at Sean. He had his left hand covering his right. I reached across and lifted his hand up and saw the bruising. Then I took a good look at his face which he'd done a good job of keeping averted. I saw a bit of puffiness pushing up his left cheek. Otherwise, it'd be difficult to tell he'd been in a fight at all. Sharon had her fingers covering her mouth.

"Who is this guy," I whispered to him. Sean shrugged. "I don't see any bleeding on you." He looked up then and gave a sly grin.

"I gave it to him good," he said. "You should have seen it, it was beautiful. Pow. Into the head. Pow. Right on the jaw. And then a good combo into his ribs and gut. It was so cool."

"Why him?"

Sean clammed up again. "He's on the football team," was all he said before Mrs. Bergamot leaned back in with a glass of water in her hand. She strode back and handed it to Sharon.

"Thank you." Sharon took a sip of the water.

Mrs. Bergamot sat herself down in front of us again so we formed an intimate circle. "You know we have a zero-tolerance policy for this sort of thing. In fact, we may have to call the police if the other boy's parents insist on it. He was taken to hospital for examination and we don't know yet the extent of his injuries."

"I see," I said, again feeling a weird sense of admiration for my son. At the same time, however, although I was satisfied he could fend for himself, yet the recklessness of it and the obvious enjoyment he took, remained disturbing. And the motive? A mystery.

"So, we'll just have to wait and see what results. As of now, Sean is being suspended from school for the next week, effective immediately. His brother will have to bring work home for him. That work must be turned in just as if he were attending school. Any failure to do so, could result in failure. Sean, will you wait outside for a moment, please?"

She had a grating voice and I could see how it could raise hackles. Sean hauled himself up, hitched up his baggy pants and ambled out, closing the door behind him. Mrs. Bergamot set her square jaw and looked at us. I wondered what she saw? Two yuppie parents who'd lost control.

"Mr. and Mrs. Goldman, I'd encourage you to talk with your son very seriously about this. We have no idea why this happened. The last thing I'd want to see is Sean in trouble with the law but with this attitude he is headed that way. The sad thing is, he is a very intelligent boy so it's a terrible waste. This was a particularly vicious beating. Apparently, several other boys had to pull Sean off. Otherwise, who knows how far it could have gone?"

"Was this other boy larger than Sean?" I asked.

"Yes. He's quite large."

"Have there been any incidents involving this boy?"

Mrs. Bergamot hesitated, then licked her thin lips. "He has been involved in one or two incidents of bullying, name calling that sort of thing. Nothing like this, however."

"But it is fair to say the boy has been known to bully and is quite a bit larger than Sean?"

"Yes."

"Then Sean may have only been defending himself, isn't that right?"

"It is possible, yes. Unless we get more information, we may never know."

"I just don't want to leave you with the impression that Sean was the aggressor or that he may have been provoked. I know my son, Mrs. Henderson. He has his faults and he is no angel certainly, but he has never done anything like this before. He is prone to mischief, yes. But I can only imagine that he was defending himself in this situation. It's the only thing that makes sense to me."

"I agree with my husband," Sharon said suddenly, and there was a flush of pride on her face.

"I understand, Mr. and Mrs. Goldman that you are now living apart?"

Sharon sucked in her breath. "Yes. What's that got to do with it?"

"I'm just wondering whether that may have had an effect on your son, his attitude or his behaviour?"

"It is possible," I admitted.

Sharon shrugged. "I don't know."

And she looked down at her feet, hands clasped in her lap. Without thinking, I reached over and put my hand on hers. It was cold. She looked up at me and smiled and in that moment, I thought my heart would shoot out of my chest.

"We'll talk to our son, Mrs. Bergamot. You'll let us know if there is anything else?"

"Of course."

"And at the end of the five days?" Sharon asked.

"He comes back to school and resumes his normal schedule but he will be very closely monitored, I can assure you."

"And the other boy?" I asked.

"The same procedure will be put into effect," Mrs. Bergamot said firmly. "We are not just singling out Sean."

I stood up. "All right, then. Thank you." I shook her hand. It was damp. Sharon nodded and we left the office together. I put my arm around her.

Sean leaned up against the wall in the corridor. I beckoned and he pushed himself off bouncing on the balls of his feet. He shadow-boxed as we clopped down the hall. Sharon held herself tall and rigid, pale and severe. Sean stopped and looked at her, he dropped his hands as he scanned her face, then followed along in a more docile manner. There was the usual clutter and clatter as kids hung out at their lockers grabbing books, jabbering, pulling on locks, slamming the metal doors. Sean knew their eyes were on him as undoubtedly, news of his exploits had made the rounds in the school. A few of the boys nodded and grinned. Sean responded with a lifting of his blonde head and a twitching of his thin lips. We made it outside and Sharon breathed in forcefully as if she'd been suffocating inside.

"That's better," she said. "I came by cab. Shall we go back to the house and sort this out?"

"Okay," I said. Sean shrugged. He hefted his knapsack higher on to his shoulder. "I'm parked over here."

Sean sat in the back. Sharon rode opposite me. I pulled out of the school parking lot and made a left turn on to Lawrence Avenue. "Did that kid threaten you?"

Sean snorted. "You've got to be joking. That fat ass?"

"Watch it," Sharon hissed.

"Okay then. I'm a little confused about what happened. Obviously, this kid did something to set you off. He's been taken to the hospital..."

"That's right," Sean confirmed, pleased with himself.

"Then what did he do?" I looked in the rear-view mirror and saw Sean shrug, then clam up.

"Sean," Sharon said. I heard the anger and tightness in her throat. "This is bloody serious. The police may be involved. You've got to tell us what happened if we are to help you. Don't you understand?"

Sean said nothing. "Sean," I said.

"I don't want to talk about it."

"Yet," I replied. "You seem plenty pleased with yourself at the outcome of this thing. I mean, a much bigger kid, jammed into a locker with maybe a broken nose. You were lathered up. A bunch of other kids had to pull you off him, right? So, what happened?"

I pulled into the drive. Sean grabbed his knapsack and jumped out slamming the door. He ran up the front steps and into the house before Sharon and I could even undo our seatbelts. I'd noticed the look in Sean's eye. It was one of fury and I began to think that this other kid had got off lucky. Sharon seemed stiff and I placed my hand on her elbow to help her out.

"I'm all right," she snapped. "I'm not an invalid."

"I didn't say you were," I replied, somewhat bewildered. Sharon faced me now on the passenger side. The door hung open and I looked at her. Her cheeks puffed up as the corners of her mouth pulled back and, to my horror, I saw tears leak out of the corners of her eyes. She put a hand to her forehead swaying slightly.

"What is happening, Bernie? It wasn't supposed to be like this."

I put my arms around her. "Unfortunately, we can't plan everything so perfectly." I held her but her body held back, rigid and unyielding, until I stepped back and together we went inside.

Felicity was sitting in the living room watching one of her shows.

"What is going on? Oh, hello, Bernie."

"Felicity. How's the leg?"

"Much better, thank you. I just saw Sean run up to his room and slam the door. Did something happen at school?"

"Did something happen?" Sharon retorted and gave a dry laugh. "I'll say something happened. Your grandson beat another boy within an inch of his life. He's in the hospital at this very moment and Sean may be arrested by the police for assault. That's what."

I put my hands up. "Now Sharon, let's not get carried away. We don't know the extent of the boy's injuries and the police angle hasn't been confirmed."

But there was no stopping her. She'd lost control. She stomped over to the bottom of the stairs. "Sean," she yelled. "Sean. You come down here this minute. Do ya hear me? I don't want to come up there and get you but I will. By God, I'll drag you down here by the hair if you don't bloody well show your face…"

At that moment, Nathan decided to show up and as he opened the door and caught the tableau of me standing there exasperated, his grandmother bewildered and his mother yelling at the top of her lungs, well a deer caught in the headlights would have been less surprised and vulnerable. Sean appeared at the top of the stairs, leaning over the railing. He saw Nathan and his expression hardened. We all turned to look at Nathan as he stood there awkwardly.

There was that shambling smile. "Hi Bernie. What are you doing here?"

"Don't talk to your father that way," Sharon said.

"It's okay, Sharon."

I turned back to Nathan and I looked at him and something struck me. I don't get revelations very often, infrequently, in fact. Then I looked back up at Sean who was staring at his brother. What would motivate Sean to do such a thing, to act with such abandoned fury with no regard for the consequences, that in a weird, misguided way, to protect the thing or person who remained closest to him, more than anything or anyone else in the world? And I looked back at Nathan and I remembered. Here was a kid who, at the age of two, folded his own underwear. He alphabetized all of his early readers. At night, he'd line up all of his stuffed animals from largest to smallest. He loved to go shopping and was very explicit about the types of clothes he had to wear. He took showers obsessively and not once had he mentioned a girl. No girls called him. The direction these thoughts took me caused my knees to buckle. I looked at him as if I saw right through his cranium into the emotions inside. I sensed his fear. It was palpable as if it rose off his skin in a cloud. He breathed noisily through his nose, panting heavily.

"Tell them," Sean said and his voice was wooden. "Just get it over with."

"Tell us what?" Sharon said and I could hear the panic in her voice mounting.

"Just say it," Sean said. "Be a man. Come on, you bastard."

"Sean!"

Sharon's face had grown white and pinched about the mouth. She turned from Sean back to Nathan who had grown very still. All of us looked at him. He was frying under the heat lamp.

Nathan swallowed hard. He dropped his knapsack at his feet with a thump. He looked handsome in his pressed jeans and tailored shirt. His thick dark hair, cut short. He'd grown in the last year, keeping pace with Sean, growing taller and still very slim. Nathan looked at me. Then Sharon. Then swallowed hard. We all stared at each other in a weird kind of triangle.

"I'm gay," he said.

From up above, I heard. "Thanks be to Christ." Felicity gasped. We'd become like one of the shows she watched on television. Sharon paled even further, her face turning to paste. I felt shocked but not surprised. I looked up at Sean who curled his lip upward, then shook his head and moved out of my view. I went over to Nathan and put a hand on his shoulder.

"Who gives a shit?" I said. "Really. Who gives a good god damn?"

Sharon joined us. "Oh Nathan. I don't know what to say. I'm all confused."

"Mom."

Tears flooded his eyes, this irrepressible and insistent child who always knew exactly what he wanted and was determined to get it, no matter what. He'd been living in a state of confusion and terror, terrified that we'd reject him.

Sharon began to cry and Nathan buried his face against her shoulder.

"It's all right. Nothing will change the fact that we love you. You're our darling boy."

Then Felicity appeared at my shoulder. "I want to hug someone too," she said. Nathan laughed and gave her a bear hug. "Not so hard, you'll crack my ribs you heathen."

I looked back up at Sean who was hovering over this tender scene from on high and our eyes locked. In a way, I had to admire him for his love and loyalty to his brother. That no matter what, he'd take his part and defend him. He read my thoughts. Then he nodded at me like a man in a bar after a fracas, and backed away from the banister. I heard the door to his room close.

After we had all blown our noses and dried our eyes, I went up to Sean's room. He lay on the bed, legs splayed out, reading a book, headphones cupping his ears. My shadow fell across the bed and he looked up. He pulled the headphones down around his neck.

"What's up Pop?"

"Sean, listen. I don't want you to get the impression that we favour Nathan in any way."

"Oh yeah?" He waited for the punch line.

"No, I mean it. I just wanted to say, although I don't condone what you did..."

"What I did..."

"Just listen a second...although I don't condone it, in a way, it was admirable. Sticking up for Nathan, I mean."

"Well, who else am I going to stick up for?" he asked, with a bit of a sneer like he'd been practicing in the mirror.

I shrugged. "You tell me."

"Whatever. Anything else?"

"Well, no, I just wanted to say that and I didn't want you to feel left out or anything."

"That's good, Bernie. Do you feel better now?"

"A little."

"Listen, just so you know. I don't like having a brother who's a faggot, all right? But he's still my brother and if anybody gets on him then I'll get in their face too."

"I get it. I'm not sure it makes me feel any better, but I get it."

He yawned.

"Somebody's got to make something happen around here." And then he paused and studied me for a minute or so. "So, you moving back in or what?"

"I, uh, don't know. It's not up to me exactly."

"Who's it up to then?"

"Well, Mom, I guess."

Sean adjusted the headphones back up on the crown of his head.

"You guys kill me." The music blared loud enough for me to hear it from his bed. "Think you know everything. You didn't know about Nathan, did you?"

"How long have you known?" I gestured at him.

He lifted a headphone. "What?"

"How long have you known about Nathan?"

He blew through his thin lips.

"Ages. Can't even remember how long its been. At least a year, maybe more, I don't know."

His answer disturbed me. It meant that Nathan had been carrying this burden with him all this time and I had no idea. He appeared as irrepressible as ever.

"You didn't answer my question," he said.

"What question?"

"About moving back in."

"Oh. I really don't know."

"That's right. You don't."

"Don't what?"

"Talk to Mom, Bernie. It's for her, not you."

"I see."

I guess I knew where we stood. Then he fitted the earpiece back on and closed his eyes to the music. I took this as my cue to leave. He effected a grim sort of smile.

I descended the stairs, slowly. Nathan had gone to his room and Felicity had gone back to watching television at 90 decibels. I found Sharon taking refuge in the kitchen.

"Fancy a cup of tea?" she asked.

"Sure."

She filled the kettle and plugged it in, then got two porcelain mugs down from the cupboard. They looked as if they hadn't been used in weeks. I guess the fact that she blew dust out of them was the main clue.

"Sorry," she said. She cut a slice of lemon for me and added milk and sugar for herself.

"Will you need a lift back to the office?"

"No, I don't think I'll go back in today."

"I see."

"How's Catherine and your Dad?"

"Uh, fine, I guess. But I haven't really seen them. I believe Catherine's coming home today. In fact," I checked my watch and it was getting on to four o'clock. "Should be home by now."

"It'll be different having a baby in the house."

"Yes, I'm not looking forward to it," I said. "All those noisy nights. Unless..."

The kettle was boiled and Sharon moved to the counter to unplug it. "Yes, unless what?"

I cleared my throat. "I was going to say, unless you'd consider letting me move back in. I mean, I'd like to but I also think that Eph and Catherine need to be on their own right now. It's a special time for them. They need their space and some privacy too."

Sharon poured the water into the pot, her brow was set and her mouth stretched into a thin line. The Maginot line, I thought. Deep thinking mode. She swirled the water around in the pot and then poured my tea knowing I liked it weak, then her own.

"I could stay in the spare room if you'd like. If that would make you feel more comfortable."

She set the pot down on the counter with a bit of a clatter, then handed me the mug.

"I don't know, Bernie. I just don't know whether I'm ready to forgive you."

I took the mug. It was very hot. "I see." We weren't going to make it, I thought. "Well, perhaps you'll think about it and let me know," I said lamely, then took a sip of the tea. Sharon averted her eyes.

On my way out, I found Nathan sitting on the cement steps. I sat beside him noticing that the day seemed to have tempered itself, the colours muted and less vivid, easing their way into night.

"So, Bernie, what do you think of all these developments?"

"I think it's not easy being a parent today or a kid. How about you?"

"I guess I'd concur with that."

"I thought you might. Listen Nathan, is there a reason you didn't tell us before? Did it have to wait until some incident happened before this would come out?"

He stared at the toes of his Nike runners.

"Well, I don't think I was ready to tell you. I don't think I knew how. And I wanted the timing to be right. Then this Bergsma fool started getting on me. You know, I didn't need Sean to beat him up for me. I could have taken him myself. I wasn't afraid of him."

"No one's saying you were."

"Well you know what people say about gays."

"What?"

"They're weak and feminine. Wusses mostly. They'll all avoid me now in gym, turn their backs so I won't see them changing." I put my hand on his knee. He flinched a little. "Hey, that tickles, Bernie."

"Sorry. Listen, I guess Mom and I are worried about you because of that. Other people's attitudes. It's never easy being different. No one likes to be singled out. Are there other gay kids in the school?"

He looked up at me, his eyes creased against the glare of the sun.

"Of course there are. Everybody knows them. They all hang around together."

"Are you friendly with any of them?"

"Not really. We don't like to do the same things. I like sports, they don't."

"This is an odd question for me but...are you seeing anyone?"

"Am I dating you mean, Bernie? You want to know about my love life, is that it?"

"I don't want to pry but yeah."

Nathan banged my knee with his fist.

"I'll let you know. So the answer is, not yet. I don't think I'm ready for it. Besides, I haven't really met anybody I like."

"Okay. That's fair. Listen, I want you to go easy on Mom, okay? She's having enough grief from Sean right now and because of our situation, she looks like she's under a lot of stress, so..."

"I wouldn't do anything to Mom."

"No, I know but this thing now..."

"My gayness?"

"Right. She, I mean both of us, are just concerned."

"Well, no one will mess with me now that Sean has beaten the crap out of that asshole Bergsma. So I'm pretty safe for now." He balled his fists up and squeezed hard. The façade dropped away as he stared off at some distant point. "He's really crazy you know."

"Who is?"

"Sean. I think you should give him away to the gypsies."

"He has his moments."

"You think I'm not serious? You should have seen the way he went after that kid. He enjoyed it. Inflicting pain, I mean."

"Are you saying he's dangerous?"

"Maybe. He just doesn't think. I don't know if he attacked Bergsma because he called me a faggot or because it gave him an excuse to fight."

Then he cleared his throat.

"I don't think he'd hurt any of us though. He just doesn't think sometimes."

I sighed.

"I wish I knew what to do about him. I just have this terrible feeling he'll come to harm one day. Bring it on himself. There's not much we can do to stop it or him. He never seems to learn from his mistakes. My real fear is he'll hurt someone else too. Hurting himself is one thing but..."

"What are you talking about, Bernie?"

"You guys will be driving next year and that scares me to death. The thought of Sean driving with passengers, knowing how reckless he is..." I just shook my head.

"Hey, have a little faith. So, are you moving back in?"

"I don't think so. Mom doesn't want me to."

"I'll talk to her."

"No. Don't do that. You'll just make things worse."

"Don't worry. I can handle it."

"Nathan."

"Being gay has its advantages. I can relate to the feminine side."

And he puckered up his face like Lucille Ball and I had to laugh in spite of myself.

"Just be sensitive when you're talking to her."

"Of course, I will. Don't worry, Bernie, I can do this."

He flung his right arm around my shoulder and squeezed. I stood up, dusting the seat of my pants.

"Back to my other world. Later."

"Don't forget to call, Bernie. Remember. Just pick up the phone. Don't be a stranger. Just call."

"I got it. I got it."

# 34

I drove to the other menagerie. Still early and I thought seriously about stopping somewhere for a quick bite but figured I should see how Eph and Catherine were coping as new parents. Catherine's Honda sat in the driveway. I parked and went in.

No one on the main floor. Then I heard murmuring upstairs.

"Hello?"

"Up here, son."

I climbed the steps and found Eph by the second-floor railing. He looked tired and frail but had a bright expression on his face.

"It's been a remarkable few days," he said. "But I'm beat."

I stopped on the landing. "I'm sure you are. How's Catherine and the baby?"

"Come see for yourself." He led me into their bedroom. There, spread out on the bed lay Catherine in sweat pants and a T-shirt, her legs tucked up under her and asleep. I peaked over her shoulder and saw the child, all swaddled up but awake and making the light grunting noises of the newborn. It seemed fascinated with its fingers.

"Who does she look like?"

"I don't know. Catherine, I hope. God forbid it should be me."

"Have you named her yet?"

Eph nodded, then stretched his face into a smile, one with a tinge of sadness. "Madeline. Madeleine Beatrice Goldman."

"Madeleine?" That was my mother's name. My face grew tight suddenly and my eyes teared up. "Madeleine?" Eph nodded and when I looked up and could see a little more clearly, his expression mirrored mine. He swiped at his eyes.

"I'm a foolish old man."

"No, you're not," Catherine said opening her eyes and yawning. "It's a beautiful name and it suits her."

"Thank you," I said.

"For what?" she asked.

"Nothing. Just thank you."

"Okay Bernie. We're going back to sleep now." She closed her eyes. As she did, the years dropped away from her.

Eph and I went down to the kitchen. "How about if I make us an omelet?"

"That'd be fine," he said and sat down in a chair to watch me. Eph had never been domesticated, never had to cook or do a dish while my mother was alive. After her death, he mainly ate out or bought pre-packaged meals that he could toss into the microwave.

"Why don't I show you how it's done?"

"Fine."

"We can do it like a cooking show on television where you'd be the guest."

"It's just an omelet, Bernie."

"But that's where you're wrong. No omelet is just any omelet."

"Okay, wise guy. Show me." Being there reminded me of when the kids were small and they'd watch me with big eyes as I cracked the eggs and beat them in a bowl, then added milk and seasoning to the mixture. I'd chop the vegetables and fry them up, then pour in the egg and let the bottom cook for a few minutes. When you saw the edges begin to solidify, then it was time to pop the pan into the oven under the broiler. This heats the omelet evenly through the layers of egg and vegetables and browns the top nicely. You do have to watch carefully. It can burn. Afterward, you spread some sliced cheese on top and once it's melted, then it's ready. I take it out of the oven and give it a minute to cool off then slice it up like pizza. Served with warm bagels and your choice of tea or coffee and it's divine.

We managed two helpings each and saved some for Catherine when she got up. We hadn't heard the baby yet but that would change in short order.

"Have you changed a diaper yet?"

Eph shook his head, his mouth full of egg.

"Not yet. Looking forward to it though."

"Oh yeaaahhh. I can't wait to see that."

"This is a pretty good omelet."

"Well, I learned a few things growing up."

"I can see that."

# 35

When I arrived at the office that Monday, I felt exhausted from the weekend. I picked up a message from Frances Schwartz on the answering machine.

"Hi Bernie. I've got some bad news I'm afraid. The sponsor's pulled the plug on the show. I really can't say why. We are all bitterly disappointed. I think it must be political or something. It certainly doesn't have anything to do with you. Needless to say, this has left us scrambling. We're supposed to go to air in five weeks. I'm looking for a new sponsor but I wouldn't want to give you false hopes or anything. I'm really sorry but this has hit us hard too. I'll keep in touch." Well, so much for my television career, not to mention the rather handsome fees that went with it. What a wonderful start to the week. No wonder Mondays are depressing. It was cool and raining too. Perfect.

Over the next few weeks, I kept my head down, focused on keeping things moving. That meant dealing with Ruth's surliness, bolstering Jessica's timidity, waking Angela up when she fell asleep at her keyboard, lashing Roberto to work better, smarter, faster. This was most frustrating. It felt like I had sunk into the morass with him. Some excuse burbled up. Some intervening factor. The computer keeps crashing, the software is out of date, he has to help his mother-in-law, his brother-in-law, his second cousin twice removed. It quickly grew into an untenable situation. I know what Sharon would have said. Confront him. Read him the riot act and move on. Easier said than done. The nights were now pierced by the cries of little Madeleine. I would hear Eph and Catherine padding around at one or two in the morning, their murmurings, the sleepy exchanges, the yawns and the cooings that kept me awake. Sharon and I had little contact. I heard a rumour she was dating. Immediately, I suspected that hunky guy I'd seen her with when I'd met Frances Schwartz for dinner. The thought of it made my guts churn.

"You look like shit," Hugo said, just before hitting with a jumper. "Nineteen."

I waved at him weakly.

"Go ahead. Sink it. It's a foregone conclusion, isn't it?"

He clapped a gnarled hand on my shoulder. It felt like a steel claw digging into bone. "All is not well with you."

"No kidding."

"Why don't you find yourself a girlfriend?"

"Are you insane? That's what got me into trouble in the first place."

"What's the matter. You don't know any girls?"

"It's not that…"

"Then what? Are you afraid?"

"I, I just don't want to complicate my life any more than I have already."

"From what you are saying, it doesn't sound like your wife is waiting for you," he said gruffly, running thick fingers through his iron gray hair. "Life goes on. Take nothing for granted. At my young age, I am ready for action."

"I don't think your wife would be happy about that."

He smiled, grey eyes twinkling. "I didn't say anything about acting on it. I said, I am ready. Of course my wife and I still have sex every day."

"Every day?"

"Naturally. It used to be several times a day but now we have slowed down."

"You're saying this isn't satisfactory?"

Hugo shrugged. "What can you do?" he asked philosophically. "We all must make sacrifices." He squeezed my neck. It felt like metal pincers.

"Yeow."

"Let's go to the pool." He swivelled and put up the last shot.

I watched it drop in. "Whatever."

I thought about what Hugo had said. Should I start dating? I didn't really want to but it didn't seem as if Sharon and I had progressed. Or should I make an effort with her first? I wasn't sure what to do. Life seemed a big swirl.

# 36

At night, the sweats came. As the baby wailed, I sat up in bed and wondered what the hell I was doing. During the day, I'd spoken to Sharon briefly, wanting to know how Sean was getting on at home. She'd been cold and distant.

"He's fine," she said. "Nathan's bringing the work home and taking back what's been completed the next day. That's it, really."

"You've grounded him?"

"Of course, I have. And Mrs. Sanchez has seen to it. Even Sean wouldn't dare defy her," she said, bitterly.

"Are you saying that he'd defy you?"

"And you," she spat. "Is there anything else on your mind, Bernie? I've got a lot to do here and I can't be wasting my time chitchatting you know."

That stung. "Well, uh, no. I guess that's it. I didn't mean to bother you."

"All right then. I suppose I'll be speaking to you later."

"Right. Uh, Sharon. Listen. I'd heard you'd been dating, is that true?"

There was a sharp intake of breath and then I heard an odd little laugh that chilled me. "What of it? Am I supposed to sit around and do nothing? Not enjoy myself once in awhile. There's plenty of men vying for my company, I can tell you that."

"All right, I was just asking. You don't have to sound so bloody proud of it."

"And why not, if it's true?"

"Sorry I asked."

"I've got to go. Bye Bernie." She hung up.

I felt ill suddenly. Ruth gave me a strange look and started to say something as I rushed out of the office but I silenced her with a malevolent look. Her jaw actually clamped shut. I made it to the loo and managed to lock the door before heaving my lunch into the toilet bowl. God, what a feeling. That had never happened to me before. Still, Sharon had given me a clear message. It was as if she'd passed out her consent and why should I feel guilty about dating?

That Saturday I met Nook at the café as per usual. Ramon was tending to his wife, who was due sometime in the next few weeks.

Nook glanced up at me and I held up a hand.

"Don't say anything. I know I look like shit. Thank you for pointing out the obvious." Then I sat down.

Nook, obviously peeved said, "I was only going to ask how you are and look what I get for my troubles."

"Sorry."

"On edge?"

"Yeah, I guess so."

I still picked up bagels and the Saturday paper but somehow as a domestic act, the bagels had become meaningless. It was now habit and some relationship with familiarity that compelled me to continue. I'd have to eat the damn things because I liked them. I went up to the counter and ordered the usual tea, then, carrying the glass mug gingerly, sat back down wearily.

"I'm not getting much sleep. Young Madeleine is exercising her lungs to the fullest."

"That's rough. We all remember those days."

"Distantly, for me," I replied, gloomily.

"How is your Dad doing?" The light glinted off his rimless spectacles as he angled his head.

I set down the mug, letting the tea cool a bit.

"He's doing great actually. They all are. After all, what else has he got to do but cater to Catherine and the baby? When he gets tired, he sleeps. He's not much more than a baby himself really."

"I was going to say that Catherine may have two on her hands."

I shrugged.

"Yes and no. Eph helps with the bathing and the diapering. He can't do much about feeding at the moment. Clearly, that's Catherine's department. He will get up and walk her in the middle of the night. He dozes throughout the day and somehow that gives him enough sleep to keep going. I feel like an intruder invading their privacy."

"Maybe you should get a place of your own?"

I looked at him, my buddha-like friend.

"I'm not ready yet. I'm still hoping things will work out with Sharon. I mean, I want them to. And I think the kids need me. Sean's been in trouble at school. He beat the crap out of a kid and has been suspended."

"Well, he's always had a restless kind of energy, hasn't he?"

"That's putting it mildly, Nook."

"Why not channel him into something positive? Like martial arts or even a boxing club?"

I'd been in the process of swallowing tea and choked at his words. "What?" I sputtered. "So, he can use that on us? Are you insane?"

"It might teach him some discipline. To focus his energies."

I dabbed at my face with a napkin. "I don't know. That kid's really on the edge sometimes."

"Well," replied Nook calmly. "Maybe some discipline would help. I'll look into it if you like. My club takes kids. I think they have a boxing program too."

"Thanks," I replied, still unsure. "It couldn't hurt I suppose."

Nook smiled in reply. "You look as if you have something else on your mind."

I nodded glumly. "Sharon is dating, apparently."

Nook's non-existent eyebrows shot up. "So, she admitted it?"

"Yup."

"So, what are you going to do?"

"I don't really know."

Nook patted me on the arm, sympathetically.

# 37

All this talk of dating got me thinking. I had to know for myself whether Sharon had told me the truth. So, I did what any wronged but sorrowful husband would do. I staked out my house so I could spy on my wife.

Eight o'clock on a Saturday evening found me discreetly parked across the street from the home I loved, the home that called me, the home I yearned for every waking moment. Knowing myself well; that I might use this stake-out as a loafable moment, I broke with tradition and sipped a coffee to go along with the Danish I'd purchased from the local coffee bar. I'd need the caffeine to prevent me from slipping into blissful unconsciousness.

I'd assembled a spy get-up, well, a black turtleneck but I'd also found an old pair of binoculars in Catherine's basement. Her kids had been into birdwatching at some point in the distant past. To keep myself focused, I turned the radio on to the local classical station, to help pass the time.

A couple of times, I almost succumbed and felt my head nodding on my chest before snapping awake. Nearing eight-thirty, the front door opened. Nathan and Sean emerged. They sauntered down the street. Headed in my direction. I ducked down behind the steering wheel and waited a few moments for them to pass by, grateful they were inattentive teenagers absorbed in themselves, oblivious to the external world.

I jumped. A sharp rap on the window. I sat up.

"Shit."

Nathan had his faced pressed to the glass on one side, Sean on the other. I rolled down the window.

"Didn't think we'd see you, Bernie? Really?"

The passenger door opened and Sean got in.

"What's up, Pops?"

"I thought you were grounded."

"I am. But you didn't answer the question."

Nathan reached inside the window and popped the button to the back seat. He climbed in too.

"Yeah, Bernie. You didn't answer the question. What are you doing here?"

Sean clapped his hands. "Say, you don't think he's spying on Mom, do you?"

"All right, you guys. Knock it off. I can park across the street from my own house, if I want to. There's no law against it."

"Apart from it being kinda creepy, you mean," Sean said.

"This seems like fun. Like a stakeout on a cop show, right Sean?"

"Weren't you guys going somewhere?" I asked. "Don't you have something to do?"

Nathan patted me on the back. "We're hanging out with you. What else would us teenagers be doing on a Saturday night?"

"Kid things. Hanging out with your friends. Getting arrested. You know, the usual."

"Funny, Bernie. Hilarious," Sean said.

The front door opened again and Sharon stepped out. She looked dressed up. Well, she wore a long coat and high heels. Her hair looked done and I spotted sparkly earrings. I think I bought them for our 10$^{th}$ anniversary.

"Get down," I hissed and we all hit the deck at the same time. Sean and I almost clanged heads. I peeked over the steering wheel. The garage door slid up. Sharon backed the Navigator out of the driveway.

"What are you waiting for, Bernie? Follow her."

"I don't think…" I sputtered.

"Come on, Bernie. We're a team," Sean said.

"Jeezus," I muttered.

Against my better judgement, I started the Saab.

"Don't lose her," Sean said.

"Now you're getting too close," Nathan piped.

"Shut up, the pair of you. I need to concentrate here."

"This is so cool," Nathan said. "Tailing Mom with Dad as the wheel man."

I tucked in several cars behind the Navigator and tried to follow discreetly. Sharon headed south, i.e. downtown. We followed along in tense silence for about ten minutes when the Navigator pulled over in front of a boutique hotel.

A tall man dressed in a midnight blue suit was waiting at the curb. He opened the passenger door of the idling Navigator and leaned in. I recognized him. It was the guy I'd seen Sharon with when I was having dinner with Frances Schwartz, the television producer.

"I knew it," I hissed.

"Knew what?" Nathan asked. "Knew what, Bernie?"

"Nothing."

"You know nothing and that's news?" Sean asked.

The tall Texan, I seemed to recall he hailed from Texas, stepped into the Navigator. Sharon signalled, then pulled away from the curb.

"You know that guy, Bernie?" Nathan asked.

"Not really," I replied through clenched teeth, as I slipped out into traffic. Where could they be going? My gut knotted like a Bosun's mate tying off a main sheet. "I saw him once before with your Mom, having dinner. A week or so ago."

"I see," Nathan said. He sounded wary, like maybe this wasn't going to be as much fun as he thought.

"I can let you guys out if you want."

"No thanks," Sean said. "We'll hang in with you. This is getting good."

"It's not a video game, Sean. Okay?"

"Yeah, whatever."

Sharon had turned down University Avenue, a broad street filled with hospitals, insurance companies and upscale hotels, all conveniently in proximity. Glittering jewels of our capitalist society. Great. Now, I sounded like a Marxist revolutionary when I was really just a now-jealous but currently, sidelined husband.

"She's getting away. Step on it, Bernie."

"Nathan, cool your jets. I see her. We're not that far back. I don't want to get spotted, okay?"

"Mom never really pays attention while she's driving," Sean said. "She's really an inattentive driver, in my opinion."

"So, you're an expert on driving now?"

"Don't be pejorative now Bernie. I know a good driver when I see one. And...I don't see one."

"Funny, Sean. Really funny."

Nathan cackled in the back seat. "I thought it was pretty good. Nice one, Sean."

"Sure," he replied, in an uber-cool sort of way.

What had I gotten myself into?

The Navigator manoeuvred into the driveway of the Shangri-La Hotel, pulling up to the valet parking. Naturally. Sharon wouldn't walk a block in heels.

Before either of them could squawk, I said, "There's a parking lot around the corner." I drove past the hotel. Sean and Nathan swivelled in unison as Sharon eased out of the driver's side while the guy did the same but opposite.

"Easy guys. Don't be too obvious."

"She's not even looking," Sean said. "I told you…inattentive…when driving and walking."

"I didn't know you were such an observer of human behaviour, Sean," as I waited for a pedestrian to cross before turning down a side street.

"Goes to show you don't know everything, Bernie. Especially when it comes to people."

I glanced at him, smirking in my direction. "Okay. I'll take that under advisement."

Nathan tapped me on the shoulder. "You can go now, Bernie. It's clear."

"So you're a back seat driver, now?" But I went nonetheless.

We found a municipal lot and parked.

"Don't forget to take the ticket," Nathan said.

"I've got it," I replied. "No need to remind me." Sheesh. I thought Eph was bad.

We walked around the corner, heading to the hotel entrance.

"What's the plan?" asked Nathan.

"Er…."

"What? You don't have a plan?" Sean asked.

"I never said that. We'll go into the hotel and look around."

Sean snorted. "That's your plan? Not much of a plan, if you ask me."

"I'm not asking you." This banter had begun to chafe more than a little.

"Don't worry, Bernie. Sean and I will check it out." Before I had a chance to open my mouth, they scampered off.

"Guys. Guys. Wait. Don't go…." Too late. They scooted through the revolving door and disappeared into the lobby. A well-dressed doorman watched them warily.

"Just full of energy," I said. "So excited to be here in this hotel."

"Yes sir," the doorman replied laconically. "If you say so."

I smiled gamely, pretending to be a long-suffering parent, which, in point of fact, bore the ring of truth.

I strode into the lobby and looked around. A swirl of people moved through the ample space. Many casually dressed but quite a few in evening clothes. It didn't surprise me, the hotel hosted any number of formal events and affairs over the course of its social calendar.

"Psst. Bernie. Over here."

I looked up. Nathan hung over a balustrade directly above me.

"What?"

"Found them. Stairs are off to the side. Come on up," he said.

I shook my head. A feeling of dread filled me. This may not end particularly well. I climbed the stairs wearily thinking how nice it would be to be at home lying on our super comfy sofa watching a movie or reading a book. I almost went limp thinking about it.

"Where's Sean?" I asked.

Nathan shrugged. "What am I? My brother's keeper?"

"Yes. Yes, you are your brother's keeper. Especially now."

"I don't know where he is. He just took off, as usual, and never said anything."

"Oh Jeez."

"But Mom and the guy are in there," he jerked his head toward a ballroom entrance. "So I'm guessing that's where Sean is too. Not a huge leap in logic, you know?"

"She can't see us here, Nathan. That'll ruin everything."

Nathan patted me on the back. "Don't panic, now Bernie. I get it but Sean, he's not that great at looking ahead or understanding consequences. He's more of an in-the-moment kind of guy."

"No kidding." I thought for a second. "Okay. We need to find him and that means going in. But for God's sake, don't let your mother see you."

Nathan nodded. "Sure. Be stealthy. I can do that."

Again, I groaned inwardly. The loudest kid in the universe thinks he can be surreptitious. I knew this was a bad idea but sometimes knowing and being able to do anything about it are different things.

"Come on," I said.

"Don't worry. I'll be invisible."

Why didn't that spark confidence?

Gingerly, I pulled open the door and slipped inside. Nathan followed right behind me. I took in a ballroom on a large scale with at least 40 or more tables. The lights had been turned down low. A band played a slow dance and couples clinched and swayed to the music. On either end of the room stood tables arrayed with food. People stood in line with plates, waiting their turn to fill them. The setting had a nostalgic feel like some bar mitzvah or wedding I'd attended in days gone past. Melvin Schwartz, I remember had a memorable affair. His mother broke a wine glass over his father's head. He'd pinched her cousin's bum, as I recall. Good times. I sunk, for a moment, into that little bit of memory.

I felt a tug on my sleeve. "Bernie." Another insistent tug.

"What?"

"You better take a look."

"What? Where?"

Nathan pointed. Oh God. Two uniformed waiters had gotten hold of Sean from either side and frog marched him toward the exit. Needless to say, he wasn't going quietly. As Nathan and I hurried over, notes of doom played in my head. The aisle was littered with obstacles, people mainly. The tables had been tightly packed together leaving scant space to navigate through. As we drew nearer, Sean pulled free from one of the waiters. I saw an arm move, a blurred fist and the waiter staggered backward heavily, falling over a wayward chair, his feet flying up into the air. The other waiter made a fatal mistake. He hitched his shoulders and moved in. After all, Sean was just a kid, wasn't he? Nathan and I had managed to get within a few feet of them. As Sean reared back, aiming what would have been a devastating kick to the waiter's balls, I grabbed him from behind, throwing him off-balance.

"Sean. Enough."

"Oh, hi, Bernie. Wondered where you got to."

I interjected myself between Sean and the waiter who panted heavily. I held up a hand. "It's okay. This is my son. Just a misunderstanding, that's all. We're leaving now."

"The kid was stealing food," the waiter spat. "Caught him red-handed."

"We are very sorry about that." I looked over. "And about your friend."

"You better watch that kid," the waiter hissed. "He's a criminal. He should be in jail."

I had turned away by then to hustle Sean away. I stopped and turned back. "What did you say?"

A small crowd had gathered. The waiter plucked up his courage. "I said that kid is a sicko and should be in jail."

I moved toward him. Reason drained away. Adrenalin took over. The stress of the previous days released a spigot of rage. Before I could take a few more steps, Nathan pushed in front of me.

"Come on, Dad, let's go. We don't want anymore trouble." His eyes went wide. "Please."

The waiter and I stood nose to nose. Finally, I nodded and turned away. I heard someone clapping and swivelled to look. A guy held a smartphone up filming the action. Of course. There stood Eric Schwilden with a crazy grin on his face. He gave me a thumbs up. I glanced over his shoulder into the crowd, locking on to the dance floor. Some overwhelming, irrational, magnetic force pulled my eyes in that direction, kind of like a tractor beam in Star Trek. Sharon and her beau stood together with their arms around each other. The expression on her face screamed fear, panic and anger. We stared at each other for what seemed an eon. My soul melted. Did I say this hadn't been a particularly good idea? Seeing her with him, like that, crushed me. I felt hot tears spring into my eyes. I turned away and marched out. Silently, both Sean and Nathan followed without prompting.

We exited the hotel and returned to the parking lot. Nathan went to open his mouth.

"Yes, I have the goddam parking ticket," I shouted.

"I was only going to say, sorry," Nathan murmured.

I hung my head. Sean lurked behind him. "I was hungry," he said. "I just wanted to get a snack, that's all."

I rubbed my hands up and down my face. I clenched my fists. I felt like I had been punched in the gut. "No," I said, finally. "It's me who's sorry. I screwed everything up and this is what it's come to. One fiasco after the other. I can never face your mother now. What would I say? How could I make any of this any better? Seeing her…seeing her…" I could barely get the words out.

Then a new voice interjected. "Seeing me, what, Bernie? Seeing me, what, exactly?"

The boys, together, suddenly looked stricken.

I couldn't turn and face her. "So, this wasn't the best idea, I'm guessing."

"Look at me, while you're talking, you bloody eejit."

I turned, glacially. I saw explosive anger, unbridled fury.

"What the hell were you thinking? Humiliating me in front of my work colleagues and clients? What the hell was that? Tell me. I demand to know."

I swallowed and shook my head, radiating with shame and embarrassment. "I...was...jealous..."

Utter bewilderment filled her expression. "What? Jealous of...what exactly?"

"You and that guy. You told me you were dating. I saw you dancing together. It seems pretty obvious."

"Are you just the biggest fool on the planet? Are you?" She took a step toward me and I cowered. Then thought better of it and turned away. A step later she stopped. "And to think," she said. "I was actually considering letting you move home. And then you do this? And you drag the boys into it as well?" She shook her head and stalked off, heels clacketing a cacophonic beat on the cement.

I drove the boys home in silence. Neither of them said a word. I pulled up to the house. They got out quietly.

"Sorry Bernie," Nathan said.

"Yeah. Sorry Dad," echoed Sean. He rarely called me dad so I believed he actually felt contrite.

I cleared my throat. "I...I...uh...don't know when I'll see you again. Just be good for your mother, will you? She deserves that. Please."

They both nodded and turned to climb the steps up to the front door.

I drove back to Eph and Catherine's. The air was cool, impregnated with moisture. I drove home in silence, willing my thoughts to disappear. But they wouldn't dissipate and a terrible, haunting feeling that I'd been trying to suppress blanketed me. When these thoughts arose, I pushed them into the background but some things were irrepressible. What if, I had thought, that some marriages were simply wrong? That the genetic intermingling produced malevolent results? Before I'd married, I'd thought that people got the children they deserved and that perhaps, within some grand, divine scheme, it was some sort of divine payback for an ill-gotten life or one of virtue. I had wanted children so badly. When I met Sharon, I had made that a condition of our marriage. She had wanted them too, but not as badly as I did. And now, looking on Sean in my mind, it was clear to me he had never been right since I could remember. There was some unnatural, vile force within him. I couldn't understand him, his selfishness, his egomania, his eagerness to hurt and inflict pain, his enjoyment of it, in fact. And what, I thought to myself, did I do to deserve this? Sharon and I both? What sort of payback was this? How had we offended in the divine comedy of life? I'd wracked my brain. I just didn't know. Driving along the darkened streets, my thoughts turned inward and I came to the conclusion, rational or not, that maybe we were an incongruent genetic mix. By marrying outside of my own faith, my own genetic code, if you will, I was being punished? Was this rational? I didn't know. It tore at me to think of it, to half-believe it. And if that were true, then Sharon and I should never have been together. Never had children. And now that we have, what will come of it? In my mind's eye, I envisioned a dark wet evening, like this one, a set of barricades across a slick roadway, flashing lights, a crowd of people silently mouthing their horror as they turned to look and stare at me. I shook my head and turned on the radio to take my mind off things. Good god, I was becoming positively Poe-like, quoth the Raven.

When I returned to Catherine's, I crept upstairs and sat abjectly in the dark, not moving, not feeling, not daring to venture a thought.

# 38

The next morning, I awoke with the thought that my theory about Sean as the product of some genetic mutation seemed profoundly absurd. I had wanted children and I must live with the consequences and not shirk my responsibilities when it came to them. I struggled with my feelings for him admittedly and found it difficult to show him affection, particularly when his sneering insolence raised hackles whenever I spoke to him. His contemptuous tone and manner led me to think that our separation wasn't necessarily a bad thing. Not to mention his impulsive behaviour. We'd been given a chilling out period. It was just the rest of the chilling out that didn't appeal to me. I ached now for Sharon and living in our house. I missed the normality of my life, yes, the routine. I didn't like change, I decided. Imposed change was the worst of all.

Gloria Martinez sat beside me in the boardroom of the mediator's office. I could hear the rustle of her panty hose as she crossed her legs. She wore a scent that I and the other men, no doubt, found appealing. Her tailored suit fitted her perfectly. The top two buttons of her crisp blouse remained undone allowing a glimpse of smooth, curved skin. Her big mane of auburn hair was immaculate. Her red nails gleamed. Not a dab of lipstick was out of place. She made me feel uncomfortable and she was my lawyer. Schwilden couldn't take his eyes off her.

I noticed a sallowness in his face, his Hugo Boss looked a bit frayed along the cuffs and the collar, and a few hairs had strayed. We had been summoned to mediation as part of the fast tracking of the case. The mediator was a tall, dark-haired lawyer named Larry Moldofsky. Gloria had chosen him from a submitted list of names. She said that Moldofsky had given over his practice to mediation almost exclusively. I could see why. He seemed good at it. I liked him and part of it meant wanting to please, I supposed. Schwilden's lawyer was a plump, pasty-faced fellow with thinning hair and dark circles under his eyes. His name, walter Grusinsky.

"Folks," Moldofsky said good-naturedly. "We're here to see if we can't settle this thing and do it quickly. Otherwise, I don't need to tell you how expensive this can get. Horrendously expensive, more than you could imagine. The costs are terrible, tens of thousands of dollars wasted. You probably could put that money to good use, in your respective businesses perhaps where it might make a positive impact rather than lavishing it on lawyers and the courts."

"We get the point," Gloria said. "Let's move on, shall we Larry?"

Moldofsky hesitated and I saw his eyes flick toward her.

"Of course. The facts appear to be very simple. Mr. Schwilden has claimed that Mr. Goldman assaulted him in the parking lot of their building. Mr. Schwilden sustained some injuries and is now making a personal claim against Mr. Goldman. He's indicated that he wants $250,000. Mr. Goldman, do you have that kind of money?"

"No."

Moldofsky nodded.

"Understandable. Few of us do. What about the charges then? Did it happen the way Mr. Schwilden claims?"

"My client vehemently denies Mr. Schwilden's assertion."

"Does he deny hitting Mr. Schwilden?"

I was about to open my mouth but Gloria put a hand on my arm. We weren't supposed to speak apparently. Only the lawyers.

"Yes, I would like to hear Mr. Goldman's version of the events," Grusinsky said. He had a slight accent.

"Please tell us what happened won't you Mr. Goldman."

I clammed up.

"Something happened. That is clear," Moldofsky said and grinned. "Otherwise, what are we doing here, right? Am I right?"

"There were no witnesses," Gloria said. "It's Schwilden's word against my client's."

"Then how did he end up in the hospital with a broken jaw?" Grusinsky demanded.

"I haven't the faintest idea, Mr. Grusinsky. Nor do I care a helluva lot, either. That's your client's problem. You just need to prove that something happened and without corroborating testimony I don't see how that's going to happen, do you?"

Gloria stood up on her four-inch stiletto heels.

"Gentlemen, we are required to be here and so here we are. I don't see any foreseeable outcome at the moment. Should you want to make a proposal or an offer, Mr. Grusinsky, you have my coordinates. I realized I was to stand up too which I did, awkwardly. I looked at Schwilden and he grinned at me, wolfishly.

"I enjoyed your performance on Saturday, Goldman. Classy. As usual."

Before I could respond, Gloria took my arm and marched me out of the office. When we hit the elevator and it was clear we were alone, Gloria asked.

"What was that all about?"

"Er, nothing. I just saw Schwilden at an event on Saturday, that's all. We never spoke."

"Okay. Whatever."

Gloria sighed. She held her Gucci attaché case in front of her with two hands. "Look Bernie. They're right in a sense. How are we going to explain Schwilden's broken jaw? We have to come up with some explanation at some point. I can obfuscate and delay as long as I can but eventually it will come down to where you were and whether the two of you were together and what happened. You will need a version of the story, whatever that is. I think you have to face the fact that this is going to cost money. How much is the issue. There's no point going to court over this. I hope we can beat Schwilden down to a reasonable amount that you can handle. At this point, that's the best we can hope for. You might want to think about making an offer."

The elevator doors opened and we stepped out into the marble and glass and steel lobby. We moved out of the flow of traffic.

"What happens now?"

Gloria shrugged.

"Somebody's got to make a move. Meanwhile the wheels of justice grind on. There'll be some back and forth and then we have to prepare for discoveries. That's where both sides get to ask detailed questions. There'll be no shirking then because you'll be under oath and it will be recorded and submitted to the court as a transcript. So we have until then to figure something out, okay?" She rubbed her palm on my jacket. "Think about it and let me know. Take some time but not too long."

"Sure."

She patted my cheek, letting her nails linger on my jaw line, then she turned and briskly walked away, her heels tapping the floor in an explosive rhythm.

# 39

Sharon and I now lived in limbo. Baby Madeleine had a really healthy set of lungs and exercised them often. No one got much sleep. I figured, because I worked and rose early, I slept the least. Eph and Catherine could nap during the day. Not so us working stiffs. I woke every day thinking of Sharon, continued to think and miss her during the day and went to sleep at night, picturing her getting ready for bed, going through her night time routine, then tucking herself into bed, glasses perched on her nose, face buried in a book, a romance novel most likely. When her feet got cold, she'd rub them up and down my legs or snuggle close. I missed those things most. The seemingly inconsequentials but the small habits and gestures that boasted familiarity, warmth and above all else, the comfort of home.

Every day I sent flowers. I had a standing order with the local florist, who loved me. Became my best friend. The flowers would bankrupt me but I didn't care. My credit card bill skyrocketed but still, I didn't care. I thought about moving out of Catherine and Eph's and getting my own place but couldn't afford it. I knew I was living on borrowed time. I tried to explain it to Eph.

"So, you can't afford to move out, is that what you're telling me?"

I nodded. That's what I'm telling you."

"And that's because you send flowers to Sharon's office every day? Every single day?"

"That's right."

"Has she acknowledged these gifts?"

"Just once. She asked me to stop sending them."

"And you haven't."

"No, I haven't."

"May I ask why?" He did seem genuinely perplexed, not something my father exuded often.

"Because it would be an admission of defeat. That there was no way forward and I'd have to give up any hope of us getting back together. I'm just not prepared to do that, not yet."

"You're not being very realistic, are you?"

"Well, call me a dreamer, Eph. Somebody's got to be."

"And that wouldn't be me, I take it?" he asked.

"Well, some of those brain cells seem to be firing still, Eph. I wouldn't call you a dreamer, no."

He sighed. "Dammit, Bernie. I want to see you two back together as much as anyone." He paused to lick his lips. "What about the boys?"

"I haven't seen them in weeks. Boys need their father. You should remember that. After the last episode, I am totally persona non grata."

Eph sighed. "You've got a steep hill to climb, my son."

"Tell me about it."

Every day that went by punctured another hole in my heart as we drifted further and further apart. I couldn't see my way back. I wracked what had been a pretty fertile and creative brain and came up empty, day after day after day. Bankrupt of plans, ideas, schemes.

The flowers had been a gesture. A nice one but perhaps something truer, something more powerful could move the mountain that had become my wife, and if I wasn't forthright, my soon-to-be ex-wife. So, I hatched a germ of an idea. I had nothing to lose. What could I do? What was I good at? In my mind, only one thing. Writing stories. So that's what I decided to do. Write her a story. And when it came to an end, then we'd see how things turned out. So I wrote Sharon a story. Every day, I sent her a new chapter. I called it, The Unrequited Idiots of the World. A bit sappy or maybe perverse, I don't know but true to the theme. It began like this:....

"Aaron sat alone on the sofa, the chattering crowd swirled around him, hemming him in tightly, compacting his solitude. He looked in from the outside but couldn't find a way to connect with anyone. The boys drank beers and the girls sipped colourful drinks punctuated with fruit and ice. Chips and dip disappeared down gullets. The others monopolized each other's company, to the exclusion of anyone else, outsiders. To the exclusion of him. He felt like a dweeb and knew that's what everyone around him thought as well. That is, if they even gave him a thought, one precious thought. Inside, he snorted. Didn't think so. Not noticeable. Not important.

Aaron's pal, Jeremy, came to his rescue, plopping down beside him. Also classified as a dweeb, Jeremy seemed to embrace his 'dweebness' and didn't seem to care about others much. Jeremy was only interested in people and things that were interested in him or to him. Which didn't leave much, unfortunately.

"Whaddaya think?" Jeremy asked.

"Of what?"

Jeremy swivelled around. "You think I'm talking about the Paris Opera? I'm talking about this, this pretty crappy party, at that."

"I'm with you. Not much really."

"You think we ought to make more of an effort?" he asked.

Aaron pondered. "No, I don't think so. Have you made an effort?"

"Sure have," Jeremy said. "I've tried to talk to at least half a dozen of them."

"What happened?" Aaron asked.

"Two guys punched me in the arm, for my trouble, so that was worthwhile." He rubbed his left shoulder. "All in jest, I assume?"

Aaron had a temper. "Which two guys?"

Jeremy shook his head. "I'm not going to tell you."

"Why not?"

"It will only lead to trouble. You know it will. We both do. After all, it wouldn't be the first time, would it? This has been going on since practically kindergarten."

Aaron stood up. He didn't look intimidating but others could be easily fooled. Pure flames burned within.

"Which two? Tell me."

Jeremy sighed. "Why make trouble? Isn't there already enough in the world?" He asked this but he knew the answer. Aaron always gave the same answer.

"A little more won't hurt."

Aaron spent his summers working in a rock quarry; rugged work that pounded and molded his slim frame. He stood taller than he appeared and boasted large, powerful hands and over-sized feet. Good anchors those feet, not to mention weapons, on occasion. They moved through the crowd. Loitering groups of teens eased away from them, like they gave off a dangerous odour, an unsettling discomfort. It seemed instinctive. The groups parted, leaving four, laughing guys in a corner downing beers.

Jeremy nodded. "That would be them."

"I thought you said there was two of them."

"Two who punched me and the other two that watched and sniggered."

Aaron turned to him. "You're going to have to step up then. All right?"

Jeremy made a face. "What? Again? You going soft on me?"

Aaron smiled. "Just be ready, okay?"

The four youths stood in a circle. They looked like athletes, burly and thick-necked. Football players, Aaron guessed. Their swagger irritated him. Good thing they were off campus in a sorority house. He sauntered up, making sure eye contact occurred with at least two of the beefy boys facing toward him.

Aaron nodded. "How's it going?"

The first two stared at him like he was an alien. Aaron imagined in his own mind what they saw. He figured they saw some geek wearing baggy dress pants, a loose white shirt with fringes hanging down, the kind that the Orthodox wore and a kippa pinned to his head. Nothing could be more foreign to them than him.

The two kept staring saying nothing while the other two turned around to look.

"Help you?" one of the boys said. Aaron wasn't sure which one spoke.

He nodded. "Actually, you can. It has to do with my friend over there," and he pointed at Jeremy, who grinned and gave a small wave.

"What about him?"

"A couple of you were a bit rude to him. I'm not sure which of you behaved that way since you all look so much alike…" The four boys started. Their expressions darkened. Aaron held up his hand. "But I have a proposition for you."

"What kind of proposition?" Aaron thought the boy directly in front of him had spoken but he couldn't be certain.

"One even you can understand. It's simple. I'm going to stand here, see, like this…" Aaron assumed a stance, leaning at a slight angle with his hands up as if pushing against something. "I'll give each one of you a turn, okay? I know you guys play football and are probably pretty strong so it should be easy for you. All you have to do is make me move, right? You place your hands against mine and push. Very simple. But you can only use your upper body. No legs, no kicking or twisting or you lose."

The four boys grinned, finally realizing that Aaron was a complete idiot to suggest such a thing.

"I'll take you on, one after the other. You've got 20 seconds each, that's the rule. Now, if I win, my buddy, Jeremy, over there, gets to give you each two shots, just like you gave him."

The boys sniggered. "I'm scared now," one said.

Another said, "What do we get when we win?"

Aaron smiled. "Then you get to give Jeremy two shots each...and me too, of course. So, what do you say?"

The first one who spoke said, "You're a kike, right?" Aaron nodded. The boy resumed. "Kikes don't act this way. Aren't you supposed to be praying or something?" He smiled and his pals sniggered.

"Or something," Aaron replied. "So. We got a deal? Think you're man enough? Huh? Tough guy football players?"

The four boys collectively rotated their shoulders and put down their drinks.

"Who's first?" Aaron asked. The first one stepped up. Aaron took his position and put his hands up. The boy opposite did the same. "Jeremy will officiate and keep time."

A crowd gathered loosely around the contestants. Out of the corner of his eye, Aaron spotted a tall girl with brilliant green hair, pale skin, freckles, startling blue eyes and elaborate tattoos up and down her arms and neck.

Jeremy stepped up. He removed a stopwatch from his trouser pocket and held it up for all to see. "Ready. Get set. Go."

Aaron maintained his position while his opponent pushed and pressed and snorted like a young bull. His pale face turned red, then purple but Aaron didn't budge.

"Time," Jeremy called. The boy pushed himself away from Aaron in disgust.

"He cheated," the boy spat.

"Next," Aaron called. The second boy stepped up. Aaron assumed his stance and the boy did the same. Again, Jeremy counted down. Again, the boy huffed and puffed and snorted and pressed. Aaron didn't budge an inch. After time had elapsed, he too looked angry, as if he'd been cheated. Aaron remained calm and relaxed.

"Let's see if one of you can do any better," he said.

The third boy stepped up. He looked confident. "Not this time," he said. "You're going down."

"Sure," Aaron replied. He assumed his position. The third boy, larger than the first two braced himself. Jeremy gave the signal and the third boy, engorged on hate and adrenalin couldn't shift Aaron in the least, not the teeniest waver. He broke away, throwing his hands up in disgust.

"I don't get it." He looked down, embarrassed and ashamed.

"Don't worry," Aaron said. "You'll get over it, someday. Next contestant."

The fourth boy stood apart. Aaron assumed his stance but watched the other boy carefully. An alert switched on in his brain. Jeremy began the countdown while the boy moved into position. Just before Jeremy gave the signal, the boy launched himself at Aaron who, smoothly, swivelled his hips to the left. The boy brushed past him, his momentum yanked him forward. Aaron stuck out his foot catching the boy's ankle. He fell, chin first, to the floor. Slowly, he pushed himself to a kneeling position and turned. Blood ran out of his mouth. He must have bitten his tongue from the impact.

"That was naughty," Aaron said. He looked at the other three. "So, you lose. Time to pay up." He beckoned to them.

The fourth boy spat out some blood. "How about we beat the crap out of you instead?"

Aaron shrugged. "That's an option certainly. But you sure you want to do that in front of all your peers here?"

For the first time it seemed, the bloodied boy took a look around him. Surrounded by onlookers. Everyone in the room had stopped to stare, to take the contest in. The girl with the tattoos stepped up. She put her hands on her slim hips and sneered. "You guys going to welsh on your bet? What kind of pussies are you? Man up, why don't ya." After she spoke, murmurs of agreement, swept through the crowd. A couple of larger boys stepped forward, crossed their arms and stared at the four who cowered.

"Pay up," one of them said.

The four boys paled but each one nodded in turn.

Aaron turned to Jeremy. "Go ahead," he said. "Do your thing." He turned to the four. "We're going to let you off lightly. It'll just be Jeremy this time."

Jeremy stepped up. The first boy offered his left shoulder. Jeremy reared back and punched him twice sparing no effort. The boy went down on his knees, hanging his head in pain but didn't cry out. The next stepped up. Jeremy put his body weight into it and he too, doubled over in pain. And so it went for the third. Only the fourth and larger boy stayed upright, gritting his teeth. "I'll remember this and you," he said. "Both of you."

"A pleasure doing business," Aaron said.

"I think we should go," Jeremy said. "We've had our fun."

"You have, you mean."

"Whatever."

"Okay." Aaron nodded to the onlookers. "See you around."

The four boys nursed their shoulders but stared malevolently at the odd pair. Wisely, Aaron and Jeremy moved quickly through the assembly, down a flight of stairs and out the front door on to the street.

Out on the street, Jeremy breathed a deep sigh of relief. "That could have gotten ugly."

"Oh ye of little faith."

"It was fun giving them the shots, though."

"Looked like it," Aaron said.

They began to walk briskly down the street back to their residence on campus. The air had chilled a little and they picked up the pace.

"Hey!"

Aaron stopped and swivelled. The tattooed girl from the party had followed them outside. Jeremy paused.

She drew near them standing awkwardly. "Hey," she said.

"Well, hey yourself," Aaron replied.

"So, that was very interesting in there."

Aaron glanced at Jeremy who shrugged. "Was it?"

"You took a risk. Those guys could have just beat the crap out of you."

Aaron nodded. "True. But they didn't."

"And why do you think that is?"

"Too many people. They don't like witnesses."

"So, how did you do that thing…that thing you did?"

"Oh that. Pretty simple really. Fulcrum theory. Basic Physics. Not difficult."

"And are you a Physics major here?"

"Uh, no. Poetry actually."

The girl's eyes shot up. "Poetry? No shit."

Aaron laughed. "Really. No shit."

"I guess, I mean, I thought…you people…your people tended to take more practical subjects."

"What people exactly?"

"You know…Jews…Jewish people."

Again, Aaron and Jeremy exchanged looks. "Oh. Those people."

She reddened. "Sorry. Didn't mean to…"

Aaron and Jeremy both laughed.

"Don't worry about it. It was funny seeing you squirm a bit. Actually, poetry is very practical in many ways."

"Say listen," she said. "What are you guys doing now?"

"Uh, heading back to residence," Jeremy mumbled. He wasn't too comfortable around girls or people generally.

"So, want to go for a drink? I know a place nearby. It's off campus."

Aaron didn't hesitate. "Sure. Let's go for a drink."

Jeremy shook his head. "Not for me. I'm heading back."

"Come on," Aaron said.

"Nope. See you." Jeremy loped off, fringes flapping at his side. The back of his shirt glowed as he passed under a street lamp.

"He doesn't like me," the girl said.

"Don't take it personally. He doesn't like anyone much. Never has."

"Say, what's your name anyway?" she asked.

"Aaron. Aaron Gold."

The girl put out her hand. "Nice to meet you, Aaron Gold. I'm Aimee."

"Aimee what?"

She shrugged. "Just Aimee, will do."

They shook hands. She had a firm grip. Aaron looked at her and her eyes widened into deep blue pools. He felt like diving in.

Aaron nodded. "Okay, Just Aimee. Let's get that drink. Where's this booze can you were talking about?"

Aimee smiled. "Not far. Just down this way a bit."

Aaron had never been to a booze can but this one, romantically dubbed The Cutty Sark, or simply, The Cutty to the locals, matched what he imagined. Dank interior, mouldy lighting, scarred laminated tables filled with dirty glasses, a long, curved bar of smudged mahogany and one harried waitress with runny make-up and sweaty armpits. An assassin behind the bar served drinks. Apart from a couple of old-timers, most of the tables were occupied by students seriously dedicated to drinking. Aaron knew the type. Those who spent seven years on a three-year degree then ended up back in their parents' basement occupying the frayed couch and surviving on take out pizza and beer.

Aaron took it all in. "Nice," he said. His crisp white shirt practically radiated in the gloom. Apparently, Aimee was a regular or at least greeted and acknowledged by a number of the current patrons, those able to sit up and utter a coherent word or two.

"Let's sit over here," she said and led him to a table in the corner.

The waitress hustled up. "Hi Hon," she said. Then eyeing Aaron, "Who's this?"

"This is Aaron," Aimee said. "How are you, Sally?"

"Yeah good. What can I get you?"

"Double Scotch for me," Aimee said.

Sally nodded. "And for the, er, gentleman?"

Aaron wanted to laugh. "You got Vodka?" Sally nodded again. "Absolut Vodka?"

"Uh-huh."

"I'll have an Absolut Vodka on the rocks with a twist, if you've got it. If you don't, that's okay."

"Don't worry," Sally said. "I'll get a fresh one from the fridge." She hustled off.

"She seems nice," Aaron said.

"Sally's okay. She works hard. Serves in this place at night and does day shifts at the Keg'N Drum over on Bleecker."

Aaron looked around. "They seem to know you here."

Aimee smiled a bit sheepishly. "Yeah. I come here pretty often. It reminds me of home."

"Ah. Tough childhood, was it?"

"No. Nothing like that. Just the sort of local bar in our neighbourhood where I grew up. Where my Dad and his pals used to hang out, you know?"

"Not really. My parents wouldn't be caught dead in a place like this."

Sally brought the drinks and banged them on the table. She smiled wanly then moved off. Aaron peeked into the glass. A reasonably unmouldy slice of lemon floated in the glass.

Aimee raised her glass. "Cheers," she said.

"L'Chaim".

They each took a sip. "What does that mean?" she asked.

"It means…to life."

"I like that."

"Me too. We should always appreciate what life gives us."

"Even if it brings bad things to you?"

Aaron nodded. "Even then. Gives us an opportunity to prevail, to overcome the negative."

"So, you don't give in, even when you feel yourself being crushed?" She looked at him seriously and he felt a chill run up his spine.

"I try not to. I'm not saying I'm always successful, or ever successful for that matter." He paused. "So, you're at school here?"

"Part-time."

"Doing what?"

"Art. I'm a painter."

"Oh yeah. Any good?"

She shrugged. "I think so."

"I figured you were kind of arty," he said.

"Why's that?"

"Oh, you know, the dyed hair, the tattoos…"

"You forgot the nose ring."

"Okay, and the nose ring."

"No stereotyping, of course."

Aaron smiled then indicated his get up. "And none from you either."

She held up her hands. "Okay. Okay. Point taken."

"We're just walking stereotypes, I guess," he said.

"So, you're really studying Poetry?"

"Yup."

"Why?"

"Because I like it. And to be honest, it pisses my parents off. I had a scholarship to law school but I turned it down."

"Why?"

"It doesn't interest me."

"And poetry does?"

"Yes. And so does art, painting in particular," he said.

"Really?"

"Well, maybe I'm trying to get on your good side, just a little bit."

"Why is your friend black?"

"Jeremy? He was born that way. Tried to scrub it off but you know, just wouldn't disappear."

Aimee downed her Scotch and held up her glass to Sally, who nodded. "You know what I mean. Come on."

"Jeremy was born in Ethiopia to a long-lost Jewish sect called the Falasha. In the early to mid-90s, there was a brutal civil war between Ethiopia and Eritrea. So, the state of Israel put together a rescue mission and evacuated 300,000 of the Falasha to Israel."

"Wow. How many were left in Ethiopia?"

"None."

"None?"

"That's right. They got all of them out. Anyway, Jeremy's family lived there for a few years then emigrated to Canada. We met in kindergarten and have been friends every since."

"You've known each other a long time."

"We have."

"I don't have any friends like that. I haven't known anyone that long except my brothers and sisters, of course."

"How many are there?"

Aimee furrowed her brow. "Oh, let's see…six…no, seven of us."

"Hmm, that's a crowd. It's just me and Jeremy too. So, we're kind of like brothers, really, being only children."

"Are your parents religious?"

Aaron shook his head. "Not at all. They're Socialists. Don't believe in God."

"And you do this to…?"

Aaron nodded and smiled. "To piss them off, yes, that's part of it. Although, it has been wearing a bit thin, lately. I thought it made sense when I was a teenager and that's what teenagers do, don't they? Everything to thwart their parents' ideas and beliefs, right?"

"I don't know. I left home at sixteen. Been on my own ever since."

Aaron looked around. "Ah, self- sufficiency, I like it."

Aimee snorted. "I don't live here, you know. Just come in for the occasional drink."

"So what were you doing at that stupid frat party? Don't tell me you were trying to fit in?"

"That's rich, coming from you. Free food and drinks were a strong attraction. Besides, on occasion there are interesting people who show up." Aimee downed the rest of her drink. Aaron still nursed the Absolut. "Hey. I wanted to ask you something."

"So. Ask."

"Will you pose for me?"

"Pose, as in...?"

"Sit in a chair while I paint you."

"With my clothes on or off?"

"On. Definitely on. It's what makes you a really interesting subject. And I've never met an Orthodox Jew before."

Aaron held up a finger. "A wavering Orthodox Jew."

Aimee smiled. "Okay. A wavering Orthodox Jew. So, what do you say?"

Aaron shrugged. "Why not? I haven't met anyone who wanted to paint me before. So, I will end up with just one head, right? Nothing Picasso-like?"

"Cross my heart and hope to die."

"Well, let's hope it doesn't come to that."

They had several more drinks, or rather Aimee had several more to Aaron's one.

"Maybe we should go, Just Aimee. I should be awake for class tomorrow."

"Okay." She lurched a bit as she stood moving and speaking, sleepily.

Outside, Aaron took a deep breath. Aimee leaned on him.

"I like you, Aaron."

"I like you too, Just Aimee."

"Is that what you're going to call me? Just Aimee?"

"It suits you."

"You're kind of funny."

"I know. So, where do you live, exactly?"

She pointed. "Just down here. Not far."

They headed down a shadowed alleyway.

"Not the best part of town."

"It's fine," she said. "And reasonably cheap." After walking for several minutes, she pulled up in front of a door. "This is me. Hmm, want to come up? I can show you my studio."

"Just Aimee. Listen. I would like to...just not this way and it's late. And you're a little bit drunk."

"Not that drunk."

"Still. As an Orthodox Jew, I still have some morals, a few, anyway. When we're both wide-eyed and clear-minded, then we can address this, uh, situation. How's that?"

"You're pretty logical for a poet."

"I never said I was a poet. Just that I liked poetry."

"You're a poet. I know you are. You are a deep soul. I can feel it."

"Okay, Just Aimee. I'm good with that."

"Goodnight, Aaron, my Orthodox Jewish friend."

"Goodnight Just Aimee, my artist friend."

She leaned in and brushed his lips with hers. He tasted Scotch and something else he couldn't identify. Then Aimee turned, unlocked the door and went inside. Aaron sighed to himself. He'd felt something electric coursing through him. It troubled him. As did she…"

# 40

The summer "blockbuster" issue of *Bookology* stumbled to completion. It had been printed and distributed to bookstores across the country and select newsstands. I felt relieved to get it over with but then came the sinking feeling upon the realization that it would begin all over again. Some days, I felt as if each new issue was standing at ground zero and we had to claw our way up through the muck to get to fresh air. Most people never realize how primeval publishing really is. And depressing too. You felt like you weren't getting anywhere, not unlike walking the treadmill endlessly. Still, that remained the glamour of publishing. Once on the treadmill, it became really tough to get off.

Over the past few weeks at the community centre, I had noticed a tall, lithe woman with long dark hair, working out. She appeared to be relentless, focused on what she was doing. I'm always curious about people and the usual cast of characters, the habitual morning-goers, were familiar to me. When a new face appeared, it became a bit of an event. Not many people liked getting up really early and who could blame them? We all remained terribly sleep deprived, zombies sleepwalking through life. It took energy and concentration to get your body moving at 6 a.m. Hugo had been off sick with the flu. I knew it had to be a serious case for him to stay home, to rob him of the pleasure of humiliating me at 21. I'd already gone through my weight routine before heading out on to the court. This gave me a chance to practice, I thought. By the time Hugo returned, I'd turn the tables on him. So, I stood there in the gym, shooting balls with varied success. Better but not great.

"You're not bad," a voice said behind me and I turned to see the lithe one standing there with her hands on her hips. She wore workout pants and a baggy grey sweatshirt.

"Not really," I replied.

"Don't be so modest," she said.

"I'm not."

"Want to shoot a few?" she asked.

I sighed. First Hugo, now her. I put out my hand. "Bernie Goldman."

"Nathalie Hunter."

She appeared completely unadorned, no rings, no nail polish, no make-up. A long and slender neck, much like her body, the nose aquiline and straight, unblinking dark eyes. Her hair streaked grey. Her hand was dry and smooth and the grip firm.

I tossed her the ball. "Break the ice," I said.

Five minutes later I still stood, hands on hips, while she drained in shots from all over the court. I hadn't moved a muscle.

She grinned at me showing crinkles at the corners of her eyes and mouth. "Twenty-one."

"Oh shit. First Hugo and now you. Will the humiliation never end?"

"Who's Hugo?"

I told her. "Maybe you should play each other. At least it would be more of a match."

Then she explained that she had played varsity basketball in university.

"Sorry. I should have told you."

"No, it's okay. You like putting men in their place. I understand that. How often does that happen in the real world?"

"Not often enough," she replied.

"Apparently not. Although I wish it hadn't been me."

"Don't sulk."

"I'm not sulking."

She began to toss the ball from hand to hand. "So, what's your story, Bernie?"

I got her meaning. "Separated. And you?"

"Divorced."

"Why?"

She shrugged. "Maybe he couldn't handle it."

"Maybe," I said. "Kids?"

She nodded. "One. A daughter, fifteen."

"Oh God, isn't that a great age?"

"You sound like you speak from experience."

I nodded. “Uh-huh.” And I told her.

“Interesting.”

“Listen, I’m heading to the pool right now. Do you swim by any chance?”

“I do. And I have my suit with me.”

“Did you swim varsity too?”

She laughed. “No. Just high school actually.”

“Oh Christ. Well come on then. I can see my humiliation has not yet been completed for the day.”

“You’re on. This is good for my ego.”

“And just peachy for mine.”

We’d fallen into a jocular banter quite naturally. It was fun. I hadn’t been this relaxed with a woman in a long time. I was also intrigued by the thought of her in a bathing suit.

She stopped me at the entrance to the men’s locker room.

“I’m not manhunting by the way.”

“Oh? I, I, …” I sputtered.

“I just didn’t want to give you the wrong impression.”

“Okay.”

“Actually, I’m gay.”

“I see.” Too bad is what occurred to me. “So, why…?”

“You looked like you could use a friend.”

“Oh. Is it that obvious?” She shrugged in response.

“So, I’m a charity case now?” I spoke to myself and my spirits, that had climbed quickly, plummeted back to their own natural subterranean level.

Nathalie put a hand on my shoulder.

“Besides, I do think you’re very cute.”

“Is that why you and your husband broke up?”

Her face tightened. “That would be it.”

“See you at the pool. Five minutes.”

When I got to the pool, Nathalie sat waiting on a wooden bench. The lifeguard, whom I hadn’t paid much attention to lately, squeegeed water off the deck. They’d filled the pool too high again and it overflowed on to the deck.

“Watch your step,” warned the lifeguard. “it’s very slippery.”

I had turned to look at her and twisted back and then forward again to look at Nathalie, who grinned at me for some reason and that’s when my feet went out from under me as my legs flew forward and my torso flipped back carried by the momentum. I remember the back of my head hitting the tiles with force and… that's all I remember.

Some time later, I listened to breathing that seemed very loud, filling up my eardrums with sound. I realized that I was lying down and there were other people in the room with me, if indeed I was in a room. Perhaps I made a noise, or groaned or farted.

"I think he's waking up," a voice said. Hushed words and muffled phrases flickered about the room.

I forced one eyelid open and I can say that everything felt extremely heavy, my head, my arms and legs, something sat on my chest which felt very sore. The images blurred at first then tightened into focus. Some photographer had adjusted my lens. Thank you. There were faces and they looked rather anxious, so I decided to open the other eye to verify what the first had seen. Yup, the view expanded and adjusted to the proper perspective but the anxiety hadn't left.

"Why are you here?" I asked.

"Why do you think?" Eph replied.

"Again, a question answers a question," I said. "The standard Goldman refrain."

"No brain damage that I can see," Eph said, and there were a few nervous titters.

I raised my head from the neck so I could peer around the room. Nathan's face suddenly appeared very close to mine.

"Hi Bernie. Dad. How're you feeling? Are you okay? Is there anything I can do for you? Get you something? A drink? A snack? What about a chocolate bar? Some fruit maybe? Or a magazine? Maybe you'd like to read something."

"Nathan." Sharon's voice rang out.

"Shut it, will ya. Your father's just come out of a coma. He doesn't need you yammering in his face." And then suddenly, there she was, leaning over me, her long hair reaching down and tickling my cheek, her hand running through my hair.

"I was in a coma?"

"Well, just a wee one."

"How long?"

"Several hours, I think. Your friend called me."

"Friend?" I swivelled my view and saw Nathalie sitting on a chair in the corner. Sean sat slumped beside her. She waved and smiled.

"Oh, you mean my new friend, Nathalie. She's gay," I said, then lay back and closed my eyes. When I opened them again, it wasn't by choice, someone slapped my cheeks.

"Bernie. Bernie. Come on now, no sleeping. You're not allowed to sleep now."

"What? Why not?"

"Because we're afraid you won't wake up."

"Oh. That." When I opened my eyes, a blinding, narrow beam piercing through. "Yeow, that's bright."

"Sorry, I'm just taking a look to see what's in there."

"Turn off the damn light."

"He sounds a little better," Sharon said.

"Sharon?"

"Mmm-hmm?"

"How long have I been here?"

"Since yesterday."

"Yesterday? Did I see you yesterday?"

"You did. And your Dad and the boys and your friend, Nathalie, who's gay."

"How did you know that?"

"You told us."

"I did?"

"Yes. You shouted it out to the whole room but she wasn't embarrassed at all. She thought it was funny actually. She was very nice. I like her a lot."

"Me too."

"Let's get you sitting up, shall we?" the doctor said, as he slipped his arm under my shoulder and helped me to a sitting position. The view didn't appear stable. Everything moved. "How's that?"

"Crappy. Everything is moving and I don't feel well."

"Don't worry. That will go away. You've had a nasty crack on the head, so you've got to take it easy for awhile."

"How long do I have to stay here?"

I finally noticed that the doctor, a short, stocky fellow with a brush cut flecked with grey, had a reassuring face. Anyone who wore a brush cut couldn't be all bad.

"Oh another day or so, just so we can observe you and make certain that nothing else has happened."

"Why is my chest sore?"

"You were given CPR," the doctor replied matter-of-factly, as if it happened all the time and in his experience that may be true but not in mine.

"What? Why?"

The doctor levelled me with a look as if to say, aren't you silly for even asking? I could see Sharon hovering over his shoulder, an anxious expression on her face.

"Well, you hit the back of your head with a lot of force and for some reason your heart stopped. Momentarily."

"My heart? Stopped? You mean I died?"

The doctor chuckled.

"No, not exactly. It just got out of synch for a moment. Luckily, help was near by."

"You mean the life guard? She gave me CPR?" And I made a mental note to thank her in person.

"No," Sharon said. "It was your friend, Nathalie. She did it. Apparently, the lifeguard was panic-stricken. She didn't have a clue. Thank god she was there."

"The lifeguard?"

"No, your friend, Nathalie."

"You mean my gay friend, Nathalie."

Sharon pulled a face.

"That's right yes. But she doesn't look gay to me."

"What does that mean exactly?"

"I'm not sure."

The doctor harrumphed.

"I don't want to get in the middle of anything here, so I'll leave you, Mr. Goldman. We're going to keep you in for 24 hours, just for observation and then we'll see about letting you go home."

"Go home where?" I asked myself, not realizing that I had spoken it out loud. The dissembled thought of returning to Eph and Catherine's made my head and stomach lurch, one after the other.

The doctor looked startled. "You do have a home?"

"I don't know where home is, anymore. I wish I did."

The doctor glanced at Sharon. "What…?"

I wandered verbally. "I want to come home. I want to come home. Just like Dorothy, but Kansas is so far away. My home is close. I just want to go there and I want everyone to be happy. Ever after. Can we do that?"

The doctor looked a bit astonished. "Mrs. Goldman?"

"Of course he has a home. With me and the children. He's just rambling now. The concussion seems to still be on, isn't it? I mean, where else would he live? His father can't look after him. He can barely look after himself and now with a new baby and all?"

The doctor gave her a questioning look. "A new baby?"

"Well, yes, Eph and his wife, Catherine, just had a child together you see. So Bernie couldn't get any rest there at all, would he?"

"Good. Well good," said the doctor. "Well, no worries there."

"Uh," I said.

The doctor turned. "Yes?"

"There's no danger of brain damage is there? I mean, I was deprived of oxygen, wasn't I?"

The doctor knit his brow, to look more serious and contemplative.

"No, you were only out for a minute, maybe less. Without your friend's intervention, however, it could have been much worse. So, there's no danger of brain damage. Just the fact you asked the question tells me you are fairly alert."

I took umbrage. "Fairly?"

The doctor smiled and pointed his forefinger at me. "There, you see." He couldn't get out of the room fast enough it seemed, and closed the door behind him. Sharon and I were alone, the first time in a long while.

"Shouldn't you be at work?"

She nodded. "But it's not every day that your husband cracks his head open on the deck of a swimming pool, is it? And gets knocked unconscious and stops breathing and then is revived by a lesbian. Now that doesn't happen every day."

"And am I your husband? Still?" I knew I wasn't being fair and that I exploited the situation but I didn't care.

Sharon came close to me now. Her face squeezed in a little and she bit her lip. Whimpering sounds came out of her somewhere and I saw large, fat tears rolling down her cheeks. She nodded in response quickly then put her head down on my chest. "Yeow."

"Sorry." And she popped up again.

"No, no. It's okay. Just move to the side a bit. You hit the sore spot."

Her head returned and I could inhale that lemony aroma that wafted from her hair. She draped herself across me for a long moment.

"I was so worried about you, you silly bugger. I was thinking, how could he do this to me and the children? But then I thought I was being unfair to you. And when I saw this Nathalie person, right away I suspected hanky panky. But she was ever so nice and comforting and in control. She took charge of everything. I was a mess. I admit it. Totally useless I was and you know how I hate the fluttering female type who flaps her hands in a crisis. That was me, I tell you."

"I'm sorry," I said.

"Ach, it's not your fault. You couldn't predict that you'd slip like that."

"No, I mean about everything else. What a mess I made of things. Of everything."

Sharon sat up straight and looked down at me. She wore a tight pullover and it didn't take much for me to imagine what she had under it.

"Ah, that."

"There was nothing to the thing with Charlotte. We just emailed each other from time to time and that was it."

"But you were attracted to her, were you not?"

"I suppose so."

"And she offered you something I couldn't?"

"No, not exactly."

"What then?"

"She just listened and seemed interested, I guess."

"And I wasn't?"

"No, not really."

Sharon rubbed the palms of her hands up and down her face. She wore little make-up, the sweater, baggy fleece pants and scuffed runners. Very un-Sharon-like.

"I was neglecting you."

"You were preoccupied. I understand that. I'm like that myself. My head is always somewhere else, dreaming, fantasizing, whatever." I paused. "Can I really come home?" She inclined her head and there was the hint of a smile. "Please. I do want to come home. I'm tired of living at Catherine's and I miss everyone, even Sean a little. Not Mrs. Sanchez though. I miss you, Sharon. Being with you. I guess that's why I followed you. It was like inflicting a wound on myself and I wanted to grovel in the pain."

"Grovelling suits you. You should indulge in it more often."

"I think I've humiliated myself enough for more than a lifetime. I was desperate, I guess. I just didn't know what else to do," I murmured.

I felt stymied momentarily. And tired. I closed my eyes. I heard Sharon's voice in my ear.

"I'm not going to let you go again, boyo. You can be sure of that and I will do better, this time, I promise. I've come to understand that family is everything and work isn't as important as I thought…" I began to drift, carried on the sound of her words but not the content necessarily. So when she concluded with, "and by the way, I'm pregnant." I was in cloud cuckoo land. I may have even snored a little. Not the reaction Sharon had wanted I don't think.

The next time I awoke I thought I saw Nathalie and Hugo looming into view.

"Hi," Nathalie said. "How are you feeling?"

"Woozy."

"It will pass," Hugo said.

"I thought you had the flu."

"I got better."

"How do you know Nathalie?"

"We have been playing basketball together. She is good. Better than you. More of a challenge."

"That wouldn't be difficult. Listen Nathalie, uh, Sharon told me what you did. That I've got you to thank for this sore chest, I, uh…"

"Anytime. I don't know what got into me actually. I took that course years ago and something just took over. I wasn't really thinking."

"Well, I'm grateful."

"Just get better," she said. My eyes fluttered closed again.

The next time they opened, I saw Eph and Catherine and the baby. Catherine was breastfeeding. This was beginning to seem like a game show. Who are our next contestants?

"Hi son."

"Dad."

"How are you feeling?"

"Better, I think. My head seems a bit better. There's less throbbing anyway. But I feel so tired."

"That comes from lying in bed all day."

"I guess. How's the baby?"

Catherine looked up. "She's wonderful. Eats all the time. She can holler like a hog caller."

"Well, a future career awaits."

"Not for my daughter," Catherine declared smiling.

"I hope I'm around to see it," Eph said, wistfully. "Now, I really want to see her grow up."

"No reason why you shouldn't, Dad." Eph shrugged but there was a curious light in his eyes. And then I thought what that must be like and that I almost didn't make it to do the same. We talked for a few minutes more and I grew tired. Catherine plucked the child from her breast and burped her, then buttoned up her blouse, picked up the diaper bag, took my Dad's arm and said goodbye.

The next time I awoke, I saw Nook and Ramon hovering over me.

"Hi guys."

"Hey," Ramon said. "You don't do things in half measures, do you?"

"Why should I?"

Nook laughed, discreetly. "Anything to get attention, right, Bernie?"

"Right."

I poked Ramon. "How are you doing? And Luisa?"

He smiled. "Better. She says she understands my point of view and we've agreed that I need some time too. So I'll be seeing you guys again on Saturdays."

"What day is it today?"

"Thursday," Nook replied.

"I've been here since Tuesday? It seems a lot longer."

"You've been drifting," Ramon said. "We've been here an hour already. We saw Sharon and the boys. They stayed for a while but then the boys had basketball practice or something. Sharon said she'd be back after dropping them off."

"Right. Basketball, I'd forgotten about that."

"So you got what you wanted," Nook said, with a sly smile.

"What's that?"

"Peace and tranquillity. The ultimate loafable moment."

"A helluva way to achieve it though," Ramon said.

"I haven't been able to enjoy it," I replied. "I don't even realize when I'm conscious or not half the time."

"Maybe that's the ultimate then," Nook said, pushing his glasses up his nose.

"Speaking of which," I said, and felt myself ease off into another space and the white cloud of unconsciousness descended. Fade.

The next time I woke I wanted to get out of bed. I wanted to get up and do things. I was tired, exhausted from lying down. How have I been peeing, I thought? And the other thing. What about that? Had I eaten anything? I don't remember chowing down. And I decided I was hungry. I looked around and saw that both my arms were hooked up to things, that there were tubes stuck into me. I could move my arms though. There was some play on the tubes, thank god.

"Hey?" I called. The sound was a little weak. Rusty pipes. I cleared my throat. "Hey?" I called again. "Anybody there?" I had no idea what time it was.

Sharon poked her head around the door. "What are you doing?"

"Calling."

"What for?"

"I want to get up. I want to walk around. I want to go to the bathroom. I want something to eat. Please. And I want to get out of here."

She gave me a curious look. "All right then. I'll go find a nurse."

"I'm glad you're feeling better," said the nurse, a large, red-haired woman with freckles dotting her pale skin. She stuck a thermometer into my mouth. "Keep that under your tongue for a moment." While I was doing that, she wrapped a blood pressure cuff around my arm and pumped it up until I thought my hand would explode. Then we watched a little squiggle on a monitor move in tight circles going faster and faster until there was a loud beep. She took the thermometer out of my mouth and ejected the plastic sheath into the garbage can.

"Vitals look good," she commented. "I'll go and call the doctor and we'll see about getting you out of here."

"How about something to eat? Can I have that?"

"What do you feel like?"

"Two fried eggs over easy, a pumpernickel bagel, lightly buttered with strawberry jam on the side and hot tea with lemon. If that's okay."

The nurse stood there looking amused. With arched eyebrow, she said, "I'll see what I can do."

"You'd think you were ordering room service at the Four Seasons," Sharon said, wryly.

"Well, I am ordering room service. It's not the Four Seasons but after a near-death experience, this isn't too bad."

Sharon paled. "Don't say that. I won't have it."

"I was just kidding."

"You've got a few good years left in you yet."

"You think so?" She nodded solemnly. "And what would I be doing with those years?"

She shrugged. "Whatever you want, I suppose."

"I feel like I've been wandering in the mist. I don't like feeling so out of it. So physically dispirited."

"I don't blame you. It must be difficult."

"It just feels odd."

One of the ladies from the kitchen brought up a tray and after taking a look, it seemed just about what I had ordered. So, it wasn't too bad. It was a bit awkward with the tubes having reined me in but otherwise I managed quite well. After I'd eaten my fill, I felt quite exhausted.

"That was heavy going. I wonder if there's drugs in everything?"

"What do you mean?" Sharon asked.

"I was wondering about the food. Perhaps it's a way to keep all of the patients docile."

"You mean, a little Prozac in the OJ?"

"Yeah. Something like that." Sharon had her hair pulled back sharply and wrapped on top of her head in a knot. She looked exceptionally girlish without make-up apart from the circles under her eyes.

"You look tired, Sharon. And I should know about that."

"I told you, I haven't been sleeping."

"Is it...?"

She nodded. "That and other things. Ma has decided to stay on longer even though her leg is fine. She and Mrs. Sanchez have become very good friends. They seem to get along well."

"That's nice for her."

"Don't be like that."

"What?"

"You know." But she smiled a little and a light came into her blue eyes. "I love you, you silly bugger, do you know that?"

"I think so."

She came around and put her arms around me. The tray full of dishes went crashing to the floor but neither of us flinched or let go.

I was released the next morning. Nathalie came to help wheel me away and pack up my things. She and Sharon seemed to have hit it off.

"You do seem to show up at opportune times."

"Uh-huh."

"Don't complain," Sharon said. "Two women fawning over you. What more could you ask for?"

"How about three women?"

"Oh, shush up. The boys will be happy to see you. I sent them to fetch your things from Catherine's, not that you had much."

"I travel light," I replied, almost sheepishly.

"And most of it needing washing too," Sharon said, sternly.

Nathalie laughed. "I like this. This is good."

"Wait until you meet Mrs. Sanchez," I said. "She is nasty."

"No, she isn't." Sharon protested, but mildly. There seemed to be a spring in her step. "Don't listen to him, Nathalie. He exaggerates something terrible."

The first day I was home, I spent sleeping for the most part. The doctor said I should get up and move around. I wondered what was happening at the office. Roberto and I had spoken briefly on the phone and he assured me that everything was okay, running smoothly and that worried me. He said that Ruth had asked about me, in a moment of weakness probably. Jessica had sent flowers, a nice potted mum, that I thought was very considerate of her. I hoped she hadn't had any more breakdowns while I'd been away.

That evening, I pulled a robe around me and went downstairs to the kitchen for dinner. Sharon had ordered in Chinese.

"Hey Bernie. Nice to see you up and around, buddy." Nathan put his arm around me and gave me a squeeze.

"You've grown in the last week," I said.

He looked me almost straight in the eye. Sean leaned back in his chair, something I told him not to do just about every day and every meal.

"Hey, Bernie. What's happening?" he asked, in that dull monotone of his. Feigning interest but really showing very little as if he couldn't care less. It was his cool persona. He spoke softly but with an edge.

"Is your house arrest up yet?"

"Yeah. I go back to school on Monday. Can't wait."

I couldn't tell if he was being serious or sarcastic.

"Been keeping up your work?"

He smiled, slyly then rubbed at his jaw.

"Of course, I have. What else have I got to do? It's like being held prisoner. I couldn't go anywhere or do anything."

"Oh? Why not?"

"Mom's been watching me like a hawk, haven't you, mother?"

Sharon wore a blue velour sweat suit. She handed round dishes and cutlery. The food was piled in bags that were set on the marble island.

"Come on, let's get organized."

"You mean, she stayed home?"

"That's what I mean, Bernie. She was everywhere."

I looked at Sharon. "Is this true?"

She looked up, licking her lips after opening the container of sweet and sour pork spare ribs. "Uh-huh."

"You took off work?"

Sharon put her hands on her hips. "I do have assistants you know. And I'm perfectly capable of taking calls and working from here too. We're online. I didn't miss much except a lot of the office crap. To tell the truth, it was a lovely break. I enjoyed it and it kept himself out of mischief, didn't it Mr. Trouble?"

Sean shrugged, then helped himself to a spring roll. "If you say so, mater."

Felicity was quiet and eyed me suspiciously. Now that I was back home, she began to feel more like an intruder, the guest who'd overstayed.

"Cat got your tongue, Felicity?"

She flushed while dishing out some beef and black bean sauce.

"No, not at all. You know I'm one for talking but I was thinking that it might be time for me to go home. I miss my little place and I'm sure it's neglected and will need some tidying up."

"Perhaps I can lend you Mrs. Sanchez for a day or two."

"Well that'd be grand, wouldn't it?"

"Yes," I said without thinking. "It would." The two of them turned and glared at me. "I didn't mean anything by it." But their eyes flashed darkly which told me they didn't believe a word.

The day floated by. I read the paper, watched the baseball game on TV, had a nap, then managed to dredge up enough energy to barbecue some chicken. After which, the boys went out to play basketball with some of their buddies and Sharon and I watched a video she had rented. It was a dreamy film about a woman who showed up with her daughter in a small town in France and opened a chocolate shop. Sharon liked it a lot and I managed to stay awake. We had a cup of tea and some biscuits, not saying much, but I realized I was content. Perhaps I spoke too soon.

"If I hadn't hit my head, would you have let me come back home?"

Sharon paused mid-sip.

"What does it matter? You're home, aren't you? Where you want to be?"

"Yes, but I just wondered, that's all. You know me, I have a restless curiosity."

"That can get you into trouble, can't it?"

"I suppose it can," I replied, noting the edge in her voice. "You're looking awfully tired, Sharon. I suppose all of this has been a drag on you."

She stared into her cup.

"It has at that. More of a burden than I realized. Looking after those two hoodlums is a chore. I'd like to think they'd be a bit more independent but when it comes down to it, you have to cater to them like they're babies."

"It wasn't that bad, was it?" I received a long look for my trouble. "They were just taking advantage of you. Trying to make you feel guilty. Kids are good at that. And they're both clever."

"What're we going to do about Sean, then? I'm worried sick about it."

"What can we do? I don't think he's going to change. All we can do is make sure he stays out of trouble while he's living with us, that's all. Once he's on his own, then who can say what will happen?"

"That sounds a bit cold. I mean, he is your son."

"I know but I'm having trouble, Sharon. I, I'm not sure I can relate to him at all as my son. I don't see any of me in him. He certainly doesn't resemble me physically…"

"You're playing favourites, aren't you?"

"It's not a matter of that. I mean, I don't see it that way, really. I just don't understand him. I don't get what he's about. Where this violent, cruel streak comes from. It's out of my realm."

"And of course there's Nathan too. I worry about him."

"At least he's sensible and grounded. Overly loud maybe but…"

Sharon banged the table. "Don't be so bloody flippant, all right? You know how kids are. How people are. Damn cruel and vicious. He's in for a rough ride. I just wish…"

"I'd like to protect him too but he's going to have to deal with it himself. He'll figure it out. It's funny, I always saw him as a parent. He's so good with little kids."

"That'll never happen now, will it?" Sharon said, wistfully.

I shook my head, "Probably not." I drained the mug. "I'm tired." I rose and opened the dishwasher, putting the mug inside. It felt like a lot of effort. "But it's good to be home. I really mean it."

I lay in bed, drifting off into blissful sleep. I could feel my muscles relax and melt into the sheets. It was the most delicious feeling. Sharon got changed into her pajamas. She pulled off her top and I happened to roll slightly to my right for a better look. Something had happened. Never flat chested, Sharon had become fuller somehow. She rolled down her sweat pants and my eyes popped open. She had a pot belly. Never had I seen Sharon with a pot belly. Oh my God, should I say something but before I could even think, she glanced over at me. Placing her hands under her abdomen and jutting her breasts, she asked, "What do you think?"

Panic. That's what it was. A man's worst nightmare.

"Well, I, uh, think you look great…"

"And…?"

"Well, perhaps, a modest diet wouldn't hurt."

"What?" Her jaw dropped and colour flooded her cheeks. "Do you ever listen to anything I say?"

"Of course I do."

"Did you not hear me in the hospital?"

"Hear you what?"

"When I told you something, you big lummox."

"No need to be insulting. What did you tell me?"

She walked and sort of waddled toward me, thrusting her abdomen practically in my face. "I'm pregnant, you fool. That's what I told you. Your third child is in here. That's another reason I haven't been sleeping and why I look like shite through and through. Can you imagine me dressing like this normally? Looking like this normally? How did I marry such an ignoramus?"

"Pregnant?" I gulped and my mind flashed back; late nights, diapers, diaper bags, changes of clothes, strollers, walks in the park, pablum splattered on the walls. "You're pregnant?

"Of course, I am. Why do you think I drove up to Haliburton that weekend? To tell you about it. I brought my suitcase and some champagne."

A long, low groan rumbled up from my toes.

"Oh my God." I sat up. "Oh my God, Sharon. How could I be so stupid…?"

"It takes quite a talent, if you ask me."

I sat up and put my arms around her, she quivered and pounded her fist into my shoulder. "Ow." But then she stopped and pressed against me and it was a lovely feeling. So lovely in fact, that… "Er, I don't suppose…?"

She laughed through her tears. "You never change, do you?"

"I guess not."

She felt down between my legs.

"Well, Mr. Winkie seems to be sending me some sort of a signal."

"Is it okay? I mean, with you in this condition?"

She gripped my arms, digging her nails in. "Tell me it's okay, Bernie. That you're happy about it."

"Well, I won't deny I'm in a bit of shock but of course I'm happy about it. How could I not?" Kiss tranquillity goodbye.

"Well, all right then. Let's lie down together. We just have to be a bit careful, that's all. No wild gyrations now."

"I'm too weak. I'm just out of hospital, you know."

"Well, we'll have to be gentle with each other, won't we?"

She paused.

"And don't forget, you owe me the ending to that story. I've been letting you off the hook while you've been under the weather but it's soon time for you to be back at it."

"You mean, you've been reading the chapters I've been sending?"

"Of course I have. And I must admit you pulled me in too. Though the characters do seem to be a wee bit familiar."

# 41

Yes, I thought. Perhaps that was the real message here, that we should all be gentle with each other. Could Sean's wildness be tamed that way? I didn't know. Could gentleness make the lawsuit disappear? Or re-form Roberto's brain into one that functioned? Or come up with a boost for business such that I didn't have to rip my hair out every month, knowing that *Bookology* had a steady revenue stream and an enviable reputation? Or that the two books I was currently writing would flow out of my fingers and on to the page effortlessly? Or that my marriage would get over the humps and setbacks of the past months? Who knew really? One thing, I didn't think the art of being gentle would tame: Ruth's irascibility. But I was wrong. Dead wrong.

The following Monday, I arrived at the office early and found a note from Ruth, stating that she wouldn't be coming in. I thought this odd. In our long association, that had never once occurred. Half an hour later and still not yet nine o'clock, a deliveryman showed up at the door with a package. It was addressed to me personally and I assumed, as I signed for it, that it was the usual buy-off from one of the publishers. When I opened it, however, I found a handsomely bound leather diary with goldleaf on the edges. The thing was practically criminal, the leather soft and supple. You wanted it next to your skin actually. I called Sharon to thank her.

"But I didn't send you anything."

"Oh."

"Perhaps I should have, to thank you for being so good in bed last evening."

"Oh? Is that an unbiased opinion?"

"It is, of course. Yes, absolutely."

"Hmm. Puzzling. I wonder…"

"Secret admirer then?"

"I don't know. I really don't know." I rang off, leaving us both in suspense. Otherwise, the day unfolded in relatively normal fashion.

When Ruth didn't show up the next day, I called her at home. The answering machine picked up. The same nasal, and flattened voice grating on your ears. I left a message and didn't think anything more of it. I didn't think she'd done a bunk or anything. That seemed out of the question.

It was on the third day that Jessica answered the phone and I noticed the colour drain out of her face. "That was the police," she began.

"What?" I said. "What did they want?" And I vaguely thought of that detective who'd been hanging around earlier.

"It's about Ruth," she replied in a small voice that seemed to close up in her throat.

"What about her?" Now Roberto had pulled himself away from whatever video game he was playing to listen.

"Well, apparently, she's dead."

"What?""

"Yes, dead," Jessica said, and nodded as if to confirm it to herself as she looked a bit wildly at the others. She stood up quickly. "Excuse me," she said and ran out of the room. I heard her footfalls clopping down the hall to the bathroom.

Roberto stood up and came over to me. "Did she say that Ruth was dead?"

"Yes, she did. The police were just on the phone."

"She never hung up," he replied and pointed.

"Oh my God," I exclaimed grabbing for the phone receiver. "Hello?"

"Yes?"

"I'm so sorry, the young lady who answered didn't tell me you were still on the line."

"Well, I am. Who am I speaking to please?" I told him. "Then you know about the deceased, Ruth Sommers?"

"Well, I just heard that she's dead, yes. It's shocking."

"And Ms. Sommers was employed there sir, is that it?"

"Yes, that's right. For the past five and a half years, actually."

"We'll need some verification of that, sir. A letter perhaps."

"Of course. Can you tell me anything? What happened, for instance?"

"Well, sir, to be honest, it looks like suicide but we won't know for sure until the investigation is completed."

"Suicide? That's terrible..."

"Do you know of any reason, sir? Anything that you can think of?"

"Well, no, not really. Ruth is, uh, wasn't a happy person. She always seemed to be fighting some demon or other."

"Can you explain that, sir?"

"Well," I struggled. Never volunteer anything, I reminded myself. "I don't know very much. I didn't know her well, actually, strange as that may sound."

"And how many are you there, sir? At your premises?"

"About six."

"Only six? And you say you didn't know her well?"

"That's right. Ruth rarely spoke about her background or her family. And she was always very testy, never in a good mood. I wouldn't say she was a very positive person."

"What can you tell us about her background, sir?"

"Not much really. Her father is deceased. Her mother is semi-blind and lives in a home. The family was well-to-do and the mother seems to be quite affluent. She has two brothers, one who is a pastry chef for one of the large food chains and another who works in financial services, I believe. The younger brother is a bachelor and lives out of town. The older brother is well-off, lives in Forest Hill. She never got along with the older one but doted on the younger, from what I gathered. But he didn't get here much."

"Very good then, thank you sir. And your name?" I told him. "Your address, sir? And phone number at home?"

"How did you know to call here, officer?"

"Well, she left a note and mentioned her place of employment. Also said something about a package she was sending as well. Did you receive anything?"

"As a matter of fact I did, but I thought it was from my wife, at first."

"And what was it, if you don't mind?"

"A rather handsome, leather bound diary."

"Expensive, was it?"

"I should think so, yes."

"Any reason you can think of, why she would send it to you, sir? Was it your birthday?"

"No, it wasn't"

"Just a parting gift then?"

"I suppose it was," I said. "But I don't know why. Maybe she felt guilty."

"Now why would she feel that way, sir?"

"I don't know. She was always snapping at me. Often made snide remarks."

"Yet you kept her employed?"

"Well, yes."

"Why, if you don't mind my asking, sir?"

"I suppose I knew, that deep down she didn't mean it. And I felt sorry for her if you must know. She seemed terribly lonely but she wouldn't let anyone get close to her either. I assumed, she'd had a difficult past and didn't want to share it. She was bitter, that's for certain."

"I see. Well thank you very much, sir. You've been very helpful."

"Will there be a funeral?"

"Uh yes, there would be I imagine, but it'll be a day or two until the body is released. We are notifying her family and I imagine they or we will be back in touch."

"I see. Thank you, officer." And I rang off.

The day of Ruth's funeral, a muddy sky complemented the damp air. It had drizzled early in the morning, leaving a drying slick on the roads and sidewalks and driveways. Now that I knew of her condition, Sharon looked visibly pregnant to me, a layer had formed around her hips, her breasts had swelled and her abdomen pushed at the waistband of her underthings. Felicity insisted on coming with us, anticipating the pleasures of a good wake. She loved nothing more than a wake. I had no such expectations but dressed in the most sombre suit I possessed, dark blue and double-breasted. We drove out to the church that had been selected for the service. It stood in the heart of Forest Hill opposite an exclusive private boys' school. Apparently, Ruth's older brother was a member of the congregation. It was Saturday morning. We discovered that Ruth had downed a mega-dose of sleeping pills, drifted off and never woken up. There had been a note but I never found out the contents as it had been read only by the police and the immediate family. A neighbour had called the building superintendent when she'd heard Ruth's cat crying and scratching at the front door. The super then called the police. And so it went. Not much of a life it appeared, sad and forlorn and neglected. I thought these things as I parked beside a number of smart-looking cars in the small lot, gleaming Mercedes and BMWs. The limousine that would carry the family to the cemetery was positioned opposite the main doors. A ramp had been placed adjacent to the cement steps to accommodate Ruth's mother I supposed.

Inside were a handful of mourners, about thirty people I guessed. Ushers stood at the doors and opened them for us, beaming sad yet knowing smiles. As we entered the foyer, a youngish man broke away from a group and came bounding up. He was plump and pasty-faced with a mop of unruly hair.

"Mr. Goldman?" he asked me.

"Yes."

He put out his hand which I took. It felt soft and moist like a bun. "I'm William, Ruth's brother. She often spoke of you."

"Really?"

"She had nothing but good things to say."

"Well, I, uh, thank you for that. And I am so sorry about all of this."

William nodded. I introduced him to Sharon and Felicity and they shook hands solemnly. "Let me introduce you to my family," he said. We were led to the small circle that comprised a large, imposing man with grey hair, combed straight back from a florid face. He filled out his suit as if it had been pumped full of air. This was Ruth's older brother, Roger. The tall woman with the large jaw and brittle hair was Roger's wife, Elspeth and the tiny woman seated in a wheelchair wearing dark glasses was Ruth's mother.

Roger nodded and shook my hand gruffly. Elspeth smiled revealing large, yellowed teeth and Ruth's mother twittered like a bird. We were thanked for attending and Roger elicited a promise from me to come back to the house after the interment for some refreshments. Despite some pressure on my elbow from Sharon, I accepted, feeling it was the least I could do. Then a sombre fellow emerged from the sanctuary, tapping his wristwatch and we all went inside and found a convenient pew.

The service was short. What we didn't know then, but found out at the "wake", put things into perspective. Ruth had been diagnosed with terminal cancer. This struck me forcefully when William revealed it. She hadn't said a word or changed anything at all. It had been over a month and so swept up in my own troubles had I been that I doubt if I would have noticed anything anyway.

William and I stood near the mantle in Roger's drawing room. Yes, some houses still had them. The fire wasn't on, thankfully, but the room must have been thirty by sixty feet and those who had returned to the house after watching the mahogany coffin descend into the earth, numbered less than twenty. It was clear that most of the guests, well-heeled and expensively dressed, were friends and acquaintances of Roger and Elspeth. I had taken a glass of wine and was munching on some brie and crackers. Sharon held a glass of orange juice while Felicity took a Scotch neat. Some light Mozart filtered through the hidden sound system. It was remarkable really. Anywhere you moved in the room, the music surrounded you.

"I had no idea," I said. "She never said anything."

"She wouldn't have," William replied. "That wasn't her way. Ruth kept a lot to herself."

"Now I feel even worse."

William drained his wine. "I wouldn't. She lived the way she wanted. She could have done much better, of course, remarried. She'd had offers." I raised my eyebrows. Sharon and Felicity listened in with quiet seriousness. "Oh yes," William went on. "But she'd been put off marriage and I supposed she had really loved Kent, that was her first husband. Ran off with his secretary, you see. I know it sounds hokey but it's true."

"What a shame," Felicity exclaimed with feeling, then went off to claim another whisky. No doubt she thought of her own cheating husband, Rory, who'd had it off with many women. William and I shook hands again, then he went off to chat with some of the other guests as the odour of flour wafted by. I took Sharon's hand. It was warm. She gave me a squeeze. That is, until I felt a blow to the middle of my back almost causing me to spill the glass of wine I held. I turned to see Ruth's brother Roger who gave my shoulders a squeeze. His eyes were slightly unfocused and it was obvious he'd had a few. It was a bit early for me.

"We never got along, Ruthie and me," he drawled, as he swayed against me and I could feel the heat of him through his suit and mine.

Sharon raised her eyebrows at me. "And why is that?" I asked.

Roger pulled at his face as if thinking this through. "I think we just detested each other, actually. Ruthie was awfully bolshie and we just didn't agree on things. Damned shame things didn't work out with Kent. He was a good fellow, a man after my own heart. We got along well, and for a while I thought she was happy. Then, for what seemed like no reason, she chucked him out."

"She threw him out, did she?" Sharon exclaimed.

Roger bowed toward her. "She did."

"And why was that I wonder?"

Roger shrugged, then slurped at his drink. "He'd had an affair or two but so what? Man's entitled to stray now and then, don't you agree, Barnard?" And he nudged me with his elbow.

"No, I don't. And it's Bernard."

"Oh, you're one of those. The faithful type." And he raised his bushy eyebrows.

At that point, his wife slid up and took his elbow, then deftly slid the drink out of his hand before it reached his pouting lips. "That's quite enough for you, Roger. We have many things to do yet and you must keep your head on," she said, crisply. "I hope he hasn't been too rude," she said to us.

Sharon smiled sweetly. "Not overly, no." Elspeth laughed. "I've always loved the Irish. You don't pull any punches."

"We try not to," Sharon replied.

Roger stood with his arms ramrod straight at his sides and balled his fists. Elspeth turned to me. "We want to thank you on behalf of the family, Mr. Goldman. Apparently, Ruth was very fond of you."

"Well, I appreciate that."

"I'm going to find Mum," Sharon said. "Our condolences once again."

Elspeth and Roger watched her go. "An impressive woman," Roger muttered.

"Yes," intoned Elspeth. "For once, Roger, we agree on something. Thank you again," and she held out her hand to me. I shook it, then went to join the ladies of my family. As I went to collect Sharon and Felicity, I thought to myself, yes, stereotypes do exist.

The ride home was fairly quiet except for Felicity who hiccupped continually.

"Something dry that I ate," she explained. "there was a cracker with something black on it and it went down the wrong tube, you see."

"That would be caviar, Mum."

"Caviar? If I'd have known I was eating caviar I might have tried harder to like it. I've never tasted anything so vile in all my life. Rubbish it was. The taste of the whisky barely drowned it out. Terrible crackers as well. Who says the rich know better, I ask you? Serving such rubbish at a wake, though I'd hardly call it a wake. Hardly anyone said anything about the deceased. Did you notice that? Shocking, absolutely shocking. It was more about stocks in this and investing in that. Renovating this, knocking down that, shopping here or there. What's the world coming to? Not a single person shed a tear. Well, that's not how it's going to be at my wake, I can tell you that. There'd better be plenty of noise and wailing and all. And music and dancing. Or else I'll come back to haunt you 'til the day you die."

"Apart from that, did you have a good time?" I asked her. She gave me a dirty look that I caught reflected in the rear-view mirror. Sharon smiled serenely but said nothing. I could read her mind though. All had returned to normal as far as she was concerned.

When we arrived home, we found Nathan sitting on the concrete steps with his chin propped up by his fist, looking very contemplative. He didn't move as we parked, then approached him as a pack.

"What's up, son?" I rarely called him that and his eyebrows shot up.

"I'll tell you Bernie. Strange things are afoot."

"And what's that supposed to mean?" Sharon asked.

"Answer your mother," Felicity chimed in.

"Now Gran, don't get all snippety on me now," Nathan replied, then pointed toward the front door. "See for yourself."

Somewhat baffled, we moved en masse to the doorway. It stood unencumbered. Open in other words. There was nothing unusual that I could see. I did notice an extra pair of runners and a knapsack. "So?" I said to the assembly.

It was then that Sean appeared from inside the kitchen. He must have heard us coming in. Trailing behind him came a slight figure in tight jeans, a tank top and a do-rag.

"Yo everybody," Sean began. "Uh, I want you to meet Spike."

Spike turned out to be a slim girl with a pierced nose, pale skin and luminescent blue eyes. She stood awkwardly by Sean's side.

"Spike?" I asked.

"Well, Melissa actually," she replied and put out her hand for us all to shake. "Nice to meet you all." Then she blushed.

"And you too, Spike."

It was funny but Sean seemed to be both proud and embarrassed at the same time. He was certainly acting strangely.

"Uh, Spike's going to stay for dinner. Is that okay?"

"Sure," I said. "I don't know what we're having yet."

"That'd be fine, hon," Sharon said, and beamed at Spike, who smiled shyly in return.

"Well," exclaimed Felicity. "This has been quite a day. I could use a nice cup of tea."

"Sounds grand," Sharon said.

"Can we barbeque?" Sean asked.

I thought long and hard about that. "I don't see any reason why not."

And then Sean said a shocking thing. He turned to Spike.

"My Dad makes a great barbecue. He's really a good cook but his barbecue is really exceptional."

I almost gagged. "Why, uh, thanks for that."

"Cool," Spike said.

"We'll be in my room." Sean took Spike's hand and pulled her along the corridor.

We stood in a still-life tableau and watched them go, in rather shocked silence.

"Told you," Nathan said, breaking the ice.

"I think I could use something stronger than tea," I said. Sharon frowned at me. "But tea will do very nicely," I added.

Sharon took my arm while Nathan took Felicity's and we marched into the kitchen, preparing to imbibe nature's own caffeine-loaded remedy. The most addictive substance on the planet.

# Epilogue

Eight months passed. On a bright Saturday morning I sat in BoBo's café with Nook and Ramon, except I had a good deal more paraphernalia than usual. This included a diaper bag and stroller and a wee chappie whose name was Ronan James, strapped to my chest like a papoose, sleeping peacefully while burbling in his dreams. He was a redhead and that meant trouble down the road. Ramon had the same get-up except his daughter, Maria Ruiz, remained quite awake and sucked on her chubby little fingers while Nook, Ramon and I quaffed our usual beverages. It felt good actually. Ronan was a good baby, only cried half a dozen times during the night but I had to admit that Mrs. Sanchez had proved a godsend. She fawned over the baby and took care of him during the day as if he were her own grandchild. The two of us haven't quite made full amends but I'd say we'd declared some sort of truce. I'd even had a smile out of her once or twice, well, Ronan did while I was in the vicinity, anyway.

Ramon and I were determined to show that we could be new dads and still maintain our independence and not alter our lifestyles. Sean was still dating Spike and she had become a fixture at our house. They got matching tattoos, a small flower on the right bicep. There'd been very little trouble with him recently. He'd been suspended only once since the last incident, for spraying water at another kid in the gym locker room. Just hijinks, nothing particularly violent, although I knew that it lurked below the surface. I didn't expect this thing with Spike to last forever but while it, did Sharon and I enjoyed the change in him. Nathan felt happy for Sean, and lonely. I could see he craved a close relationship with someone. Unfortunately, Sharon and I felt helpless. We were out of our depth in that department but as luck would have it, help was close at hand.

"Hi guys. Sorry I'm late."

"Hi Nat."

Natalie came in wearing sweats and a baseball cap. She plunked herself down and grinned.

"Look at the babies. They're adorable as always." She reached over and grabbed a piece of Maria's cheek.

"Ramon, I could eat her up. Anybody want anything?" We all shook our heads.

I raised my mug. "I'm still working on this one."

"And how's little Ronan?" Natalie asked.

"He's doing well. Really well, actually."

"Looking more like you all the time."

"You think so? He's rather pale, I'd say."

Natalie laughed. "Don't be silly. He's almost you."

She went off to get her usual cappuccino. As I was saying, Nathalie had been a good friend to me, and all of us, and particularly to Nathan. He'd become good friends with her daughter, Barb, who, I gathered, gave him another perspective on alternative lifestyles.

As for *Bookology*, I put myself out of my misery and sold it to a rival publisher. I convinced them to keep all of the staff, even Roberto. The magazine is actually doing much better. I'd too many split priorities I supposed, not to mention, distractions in my life. I didn't get much for it, just barely enough to pay my liabilities but felt I'd walked away free and clear and could do what I wanted. I moved my office back home so I could look in on little Ronan, take him to the doctor and go for walks. In fact, Eph and I would rendez-vous at a central location and take our babies out together for a jaunt in the park or along a section of town we found interesting. In a bizarre way, it has brought us closer together.

I'd also managed to finish the two manuscripts I'd been working on haphazardly and worked through sets of revisions. De Groot hectored me for a firm publishing date and we'd settled on early fall for *Memories*. That suited me. I'd hoped to have the revisions on *Das Vidaniya* finished by the Spring. Then, all going well, it would come out the following September. So, I'd have the two book releases just a year apart. That made me both pleased and satisfied.

The lawsuit would probably never end. Gloria was a master of dragging things out. In the meantime, I'd heard a few interesting things. Schwilden was being sued for sexual harassment by several of his female employees. Caroline, the eyewitness to that fateful punch, had quit the firm and told me about it. She joined as a plaintiff on the case. She also told me their business had taken a dramatic downturn given the high-tech meltdown in the markets. Eric's Porsche and lifestyle had been purchased with venture capital money, money that he and his partners burned through faster than the disappearing ozone layer. I related this to Gloria, who surmised he'd hang on because he really needed the money. This turn of events might open the door to a substantially reduced offer for quick cash, however. I left it in her hands. Lawyers were the only ones who benefited anyway.

Recently, I'd attended a book launch, one of my last official functions as editor and publisher of *Bookology.* I was chatting up the very attractive publicist for Stewart House when I felt a sharp tap on my shoulder. When I turned around, I couldn't have been more surprised.

"Charlotte?" She beamed up at me and instinctively I went to give her a hug. "What's this?" There was more to her than I realized.

"I'm preggers," she laughed. "Can you believe it?"

"No, not really. What happened?"

"Well, Michael came home from another business trip and I was in a pissy mood and I told him that this wasn't a marriage, it wasn't even a relationship and that I was going to leave him. Well, I guess that shook him up quite a bit. He'd been taking me for granted for a long time. Anyway, I didn't realize that he was unhappy too. He hated the travel and being away so much. So, he went and talked to his boss about it and they rearranged his travel schedule. He still travels but not nearly so much and then we had more time together and that was really nice. Once thing led to another and then, whoops, I missed my period. Michael was over the moon. He'd wanted children but didn't think I did and we'd never really talked about it seriously, or anything seriously, and now we're going to have a baby and I'm very scared but very happy too. And that's it," she finished with a flourish.

I gave her a peck on the cheek. "That's marvellous. I'm very happy for you. I'm a new Dad too, by the way. We had a little boy, Ronan James, not more than a month ago."

"I know."

"You do?"

"I still keep in touch with people at Cablestar. I know what's going on."

"Anything I should know?" I laughed, then drained the wine glass I'd been clutching.

"Not a thing."

We chatted on for a few minutes. I told her to keep in touch and then we parted as warm friends. Now that was a surprise, but altogether a pleasant one.

I still seek that perfect moment of tranquillity. Since moving back into the house, it has been elusive. Just when I begin to drift into that warm space on the edge of consciousness, I hear the cry of Ronan in my ear. New life. New beginnings. The horror had just begun.

Dear reader,

We hope you enjoyed reading *A Loafer's Guide To Living*. Please take a moment to leave a review in Amazon, even if it's a short one. Your opinion is important to us.

Discover more books by W.L. Liberman at https://www.nextchapter.pub/authors/wl-liberman

Want to know when one of our books is free or discounted for Kindle? Join the newsletter at http://eepurl.com/bqqB3H

Best regards,
W.L. Liberman and the Next Chapter Team

You might also like :

Looking For Henry Turner by W.L. Liberman

To read first chapter for free, head to:
https://www.nextchapter.pub/books/looking-for-henry-turner

# About the Author

W.L. Liberman believes in the power of story telling, but is not a fan of the often excruciating psychic pain required to bring stories to life. Truthfully, years of effort and of pure, unadulterated toil is demanded. Not to sugar coat it, of course, writing is a serious endeavor. It is plain, hard work. If you've slogged away at construction work, at lumber jacking, delivery work, forest rangering, sandwich making, truck driving, house painting, among other things, as he has, writing is far and beyond more rigorous and exhausting. At the end of a long, often tedious, usually mind cracking process, some individual you don't know pronounces judgment and that judgment is usually a resounding 'No.' This business of writing is about perseverance and stick-to-it-iveness. When you get knocked down and for most of us, this happens frequently, you take a moment to reflect, to self-pity, then get back at it. You need dogged determination and a thick skin to survive. And an alternate source of income.

W.L. Liberman is currently the author of nine novels, ten graphic novels and a children's storybook. He is the founding editor and publisher of TEACH Magazine and has worked as a television producer and on-air commentator.

He holds an Honours BA from the University of Toronto in some subject or other and a Masters in Creative Writing from De Montfort University in the UK. He is married, currently lives in Toronto (although wishes to be elsewhere) and is father to three grown sons.

# Also by the Author

- Dasvidaniya
- Looking for Henry Turner
- The Global View (The Goldman Trilogy Book 1)
- A Loafer's Guide To Living (The Goldman Trilogy Book 2)
- Dead Fish Jumping On The Road

Lightning Source UK Ltd.
Milton Keynes UK
UKHW012115280720
367329UK00005B/83